Kathryn started her working life  soon realised trying to decipher de for her. In 2011, backed by her fam..., pharmaceutical science to begin life as a self-employed writer.

Also by Kathryn Freeman

The New Guy

Up Close and Personal

Strictly Come Dating

Mr Right Across the Street

The Beach Reads Book Club

The Italian Job

Nobody Puts Romcoms In the Corner

WAS IT GOOD FOR YOU?

KATHRYN FREEMAN

One More Chapter
a division of HarperCollins*Publishers*
1 London Bridge Street
London SE1 9GF
www.harpercollins.co.uk
HarperCollins*Publishers*
Macken House, 39/40 Mayor Street Upper,
Dublin 1, D01 C9W8, Ireland

This paperback edition 2023
First published in Great Britain in ebook format
by HarperCollins*Publishers* 2023
1

A catalogue record of this book is available from the British Library

ISBN: 978-0-00-8560355

Printed and bound in the UK using 100% Renewable Electricity
by CPI Group (UK) Ltd

Chapter One

Tinkerbell jumped gracefully onto the sofa and curled up next to her. Sophie gave the pretty tabby a distracted stroke as she stared at her computer screen in smug satisfaction. This could be her proudest achievement to date. Okay, maybe that didn't say much for the last twenty-nine years, but the work of art in front of her was her creation, her baby.

The way things were going, it was likely to be as close as she was going to get to one.

'Isn't it beautiful?'

She angled the screen towards Tinkerbell who glanced up, bestowing her a look that could have said *You're a genius* – though possibly also *You're weird*. Then promptly settled down to sleep.

Ah well, maybe the feline world wasn't ready for spreadsheets. As for humans, her spreadsheets had never failed to elicit a reaction. Granted, it wasn't always positive, but then some poor souls didn't understand what an absolute game changer, even a life saver, a perfectly executed spreadsheet could be. Some even doubted that the time she spent creating it, and religiously updating it, was compensated for by the time it saved her. Yet how could it not, when she had her whole life in one easily accessed, perfectly ordered, repository?

And she really meant her whole life.

Tab one held her financials. What came in, what went out. Next was her meal plan, organised for the week to ensure she had the right balance of nutrition depending on which diet she was following. Tab three was her exercise plan, including boot camps and the routine Zumba, tennis and Pilates lessons. Personal care in tab four was all about making sure her hair, bikini line, eyebrows, nails and weekly massages were up to date. Then she had a tab for her holiday plans and one for the places in the UK she'd earmarked to visit each month. There was also a tab for gifts – what she'd given to who – and one for her social life which kept a record of best bars, restaurants, clubs, activities, when she'd visited and which she'd plan to visit again. Finally there was the most recently added tab, Love Life. Created six months ago following repeated nagging from flatmates Ava and Grace to get out there again.

Will, they assured her, had not been worth any further moping.

At the time it had felt like good advice. But. After quickly inputting the scores from last night's lacklustre date into the spreadsheet, she fell back against the sofa and sighed. There, in bold red, was the reason she should have ignored her friends.

Dating was the one area of her life not going according to plan.

'Hey, come on Soph. We're going to be late,' Grace yelled,

walking into the living room. 'Oh.' She peered over Sophie's shoulder. 'Callum didn't make it, huh?'

'Nope.'

'What went wrong?' Ava, the third Musketeer, the Wonder Woman to their Superman and Batman (though on some days it felt more like they were The Three Stooges) came to join them, water bottle tucked under her arm.

Sophie pointed to the spreadsheet where Callum's overall score had gone from eight out of ten after date three, to six out of ten and an automatic red line from last night. 'He kissed me, and it was really mediocre. I mean, I gave it a three but that was being kind. Plus, we'd started to run out of conversation. First few dates I was kind of interested in his snowboarding and I'm not going to lie, the body building sounded sexy.'

'*Sounded* sexy?' Grace scoffed. 'You so wanted to see him without his shirt.'

'Fine, I did. Past tense. After last night, we're done. No male body is sufficiently drool worthy to make it worth spending my Sunday evening listening to repeated tales of how he nearly got caught in an avalanche, or how much weight he can bench press.'

Ava scrunched up her face as she peered at the spreadsheet. 'I still maintain it's weird Soph, giving guys scores after every date.'

'Why? It's only putting a numerical figure to all the stuff that goes on in my head. You know, *I like this about him but I'm not sure about that*. Using the spreadsheet just organises those thoughts, plus it takes all the stress out of the decision of whether to see the guy again. His average score goes below seven out of ten and zap, it's over.'

'But what if you found some guy was scoring you?' Ava persisted. 'I'd be mortified if Ethan was doing that to me.'

'Come on Ava, they always score us,' Grace interrupted. 'How many times have you heard them say she's a six, or a nine. I think there was even a film made in the seventies about a woman who was a ten.'

'And that was just based on looks.' Sophie pointed back to the spreadsheet. 'This is way more sophisticated than that. Besides, it's only for me. A kind of mathematical brain dump of what I'm thinking. They're never going to see their score, but I get an instant decision on whether to keep seeing them. No more time wasted on unsuitable guys or drifting into relationships that ultimately aren't going anywhere.' Like Will, and Chris before him. And the two before them. The months – the years in Will's case, she thought with a familiar feeling of loss and anger – that she'd wasted dating guys who'd turned out to be not who she'd first thought. Or who she'd subconsciously probably known weren't quite right but had never been able to put a finger on why, so she'd kept seeing them through habit, or that fundamental need for companionship.

'You're so obsessed with saving time.' Ava gave her a concerned look. 'I'm worried with all this documenting, analysing, ticking off and moving on, you're forgetting how to *live*.'

Unconsciously Sophie's gaze flew to the photograph on the shelf to her right. Two fresh faced twenty-one-year-olds grinned into the camera with identical smiles. Her heart twisted, the feeling familiar, dimmed a little by time but still leaving a hollow ache that could never be filled.

Ava must have noticed because she squeezed her hand.

Then she felt Grace wrap an arm around her shoulders. 'We get it. Just, you know, try to dial down the nerd part of your brain every now and again.'

'Efficiency isn't nerdy,' Sophie protested, swallowing down the lump in her throat and forcing her gaze away from the photo and back to her computer. Quickly she saved the file and closed it down. 'Right, I'm ready. Let's get to Zumba. Jade will make us go to the front if we're late.'

Jade was their five months pregnant, rocking, larger than life, highly enthusiastic Zumba teacher. Rich brown skin, afro hair in a tumble of corkscrew curls, she had the widest, brightest smile Sophie had ever seen. It was impossible to go to Jade's Monday evening Zumba class and not laugh, not come out feeling a million times better than when she'd gone in.

They bundled into Grace's sporty new BMW – people who didn't know her, called her spoilt. After all, she owned the three-bed flat they shared, together with a wardrobe of designer labels, and a bank account with far more zeros than Sophie would ever possess. But Sophie knew Grace would have traded all her trust fund to have a dad who actually gave a damn.

Fifteen minutes later they pulled into the leisure club car park.

'Well, well, it's the troublesome trio.' Jade waved them inside and pointed to the front. When they all groaned, Jade's smile grew wider. 'I want to see your sweaty red faces when we try out the new routine.'

'You're getting meaner,' Sophie grumbled as she trudged to the front. None of them wanted to be on show, and it wasn't because they were shrinking violets, oh no. Sophie and Grace were more than happy to strut their stuff in front of the class

(Ava, not so much). But they also liked to chat, to get distracted by the sight of the guys turning up for football training.

'If I was mean,' Jade declared. 'I wouldn't be about to give you the number of the nicest guy you'd ever hope to meet, would I?'

Sophie narrowed her eyes. 'If he's that great, why is he single?'

'Hey, I'm great and single,' Grace interrupted. 'Maybe you should give his number to me.'

'Err, I think Daniel would dispute the single part,' Sophie interrupted.

'Nah, we're casual.'

Jade turned to Grace, her wide smile slipping a little. 'No offense Grace, but my guy, he's kind of on the quieter side. Not sure the pair of you would get on.'

Grace, a tall, leggy blonde with a no-nonsense attitude, frowned. 'Sophie's not exactly shy and retiring.'

'No, but you're loud, wild and a bit scary.' Grace's eyebrows flew to her hairline but Sophie and Ava giggled because the description was deadly accurate. 'Sophie, she's more … bouncy.'

'Bouncy?' Sophie stared down at her A cup chest. 'The only time I give myself a pair of black eyes doing Zumba is in my dreams.'

Jade hooted with laughter. 'Damn girl, that's what I'm talking about. You're fun. And chatty. Michael could do with a bit of fun and chatty in his life.'

Sophie privately thought nice, quiet Michael sounded like the type of guy she took pains to avoid. And would be red-lined after one date. 'How do you know him?'

'He's Dave's brother.'

That made her perk up a bit. She'd met Jade's husband and aside from being tall and good-looking, he had a wicked sense of humour. 'Okay, fine. Send me this paragon of virtue's number and … wait, he wants to do this, yes?'

Jade's big brown eyes darted briefly away before coming back to rest on Sophie, the big smile firmly in place. 'He's really looking forward to meeting you.'

———

Michael stood at the door and jammed the key into the lock while juggling bread, milk, a box of eggs and his briefcase in his other hand – why hadn't he decided to sod the environment for once and ask for a carrier bag?

Finally he heard the blessed click, and he pushed the door open. A bundle of fur darted out from the living room and began to yap, running in and out of his legs.

'Princess, stop that.'

But the aptly named long haired chihuahua ignored him and tried to climb his leg.

Sure, she was a tiny thing, but the motion was enough to unbalance the bread/milk/egg/ stack and the egg box fell out of his hands. Not just that, but in synch with the luck he was having recently, it landed upside down, the lid opening just enough to leave a trail of splattered egg. 'Damn it.'

His exclamation was too loud. Princess backed away, little legs trembling. And then pissed all over the floor.

Okay. Michael inhaled a deep breath, let it out slowly until he felt his shoulders come down from his ears. Then he dumped everything else he was carrying onto the floor and reached to pick up the now worried looking pooch. 'Sorry, gorgeous.' Ruffling her head, taking care not to mess with the pink spotted bow his gran insisted on tying in her hair, he stared back at the puddle of dog pee. 'She forgot to let you out again, huh?'

Clearly forgiving him for raising his voice, Princess licked at his hands.

Just then Fudge padded into view. The polar opposite of Princess, his brown lab was quiet and unassuming. About the only woman in his life who was, he thought with a wry smile.

After giving Fudge an affectionate rub, he raided the kitchen for paper towels and cleaned up the egg/dog pee mess. Then, dogs in tow, he went in search of the third female he shared this creaking cottage with.

He found Betty asleep on the sofa in the living room, newspaper spread out on her knees, reading glasses hanging on a chain round her neck. His gran was eighty-five now, but he'd never been allowed to call her Gran because *I'm not old enough to be a grandma.*

His heart squeezed as he stared at her. Ever since the fall, she'd seemed frailer and yes, old. Two words he'd never associated with her before. She must have sensed he was watching because her eyes fluttered open.

'Ah, just the man I've been waiting for.'

Typical that she wouldn't admit she'd fallen asleep. Just as she'd never admitted she'd been finding life harder, living by herself. It shamed him that it had taken a fall and a broken hip for him to realise she needed more help from the two boys she'd raised since they were teenagers. Dave, his brother, lived in London with his wife and daughter so he had his own family to focus on. Michael was single, plus the one with the medical degree. And really, moving back down from

Manchester to take care of her had been a small price to pay for the years she'd given up looking after them.

'How many other men have you got visiting this evening?' he asked dryly, bending to kiss her cheek.

'That's my business.' She pushed herself up from her slightly slumped position. 'I wanted to play back that Loose Women programme we recorded but I don't know how on this fancy system you've put in.'

When he made the decision to come and live with her, he'd decided two things were needed to stop him going stir crazy. First was a huge extension to the cottage so they each had their own space. Second was installing the latest TV technology so he didn't have to resort to watching what she watched.

'You mean the programme *I* recorded for *you*,' he clarified. He knew from experience if he didn't correct the phrase now, she'd be repeating it to everyone in the village. Just as she had when she'd informed Kath in the post office *they* would be going to bingo (err, he would drop her off and pick her up). Or when she'd told Sid in the village club that *they* planted their bedding plants last week … and okay, he had shoved a bunch of flowers in because she couldn't bend down easily, but only under *her* direction.

She waved his comment away. 'Same difference.'

'Not when you're my age.' He wanted to at least give the impression he had one foot still in his thirties and not both firmly planted in middle-age. Even though at times reality felt otherwise.

He'd just found the recording for her when his mobile rang.

Betty peered over at him from the top of her glasses. 'Who's that?'

'Jade.' There was no point reminding his gran that he was

thirty-five and entitled to a bit of privacy. She'd only wheedle the information out of him later. 'Wonder what she wants.' He glanced over at Betty but her gaze remained firmly on the TV screen. 'You're looking shifty. What do you know that I don't?'

'Nothing.' Her expression was deadpan, but when she turned her head briefly to look at him, a pair of faded blue eyes twinkled back. 'At least I won't know any more than you once you've answered your phone.'

With a sigh he pressed answer. 'Hello Jade. What have you and Betty been cooking up?'

Jade's full-throated laughter echoed down the phone. 'I told her not to say anything.'

'She hasn't. Wait.' He stared at Betty, who was studiously watching the TV again, though he knew she was listening. 'Why would you not want Betty to say anything?'

'Because I knew if she told you I'd given your number to a gorgeous woman who I happen to think would be perfect for you, there was a chance you'd not answer when I phoned.'

He cursed silently, drawing a hand down his face and fighting to retain the calm he was renowned for. 'Why would you do that?'

'Because it's been over three years since that bitch did the dirty on you and you've not made any attempts to date since. Because I think I'm an expert matchmaker and you can't disagree with a pregnant woman. Because Sophie isn't just gorgeous, she's bright and bubbly and I like her so I think you will too.' She paused, let out a deep breath. 'Because I want to see my awesome brother-in-law happy, and right now he's not.'

Jade was loud, extrovert and pushy. He was ashamed to say she'd scared him a little when his brother had first introduced her. But five years on, he'd got used to her loudness, and had come to realise her pushiness came from a desire to help. His sister-in-law had a huge heart, and his brother was a lucky man. 'Awesome huh?'

'You know it. How many other people let me ramble on without interrupting?'

He smiled, recognising the truth behind her jokey comment. His brother was a chatty, social animal where he was … not. 'Well thanks, I guess.' Though he wasn't convinced either he or the bright, bubbly Sophie, would be thanking her later.

Ending the call, he turned to find Betty frowning over at him. 'Stop it.'

He blinked. 'Stop what?'

'Stop thinking yourself out of this before you've even met her. You need to get out more.' She patted at her short, silver hair. 'You're cramping my style.'

'Sorry?'

'How am I supposed to have gentleman friends over if you're here every evening like some Victorian chaperone?'

Though there was humour in her tone, coming on the back of the phone call, the words grated. How had his life come to this? Family plots to get him out of the house on a date because he was getting in the way of his eighty-five-year-old gran's love life? A date they had to arrange because they thought he was too incapable to find his own?

Chapter Two

Sophie took another sip of her wine and looked down at the time on her phone. Jade's brother-in-law might be a nice guy, but he was also late.

Uninterested, she thought, remembering the stilted conversation she'd had with him two days ago. So why not just say that? Why arrange to have dinner with her Friday night? And as an aside, what a terrible decision *that* had been. Why hadn't she stuck with drinks so she could have ducked out early, though as it looked like he had no intention of turning up, the point was moot.

With a huff of frustration, she opened the spreadsheet app on her phone, her finger hovering over the column headed punctuality, but then she closed the app and set her phone back on the table. He might not even turn up, in which case she didn't need to bother scoring him for anything.

The door to the pub opened again and a guy walked in. Tall and lean with short fair hair, he wore a crumpled dark suit. Beneath it was a white shirt, open at the collar, and a grey striped tie that had been yanked down, like he'd wanted to take it off but couldn't be bothered pulling it over his head. His gaze darted around the room and … her heart jumped as a pair of bright blue eyes locked on hers. Okay, she wasn't expecting *that* reaction. Weird because she liked tall, dark and handsome. Not tall, blond and … there was no denying it, he was attractive. Not handsome in the classic sense, but there was something, probably those vivid eyes, or the square jaw. *Something* that made her stomach flip flop as he strode towards her.

'Sophie?'

'That's me.' Prepared to forgive his lateness, she gave him her wide smile but he only nodded back.

'Sorry I'm late.'

She waited for the explanation, but instead he busied himself taking off his jacket and draping it round the back of the chair. Then he sat down, exhaled a deep breath and drew a hand down his face.

'Bad day?'

'Bad end to it.' Charming. He must have seen something in her expression because he grimaced. 'I didn't mean…' He exhaled, rubbed at the back of his neck, then nodded over to her half full glass. 'Can I get you another drink?'

'Thanks. I'm on the red. This one is a merlot but to be honest I don't mind what grape it is. Or from which country. I guess you could call me easy.' Her smile froze when he stared back at her, looking completely nonplussed. 'But only when it comes to wine,' she added quickly. It earned her a half smile, which felt like one of those awful consolation prizes given to people just for turning up. 'How about you?'

'Me?'

'Unless you want to ask anyone else about their drinking habits?' The more he looked at her as if she was talking a different language, the worse her jokes became.

'Sorry.' He appeared to shake himself. 'I'll get the drinks.'

The chair scraped and he stood up again. She watched him stride towards the bar – nice broad back view – then glanced down at the notification on her phone.

Jade: Is there chemistry? Please tell me there's chemistry. You two were made for each other xx

Either Jade was going through some hormonal pregnancy melt-down, or there was, maybe, possibly, more to the sullen guy at the bar than she'd seen so far.

He came back clutching a bottle.

'Wow, is it going that badly?'

'Pardon?'

Maybe she'd lost her touch. Or maybe Michael didn't have a sense of humour? 'It was a joke. You know, the date is turning out so badly you resort to getting drunk?'

He looked at the bottle, then at her. 'I thought we'd share it?'

'Oh, right. Date not going that badly then.'

The tight-lipped smile he gave her could have meant anything. *It's going worse than badly. I just want to get out of here.*

He set down a second wine glass on the table, then unscrewed the bottle and began to pour. She wasn't usually stuck for something to say, but in his guarded company she couldn't find her ease, her flow. 'I guess we should find out a bit about each other before we order our food.'

He nodded, reached for his glass and took a big gulp. But didn't say anything.

'Why don't I start? I'm twenty-nine. I live with my two best mates Ava and Grace in Mayfair. And yeah, I know that sounds posh but it's Grace's flat and she rents the rooms out to us for way less than she should because she doesn't need the money but she likes the company.' He nodded again, watchful, definitely listening, which was something. Even though he didn't look like he was actually going to say anything. She ploughed on. 'I work as a colour consultant so I basically spend my days going to people's houses and recommending paint and wallpaper colour schemes. I suppose it sounds trivial, and sure, it's not rocket science but I get a real buzz from giving people ideas and helping them improve their space. And anyway, what can be more important than having a place to come home to that calms you, inspires you, relaxes you?' She watched as he took a swig of his wine before glancing down at the phone he'd left on the table. Way to make her feel like she was boring him. 'What about you?'

The pause was so long she wondered if he understood the question. But then he spoke, his voice deep, yet soft, quiet. 'I'm thirty-five.' His gaze drifted over her shoulder. 'I live in a village in the Chilterns.' He cleared his throat. 'With my grandmother.'

She nearly choked on the mouthful of wine she'd just sipped. What had Jade been thinking? But okay, maybe she was being too judgey. There was probably a good reason he lived with his gran. In the sticks. 'I'm a real city girl. What's it like living in a village? I bet you have a dog, huh?' She didn't like dogs much. In her experience they were too much effort, barking at the slightest noise, needing walks, fawning over their owners, leaping up and slobbering over you. And that was before she thought about having to pick up their poo and shove it in a bag. Cats got on and did their own thing, including managing to exercise and poo without needing help. All they asked for was a bit of love, a warm spot in the house to curl up, and to be fed twice a day.

'I have a brown Lab. Fudge.' His phone buzzed and he looked down at the screen. 'Sorry. I need to take this.'

He clasped the phone to his ear and walked off, not sparing her another glance. With a sigh, Sophie reached for the bottle and refilled her glass, noticing he'd barely touched his. Then she opened up the spreadsheet on her phone, typed Michael's name into it. And began to score.

Michael waited until he was outside before he pressed answer.

'Gill, how is he?'

'He's okay.' Relief coursed through him and Michael sagged against the wall. 'In fact he's even been laughing with the nurses,' Gill added. 'He's going in for an angioplasty soon which they say should help him recover.'

'It will get the blood moving through the coronary arteries. They might add a stent, too, to reduce the chances of another heart attack.'

She let out a half laugh. 'That would be good. I definitely don't want to go through this again.'

Me neither, he thought. He might be a doctor, but it had been years since he'd performed CPR, or even had an acute emergency to deal with. 'Thanks for letting me know. I appreciate it.' He'd been on tenterhooks ever since he'd watched the ambulance disappear down the road. Roger wasn't just a patient at his GP practice. He and Gill had lived in the village for years. When he and his brothers had gone to live with Betty after their mother's death, Roger had taught him how to play cricket.

'Michael.' Gill's voice faltered for a moment. 'I wanted to thank you. I was in such a blind panic. He kept telling me he was fine, but I knew he wasn't and you were the first person I thought to call.' A quiet sob echoed down the phone. 'You saved his life.'

Emotion threatened to break through his carefully constructed clinical detachment and Michael briefly closed his eyes, pushing back the images of the last few hours. Gill's distraught expression when he'd raced over to their house the moment he'd got the call. Roger sat on the sofa, face pale and clammy, clutching at his chest. 'I'm just glad he's going to be okay. Tell him I'll call in on him once he's back home. Check he's behaving himself.'

He tucked the phone back in his pocket, rubbed a hand down his face and took a few minutes to compose himself before going back in. To his date.

His sister-in-law had been right. Sure, he'd arrived stressed from having to dash straight to the station from Roger's house, but it hadn't stopped him registering how gorgeous Sophie was. Short dark hair framing an angular face that was striking rather than pretty, and all the more attractive for it. Add in a wide smile and clear grey eyes that seemed to spark every time she spoke. Which was a lot. If he had to describe her personality, it would be a woman running on a double espresso topped up with Red Bull. He didn't mind that though, at least it was better than having to force a conversation. It's just, when he added the lingering shock of the last few hours to his natural tendency to want to think before he spoke, and her non-stop chatter that prevented him from being able to actually say much … he wasn't sure what sort of impression he'd made.

Still, he had the rest of the evening to improve on it.

Feeling a lot better than when he'd arrived, he strolled back through the packed pub to the slim, dark haired woman sat on a table by herself, head bent as she typed into her phone.

Clearing his throat, he slid back onto the chair he'd vacated. 'I'm sorry about that.' How to explain why he'd taken the call without sounding like a pompous arse?

'No problem.' She slid her phone back into her handbag and spoke before he'd managed to get his brain into gear. 'Sometimes phone calls are important. More important than the person sitting in front of you. And I get that, I really do. It wasn't a dig.'

'That's not what … well I guess it was, sort of, but …'

'It's fine.' She drew in a breath, gave him a wry smile. 'This clearly isn't working, is it?' He wondered if it was a question, but if it was she didn't give him time to answer. 'I suspect Jade pushed you into seeing me.'

'Err.'

She rolled her eyes. 'I knew it. She assured me you were up for it, that you were looking forward to meeting me, but it's beyond obvious this is the last place you want to be.'

'Wait.' Okay, he had her attention. Now he needed to find a way to salvage the date. 'At least let's finish the wine.'

'I think this is where I say … oops.' She glanced over at the bottle, and he realised his mistake. She'd managed to drink most of it already, so now his comment sounded like he, too, wanted to leave as quickly as possible when actually he'd been thinking the opposite. That they could linger over finishing the bottle, which would hopefully give him time to dust off the charm he thought, maybe, he'd once been able to produce, before they moved onto dinner.

'For the record,' she said, topping up his glass and then pouring what was left into her own, 'this was a very nice wine. Slipped down a little too easily.'

He recalled her joke from earlier about a date going badly and resorting to getting drunk. At least now he knew what impression he'd made.

'What shall we tell Jade?' Sophie pulled a face. 'She's bound to want to know why we're not seeing each other again and it would be good if we had the same story.'

The evening was pulling away from him and he had no clue how to drag it back. 'We could tell her we will see each other again?'

Sophie's eyes widened. 'Holy moly, you mean lie to her? Your sister-in-law and the woman who puts me through tortuous exercises every week even when she's in a *good* mood?'

He considered himself reasonably smart, but it was a struggle to keep up with this conversation. 'I wasn't thinking it would be a lie.'

'Oh, sure, I can totally see you wanting to come all the way into London again from…' she flapped a hand at him. 'Wherever it was you lived, to watch me guzzle my way through your bottle of wine.'

'Our bottle,' he corrected, then wondered why he was focussing on that and not on trying to stop this runaway train of a date from crashing.

'Yes, sorry, only you didn't drink much of it, did you? Most of it ended up in my glass because—'

'Bad date.' He crooked her a smile.

'Exactly. This is a bad date.' She pounced on his words with the alacrity of a cat finding a fat, juicy mouse.

Only she'd got the wrong mouse. 'That's not...' what I meant. He swallowed the words because she was already moving, grabbing at the handbag she'd slung over the back of the chair. Jumping to her feet. All that Red Bull mixing with the wine.

He stared in bewilderment as she held out her hand for him to shake. 'It was good to meet you, Michael.'

He'd had a date with a gorgeous woman and it was ending early, on a hand shake? How had he managed to cock this up so badly, so fast? 'And you.' At least one of them meant it, he thought ruefully.

'I'll tell Jade you were a nice guy but the chemistry wasn't there. Does that work?'

Nice guy, but. The words scraped over him like nails picking at a scabbed wound. 'Fine.'

He slumped back onto his chair and watched her trim figure make its way out of the busy pub. And yep, his weren't the only male eyes following her.

He was out of practice, that was all, he tried to reassure himself, but the words were hard to believe when he couldn't put any conviction behind them. Picking up his glass he drained it in one long, cheerless swallow. Then, ignoring the rumble in his stomach – he was not going to sit and eat alone like some sad git who'd just been stood up – he pulled out his phone and checked the time of the next train back.

Fucking great. He'd just missed one.

But Roger is going to be okay.

The thought pushed him out of his bad mood and he reached for his jacket. He'd walk the long way round to the station. And grab a McDonalds while he waited for the train.

A fitting end to a shite day.

As he walked he scanned his messages and saw he'd missed one from Jade.

Jade: Hope you found Sophie. Keeping all my extremities crossed. I have a good feeling about this. Jx

He thought about replying with Sophie's *the chemistry wasn't there* cop out, but Sophie was right, he couldn't lie to Jade.

He *had* been interested. Had felt something.

Deciding it wasn't a message that needed a reply, at least not right now, he shoved the phone back into his pocket and kept on walking.

Chapter Three

The following morning, Sophie was running late. A terrible thing for a woman who prided herself on meticulous organisation. But one thing her spreadsheets didn't do was account for clients who couldn't make up their minds. And yes, she understood choosing between walls painted *raspberry ripple* or *candyfloss creation* was difficult, but at some point, you had to make a decision. Even if you were only ten.

As she jumped back in her car following the first appointment of the morning, her phone buzzed with missed call messages from Ava and Grace who'd clearly just woken up. The joys of not having to work on a Saturday. To be fair, she rarely worked Saturdays, too, but only because she could usually persuade clients to meet her on week days. Better an evening appointment than one crashing into her Saturday morning "hangover" lie in.

Having set the sav nav up for the next client, she pressed Ava's number on her phone. 'Hey, I'm dashing between appointments. What's up?'

'Nothings up, we're just bummed we haven't caught up with you yet for the date dissection. Wait, I've got Grace here.'

There was a shuffling sound and Grace's voice came over the handsfree. 'Missed you last night. Ava is no fun. She left me dancing on the table by myself, the wuss. That date had better have been worth it.'

Friday nights usually involved drink, dancing and catching up with an ever-expanding group of friends at The Drunk Flamingo bar. It was where Sophie should have been, rather than in a pub, drinking most of a bottle of wine by herself and having a stilted conversation with a guy who hadn't wanted to be there.

'I can't go into it now, I'm running late and my next client is only a few minutes away.' Two minutes was not enough time to fully offload, especially as Michael was Jade's brother-in-law so there was a certain sensitivity to it.

'Oh wow,' Grace exclaimed. 'You're really going to leave us hanging? That's harsh.'

'And by the time you're back I'll be out with Ethan,' Ava complained. 'I can't go the whole day without knowing. You've got to give me *something*.'

'Okay, okay, I get the message. Now go away. Some of us have to work today.'

After squeezing her Mini into the one remaining space outside the next appointment – parking in small spaces was becoming her superpower after three years of this job – Sophie hastily found her spreadsheet and pinged it to Ava.

Here you go. See for yourself how it went, S x

It was only when she parked up outside their flat a few

frazzled hours later, that she thought to look at her phone again. And saw that it had exploded with notifications.

Holy cow, since when had she become so popular?

She opened the first message.

Mum: How what went? What am I seeing for myself? You know I don't like to wear those reading glasses. Love you x

What? Then she saw the one from her step mum:

Patricia: Impressive spreadsheet, Sophie. But what am I looking for?

And from her father:

Dad: I'm going to pretend I didn't see this. Dad x

Confused, she skipped to the one from her boss:

Trevor: Are you sure you meant me to see this? We need to discuss the scheduling of some of these appointments.

Alarm shot through her. Shit, what had she done? That's when she saw the seven missed calls from Ava. And finally a message from her.

Ava: READ THIS NOW! You sent the spreadsheet to EVERYONE!!!!!! DELETE, DELETE, DELETE!!!!! Ax

Shit on a candlestick – instead of sending the spreadsheet to Ava, she'd sent it to All contacts. A great, time saving idea when it came to asking for donations for her charity walks. Not such a great group to send her very personal spreadsheet to.

Her heart thumped wildly and her fingers felt like they belonged to someone else as she scrambled to find the original message and delete it.

Okay, breathe. This actually wasn't a disaster. Fine, she had an uncomfortable conversation with Trevor about bikini waxing to look forward to. But aside from that, surely not many people would have seen the message, and even fewer would have read it?

Except, there were more notifications.

Patricia. Your Christmas present to me was the jumper your mum gave YOU???

Damn it, that was two uncomfortable conversations. But hey, the jumper was cashmere and suited Patricia way more than it had her.

Callum: You scored me?????????? And our effing kiss???????

Okay, make that three uncomfortable conversations.

Mum: Who is this Johnathan my daughter had mediocre sex with?

She closed her eyes and let her head fall against the steering wheel. Bugger, bugger, bugger. Wearily Sophie climbed out of the car and made her way up the stairs to the flat. Ava and Grace dashed to see her the moment she opened the door.

'Oops.' Grace was clearly struggling not to laugh.

Ava looked more sympathetic. 'What a nightmare. I told Ethan, I can't see him until I know you're okay. Did you delete it?'

'Yep, but not fast enough to escape a few embarrassing questions.'

Grace pulled a face. 'Did Johnathan see his score?'

Her stomach fell out and onto the floor. Just when she'd thought this couldn't get any worse. Why had she added the last few dates to the blasted All contacts list? That's what she got for trying to wangle money out of people.

Ava must have seen how pale she looked because she squeezed her hand. 'He's probably not seen it. Come on, you can check on your phone who's seen the message.'

Okay, that was a good idea. At least then she'd know what she was up against.

They all peered at her screen as she checked through the list. Her heart rate began to settle as she realised the *read by* list wasn't that long and it didn't include Johnathan's name … but then it faltered when she saw two of her other previous dates, Joshua and Michael, were on the *read by* list.

'I want to say oops again,' Grace said. 'But I think you might hit me.'

'Just because they've seen the message doesn't mean they've accessed the spreadsheet,' Ava added more helpfully.

'But it does mean I need to talk to them.' Unbidden, an image of Michael popped up in her head. Shit. She'd been surprised how low his score had come out. 'And to my boss, and Mum and Dad, and Patricia. And Callum.' She scanned the read by list again, which also included three customers. 'And these people.' Inhaling a shuddering breath, she pushed the phone into her pocket. 'But first I need something brimming with calories, washed down with something very alcoholic.'

Grace laughed. 'Of course you do. Sit down and I'll get the gin bottle. Then we'll work out a plan of action.'

Half an hour, a donut and a very stiff gin and tonic later, Sophie had a running order of people to contact. And she'd thought her morning had been bad.

Picking up the phone, she started with the easiest.

'Hi Mum.'

'Darling, I'm glad you called. That message you sent was so confusing but if I read it right, we really need to discuss your sex life. You can do so much better than five out of ten sex. Even your father was better than that.'

She loved her mum, but at times she did wonder if she was on the same planet as everyone else. 'Can you forget you saw that spreadsheet. Please.'

'Oh.' A pause. 'Why did you send it to me then?'

'I meant to send it to Ava, but I did it in a rush and I pressed *All* instead.'

'I see.' Sophie can almost hear her mother's brain creaking. 'So *everyone* knows my daughter was having five out of ten sex with a man called Johnathan?'

Sophie groaned and took another slug of her gin with a tiny bit of tonic. 'Seriously Mum, do you have to keep mentioning sex?'

'Well you did send me a spreadsheet with the title Love Life.'

'There were eight other spreadsheets!' She took a breath.

'Look, I just wanted to explain that you received that message in error. Now please forget you've seen it and we can talk about usual mum/daughter stuff like shopping. And casseroles.'

'I've never made a casserole in my life. So what about these other men you've been seeing and haven't had sex with. Why weren't they any good?'

Sophie hung her head. And this was the easiest of the calls she had to make today.

Michael couldn't help it. He kept thinking of that bloody spreadsheet. Sophie might have deleted the message, but the contents were already indelibly burnt into his retina. Two and a half out of ten. Yep, a fucking two point five. He'd never got below sixty percent in *anything*.

'Darling, whatever it is that's got you all wound up, can you take it out on the weeds and not my begonias?'

He glanced up to find Betty with a concerned expression on her face – whether it was concern for him, or the begonias, he wasn't sure. 'Sorry.'

She looked like she wanted to say something else, but she must have sensed his mood because she stepped back inside and left him to his gardening therapy.

He shouldn't have opened the message. It had clearly been sent in error, but the wording *see for yourself how it went* and the timing, the morning after their date, had felt like too much of a coincidence. Besides, it had come from the woman he'd spent the hour-long train journey home thinking about, so he couldn't *not* open it. Couldn't miss the opportunity to find out what she'd thought of him.

Well, now he knew. He also knew a hell of a lot more about her.

She'd dated four guys in the last six months, one of whom, Johnathan, she'd clearly liked enough to have sex with. Then presumably disliked that enough to dump him, judging by the poor sod's five out of ten for *sexual performance*.

That being said, judging by their overall scores, none of the guys she'd dated recently had been as much of a dead loss as him.

Wounds he thought had healed, ripped wide open again and he grabbed hold of a clump of bind weed and gave it a vicious tug.

As an aside, he'd also found out she was obsessively organised – who else put their entire life into a ruddy spreadsheet? And rigidly disciplined – a food plan and exercise schedule that even the doctor in him thought was over the top.

He wasn't going to think about the bikini waxing.

She'd marked him three out of ten for style? *Three?* Taking the spade, he thumped it into the ground he'd cleared. Sure, he was a bit conservative with his clothes, but he'd come from work, for fucks sake. Punctuality, fine, he'd accept a two for that, though she hardly gave him a chance to tell her why he was late. As for humour and charisma...

His mobile rang just as he was taking another bout of frustration out on the soil. When he saw who it was, he almost laughed. Definitely considered not answering.

The only reason to, was because she was Jade's friend. 'Hello.'

'You answered.'

He leant against the spade. 'Why wouldn't I?'

'Err, no reason.'

'You called me just to find out if I'd answer?'

'Of course not. That would be ridiculous.' She hesitated. 'I called to apologise for sending a message to you in error. I've got a friend called Ava and I meant to send it to her, but I accidentally sent it to All contacts.'

'You've created a group for all your contacts?' Then again, why was he surprised. She'd created a spreadsheet for her love life.

'All my active contacts, yes.' There was no defensiveness to her tone. If anything, she sounded surprised that he'd asked the question. 'It can be a really efficient way of communicating. Like, for example, if you change your address, or want some help with something, it saves sending loads of individual messages...' She trailed off. 'Anyway, I just wanted to explain why you got this weird message from me.'

'Asking me to look at a spreadsheet?'

He heard a quick inhalation and then a cautious. 'Yes.'

'To see how *it* went?'

He was sure he heard her swallow. 'Yes.'

'*It* didn't go well, from what I saw.'

A muffled curse. 'Bugger, you opened it, didn't you? I was really hoping you hadn't. Now I'm super embarrassed and also really sorry that you had to read ... well, stuff that I never intended for you to see.'

'You didn't want me to know I was the worst date you'd had in the last six months?' It was hard to speak, his jaw was so tight. 'Or that in your opinion I lack humour, have no style and am not remotely interesting?' He nearly choked on the last words.

'Now wait a minute, I didn't say any of that.'

'What *does* two out of ten say then?'

A huff of breath, followed by a long exhale. 'It says I wish to God I'd not sent the spreadsheet in a rush. And I'm really, really sorry you saw that. Obviously it was only my opinion, after one drink where I did ninety percent of the actual drinking. I mean, I can't imagine you would have rated me any higher. And I did mark you 8 out of ten for looks.'

'Am I supposed to be grateful?' he asked incredulously.

'No, that's not what … I didn't mean to imply that.' Another deep sigh. 'I can only apologise again. I'd like to meet up and do that in person. And buy you a drink. One that you actually get to drink yourself this time.'

Beneath the attempt at humour she sounded subdued, which niggled at him. He wasn't usually this harsh or unforgiving over what had clearly been a mistake. It wasn't like she'd intended to cause offense. The fact she'd hit on a raw nerve was his issue, not hers. What Jackie had done … he should be able to push past it by now. Yet here he was, feeling not only insulted, but *diminished* by the opinion of a woman he barely knew. 'You can save the drink buying for Johnathan. He possibly needs it more.' Call him shallow, but he'd rather have a two out of ten for interest than a middle of the road score for sex.

Her voice became quiet. 'Thankfully I managed to delete the message before Johnathan saw it.'

'You got lucky then.'

'Lucky?' Her voice hitched. 'There's nothing lucky about

everyone in my contact list seeing a highly personal spreadsheet. Or finding you've upset a load of people.'

The comment made him pause. 'No, I don't suppose there is.'

'Anyway, it's my own fault so I'll stop whinging. I just … I really am sorry. That must have been shit to read.'

'It was.' The nerve she'd struck hurt too much for him to be gracious. 'Good luck with the rest of the grovelling.'

It gratified him that she laughed. *See I have got a sense of humour*. 'I think I'm going to need it. Next on my list is Dad, who I suspect will never be able to forget seeing a sex rating for a guy his daughter dated.'

'Ouch.'

'And then I've got my step mum, who's going to want an explanation for why her Christmas present from me was a present I recycled from my mum.'

He felt marginally better knowing she was having a tough time over all this, too. 'Do they get on?'

'Can't stand the sight of each other. So, anyway, sorry again and thanks for not ignoring my call.'

It was only when the line went dead that he realised they'd probably spoken more in the last few minutes than they had on their ill-fated date. Maybe if she gave him another go … he looked down at his worn, scruffy gardening clothes, the fact that he was gardening at all, and exhaled heavily. In her world he'd still be a blasted two and a half out of ten.

Chapter Four

Sophie walked past the rows of colour swatches and wallpaper displays, and into the office at the back of the showroom where her boss, Trevor, was waiting to see her.

Yep, the repercussions from her spreadsheet debacle just kept on coming. Thank God the customers who'd received it had laughed and assured her they'd known it wasn't meant for them so just deleted it. If only others had been that courteous.

'Good afternoon.' She pasted on her *I'm so happy to see you*, smile.

'Take a seat.' Trevor was in his late fifties, receding hair, overweight and basically waiting for retirement. Until he got there, he bided his time making his staff miserable.

'I'm really glad you asked to see me,' she began, determined to have her say first before he made any of the sarcastic barbs she knew were coming. 'If you hadn't, I'd have made an appointment with you myself. Important to clear up what you might have seen on the spreadsheet I had the...' *stupidity*, 'misfortune to send out.'

'Got yourself into a right pickle with it, I bet.' He smirked, which could look hot on a good-looking guy, but on Trevor made him look like he'd just stood in a pile of maggots. 'That Johnathan bloke can't have been happy. And what about Michael, eh?' He chortled. 'Reckon I could get more than two and half out of ten.'

Not in this universe or the next. 'I don't think you've asked me here to talk about...' *my love life*. 'That particular spreadsheet.'

He nodded, an evil glint appearing in his dishwater brown eyes. 'You're right. I've asked you in today to discuss your bikini waxing.'

Oh, for God's sake. 'My personal care spreadsheet,' she corrected him, then bulldozed on before he could make any more inappropriate, sexist and frankly *creepy* remarks. 'I admit at first glance it must appear like I've used company time on occasion to go to some of these appointments, but I want to reassure you that all the appointments are done in my lunch hour. Sometimes I have a late lunch,' she added, aware that two o'clock could sound a teeny bit like she should be working.

'I see.' He tapped his fingers on the desk, which was frigging annoying. 'Do you enjoy what you do, Sophie?'

She swallowed. 'Yes. I love my job.'

'Good. And you're aware there aren't that many colour consultancy jobs flexible enough for you to have a pedicure at two o'clock in the afternoon?'

'I'm aware, yes. And very grateful.'

'I'd ask how grateful, but I don't want to be accused of sexual harassment.' He chuckled, and it sounded like a cross between a Bond baddie and The Joker.

'Grateful enough that I will continue to do my job to the very best of my ability, in turn ensuring you continue to get the uplift in paint and wallpaper sales that has been a consistent benefit of my work here.' Yep, take that. If he pushed her out, she wouldn't be the only loser.

He blinked a few times, then muttered something that sounded like "Good to hear", but could have been *Bugger, you have me there*.

'Was there anything else?'

He shook his head and she scarpered as fast as her neat pencil skirt and heels allowed. Worn in a desperate attempt to at least look professional, even if she was discussing bikini waxing and pedicures.

Giving a cheery, *All good here, nothing to stress about* wave to Alison in the shop, Sophie's legs felt like they did after a Zumba workout as she walked towards her car. She'd not lied to Trevor, she did use her lunchbreak for the appointments, but coming after all the flack she'd received from everyone she'd phoned to apologise, she felt evil. Like she'd deliberately set out to piss people off.

Her stomach rolled over as she thought of the call she'd made to Michael. That conversation hadn't gone at all well. Callum had been nearly as angry, even though he must have known the kiss was lacklustre because he'd not exactly disagreed when she'd said she didn't think it was working. Now she had to face him again because unlike Michael, he'd taken up her offer of a drink, probably just so he could humiliate her and not turn up. She also had to face Joshua, though he'd been more kind about her apology. Then again, maybe he'd looked at Michael's scores and figured he'd done okay.

Speaking of Michael … she glanced at her watch. She was due at Zumba in an hour. If Jade had found out about the spreadsheet, she was going to get crucified.

Two hours later, Sophie sat on the floor of the exercise studio and struggled to drag air into her lungs.

'Whoa, Jade really had it in for you today, huh?' Grace gave her a sympathetic look.

'Ah, it was nothing.' Sophie heaved in another breath. 'I can take whatever she dishes out.'

Beside her, Ava giggled. 'Sure you can. That's why your face is fire engine red and there's like a gallon of sweat pouring off you.'

'Yeah, well I'd like to see how you looked if you had to demo all those routines as well as actually do them.'

'Ava wouldn't need to,' Jade cut in, sauntering over to them, all feline grace, cute baby bump and knock out long legs encased in brightly patterned leggings. 'Because Ava wouldn't be mean enough to upset my brother-in-law.'

'Upset how?' Sophie asked. She knew Jade hadn't read the message. 'We both agreed there was no chemistry.'

Jade gave her a quelling look. 'And did you agree to score each other at the end of the date?'

Grace whispered another of her unhelpful *oops*, and Sophie let out a deep sigh. Oh joy, another uncomfortable conversation. And she wasn't talking about the sweat now sticking to her skin. 'I don't know what Michael told you, but it was all a huge mistake. The scores were my private thing, I never meant for him to see them. I did phone to apologise and, well, I know he wasn't happy but I thought we left things okay.'

Ava and Grace glanced at each other and, through some unspoken agreement, drifted away, leaving her to face the wrath of Jade alone.

'I'm really bloody sorry, Jade.' Fresh waves of guilt rolled through her and for the millionth time since Saturday, Sophie wished she could turn the clock back to just before she'd pressed send on that frigging message. 'I never intended to upset Michael. He's a nice guy. Just a bit stand-offish and uninterested, if I'm honest.'

Jade's eyebrows flew upwards. 'Uninterested? That doesn't sound like him. Stand-offish, I can understand because he's naturally quiet and can come across that way. But uninterested, no. One of his superpowers is listening. It's why he's such a great doctor.'

'Doctor?' Sophie felt a ripple of unease. How had she not even known that about him? And holy shit, she'd banged on about how important her job was. He must have laughed his head off. Assuming he was capable of laughing.

'He's a GP.' Jade gave her a questioning look. 'You really didn't talk much, did you?'

'No.' She'd tried, she reminded herself. It wasn't her fault he'd not exactly been forthcoming.

With an alacrity Sophie could only dream of, Jade swooped down to join her on the floor, crossing her legs in a way only bendy people could do. 'Look, he'd hate me for saying this, but he seemed really unsettled when we saw him yesterday. Like he was bothered by something but didn't want to be.'

Sophie's stomach fell. 'And you think that something was the spreadsheet?'

She nodded. 'He didn't say much at first, just that the date was a disaster and it wouldn't be happening again. Of course I wouldn't let him wriggle out of that so easily, so I told him he didn't know that for sure.'

'And he said he did,' Sophie filled in flatly. 'Because he'd seen how I'd rated him.'

'That's the short version, yes. The long version went along the lines of him saying, *Trust me Jade, I know*. To which I replied, *Of course you don't*, and his brother piped in with something unhelpful like, *Well he will if he was his usual monosyllabic self*. Then Michael told us both to leave it, which I didn't because, come on, this is me. Finally, in a rare burst of anger, he ground out *She didn't like me being late and said I have no sense of humour*, both things I find freaking hard to believe because I can set my watch by him when he looks after Olivia for us, and his dry quips crack us all up no end. When I asked *how* he knew, he admitted he'd seen some sort of score that he wasn't meant to see.'

Guilt wriggled again in her belly, along with a smidgen of respect that he hadn't just thrown her straight under the bus. 'He really shouldn't have taken it so personally.'

'No.' Jade sighed and looked troubled. 'But there are reasons he might have taken this to heart more than he should.'

Sophie groaned. 'I feel terrible. My only consolation is I know he wasn't interested in me. He spent most of the date looking at his phone, then he went off to answer a call.'

Jade frowned. 'Did he say who the call was from?'

'Nope.' Had she given him the chance? The guilt burrowed further.

'Maybe if you knew, it would explain why he was late and

distracted.' Jade jumped up. 'Anyway, sorry about tonight. I guess I felt a bit peeved for his sake, but I've exacted my revenge so no hard feelings. Just a shame you guys didn't work out.'

Sophie scrambled much more slowly to her feet. 'Does this mean you'll take it easier on me next week?'

Jade gave her an evil grin. 'Oh no. Now I know you can take it, I'll be pushing you every week.'

Friday, at last. Michael tugged on his jacket and zipped up his briefcase ready to head home.

'Are you off, Dr Adams?'

He looked up to find Hattie, their receptionist, standing in the doorway. 'I am.' There was no point asking her to call him by his first name. He'd tried in the first year he'd joined, but she'd stubbornly refused. In her early forties, single and dedicated to her job, she was the one who kept the engine of the surgery running smoothly in the background.

She narrowed her eyes at him. 'Did you sign all the scripts I left?'

'I did.'

'And sort out those three referrals?'

'Affirmative.'

She didn't crack a smile. 'I'll see you Monday, then.'

'You will. Don't stay too long.'

'I'll stay until the work is finished.'

Yes, she was an absolute godsend. But so meticulously efficient, she terrified him.

He felt his body sag with relief as he walked towards the

exit. It wasn't the job he was glad to see the end of for a few days. Sure, there were the time wasters, but in the main the people who came to see him were sick or worried and in need of help. He deemed it a privilege that he was in a position to provide it, though it was also a source of great sadness and frustration that sometimes he couldn't.

No, his need to put this week behind him came from another source. Sophie and her blasted spreadsheet had been preying on his mind. He wanted to dismiss the whole thing as a bad first impression, but it had woken insecurities that should have been put to bed by now. He wasn't the first guy to have been betrayed, so it angered him beyond belief that those scars hadn't fully healed three years later. Yet it didn't seem to matter how much he told himself *quiet* did not equal *boring*, those blasted insecurities kept whispering in his ear. What if in his case, it *did?*

'Michael.'

He nearly jumped out of his skin as he pushed open the surgery door to find the woman he'd been thinking about, standing outside. Dressed stylishly in cropped white jeans, blue and white striped T-shirt and a soft suede jacket, Sophie looked good enough to snatch his breath away.

'What are you doing here?'

She flinched, and he realised the shock had made his tone too harsh. 'I wanted to talk to you.'

'Oh, right.' His mind whirled with possibilities, but there was only one that made sense. 'Should we head back inside?'

'What?' Her brow wrinkled in confusion.

He glanced back at the surgery. 'Get my stethoscope out?'

'Oh, God, no, nothing like that.' She began to laugh. 'Wow,

you really thought I'd come all the way out here just to grab a bit of free medical advice?'

'It's hardly the end of the earth.'

'Kind of feels like it,' she muttered, glancing around her. 'I mean, does anyone actually live here, because I've not seen a soul so far? But no, I don't need medical help, though it was interesting to find out from Jade that you're a doctor. You left that out of the five-word description you gave me of yourself.' *I was distracted. You put me on the spot.* As both sounded lame, he kept quiet. 'I came to buy you a drink.'

'I thought I'd said no.'

'You said to save it for Johnathan. Well not to brag or anything but I'm not so destitute that I can't afford to buy *two* drinks, so here I am.' She gave him a hesitant smile. 'I wanted to apologise in person.'

He exhaled heavily. 'Jade put you up to this, didn't she?'

Sophie's cheeks turned a delicate shade of pink. 'Not exactly.'

Well great. This was fucking embarrassing. He loved his sister-in-law, but right now he wished she'd never met his brother. 'Well I'm sorry you felt you had to come *all the way out here*. I'll take you back to the station and tell Jade I appreciated the gesture.'

She gave a shake of her head. 'Nope, that's not going to work. I've come straight from my last appointment and I'm not about to head back into town without a drink and something to eat.' Her hands twisted in a nervous gesture at odds with the bold way she looked him in the eye. 'I'm kind of hoping you'll tell me the best place to go. And join me. I'm buying.'

'Best place is The Royal Oak,' he informed her, wishing

she'd take the bloody big hint he'd given her, and go. 'And thanks, but I need to head home.'

Her face fell, making him wonder if she was as scared of Jade as he'd once been. 'That's a shame. I was really looking forward to talking to you.'

He couldn't help it, he barked out a humourless laugh. 'Sure you were.' His fingers tightened round the handle of his briefcase. 'Sophie, I don't want to be rude, but we both know this is a pity date and … well…' He swallowed, humiliation licking at his insides. 'That's even more excruciating than being rated two and a half out of ten.'

Her jaw dropped and she stared at him in horror. 'Oh my God, that's absolutely not what this is. I came out here to try and explain to you about the spreadsheet, to work out why I probably got some of my wires crossed and scored you low where I shouldn't have. I didn't, Jade didn't … crappity crap, crap.' She waved her hands in the air. 'You're more than capable of getting yourself a proper date with someone way better than me. I mean, you're great looking – I only scored you 8 because I prefer dark hair. And you're a doctor. Doctors are what loads of women go ga-ga over.'

He didn't know whether to feel further insulted – all he had going for him was his medical degree? – or faintly amused at how flustered she appeared. He certainly didn't know how to reply, but that didn't seem to be a problem because she was talking again.

'Damnit, I've mucked up again, haven't I? I didn't mean to imply…you absolutely have more to offer than your job description. I just used that as an example of how eminently dateable you are.'

'Eminently?'

She flapped her hands again. 'I'm totally on the back foot here and when that happens I apparently come out with posh long words.'

'Evidentially.' Amusement won and he found himself smiling at her. When she returned it, something sparked, hot and punchy, in his gut. Arousal, he realised with surprise. It had been so long, he'd almost forgotten what that it felt like.

'So, will you save me from the ignominy.' She screwed up her face. 'Oh God, there I go again. Will you save me from the embarrassment of eating alone?'

Clear grey eyes landed on his, and even if he had been able to ignore the plea in them, he was helpless against their glittering vitality. She wasn't here because she wanted to be, they both knew that, but maybe even a pity date was better than another night in with an eighty-five-year-old and two canines.

'I need to go home first.' Unconsciously he looked down at his suit.

'You don't need to change. I mean not on my account.' A flush crossed her face. 'I won't be scoring you this time.' She threw a hand over her mouth and groaned. 'You came straight from work for our date, didn't you?'

'I hadn't planned on it, but yes.'

Her teeth sunk into her lush – yep, he'd noticed – bottom lip. 'You must think I'm a total bitch, scoring you like that.'

'Not a bitch, no.' He studied her, trying to work out how the woman in front of him, chastened, embarrassed, could be so cold as to score him on a spreadsheet. 'I don't understand how you can use a spreadsheet to determine something as personal as attraction.'

She nodded. 'That's fair. And if you decide to let me buy you dinner at that pub you mentioned, I can try and explain.'

'Okay.' Should he invite her back while he changed and took the dogs out for a pee? But he'd also have to introduce her to Betty, explain where they were going … it wasn't hard to visualise how *that* conversation would go. 'I'll see you at The Royal Oak in half an hour?'

'Thank you.' If she was surprised not to be invited back, she didn't show it. More likely she was relieved that he was keeping things impersonal.

'Do you know where it is?'

She waved her phone. 'I've got Google and half an hour to kill.'

Guilt wriggled in his gut. He really should ask her back. 'Will you be okay?' He settled on instead.

'Absolutely.' She nodded vigorously, like being stuck in a place she didn't know was the height of excitement. 'I'll check out the village hot spots. See what you guys do for entertainment round here.'

He decided not to tell her that the pub *was* the hot spot. Let her think she'd just looked in the wrong direction.

Chapter Five

Sophie sat back on her chair and cast her eyes around The Royal Oak. In London there was always a buzz when you stepped inside a pub. Chatter, laughter, energy, all fuelled by Prosecco and cocktails. This place was more occasional murmur about the weather and pensions, fuelled by sherry and stout.

'You said this was the best place to eat in Little Brook.' She glanced back at the man opposite her, who she noticed had changed into a sky-blue polo shirt and chinos. It wasn't exactly top fashion, but actually the classic look suited him. 'Is it also the only place to eat?'

He took a sip of his wine and gave her a small smile. 'Only *and* best.'

'And what else is there for entertainment out here?' Along with the pub and a GP surgery, as far as she could work out Little Brook had only a small parade of shops, a hairdresser and a cricket ground.

How could any sane single guy want to live out here? It

was like one of those TV programmes set in a cosy village where everyone got murdered despite there being only a handful of locals.

His gaze dropped to his glass. 'I think we've established you won't be moving here in a rush, so why don't you say what you came here to say?'

There had been a moment earlier, outside the surgery, when he'd smiled and she'd thought he'd forgiven her. Because the smile had caused her pulse to race unexpectedly, she'd even wondered if her spreadsheet had been wrong, and they should have tried another date. Now she realised the best outcome was to get on a train back to London as fast as possible. 'Okay, so I dated this guy Will for two years and, well, I thought we had something real. I mean, nobody stays with someone for 700 odd days if they don't feel connected, right? Wrong, because when I suggested we take our relationship to the next level and move in together, he looked like I'd asked him to wade through sewage with me. Then he dumped me.' Her heart faltered as she remembered her excitement at asking him, quickly crushed by Will's horrified expression. 'Apparently he liked me, I was fun to be with.' She swallowed down the ball of emotion. 'But only in small doses.'

Michael said nothing. No soothing words, not even a look of sympathy from those heavily guarded eyes. Eyes that were a shockingly gorgeous shade of Mediterranean blue, she thought idly, then shook the thought away. It had to be the shirt making them pop. 'Anyway, when I thought of how much time I'd wasted dating him, and the guy before him, I was horrified. I decided that was it, I wasn't going to date again, but my friends—'

'Ava and Grace.'

She blinked. So he had been listening. 'Yes. They kept pestering me to give dating another go, so I figured if that was going to happen, I'd do it differently. No more wasting time on guys who weren't going to work in the long run.'

'Like me.'

'And Johnathan, Callum and Joshua,' she felt compelled to point out, even if it did sound like she went through men like a knife through easy spread butter.

'You really think a spreadsheet is the answer?'

She ignored the derision in his tone. 'I do. I already have a thing for them...'

'I noticed.'

'Yes.' She willed herself not to blush. 'You and an embarrassing number of others now know far more about me than I ever intended.'

He fiddled with his glass, turning it round and round before finally lifting his eyes to hers. 'I guess that nearly makes us equal in the humiliation stakes.'

Heat scorched across her cheeks. 'I didn't...humiliating you was never my intention.'

He sighed heavily. 'I know.'

Thank God for the arrival of their food. As nothing on the menu had corresponded to the baked salmon, new potatoes and kale she'd assigned for tonight on her spreadsheet – no, she didn't want to lose weight but yes, she did want to live until she was a hundred – she'd had to improvise. 'Wow.' She gulped when her meal was placed in front of her. 'That's more shark than fish.'

He looked over at her plate of fish and chips. '*Out here* we like our food.'

Jeepers creepers. She'd apologised, grovelled. It wasn't her fault he took everything she said so personally.

'And we like our batter,' he added, his expression turning to one of mounting horror as he watched her carefully scrape it away from her fish.

'In the city we like our arteries unclogged,' she countered. 'As a doctor I thought you'd appreciate that.'

'Then why choose fish and chips?' He glanced pointedly down at his steak.

'Today was a fish day.' He frowned, but before he could start to question her about what she knew was a perfectly sensible diet plan, she changed the topic back to the one she'd come *all the way out here*, to discuss. 'Anyway, to answer your earlier question, yes I do think a spreadsheet is the answer. It takes the guesswork out by putting a numerical value on the dates. No more wondering if I should keep seeing a guy. No more letting my heart rule my head. If it's not going to work out, the spreadsheet tells me and I can nip it in the bud.'

'With a red line.'

'Yes.' Did it sound a bit dramatic? 'Is the colour a problem? If I'd used blue…'

He gave her a weighted look, which she took to mean *You're being ridiculous*. Then he speared a slice of steak with his fork, popped it into his mouth and chewed slowly. It was unnerving, how perfectly happy he seemed with long, silent pauses. 'What about feelings?'

'Sorry?'

Another pause while he sipped at his wine. 'What about what your heart says?'

'Hello, were you listening when I told you about Will? I've

tried that and it didn't work. A scoring system is a better judge.'

He took another mouthful, another slow chew. Clearly the guy never got indigestion. 'You think it was right to red line me following one drink after work when I was feeling shite?'

Wow, the anger was still there then, quietly simmering. 'It wasn't like that. We agreed the date wasn't working.'

He gave her a bland look. 'Did we?'

There was something about the intensity of that blue-eyed stare that made her heart jump. 'You weren't interested in me. You kept looking at your phone...' she trailed off, remembering Jade's words. 'I thought you didn't want to be there.'

'I'd come straight from giving CPR to a patient, a *friend*, and saw him go off in an ambulance. The call was from his wife.'

Shame bulldozed through her. 'Oh God, I'm sorry. Was he ... is he...'

'He's going to be okay,' Michael cut in quietly, helping her out.

She felt the sting of tears and dropped her face into her hands, feeling utterly awful.

'You didn't know.' When she dared to look up, he gave her a wry smile. 'I couldn't work out how to tell you without coming across as an arrogant prick.'

'Instead you came across as not wanting to be there.'

Her words hung in the air between them. For once she didn't know what to say.

And for once he broke the silence. 'Would it have made a difference to my score if I'd explained?'

'Probably.'

He lay down his knife and fork and stared at her. 'Then you've proven you can't judge a potential date using a spreadsheet.'

'Hey, wait a minute. That's a huge leap to take.' She met his gaze head on, unwilling to back down on this. 'I concede I may have proven one date wasn't enough.'

'How many then? Two, five, ten?' He shook his head. 'It's ridiculous, you can't put a number on any of this.'

'Ten.' Those bright blue eyes blinked back at her and Sophie felt her heart race. Even for her, this was a rash move. Was she doing this out of a compulsion to prove her spreadsheet was right? Or the fascinating possibility that it could be wrong. That she'd waved goodbye to some of her last few dates too early; Johnathan, Callum, Joshua ... no, surely not. Michael. Her heart gave an unexpected bounce. 'Let's see what the score is after ten dates.'

Michael's heart thumped. What in God's name had he got himself into? Had he jammed himself into a corner, taunting her like that? Did he now have to suffer ten more dates with a woman who wasn't interested in *him*, just to prove that she was right and he was wrong? Or ... had he just gained a reprieve, a chance to show this attractive, gregarious, spreadsheet obsessed woman that he wasn't the dull guy she'd pigeon-holed him as?

Not that it mattered what she thought, he reminded himself. This was about the principle of using a spreadsheet to rate a date.

He took a measured sip of his wine and considered his

options. 'I get to choose our dates.' If he was doing this, being in his comfort zone would make it marginally less painful.

'You get to choose half.' Sophie's lips tilted in a wry smile. 'If it's a disaster, at least half the time both of us will be doing what we want to do.'

And she was expecting a disaster. He glanced away, determined not to let her see how mortifying that was. 'I'll think about it.'

'What is there to think about?' Her eyes flashed back, challenging him.

It was alright for her, this was just a game. Ten more dates with the dud one to prove she'd been right to get shot of him all along. For him though ... he felt his ego shrivel further. No, damn it, he'd make her sorry she ditched him so fast. 'Fine. I go first.'

'Deal.' She beamed, making her eyes spark. And awareness zing through his belly. 'We'll pick five dates each and I'll see if the scores improve after each one.' She gave him a speculative look. 'Do you want to know the running total, or keep it as a surprise until the end of date ten?' He didn't have time to hide his reaction and she grimaced. 'Yikes, that sounds a bit callous, doesn't it?'

'You think?'

'Ordinarily, the guys I date wouldn't know I'm scoring them, never mind see their scores. Of course now you have, it makes all this a bit awkward.' She frowned and bit into her bottom lip. He wished, really wished, the action didn't wake up hormones he'd forgotten he had. 'You need to remember this isn't personal. You should look at it as ... I know, as a trial. Being a doctor, you know all about them.' She smiled, looking satisfied with her summary. 'It's a trial to see if my spreadsheet works.'

'A trial where I'm being scored.'

Her face fell and she had the grace to look embarrassed. 'I can't escape that part, can I?'

Nor could he. 'Remind me what I'm being judged on again.'

She flinched as she picked up her phone and opened the spreadsheet. 'I hate that word.'

'That's what you're doing, though, isn't it?'

'I'm doing what anyone does when they go on a date,' she countered, meeting his stare head on. 'I'm forming an opinion about the person I'm meeting. The only difference is other people don't put their thoughts into a spreadsheet.' She glanced down at her phone. 'Okay, so I've got; looks, style, punctuality, sense of fun, sense of humour, charisma, compatibility, sociability, interesting?, spontaneity, cat or dog lover.'

'I get marked down for having a dog?' he asked incredulously.

'Well, this is *my* spreadsheet with all the things *I* think are important. In my opinion, cats are way cooler.' She shrugged. 'But obviously you're not going to get rid of your dog, so for the purposes of this exercise I'll drop that one.'

'Fudge says thank you,' he countered dryly.

She hesitated, stared back down at the spreadsheet. 'There's also kissing expertise, naked appeal and sexual performance.'

'Ah, yes.' Poor Johnathan. At least they wouldn't get that far.

She gave him a long, searching look. 'You know you could always create a spreadsheet for me, too, just so we're even.'

He swallowed, hard, her grey gaze causing an unwanted reaction in him. 'I don't need a spreadsheet to gauge whether I'm interested in you.' Her eyes widened, and though he read the question in them, he kept quiet. His interest was purely physical, he told himself. There was nothing remotely relaxing about being with her. Dating her would be like plugging himself into a live socket. Not what he wanted after a hard day at work.

Silence descended, his words creating a hum of awareness that he doubted her numbers could quantify. He decided to focus on finishing his steak, though he was no longer hungry.

The clutter of cutlery onto a plate signalled that she'd finished and when he looked up he found her staring at him. 'We don't have to go through with this.' She gave him a sly smile. 'You could just admit my spreadsheet works and then you'd never have to see me again.'

He was close, so close, to agreeing. But where would that leave him? Licking his wounds over his two point five out of ten in a year's time? Those eyes blinked back at him and the challenge, the mischief she didn't try to hide, egged him on. 'I can't agree that it works without a proper trial.'

Her grin made his breath hitch. Like her, it was bold, fresh. A promise that their next ten meetings wouldn't be quiet, or easy. He was about to be plunged into an ice bath, then dragged through a tornado and when he was finally spat out, he wouldn't be the same again.

The prospect was unnerving, yet his life had become staid – he'd become staid. Perhaps he needed a dose of short, sharp shock treatment to get it starting again.

Sitting back on her chair, Sophie folded her arms. 'So where are you taking me first?'

And apparently that shock was starting already. Shit, he was ridiculously out of practice at all this. 'I don't know.'

'You don't have a usual date venue?'

He thought of the last time he'd taken a woman out. Jackie. 'It's been a while.'

'Don't be coy now. Define a while.'

He shouldn't be embarrassed. He'd been too busy, that's all. 'Three years.'

Her eyes rounded. 'Wow, that's a long time to be without … a date.'

Sex. He knew what she was thinking, but in reality he'd not really noticed the time passing. Betty had taken her tumble a few months after the ending of his relationship with Jackie. Then there had been the move from Manchester, taking care of Betty when she'd come out of hospital … and after that, he guessed his life had drifted, his thoughts rarely turning to sex. Until now. 'I'm aware.'

She glanced around her, then whispered. 'Are you going to make me come out here again?'

'Here is where I live.'

'Yes, sure, okay.' She smiled brightly, as if determined to convince herself this really was a great idea. 'I'm sure you can come up with something first date suitable.'

'Technically it'll be our second date.'

'I suppose, but that kind of crashed and burned, didn't it? We're starting again. A whole new row in my spreadsheet.'

He wasn't sure how to react to that. The circumstances would be different next time they met. He'd be on home turf, hopefully without any prior emergency. But he wouldn't be different. And neither would she.

They halved the bill – he'd never let a woman pay for his

meal and he wasn't about to start now. The gentleman in him found it hard enough to let her pay for her share, but the guy who'd been publicly red-lined decided it was fair. He did walk her back to the train station. And he did try not to smirk when the sexy but impractical high shoes she wore snagged in a pothole.

'We're not used holes in the road in London,' she muttered, glaring up at him.

'No. I suspect you're not used to sheep, either.' He slid his hands into his pockets and came to a decision. 'Maybe I'll show you some on our first date.'

'The anticipation will kill me.'

He tried not to smile. And failed.

Her arm bumped against his. 'See, this is already better than last time. You've actually smiled.'

Does that improve my score? It annoyed him that he wanted to ask. 'When are you free to venture out here again?' he asked instead.

Immediately she pulled her phone out of her bag and began to tap. 'I'm out Saturday, got a sponsored run on Sunday. Monday is Zumba, Tuesday I have a saxophone lesson, Wednesday there's a tennis match, Thursday I'm seeing a couple of the girls from work. Oh and damn, I need to re-arrange Joshua because we tentatively agreed Thursday for a drink.'

'Joshua?'

'He's one of the guys I dated before you.'

Now he realised why the name rang a bell. 'Started at seven out of ten. Got red-lined in his fifth and last date.' But a seven versus his two point five. The thought stung.

'Umm, yes.' Her eyes darted away from his. 'So anyway, I

can't do Friday either because it's always The Drunk Flamingo and on the Saturday Grace's sister is having a party which will be an absolute riot because Tanya is like Grace, only three years younger and even more crazy.' She tapped again, nodded and glanced up at him. 'I can do a week on Sunday?'

His mind felt like a spinning disc – so much information it was hard to grasp any of it. 'Okay.'

'Are you sure that works? You don't need to check your diary?' She gave him a wide grin. 'Or your spreadsheet?'

Dimples, he thought. Then looked away before he could get lost in them. 'I'm good. It's all up here.' He tapped his head. Easy to carry his diary there when all he had in it was Monday to Friday, work. Saturday and Sunday, catch up on stuff – shopping, paperwork, exercise. Repeat.

'That's a plan then. I'll see you a week on Sunday. And, err, maybe some sheep?'

With another of her smiles – a dash of humour, a dollop of cheeky, a hint of sexy – she waved him goodbye and headed to the platform.

As he strolled back home, his step felt lighter than it had a few hours earlier. He'd just opened the door when his phone pinged.

Sophie: Do you still want to stick pins in my effigy?

He let out a bark of laughter. Then shot off three messages.

I never wanted to do that.

Okay, maybe I did once.

56

Or twice.

She was clearly bored having to sit down for an hour on a train because she immediately pinged back.

Sophie: And now?

He shook his head and, smiling, rattled off a reply.

I'm considering taking down the dartboard with your face on the bull's eye.

'Is that a smile Michael Adams?'

He looked up to find Betty watching him. 'It has been known to happen.'

She made a dismissive noise. 'Not in a while.'

Her gaze sharpened, but before she could ask any questions, he went to kiss her cheek. 'I'll go and take the dogs out.'

On his whistle, Princess and Fudge scampered over to him. In his pocket, his phone pinged again.

He forced himself to wait until he was outside, the dogs doing their business, before he glanced at the message.

Sophie: Should I be afraid? Or is that you proving you have got a sense of humour?

He considered for a moment, then typed back.

Time – and maybe your spreadsheet – will tell. See you a week on Sunday. Bring shoes you can walk in.

Chapter Six

The following week, Sophie woke on Sunday morning with a hangover. It wasn't that unusual an occurrence, especially after a party at Tanya's where champagne was drunk out of bottles as if it was beer.

She reached for her phone and checked out her planner. Crap, she had to get on a train in a few hours to see Michael.

With a groan, she sunk further under the duvet.

'You sound like I feel.' Grace appeared in the doorway to her bedroom, long blonde hair a riot, her beautiful face pale, blue eyes bloodshot. 'I want to puke, but I don't think I've got anything left in my stomach.'

Sophie waved her away. 'If you talk about puking it will make me want to puke.'

'Sorry.' She came in and climbed gingerly onto the end of the bed. 'I announce today an official slob day. Let's drag our duvets into the living room and watch back to back Bridget Jones films. Followed by the entire series of Lucifer because nobody can feel bad when they're watching him.'

'Did someone say Lucifer? Count me in.' Ava joined them on the bed, face slightly less pale than Grace, though her hair was similarly tangled. Sophie patted at her own cropped locks. This was why she kept her hair short. Who had time to brush and blow dry?

'Yeah, well as good as all that sounds, I can't join you both.' She groaned again and flopped back onto the pillow. 'I've arranged to see Michael.'

Grace's eyebrows shot up. 'Two and a half out of ten man?'

'Yep.' It niggled at her, hearing him called that, even though she was the one who'd scored him.

Grace shook her head. 'Err why have you decided it will be a good idea to see a bloke you didn't like, for another date?'

'Not just one.' Sophie shut her eyes, feeling the room start to spin. 'Ten.'

'Holy shit, Soph,' Grace exclaimed. 'Have you gone mad?'

'Possibly.'

'I thought the point of this spreadsheet was to stop you wasting time on dates with guys who weren't ever going to be The One,' Ava added, miming quotation marks.

'It is.' Sophie searched her alcohol addled brain for the reasons why she'd committed herself to this. Nope, nothing. Nada. 'I don't know how it happened. You know I went out to see him to apologise last week.'

Grace scrunched up her forehead. 'I remember. You said it went okay.'

'It did, at least by the end. What I didn't say was that we got into this discussion about the spreadsheet and he argued it couldn't be used to judge a date.' Ava cleared her throat pointedly and Sophie shrugged. 'So, the pair of you are in agreement. Doesn't make you both right. I did concede that using it for one date possibly wasn't enough.' She rubbed at her temple, feeling the beginning of a headache. 'Before I knew it, we'd agreed to review it again after ten dates.'

'Ten dates?' Grace looked aghast. 'You don't even like him that much.'

'I know, but it's to test the spreadsheet.'

'Hang on.' Ava's brow wrinkled. 'What if you find he's a seven out of ten after ten dates? Are you really going to carry on seeing a guy you told us has no sense of humour, was dead quiet and lived in the sticks with his gran?'

'And his dog,' Grace supplied unhelpfully. 'Don't forget the man got a zero for being a dog-lover, though I guess he could get rid of the dog if he was really keen on you.' When Sophie and Ava both inhaled sharply, Grace rolled her eyes. 'Duh, I meant give the dog away. Obviously you're not going to carry on dating a dog killer, even though you don't like our canine friends.'

'You're making me sound like Cruella's evil sister,' Sophie protested. 'There are dog people and cat people and I'm a cat person. But that's beside the point. Obviously he's not going to be a seven out of ten at the end of our dates because, guess what, the spreadsheet doesn't lie. All I'm doing is proving to him, and to you guys, that it's a bloody good idea.'

'So are you going to give the other guys ten dates as well?' Ava asked, always the fair one.

'God no. I found Johnathan on a dating site. He doesn't know any of my other contacts and didn't read the message so he's no clue about the spreadsheet. I intend leaving it that way. I am going to see Joshua and Callum to apologise in person, but there's a reason the spreadsheet red-lined them.'

'Just as it red-lined Michael,' Ava pointed out.

'I know, I know. But he knows Jade, and we only had one drink together, and...' She heaved out a sigh. 'Maybe when I see Joshua and Callum I'll figure I should see them a few more times, too. I don't know.' But she couldn't forget that zap she'd felt when she'd first seen Michael, before their date had gone downhill. A zap, and a looks score that none of her other dates had come close to.

She glanced at the bedside clock and swore. 'I need to get moving because I've got a ruddy train to catch.'

'A train?' Grace looked at her as if she'd gone mad as she and Ava wriggled off the bed. 'You're not seeing him here, where there is actually stuff to do?'

'We're taking it in turns to choose the date. Apparently today I get the joy of going for a walk somewhere.' Sophie grimaced. 'And he thinks he can prove my spreadsheet wrong.'

Grace burst out laughing. 'I feel sorry for him. He's probably got this sweet date planned, like a picnic in some idyllic field, and you're going to hate it because you're allergic to quiet and peaceful. Plus you'll probably end up treading in sheep poo.'

'Better than dog shit.' Ava gave her a sympathetic smile. 'Have fun. We'll think of you as we binge on Lucifer.'

'Thanks.' What *was* she doing? She was certifiable. 'Hopefully I'll be back in time to catch the last few episodes. I mean, how long can it take to eat a few sandwiches?'

She'd cancel, Sophie thought as she stood under the shower. It wasn't like either of them really wanted to go through with this. They'd arranged the date not through a desire to see each other again, but to prove a point. It was a terrible reason to drag her hungover body out of bed on a

Sunday. Having dried off, she shrugged on her big towelling robe, reached for her phone and clicked on the message app.

Automatically she began to read their last string of messages. And found herself smiling.

Okay, maybe seeing him today wouldn't be that bad. He … intrigued her. They weren't heading for romance, but she was interested to see whether his score would improve the more she saw of him. Before she knew it, she'd tapped out a message to him.

Got a good cure for a hangover, Doc?

A few seconds later she received a reply.

Michael: Don't drink.

She laughed out loud and went to search her wardrobe for something picnic suitable.

―――――――

Sat at the kitchen island, Michael stared down at Sophie's message on his phone. Was it too late to cancel today? It's not like he'd be letting her down. In fact it was quite possible her message was a subtle hint that she wanted to cry off. Let's face it, hangover or not, she didn't want to come out here for a walk with him. So why put himself through this charade? In the most likely scenario, he'd come to the end of ten dates and still be a two and a bit out of ten, thus feeling even more shite…and proving her right. If by some miracle he came to the end without a red-line, what then? He'd be able to say he was right, that spreadsheets were a crackpot way to determine compatibility – something everyone with an ounce of common sense already knew. It wouldn't alter the fact that they *weren't* compatible.

He snatched up the phone and called her number.

'Ah, it's the good doctor. Got that hangover cure for me I hope?'

'Err.' He had a brain, one that had been good enough to get him into medical school. So why didn't it work when she spoke to him? 'Drink lots of water.'

'That's the best you can come up with? Got to admit, I'm disappointed. Thought with your medical degree you'd have a few clever solutions, like, I don't know, an Alka seltzer mixed with two spoons of sugar and the leaves of a yew tree.'

'I'm a doctor, not a witch. And yew tree leaves are poisonous.' He dragged in a breath, trying to find his balance. He was used to talking to people, had even been told he had a great bedside manner, yet Sophie turned him into this stiff, humourless prick. Probably because he felt on the backfoot with her, like he somehow had to impress to get his ruddy score up. Another reason to get out of this charade now. 'Best cure for a hangover is to go back to bed.'

'Ha, but I can't, because I'm seeing you.'

'About that.' The words, *let's forget this*, hovered but he realised they sounded too harsh when said on the phone, especially as it was only a few hours before they were due to meet. As he searched his brain for a softer excuse, Betty appeared in the doorway, wrapped in her dressing gown still. The Betty of ten years ago would have been dressed and out by now, but this older, post-fall Betty took longer to get going in the morning.

'Hello, are you still there?' Sophie's voice rattled him out of his thoughts.

'Yes, sorry.' He smiled at Betty, brain finally starting to work. 'I'm afraid I'll have to cancel today. My grandmother isn't well and I don't feel I should leave her.'

Betty's gaze flew to his, a frown deepening the wrinkles on her forehead. 'Who's that you're talking to?'

He shook his head at her, turning away as he listened to Sophie.

'Oh no, your poor gran. I hope she gets better soon…'

He didn't hear what Sophie said next because suddenly the phone wasn't in his hand. It was in Betty's.

'Hello dear, is that Sophie? It's Betty here, Michael's gran. He's been telling me all about you and I know he's really looking forward to seeing you today.' Fuck. He tried to snatch the phone back, but he received the hard stare he'd had as a kid when he'd pinched a third biscuit from her cookie jar. 'Oh, don't you worry about me. My grandson is a fuss pot. I'm right as rain. You two young things enjoy your day.'

With a satisfied humph, she thrust the phone back into his hand.

Great. Now it was bloody obvious he'd tried to wriggle out of today. Worse, he'd been thwarted by an eighty-five-year-old who'd called him a fuss pot to the woman he was trying to prove had got him wrong in her first damning assessment.

'She sounds lovely, your gran.' Sophie's voice echoed back at him. 'Lovely and not at all unwell.'

He dropped his head to the worktop, barely resisting the urge to bang it, repeatedly. 'Yes. When I took a cup of tea to her this morning, I thought she was having one of her dizzy turns.'

Could he sound any more pathetic? 'But apparently she's okay.'

There was a long pause during which he died a thousand deaths, knowing damn well his lie was about as believable as finding nightlife in Little Brook.

'You must perform medical miracles, Doc.'

There was another heavy pause and guilt squirmed in his gut. This time he was the one who'd hurt her feelings. She'd been willing to get on a train, despite her hangover. 'I'll see you at the station then?' He exhaled, that guilt wriggling some more. 'If you're still happy to come over.'

Silence. He didn't know which was the worst outcome, her telling him to bugger off, or her agreeing to go through with this date neither of them wanted to be on. 'Yes, fine. I'll see you in a bit.'

'Well.' Betty gave him a disapproving look as he clattered his phone onto the worktop.

He groaned, hanging his head, feeling like a kid again. He'd always hated disappointing her. She'd never had to say much. Like now, her look had always been enough. 'I know, I know. I just … this isn't about her wanting to see me.' And his ego needed his date to want to be with him.

'Nonsense. She came out here to ask you to give things another try. Now it's up to you to show her who you really are.'

And what if who he was, still wasn't up to much? He shook the thought away, disgusted with himself. He was a decent guy. One day he'd find a woman who appreciated his brand of … quiet.

'She wants to prove her spreadsheet was right in the first place,' he corrected. 'I told you, that's all this is.'

Betty hmphed. 'A woman doesn't agree to keep seeing a man only to prove a point. She likes you. Or at least she thinks she could get to like you.'

The thought there might be some truth in the statement, that there was a chance, even a vanishingly thin one, that these next ten dates could lead to something, made him pause. But then he remembered he'd rated the lowest of the dates she'd been on. And how she was seeing Joshua again. Joshua who she'd liked at least twice as much as she had him.

An arm wrapped around his shoulders. 'At the very least,' Betty said quietly. 'At the end of this you'll have had ten dates with a woman who makes you smile.'

He frowned. 'How do you know that?'

She nudged him. 'It was her messages I caught you reading last Friday, wasn't it?'

He let out a heavy breath, aware his answer was only going to feed his gran's false romantic notions. 'Yes.'

'Well three years is plenty long enough to lick your wounds.' Betty squeezed his shoulder. 'It's past time you put all that business with Jackie behind you and started to live again.'

She was right, he thought as he watched her fuss about making herself a drink. And it's not like he hadn't thought of dating again – it's why he'd gone along with Jade's suggestion in the first place. Yet he and Sophie were hardly well matched, and even if he looked past that, past the fact he'd never be able to relax with her, she wasn't interested.

With a heavy heart he trudged up the stairs and headed to his shower. This was going to be one hell of a long day.

Chapter Seven

Sophie's pulse did an odd kick as she stepped off the train to find this tall, fair-haired figure dressed in shorts and a polo shirt waiting for her at the end of the platform.

Yep, he was too quiet and reserved for her taste, but looks wise he was easily an eight out of ten.

And legs ... wow. Who'd have thought beneath that crumpled suit he had such frigging sexy legs? Tanned, with a pair of calves so well defined she could appreciate them even from this distance.

He put up a hand, like he wasn't sure she'd seen him even though he was the only person in the station.

'Hello there, Doc.'

That kick happened again as he gave her a small smile. 'Hello.'

They began to walk out of the station, which wasn't a station by any usual definition. Where were the passengers, the staff, the obligatory Starbucks/Café Nero/Costa coffee? 'How's your gran? Any more dizzy spells?'

A flush crept up his neck. 'She's fine. Thanks.' He let out a long exhale and jammed his hands into the pockets of his shorts. 'She was never ill. But then you knew that.'

She tried not to smirk. And failed. Really, she shouldn't wind him up, but after all the grovelling she'd had to do, it was good not to feel at a disadvantage for once. 'Why did you want to cancel? Did you decide you had no hope of proving my spreadsheet wrong? Or was the thought of ten dates with me so bad it wasn't worth trying?'

The flush on his neck deepened and he sighed. 'Neither.'

'What then?' When he remained silent, she gave him a nudge. 'Come on, spill. Because if you really don't want to do this...'

'I do.' He halted, bright blue eyes finally finding hers. 'But do you?'

'I'm here, aren't I?' He blinked and looked away, and suddenly she got it. 'If I hadn't sent the spreadsheet out by mistake we'd not be doing this. We both know that. Plus, it must be really shitty having to keep seeing this bitch who only scored you two and a half out of ten, but I'm game to go through with these ten dates if you are.' She sighed, annoyed with herself. 'And me continuing to mention that score isn't helping, so I should admit now that I was wrong to assess you like that after only knowing you a few hours.' She tapped his arm, bringing those cautious blue eyes back to hers. 'I wouldn't have agreed to see you ten more times if I thought I'd have a shit time.'

His jaw muscle bunched. 'Careful. Flattery will go to my head.'

She didn't know whether that was his version of humour, or his version of still annoyed. 'All that aside, if I'm going to use the spreadsheet to find my partner in life, it's important for me to know how well it works.'

He gave a slight shake of his head. 'I can save you the effort of ten dates. It doesn't.'

Laughter burst out of her. 'Well that's not very scientific of you, Doc. I need more proof.'

Another head shake, though this time his mouth twitched upwards. 'Okay.'

'Is that, "Okay Sophie, let's see where these next ten dates take us and I promise not to use my grandmother as an excuse to duck out of any more of them?"'

God, those eyes of his. They really were beautiful. Bright and blue and right now, as they caught hers, sort of shimmery. Like the ocean on a sunny day. 'No more excuses. I've got it.'

'Great, so let's get cracking with today.' She gazed around her. 'Where's your car?'

'Car?' He nodded down to his feet, and for the first time she noticed his sturdy walking boots. 'We're walking.'

'From here?'

'I thought so.' He cleared his throat. 'But we'll head to mine first to pick up Fudge. And so you can freshen up.'

'Freshen up?' They started off in the direction of what she assumed was his house. The one he shared with his gran. 'Oh, you mean go to the loo. Thanks, yes, that would be great. Better than having to squat behind a bush. I might get attacked by one of your sheep.'

'Walking in the countryside can be a dangerous business.'

She glanced sideways at him, experiencing another jolt as she took in his handsome profile. 'I never know if you're kidding or not.'

He quirked an eyebrow. 'I have no sense of humour, remember.'

She groaned. 'Oh God, please can we forget all about the spreadsheet today and just, well, try and enjoy ourselves.'

'That depends.'

That poker face of his was going to be tough to crack. 'On what?'

'On how many times we're savaged by sheep.'

His eyes flicked over to hers, and when she saw the glint of amusement she realised he wasn't humourless. His was just a brand of humour that took a bit of getting used to.

They turned down a small leafy lane and stopped outside a sprawling brick, flint and stone house. It was like something from those TV programmes again. Not the one where everyone was murdered this time, but the one where the couple decide to move from the busy, noisy city to the country to live this idyllic life with their dog and two unruly kids. Planting vegetables during the day and watching a roaring fire in the evening because with one sad pub and a truly abysmal broadband signal, there was nothing else to do.

The house was pretty though. Even had roses round the door and tidy flower beds running along the front. 'This is where you and grandma live?'

He nodded and pushed open the front door, standing back to allow her in first. As she passed him she inhaled a hint of his aftershave, or maybe it was his shower gel. Whatever it was, it suited him. Subtle and outdoorsy. She liked a bolder, more sophisticated aftershave, a scent that said take notice of me, but his was … pleasant.

'Who's the gardener?'

'I am dear.' A petite elderly lady stepped into the hallway, silvery grey hair cut very short, eyes a faded blue but which she suspected had once been as bright as her grandson's. 'But Michael's very good at pruning roses and putting in bedding plants.'

Behind her, Michael let out a sharp exhale, followed by a quietly muttered *Seriously*, and Sophie had to supress a giggle. 'You must be Betty, the famous grandma.'

She received a beaming smile. 'And you must be Sophie. The one who's got my grandson into all of a lather over some scores.'

Oh God. It was her turn to feel a wave of embarrassment, but before she could say anything, Betty waved her hand. 'Don't you fret, he can give off a terrible first impression but at least now he has a chance to redeem himself. Would you like a drink before you head off, dear?'

'Betty.' Michael's voice held a note of warning.

The older woman's eyes found hers, the spark in them proving age was no barrier to mischief. 'And now he's annoyed with me for interfering. He wants to whisk you away so I won't ask any awkward questions or say anything embarrassing.'

Sophie grinned. 'You know what? I'd love a drink.'

Michael huffed out a breath and this time she heard him mutter a faint *Christ*.

'Come on into the garden Sophie, while Michael makes us all some tea. He's got quite proficient at it now I've taught him to use a teapot and warm it first. While we wait I can show you the rose bushes he helped me cultivate and the begonias he planted the other day. He's becoming a real gardener, though he still needs a lot of direction. Oh and you need to meet Princess...'

As Betty ushered her through the living room and out of the big French doors, Sophie glanced behind her and saw Michael give a weary shake of his head.

Michael wanted to dump three tea bags into three of the grottiest mugs he could find. Without warming them first. No, wait, what he really wanted to do was open the front door and go for a very long walk. Alone. He looked up at the sound of nails scratching on tiles to find Fudge had come to join him from where she'd been taking a nap in the front room.

'Okay girl, I'd take you with me.' He gave her ears a rub, just how she liked it. 'You're the only female round here who doesn't get pleasure from embarrassing me.'

With a sigh he stretched up to pull the fancy teapot out of the cupboard. And the matching bone china cups and saucers Betty liked to drink out of. The same Betty who'd put her life on hold to take in two grief-stricken boys after their mum had died. So it didn't matter how much she was unwittingly taking his street cred score down from around two to something into the minus marks. He'd make the tea how she wanted it, because he loved the lady to bits. Never mind pruning her roses for her, he'd move mountains.

By the time he carried the tray outside – rose patterned tea pot, matching cups, saucers, milk jug and sugar bowl – Betty and Sophie were sat on the wicker chairs he'd insisted on buying to replace her painfully uncomfortable antique wrought iron set. His eyes automatically zeroed in on the slim, shapely legs he'd noticed the moment Sophie had stepped off the train. Silently he thanked the weather Gods for sending him a June Sunday warm enough to inspire her to put on a pair of denim shorts that could have come from Daisy Duke's wardrobe. At least if they couldn't manage conversation, he'd have a lovely pair of legs to stare at.

That's unless she fell over and broke one, considering she was only wearing a pair of flimsy converse trainers.

As he neared, he could hear Betty in full flow. From the way she was now detailing how proud she'd been when her *eldest chipmunk* had got into Cambridge to study medicine, he guessed she'd moved on from roses to giving him the big sell.

His ego shrivelled a little more. Dear God. The fact she thought he needed it, added to the obvious way she was going about it. The chance of him improving the impression Sophie had of him after today was vanishing faster than England's hopes of winning the next test match.

'Thank you, dear.' Betty scanned the contents of the tray and let out a satisfied hmph. When he risked a glance at Sophie, he saw her pretty grey eyes were as wide as the saucers Betty insisted on using. 'I was just telling Sophie how good you were as a boy. Never had any trouble getting you to do your homework or revise. Now if you'd asked me about his brother, it would be a different story. Always up to mischief, Dave was, staying out all night at parties, sneaking off with the girls, obsessed with playing football. I was at my wits end trying to get him to study for his exams.'

Michael tried not to wince. Being studious didn't mean he was boring.

Sophie smiled as Betty poured out the tea. 'I drove my mum mad, too. Books, studying, it was way too dull. Far more interesting things to do.'

Well, that told him.

'Did you have any siblings helping to distract you?' Betty asked, handing him a cup but not looking in his direction. As he sat down on the spare seat, Fudge curling round to sit at his feet, he wondered if either of them would notice if he took that walk now.

'Umm, yes. A sister, Rosie.' Because he'd been watching Sophie carefully – hers was a face he could enjoy watching – he saw a shadow pass over it. Fleeting, but raw.

He'd never know if she was planning to expand on what was clearly a traumatic story, because Princess chose that moment to make a fuss, yapping over some bird, squirrel, butterfly – the dog was easily distracted.

As Betty rose to quieten the pint size Chihuahua, Fudge looked up at him and Michael swore she rolled her eyes.

'So, umm, I presume that's Fudge.' Sophie waved a hand at the brown lab still sat obediently on the grass.

'It is.' He looked down into a pair of intelligent brown eyes. 'Fudge, introduce yourself to Sophie.'

The dog immediately climbed to her feet and he watched with what he guessed was something akin to fatherly pride as she sat, raised a paw and placed it on Sophie's lap.

'Oh, okay.' Rather than being impressed, Sophie looked like she wasn't sure what to do, and he belatedly remembered she was a cat person. 'Hello Fudge.'

His dog – his beautiful, obedient, docile, loyal, big-hearted dog – gazed up at her and Michael thought Sophie had to have a heart of stone to ignore that look. He sure as hell melted every time. But no, Sophie was staring at her, like she'd never seen a dog before. Just when he thought maybe she *was* that cold, she reached out and gave Fudge a tentative pat.

'She likes her ears being fondled.'

Sophie's eyes bounced to his. 'Fondled how, exactly?'

The softly spoken word on her lips tugged an alarming reaction out of him. One he recognised as lust. The re-awakening of a libido that had been in deep freeze for the three years. Unbalanced by it, he cleared his throat and bent towards Fudge to give Sophie a demonstration of what fondled meant to Fudge, shaking his head fondly when the dog's tongue lolled out of her mouth as she moved her head to encourage him.

'Ah, right. I think I've got it.'

Sophie reached to rub gently at Fudge's ears, and Michael found himself wondering what those long, slim fingers would feel like rubbing him…

'Michael?'

He gave a guilty start and looked up to find Betty watching him curiously. Please God she hadn't read his mind. 'Sorry. What did you say?'

Those eyes twinkled knowingly back at him. 'I was asking if you were going to take Princess with you on this walk of yours.'

His gut reaction, *fuck no*, was not one his gran would want to hear. It also made him shallow, but he could live with that. He was, after all, trying to prove this ruddy spreadsheet *wrong*. 'I'm afraid we're going too far for her little legs.'

'We are?'

Sophie looked startled which was odd because he knew from Jade that she was fit. 'Only far in Chihuahua terms.'

'Where are we walking? Is it somewhere notable?'

What on earth? 'Sorry?'

'I mean is it somewhere I can put on my spreadsheet. And then cross off that I've done it?'

He stared at her incredulously. 'You do that?'

She shrugged. 'Not as a rule. I compile a list of twenty places I want to see during the year, and cross them off as I go. But sometimes it's hard to cram them all in. This way I can still achieve my target.'

He didn't know whether to be impressed or horrified. 'We won't achieve anything if we don't get a move on.'

Sophie looked about as reluctant to go with him as Betty was to see them both go. Only Fudge shot to her feet and gave her tail an excited wag.

Maybe he'd cut the walk short. Put Sophie out of her misery.

Chapter Eight

Sophie was as disciplined about exercise as she was about everything else in her life. She ran, did Zumba, Pilates … she was fit. So it wasn't the effort of putting one foot in front of the other that she wasn't looking forward to. It was the time it was going to take them.

'How long is this walk, exactly?' she asked as she watched Michael climb over the stile, eyes glued to his legs because who wouldn't look at legs like that if they had the chance? Tanned and dusted with fair hair, his muscles tensed and rippled with every stride. Of course maybe they only seemed great because they were so surprising.

'Worried it's too much for you?'

'Hardly. I run half marathons for fun.'

He nodded. 'That leaves the sheep.' He slid her a look. 'Or the company.'

'Sorry?'

'The reasons you want to cut the walk short.'

'I didn't say I did.'

He let out a low laugh. 'We both know this isn't how you want to spend your Sunday.'

She was starting to get frustrated. 'I told you, I wouldn't be here—'

'If you thought you'd have a shit time,' he finished for her. 'But mediocre is okay?'

'Maybe I have more faith in your ability to entertain me than you do.'

His eyes flashed with an emotion she couldn't put a finger on. She wasn't sure she'd ever be able to read him. 'I thought we'd walk through the fields to the pub in the next village and have lunch there. We can hike back a different way, or catch the train back.' He gave her a half smile. 'Depending on whether your faith is misplaced.'

'No picnic?'

He frowned. 'Should there be?'

'No. It's just the girls thought we'd be having one. A picnic in a field, and me stepping in sheep poo.'

He considered her with a deadpan expression. 'We can still manage the latter.'

'Oh goodie. I'll look forward to it.'

They walked on in silence for a while, Fudge trotting ahead, halting every now and again to sniff before chasing after a bird for a few minutes, then obediently coming back to her master's side. Kind of sweet, really. If dogs were your thing.

She tried to appreciate the quiet, interrupted only by the gentle sounds of bird song and leaves rustling in the light breeze. No noisy traffic here, no honking horns. But her brain was wired for noise, conversation. Something to look at besides grass in fields. 'So, Cambridge University, huh?'

He gave a start of surprise, like he'd not been expecting to actually have to talk. 'I was the studious one, remember.'

'Yeah, but were you studious because you didn't like sport, or parties, or girls? Or because you wanted to be a doctor?'

He caught her eye, gave her a small smile. 'Thank you.'

'For?'

'Giving me an out.' His shoulders lifted in an awkward looking shrug. 'The truth is a bit of both. I wanted to be a doctor. And I hated parties.'

'But not sport and girls?'

'Sport I enjoyed, but I was more bat and ball.'

'And girls?' She didn't usually have to fish for information. In her experience guys liked nothing more than talking about themselves, yet she was finding the less Michael told her, the more interested she was.

Another small smile. 'Girls came later. At university.' He turned to her. 'What about you? How did you get into colour consultancy?'

She listened for any hint of derision in his tone, but found none. 'Well, we've already established I didn't work at school, so I was never going to go to university.'

'You were more hands on. Creative.'

She let out a surprised laugh. 'And now it's my turn to thank you for the out. But yes, let's be generous and say I always enjoyed the arts more than the text books. Even at six I was designing my own bedroom, which drove my parents nuts. Mum wanted to paint it pink and slap a few Disney transfers on it. I was all about messing with colours and painting a feature mural. By the time I hit eighteen, I'd re-decorated every room in their house, some that worked, and some, like the jungle-themed spare room complete with zebra wallpaper and bamboo headboard, that didn't. I suppose it was no surprise that when I left school I went to work in home furnishings, first in retail, then as a buyer and for the last five years as a colour consultant.' She remembered back to the first time she'd met him, and gave him an apologetic smile. 'I cringe when I think of how I mouthed off about how important my job was, while you were sitting there, having saved a guy's life.'

He came to an abrupt halt. 'Don't.'

'Don't what?'

'Make comparisons like that. A world full of doctors would be very dull indeed.'

It was true, but she appreciated him saying it. 'Well it's certainly my aim to add colour to it.' She crooked him a grin. 'Who gets the say on decorating your place, you or Betty, because I can totally see your hallway in sunflower yellow.'

He gave her a pained look. 'I'm not sure I should admit this, but that's Betty's remit. I get no say.'

Interesting. 'So what's the story there, with you and Betty?' Silence. She looked over at him, tried to work out if he was deliberately ignoring her, or thinking how to answer. 'It sounded like she brought you and your brother up?'

He picked up a stick and threw it for Fudge to chase after. The dog was growing on her. Quiet, like it's owner, but she figured in a dog, quiet was good. 'Mum died when I was fourteen, Dave only eleven,' he said finally. 'We went to live with Betty.'

'I'm sorry. That's a tough age to lose a parent. And your dad?'

'Left when I was seven. We never heard from him again.' He kept his gaze forward, expression neutral, though the tense set of his shoulders was like a big warning sign. *These questions are getting too personal.*

She decided to move to easier ground. 'Betty seems like a real character. I bet you had some interesting times, growing up with her.'

'You could say that.'

She glanced again at him, and the fondness in his expression was so sweet, so touching, that for a few moments she couldn't look away. That had to be the reason she found herself stumbling over the rock that had suddenly landed in front of her.

'Are you okay?'

'Yep.' Embarrassed, she waved away his concern. 'I'm a mountain goat, me.'

She slipped on the next rock, nearly twisting her ankle. God, where had all these boulders come from? 'As I said, mountain goat.'

'Clearly.'

Crap, why did her trainers suddenly have slicks for soles instead of treads? 'Maybe I'm a goat that hasn't quite found her footing yet. A young, goat. A mountain kid.'

There were only so many times a man could watch a woman stumble and not do something about it. Apparently for him, that number was four. He'd forgotten this route sent them through the derelict quarry.

Her cute but useless trainers slipped again on the next rock. 'Here, take my hand.' She grasped it as if it was a lifeline, her grip strong, her hand warm and ... yes, tingles now raced over his skin from where their hands joined.

Funny how this feeling he remembered as attraction, could come from a woman so absolutely wrong for him.

For a few minutes they walked side by side, hand in hand, her focussed on the rocks. Him on the feel of her fingers wrapped round his. When the number of rocks in their way began to dwindle, he reluctantly let go – he wasn't going to think too much on *that* – and they came to a halt at the stream.

'Please tell me we don't have to cross that.'

It was racing faster than he remembered last time he'd walked this way. And the stepping stones, while perfectly okay for walking boots, were wet versions of the boulders she'd already stumbled her way over. 'I could say we don't. But I'd be lying.'

She screwed up her face. 'And this is what you guys do for fun out here?'

His heart sunk a few inches in his chest. She was hating this. He'd genuinely thought she might enjoy it – she liked exercise, fresh air had to beat exhaust fumes, and the scenery was surely far superior to the concrete jungle of London.

As if to prove his point, she took out her phone and snapped off a few photos. When she caught him watching, she laughed. 'Just taking a photo to put on Instagram. You know, so when I'm in hospital with a broken ankle I can point to where it happened.'

At the sound of a splash he looked over to find Fudge had bounded into the water, tail wagging. 'At least someone's enjoying it,' he remarked.

'I didn't say I wasn't.' She tucked the phone back in her pocket and sighed. 'Okay, so maybe I'm not having the best time. It's just … I'm embarrassed I've been so crap today, to be honest. It's not like I'm unfit, but so far I've been like that stereotypical city person who makes a tit of herself when she tries to go horseback riding, or camping.' Another sigh. 'Or apparently just for a walk.'

He wanted to dismiss her, to pigeon hole her into that very stereotype, because then it didn't matter that he found her attractive. He'd never be in trouble if he didn't like her. But it was impossible not to smile at her now. 'You'll be able to get your own back.'

She pursed her lips, which then curved into a mischievous grin. 'Oh yes, what was it you said earlier? You hated parties? I'll have to remember that.' Instantly his mind conjured up the image of a party in full flow, her dancing with her friends, him sat in some dingy corner like a sad git. Thankfully he was dragged out of it when she spoke again. 'Meanwhile, how do you suggest we get across here, Bear Grylls?'

'No more Doc?' He'd never liked the shortened phrase, so it was odd that he suddenly missed it.

'I thought Bear Grylls would be useful right now.'

He cast his eyes over her slim frame – no hardship – and made a snap decision. 'Jump onto my back.'

'You … what?'

She was looking at him like he'd made some sort of weird sexual reference. 'I'll carry you across this.' When she still stared at him, he added. 'Piggyback.'

Her gaze left his and eyed up the wet, slippery stepping stones. The fast-moving water. 'You could drop me.'

'I could.' He looked pointedly down at his boots. Then her trainers. 'Then again, you could fall in without my help.'

'You said bring shoes I could walk in. Not climb over giant boulders and cross treacherous rivers.'

It was a fair point, he guessed. For a city dweller. 'I also said we'd see sheep. You don't get them on pavements.'

She indicated ahead. 'Apparently you don't get them in the countryside either.'

He placed his hands on her shoulders and turned her ninety degrees. 'Short legs. White woolly coat.'

She huffed out a breath. 'Fine. Maybe I missed them earlier, what with trying to avoid breaking my neck.'

He inhaled, about to say something about mountain goats not being known for breaking their necks, but halted when he caught her scent; bold, spicy. If he'd smelt it from a bottle he'd have turned up his nose, but on her skin? And with the feel of that warm skin beneath his hands, even through a layer of cotton? The combination caught him by the balls.

Hastily he dropped his hands. He'd been mad to offer a piggyback.

'You really reckon you can carry me across without either of us face planting in the water?'

Ego vied with common sense. 'Yes.'

She gave a brisk nod. 'Okay then, let's do this. But if I end up in the drink, you're heading to the loudest, most raucous, pretentious party I can find.'

He considered it a minor miracle that he made it across without slipping. Not because of her weight – she wasn't heavy – or because it was treacherous. The hardest part hadn't been finding his balance on slippery rocks. No, it had been finding his balance with fifty odd kilos of warm, supple woman wriggling around on his back, her scent in his nostrils, the smooth skin of her legs against his palms.

If she noticed he was quick to release her at the other end, she didn't let on. Just carried on talking with the same rush of words she had since he'd met her off the train. He wondered if she talked in her sleep. Which then got him thinking of her in bed, and whether she talked during...

'Err, Doc, where have you gone?'

Grey eyes sparkled back at him, amused, curious. Thank God they weren't psychic. 'Sorry.'

'Thinking about the party I've got lined up for you?'

'Something like that.'

She studied him, and he tried not to squirm. 'I was asking how much further to the pub. Not that I'm bored of this Country File outing, but I'm hungry.'

'It's not too much further.' He gave her a sly glance. 'Round the next corner.'

She groaned. 'Oh please, that's what my parents used to say to us.' *Us*. He didn't think she was aware of it, but her body tensed for a moment. 'It's probably why I ended up living in London, just so I wouldn't have to go on walks where I had no clue how far it was to the end, and no civilisation in sight.'

He was a guy who hated talking about himself so he could totally understand her need to keep certain parts of herself private. It appeared her sister was one of those parts, so he ignored the urge to probe her further. 'Disappointed I didn't do a picnic?' he asked instead.

'If you asked my stomach right now it would say yes. But by the time I'd been stung twice by wasps, sat in an ants' nest and then stood in sheep poo trying to escape it, I'd say the pub was a better choice.' She slid her phone out of her pocket and tapped it a few times. 'As long as it has a no carb option.'

'Did you just check your spreadsheet?'

'Of course. I designed a weekly meal plan to ensure I have a balanced diet. Spreadsheets are brilliant for more than just determining the suitability of a date, you know.'

She winked and gave him a cheeky smile. The combination caused a disturbing flutter in his chest. Quickly glancing away, he pointed to the thatched building ahead of them. 'You can see the pub now.'

'Oh wow. Great. Looks like you were right about the "round the corner" part.' She mimed quotation marks.

'Might not be the only thing I'm right about,' he countered mildly.

She smirked, and he realised the curl of her upper lip, along with the twinkle in her eye, was growing on him. 'I believe you've got another nine and a half dates before you can make that claim.'

He had to admit this one hadn't gone swimmingly, what with Betty and her embarrassing attempt to big him up – begonia planting aside – followed by Sophie stumbling across rocks, having to be carried over a stream and her clear dislike of the countryside in general. Yet, if he forgot about why he was doing this and focussed instead on how this compared to a usual Sunday, he could honestly say he'd enjoyed himself so far.

Turns out the company of an attractive woman, even if she wasn't into him, and even if she was too loud for him, was better than his own company.

Fudge chose that moment to squat.

'Oh, is she…' Sophie turned away. 'Yep, she really is.'

Fudge gazed back at him, totally unfazed at taking a shit in front of this new addition to their walk.

'Why don't you go on ahead,' he waved towards the pub that was only a few yards away now. 'Find us a seat in the garden. I'll … take care of this.'

'Good plan.' Sophie charged off, turning round only when she got to the pub gate. 'FYI, that's why cats are cooler. Pooping in a litter tray in private is way more dignified.'

When she was out of sight, he stared down at Fudge, who'd finished and was wagging her tail, tongue lolling out of the side of her mouth. 'Seriously? You couldn't have waited? You had to do it just before we ate?'

She let out a little bark, then wagged her tail again, nose nuzzling against his hand. 'Okay, okay, you didn't know I was trying to impress her, huh?'

Digging the bag out of his pocket, he scooped up the poo and tied it up. Now he just had to hope there was a nearby bin. Eating while trying to be interesting and charismatic were hard enough for him to pull off anyway – though her two out of ten for both still rankled. With a pocket literally full of shit though, he couldn't see either score improving.

Chapter Nine

Wednesday night, and as Sophie got ready to meet Joshua for the drink she'd promised him, her phone buzzed with a message from the only other man she'd so far met in person to apologise.

Michael: I can do Friday.

She shook her head at his typically minimal response. It had been coming up for two weeks since their walk, and they'd had a bit of toing and froing over when he was coming to London. Looks like they finally had a date.

Sitting on her bed, she typed back.

Excellent. We'll hit The Drunk Flamingo. You can meet the gang.

She paused, then, smiling to herself, added.

You'll love it.

A few moments later she received another message.

Michael: I doubt it.

She giggled, imagining his dry smile.

'Umm, what are you laughing over?'

Sophie looked up to find Grace standing in the doorway. 'Nothing, just a message.'

Her gaze narrowed. 'Message from who?'

She didn't know why it felt awkward. 'Michael. He's coming to The Drunk Flamingo with us on Friday.'

'He's going with *you*.' She tapped her index finger to her lip. 'Is this date two of ten then?'

'Yep.'

'So even though the original date was such a disaster you didn't want to see him again, and the revised first date was, by your account, boring and involved you nearly twisting your ankle, you're persisting with seeing him nine more times?

'I didn't say last Sunday was boring.' In fact she'd enjoyed some parts. The pub lunch. Meeting Betty, who was a scream. *The piggyback ride.* Yep, she wasn't going to think of how her heart had sped up when she'd settled her legs around Michael's waist. Felt his hands on her thighs. Put her arms around shoulders that had been broader, stronger than she'd thought. 'I'm just not a fan of walking, unless it's to actually get somewhere, you know like a bar, or a concert. Or the shops. And anyway, you know why I'm still seeing him.'

'I know you have some weird hang up about proving this bonkers spreadsheet theory of yours right.'

'Wow, don't you go all polite on me now, Grace. Say it how you mean it.'

Grace rolled her eyes. 'That *was* me being polite.'

'Well for the record, I totally dispute the words weird, hang-up and bonkers. I have a perfectly sensible determination to see whether I can use my genius spreadsheet to slash the time wasted in getting to know guys who ultimately turn out to be duds.'

'I'll tell you an easier way,' Grace supplied. 'Short-term hook ups. Never last long enough to get boring or as you'd say, waste time.'

Ava popped her head round the door and had clearly heard Grace's statement because she looked at Sophie and raised her eyes to the ceiling. Grace's supposed short-term hook up, Daniel, had been on the scene for several months now and Grace showed no sign of getting bored.

'Are you sure that's all there is to this thing with Michael?' Grace pressed, her expression turning serious. 'You're not secretly going to fall for him, are you, because I'm telling you now, from what I've heard so far, I'm not going to like him. And I'll like him even less if he takes you away from us and forces you to live in some village where your only entertainment is seeing how big a marrow you can grow.'

Sophie burst out laughing. 'Oh my God, stop talking, you daft cow. I'm definitely not going to fall for him. You do remember his spreadsheet score? And sure, there were reasons he turned up late and distracted, really good reasons as it happens,' she added, remembering with shame how she'd thought him rude, when really he'd just been concerned about a patient. 'But I revised it again after the walk and guess what, he's still only three and a half out of ten.'

'He's gone up though?' Ava asked.

'A bit. He was on time to meet me at the station and he wore these shorts and a polo shirt which, though a bit conservative, did look good on him and were definitely a step up from the crumpled suit. Plus he's got these phenomenally good legs, though I don't have a category for that. Maybe I should have.'

'What about his sense of humour?' Grace prompted. 'His message clearly made you laugh.'

'Well yes, but I wouldn't describe him as funny. He's so dry, half the time I don't even know if he's being funny or serious. And his idea of a good time is going for a walk with his dog, so he's hardly compatible with me or my mates.' She glanced at her bedside clock. 'I have to go, or I'll be late for Joshua.'

Grace screwed up her face in a frown. 'Wait, I remember him. He was a bit of a laugh, especially when we got him dancing.'

'He was,' Sophie agreed. 'But by date five I realised I didn't want to kiss him, you know? High rating for fun and spontaneity but though his charisma and looks were okay, the whole package just wasn't enough of a turn on in the end.'

'Well you'd better go meet him before he marks you down for punctuality on *his* spreadsheet,' Ava remarked with enough of an edge for Sophie to know she still didn't approve of the whole scoring thing.

Once the pair of them had ducked out of her room, Sophie went back to the task of deciding what to wear. Plumping for her strappy jumpsuit, she teamed it with a pair of wedge sandals, and headed out of the door. On the tube she fired a quick reply to Michael's last message.

Of course you'll enjoy our date. You'll be with me. The Mountain Goat. We're bound to have a laugh.

She tried not to keep glancing at her phone for a reply. And tried not to be disappointed when no message came back. Maybe it was because of the dodgy reception.

Joshua was … nice. Sophie found it strange being back with him again after Callum. And after Michael. Callum was the more dynamic of the three. Joshua was fun, easy company but her pulse still didn't quicken when she looked at him. Michael was by far the most attractive, physically, yet also the least sociable, the hardest to talk to, and the most serious.

As looks faded, it was right that her spreadsheet was weighted towards the more important attributes like charisma, sociability and compatibility.

'I still can't believe you scored our dates.' Joshua shook his head, dark hair flopping over his forehead. 'I get the spreadsheet thing, I use them all the time at work, but to use it for analysing a date. Isn't that a bit, you know, clinical?'

Why didn't people get it? 'Maybe. Maybe not.' She made to catch his eye. 'What did you think of me? Were you gutted when I suggested not seeing each other anymore?'

He shrugged. 'I guess not. I mean you're hot, probably way out of my league if I'm honest. And you were funny, made me laugh, but you're not really my type. I prefer my women more … chilled. Plus I never really got what you did for a living. Colours and paints and all that. Woman I saw last week was a software developer. It was so cool watching what she could do with algorithms…'

There, she wanted to say. It might not have been numerical but he'd judged her, just as she had him. And they'd both found the other okay but that was all. If she'd not had the spreadsheet they might have even carried on seeing each other because … again, they'd got on. But it was just as obvious now that nothing would have come of it in the end.

As Joshua continued to sing the praises of his computer geek date, she was aware of a buzz in her pocket. Had Michael finally replied?

The need to take a look was almost overpowering, but aware she'd accused Michael of being rude for looking at his phone, she ignored it and focussed instead on Joshua, who'd now moved to talking about the latest machine learning … something or other, and how it fascinated him. Odd that he didn't get her spreadsheet, considering how much he was into tech.

That compatibility score she'd first thought was a seven? It was now down to three. The interesting score? Right now she was thinking a two.

When she couldn't take any more, she pleaded a need to go to the toilet. As soon as she closed the door behind her, she snuck a look at her messages.

Michael: Mountain goats aren't good in bars. Maybe we should try another walk.

Laughing to herself, she messaged back.

Nice try Doc but we have a deal.

Then, because she couldn't resist teasing the serious guy, she added.

What are you up to? Planting begonias again?

––––––––––––––

Michael looked down at his phone and gave a shake of his head, not knowing whether to be amused or insulted at Sophie's latest message.

'There he goes again.'

He looked up to find Jade smirking at him. 'What?'

'I've never seen you so glued to your phone. Even when you're on call you don't check it as often as you have this last half hour.'

Feeling guilty, and a little embarrassed, he was about to slip it back into this pocket when his brother put a hand on his shoulder. 'Not so fast. We need to see who you're messaging.'

'No you don't.'

'Ah, but we do. That way we can relentlessly take the piss out of you for the rest of the evening.'

'Unkey Mikey.' The reason he'd come out to his brother's tonight stood on the top of the stairs, the giant furry octopus he'd bought her for her birthday, firmly nestled under her arm.

The sight caused a squeeze on his heart. 'Hey Olivia. You ready for that story?'

She nodded. 'I want "Inky Octopus".'

'Then you've got it.' He rose to his feet, gave his brother a smug smile. 'Sorry, got to go.'

'The questions will still be here when you come back

down.' His brother waved up at his daughter. 'It's late, so one story only, yes?'

'But I'm four now.'

Michael bit back a grin. His brother had two strong-willed females in his life. And a fifty-fifty chance of there being three in a few months.

'Fine,' his brother replied with the weariness of a father who knows it's a battle he won't win. 'Two stories, tops.'

'You're such a sucker,' Michael whispered as he walked past.

'Me? You're the one who bought her a birthday present full of suckers.'

Laughing, Michael jogged up the stairs. God, but his niece was adorable, he thought as he followed her pint-sized figure to her room. He'd bought her the octopus because she'd been so fascinated with it when he'd taken her to the London Aquarium a few months ago. Once a month he took Olivia out for the day, ostensibly to give Jade and Dave a day off from parenting, but really because he just plain adored spending time with her.

'Have you got a name for your new pal yet?' he asked, indicating towards the bright orange octopus as he settled on the bed next to her. She shook her head, brown curls tickling his chin as he put his arms around her. 'That's okay, plenty of time. Names are important, you don't want to get it wrong.'

He opened the book – another present from him – and began to read. He'd got to the part where Inky squirted his ink when Olivia started to giggle. 'Squirt.' She patted the furry orange head. 'His name is Squirt.'

'An excellent name for an octopus.' He kissed the top of her head, feeling a wave of love. And hot on its heels, an acute pang of something he could only describe as longing. Would he ever have a family of his own? He was the oldest brother, but also the one not settled. It hadn't bothered him while the painful split with Jackie had been so raw, especially as his worries for Betty and the move down had been at the forefront of his mind.

Yet now, as he held this precious bundle, felt her body relax with sleep, he wanted with an ache he could feel deep in his chest.

After settling Olivia into her bed and Squirt on her pillow – he hoped she didn't wake up in a panic with those big eyes staring at her – he was about to head downstairs when he remembered Sophie's message. Something about begonias. Thanks Betty.

Quickly he typed out:

No begonias tonight. With Jade and Dave. You?

Should he be flattered she'd carried on the virtual conversation? It pissed him off that he was so keen to change her opinion of him. At the very least, to get her to admit he was higher than two and a half out of frigging ten.

He shouldn't care. He should be focussing his energies on finding a woman who actually liked him from the start. Who recognised his quiet, his reserve, as traits that were every bit as worthy as … what was in her spreadsheet? Oh yeah, charisma, sociability. Spontaneity. Who the hell looks for spontaneity in a date? Wasn't it better to be well thought through? Organised?

He was walking down the stairs when he received a message back.

Sophie: With Joshua. Apology drink [monkey hiding eyes emoji]

He felt an uncomfortable twinge in his gut. Probably the triple chocolate birthday cake.

Before he could stop himself – very unusual for a man who always thought long and hard before he spoke – he'd punched out a reply.

No dinner?

'You do realise you're not leaving this house before giving us the low down on who you're messaging and when you met them.' Jade greeted him at the bottom of the stairs, hand on her hip, right brow arched. 'Oh and when *we* get to meet them.'

Damn it. He was not ready for Jade's inquisition. He was way too embarrassed. Easy for Sophie to explain why they were still seeing each other; *He told me a spreadsheet couldn't judge dating compatibility. I thought it would be a bit of a laugh to see him again to prove him wrong.* But for him? However he phrased it, there was a smack of desperation to a guy continuing to see a woman who'd so clearly written him off.

'Oh my flaming God, it's Sophie, isn't it?' Jade, the apparent mind reader, gaped at him. 'That's why you're looking like Olivia does when I catch her sneaking an extra biscuit when my back is turned.'

He swore under his breath and went to sit on their big leather sofa. When he snuck his brother a pleading sideways glance, Dave shook his head. 'Don't look to me to help you out bro'. I'm as invested in finding out what's going on between you and this mystery texter as my wife is.'

'Nothing is going on.' He sighed, dragged a hand through his hair and waited for them to ask another question or hey, change the subject – he could be optimistic. But he was hit with a wall of silence. Sat together on the opposite sofa now, they both gave him *the* look. Dave had been doing it since he'd turned teenager, but more recently Jade had perfected it, too. It said *We know you're waiting for us blabber mouths to talk, but we're smarter than you think. We've learnt to bite our tongue and wait for you to cave.*

He sighed again. Crossed his legs at the ankles. Wondered how bad form it would be if he left now.

'No way.' Jade, spotting his not-as-surreptitious-as-he'd-hoped glance at the door, gave him a hard stare. 'You go now, you can cross Olivia off your play date list.'

He laughed incredulously. 'You'd use your daughter to blackmail me?' His gaze jumped from Jade, to his brother.

'I told you, I'm not helping. I'm as scared of her as you are.' Dave waggled his eyebrows at Jade. 'Plus maybe a bit turned on.'

'Jesus.' With a final deep exhale, he gave them what they wanted. 'Fine. Somehow, I got roped into seeing Sophie ten more times, so she can prove her spreadsheet right. Or wrong.'

'Ten.' Jade's eyebrows bobbed up and down. 'That's a lot of dates for a couple who don't like each other.'

'We're hardly a couple.' He heaved out another breath. 'And I never said I didn't like her.'

'Interesting.' Jade's eyes zeroed in on his. 'Does Betty know about this?'

'Yes.'

'Wow.' Dave rocked back. 'And she didn't tell us?'

'There's nothing to tell.'

His phone buzzed again and both their eyes fell to where it lay on the sofa next to him. 'That's Sophie again, isn't it?' Jade asked, almost bouncing up and down.

'We're just finalising the date and time for our next … meeting.' It was sort of the truth. And he refused to call it a date, not in front of them.

'Okay, what does she say?'

Because he was interested, he took a look at Sophie's reply to his question about Joshua and dinner.

Sophie: He didn't warrant a meal. See u Friday [smiling face emoji]

He could read it a number of ways. Joshua hadn't needed as much pacifying. He hadn't deserved a meal as he'd not been humiliated. She hadn't *wanted* to eat with him. He hated that it was the latter he focussed on.

'So?'

'She says she'll see me Friday.'

They gave him the squinty eye, but this time he didn't flinch. The next nine *meetings* were going to be tough enough without his family sticking their noses in.

Chapter Ten

Friday had arrived and Sophie's friends were driving her crazy. Ever since the pair of them had come home from work – Grace from her job as a receptionist (because she wanted to be like a normal person, even though she was loaded) and Ava from the accountancy firm she worked for – they'd done nothing but ask questions about the man they were going to meet.

It wasn't as if she knew many of the answers. Thanks to Betty and Jade, she could tell them Michael's age, what he did, where he'd studied. The fact he and his brother had been brought up by their grandma since Michael had turned fourteen. She couldn't tell them what he did outside work, other than walk and plant begonias. Nor did she know his relationship history – just that he'd not been on a date for three years. She still had no clue why a single man in his thirties lived with his grandma in some quiet village with no night life.

From the silent communication between Ava and Grace

after she'd admitted this, she had a feeling she'd have more answers by the end of the evening.

They'd agreed to meet at The Drunk Flamingo because, as Michael had been at pains to point out, he couldn't say for definite which train he'd be able to catch. He hadn't added that this wasn't because he didn't believe in being punctual, but because he had a job that sometimes involved saving lives. The omission would have earned him a high score in the column of her spreadsheet marked *gracious*. Had she had one.

The bar was heaving, which was standard for a Friday night. Worried she might not spot Michael, she'd chosen a table next to the window so they could keep an eye out for him.

'What are we looking for?' Grace asked, eyes scanning the pavement outside. 'Other than an eight out of ten?'

'Tall. Mid-thirties. Fair hair. Possibly wearing a crumpled suit,' Sophie added, aware he might have to come straight from work again.

Ava gave her a curious glance. 'What happened to tall, dark and debonair?'

Sophie took a sip of her cocktail. 'I'm still waiting to find him.'

Yet her heart gave a little jump as she saw a familiar figure cross the road towards them. 'That's Michael.'

'Oh.' Grace frowned and turned to scrutinise the man who'd just walked in. Thankfully there was no suit. Instead he'd put on a pair of dark jeans and a casual grey shirt over a plain white T-shirt. 'Ooh,' Grace repeated. 'He's actually kind of hot looking.'

'I know.' In fact tonight he looked like a guy she should

have given at least a nine out of ten to in terms of looks. And an eight for style.

'He doesn't seem like a guy who only rates two and a half out of ten,' Ava added quietly.

'Agreed.' Sophie watched him look round, then nod when he caught her eye. There were men who strolled into the bar like they owned it. Men who strutted in, determined to attract attention. Men who sauntered in, drawing the eye. Michael didn't do any of those things. He was … unassuming. So much so that, as he slowly picked his way through the throng of Friday night drinkers towards them, most women didn't even notice him, which was a shame. She'd meant it when she'd told him he'd be a good catch for someone.

'No emergency dashes tonight then, Doc?' she asked in lieu of a greeting, pointing to his jeans.

He frowned. 'No, I…' His expression cleared. 'Ah, I see what you mean.'

He gave her an awkward smile, his gaze jumping from her to the two women beside her who were currently staring at him like he was a rare species they'd not seen before. 'So, these are my friends. Ava's the brunette and likely to give you the easiest time. Grace is the blonde who makes me look shy and reserved.'

He inclined his head. 'Good to meet you both.'

A strained silence followed his words, something that just didn't happen when the three of them got together. It was like his quiet was rubbing off on them.

'What are you drinking?' She waved her nearly empty glass in the air, trying to break the tension. 'We can recommend the cocktails, can't we girls? Cost almost as much as a month's rent mind you, but totally worth it. Especially when we're celebrating.'

He eyed her like he wasn't sure what species *she* was. 'What are you celebrating?'

'The fact it's Friday, obviously.' She drained the rest of her drink. 'We're on the Porn Star Martinis tonight. You should totally try them.'

Grace nodded enthusiastically. 'Absolutely. They put hairs on your chest, so I'm told. That is if you haven't got hairs on it already.' She giggled. 'You should be warned, Sophie does like a hairy chest. Not too much, mind you. Just enough to say I've got plenty of testosterone.' She dug Sophie in the ribs. 'You should add hairy chest to your spreadsheet, Soph.'

'Thanks, but I think naked appeal covers it,' Sophie replied dryly, used to Grace's sense of humour.

Michael's ocean blue eyes nearly popped out of their sockets. 'Right, well…' he glanced towards the packed bar. 'I'll get us all a drink.'

As they watched him head off, Sophie felt a tug of sympathy for him.

'Doesn't talk much, does he?' Grace observed, which made Ava laugh.

'You hardly gave him a chance.'

'I thought I should warn him what he's up against if it gets as far as him taking his clothes off,' Grace protested.

'He might have hairs on his chest.' Sophie didn't know why the thought of seeing his chest sent a rush of heat between her legs.

He must have more presence than she'd given him credit for because he returned with the drinks a few minutes later. 'Wow, that was quick.'

'I got lucky.'

Not luck, she thought, as she caught the pretty redhead bartender staring over at him. And apparently not unnoticeable. 'Hey, where's yours?' she asked as they all grabbed a cocktail glass filled with fizzing orange liquid, topped with a slice of passionfruit. Thanking him effusively because of the aforementioned eye watering cost.

He sat down on the chair they'd snagged him and tugged a bottle of lager out of his jeans pocket.

She smiled. 'Ah, did we scare you off the cocktail?'

'Looks like he's got the chest hair covered already,' Grace added with a grin.

Michael shrugged awkwardly. 'I prefer beer.' As if to confirm his statement, he took a swig from the bottle, and yes, there was something sexy about watching the way his throat moved as he swallowed.

'Soooo.' Grace gave Sophie a sidelong glance, which she easily interpreted as *this guy is hard work*. 'This is the stage in the evening when we get to do a quick-fire Q&A, so you need to be sitting comfortably.'

His eyes widened and, when he looked her way, Sophie gave him an apologetic smile. 'Sorry, I can't defend you from this. It's kind of a tradition that they quiz my dates.'

'As long as the guy has survived to date four,' Ava added unhelpfully, making her sound like a serial dater.

He frowned. 'But this is only two.'

'Technically it's the fourth time we've met, though.' Sophie ticked off the occasions on her fingers. 'Number one was the disaster date, number two the apology meal. Number three the dangerous walk through fields of savage sheep.'

'A walk I'm unlikely to forget,' he murmured.

Was he amused? Was that a fond *unlikely to forget*, or a left a nasty scar, forget? It was so darn hard to work him out. 'Do we have your agreement to continue with the quiz on that basis?'

His gaze jumped from her, to Grace, to Ava. And back to her. 'Technically, we're not dating.'

She waved a hand at him. 'There's no escaping the quiz over a dodgy technicality. Only death, near death or the bar catching fire are valid excuses.'

He swallowed, nodded. 'Do you have a match?'

His expression was so deadpan for a split second she wondered if he wanted to chill and light a cigar. 'Good try, but none of us smoke.'

Grace levelled him a look that Sophie swore was part evil. 'Settle back, doctor. This won't hurt at all.'

It wouldn't hurt, the blonde had said. The one who talked even more than Sophie did. And maybe if Michael had had as many cocktails as they had – they were now on their fourth – the alcohol would have acted like an anaesthetic. But his two lagers weren't cutting it.

Up to now, the questions had been banal. Favourite colour – blue. Film – The Dark Knight, or The Dark Knight Rises. No, he wasn't a Batman fan particularly. Just a fan of a well-made film. Food – steak and chips. Drink – tea. When they'd shaken their head at him, he'd given them Peroni, though he had argued he didn't fancy a lager with his cornflakes.

'Come on, this is supposed to be quick fire. Answer the question.' Grace, definitely the scarier of the two, tapped her fingers on the table. 'You must have thought about what score you'd have given Sophie after that first date.'

'I haven't.' But he had thought about the fact he'd wanted to see her again. Until he'd found out what she'd really thought of him.

Sophie, sitting opposite him, buried her face in her hands. 'Can we move on from scoring. Please?'

Silently he agreed with her.

'Fine,' Grace conceded. 'We probably only have time for a couple more questions anyway before the rest of the gang arrive.' There were more of them? His heart plummeted so fast he wondered if they'd see it rolling about on the floor by his feet. 'Ava, your go.'

'Okay, let me think.' Ava flicked back her long, dark hair. 'What do you do for fun?'

He took a drink of his beer. 'Besides answering personal questions?'

A low huff of laughter left Sophie's lips. It was a little embarrassing to admit how pleased that made him. Purely because he'd proved he *could* make her laugh, he reasoned.

Ava gave him a warm smile. 'Beside that, yes.'

'I walk. Play cricket.' One look at their expressions and he dropped his other favourite pastime – reading.

'Hey, there's Ethan, with Jacob and Daniel.' Ava waved over to the three men who'd just walked in. Skinny jeans, white trainers, cool jackets. They all had a look, a vibe, that said *I'm hip*. He wondered if his vibe said *I've got a dodgy hip*.

'Okay, nearly finished.' Grace's blue eyes zeroed in on his. 'Ever been married?'

His heart faltered. Taking care to keep his face bland, he

took a sip of his beer, hoping it would help lubricate his very tight throat. 'No.'

She nodded, and he thought he'd got away with it. But then he stupidly glanced at Sophie, and saw she was watching him with hawk like vision.

'Okay, final question.' Quickly he focussed back on Grace. 'Who was the last woman you dated and why did it end?'

'That's two questions.'

'*Technically*, and we know you're a big fan of the technicalities, it's one question in two parts,' Grace countered. 'And you know all about Soph's last dates, maybe more than you want to,' she added with a giggle. 'So it's only fair she knows something about yours.'

He could see this was a game to her. To all of them, he added as he watched Sophie and Ava nod vigorously in agreement. And maybe it wasn't such a big deal, discussing exes. Being best friends, all of them outgoing, they probably swapped stories of failed relationships all the time.

But he didn't. More, he had no wish to discuss that particular part of his life with anyone, ever again.

He'd also had enough of being the focus of attention, dancing to their tune.

'Jackie was the last woman I dated.' He rose stiffly to his feet. 'Who wants another drink?'

His credit card took a further hammering at the bar – bloody London prices, unbelievable – but he figured the escape was still worth it.

By the time he returned to the table with the drinks – the redheaded bartender was now flirting with another guy, which seemed to be the story of his life – he found it deserted, except for some empty cocktail glasses.

Looks like he was drinking alone then. Beer bottle in hand, he settled back in the chair and stared over at the small dance floor which was now thronging with people. They all writhed to the beat, their bodies moving in ways his had never learnt to.

And in the middle of it all, laughing, hands raised in the air, her body doing a sensuous glide, hips swaying, was Sophie. Centre of attention, she danced with rhythm yet also in a way that didn't take herself too seriously. Sexy, but approachable. A fact that didn't go unnoticed by the men practically falling over themselves to get close to her.

His gut twisted. He was jealous, he realised. Not of the guys vying for her attention, but of her cheerful confidence. How at ease she was in her skin. He was only six years older, yet the gap between them felt like a chasm as he watched her laugh with her friends.

It was blindingly obvious he didn't fit in this bar, with these people. Or with her.

Yet where did he fit? Was he really ready for planting begonias, Friday nights in with a good book? Saturdays walking his dog? Washing his car?

Sophie's gaze collided with his from across the room and a buzz of awareness shot through him. She waved, beckoning him over, but he shook his head. It was one thing feeling lonely. Another feeling a fool.

She wasn't going to let him sulk quietly, though. Of course she wasn't. He watched with trepidation as she walked towards him, long shapely legs looking dynamite beneath her short red dress.

She was attractive, no question, but it didn't mean *he* was attracted, he reminded himself as his eyes refused to stop staring. He'd always preferred substance over looks. Relaxing company over challenging. Quiet over loud. Still, he wriggled his tongue, just to make sure he hadn't swallowed it.

'I've come to grab you for a dance.' She stood before him, all legs, brimming confidence and beaming smile.

'Thanks, but I'll pass.'

He'd shut her down, yet her smile didn't waver. 'Sorry, no passes allowed. I didn't pass on the walk, even when faced with a treacherous, swirling, fast-flowing river.'

'A stream. And I gave you a lift.' He'd thought of those legs wrapped round his waist more often than he wanted to admit.

She waved her hand in front of his face. 'Take my hand and I'll help you this time.'

His ego smarted. 'You think I need it?'

'Well come and prove that you don't.'

Her eyes twinkled, challenging him, and before he knew it, his body had propelled him out of his seat. Giving him a satisfied smile, she took his hand and as her fingers curled round his, he felt the connection zip down his arm.

As they neared the small dance floor though, he halted. 'I'm not doing that.'

She tugged at his hand and a zing raced across his skin. 'No ducking out, remember.'

'If I'm dancing, I'm doing it my way.'

Her face lit up. 'Show me your way then.'

Feeling horribly self-conscious, he shifted them both so he held her left hand, his right sliding around waist. Her eyebrows bumped upwards. 'Ballroom? Seriously?'

Slim, toned. That was how she felt beneath his palm. Involuntarily his fingers pressed further and he added supple and sexy to the list. 'My only real dance moves come from Betty.'

'Oh wow, this I have to see.' She placed a hand on his shoulder and he felt the heat of it through his shirt. 'Show me those moves, Doc.'

He did, at least as much as he could remember Betty telling him. He stumbled a few times, but then so did she. It didn't seem to matter, not if her giggles, or the brightness of her eyes were anything to go by. Gradually he began to feel less awkward, his body relaxing, enjoyment replacing his initial wariness. No longer was he lonely. And far from feeling like a fool, dancing with Sophie made him the envy of most of the men in the room.

It was with a surprising reluctance that he realised it was time for him to leave to catch his train. He indicated for her to carry on dancing but she shook her head and walked with him to the door.

For a few beats they looked at each other and he felt this odd tug in his chest. Perhaps because she'd been kind enough to make him feel included. Perhaps because he'd enjoyed tonight more than he'd expected.

Or perhaps because she looked so radiant in that red dress, her eyes wide and sparkling.

'So, date two done.' She smiled, and that feeling in his chest intensified. So much so he didn't even want to correct her about the use of the word date. 'Shame I didn't have a column for dancing skills on the spreadsheet. You'd have aced it.'

'I'll tell Betty.'

Her eyes searched his. 'I've got to admit, I didn't have you down as a dancer. Maybe I'll have to up a few of those scores when I get home.' Her smile grew playful. 'Do you want me to send you the updated version?'

The reminder of why she'd spent time with him tonight was as effective a mood dampener as having a bucket of cold water dumped on his head. Sure, she'd see him again, but only because he was her spreadsheet guinea-pig. Not because she felt the same pull, the same attraction that he did. 'I'll wait till the end.'

Avoiding looking at her, he gave her a curt nod, shoved his hands into his pockets and strode off. Half way to the station, he made a promise to himself. He wasn't only going to prove that her spreadsheet was wrong. He was going to prove that quiet did not equal dull.

Maybe in the process, he'd prove it to himself, too.

Chapter Eleven

Sophie tried to concentrate on what her mum was saying, but her brain wasn't that interested in speed dating for the over 50s. It was still obsessing about last night. And her dance with Michael.

She'd not known what to think when he'd declared he was doing it his way, a defiant look on his handsome face – yes, his looks were now a nine out of ten on her spreadsheet. She'd baulked at a ten because it felt like a score only Chris Hemsworth should have.

She'd not been able to think at all when he'd placed his hand on her waist. Talk about tingles. That thrilling rush of blood, of heat. But she knew better than to trust in the indefinable chemistry that had let her down too many times in the past. The spreadsheet gave her a tangible score, rather than intangible "feels". So it had been reassuring to find that, despite the mark she'd added to Michael's looks, the six she'd given him for style (he'd looked good in those jeans) and the increase to four in humour (she still wasn't sure if it *was* humour), he was still only a four out of ten overall.

She hadn't needed the extra dates to prove he wasn't right for her.

Yet she had to concede the dates had given her *something*. That unexpected thrill when he'd lead her round the dancefloor. A giddy feeling of arousal as his body had touched hers.

'Are you listening to me at all?' Guiltily she looked across the restaurant table at her mum, who had a pouty look on her still very attractive face. She was known in her social circle as Mini Mirren because she had the look of Helen Mirren in her sixties. 'I don't mind if you're not paying attention, you know me, I'll happily talk to myself. But as we're supposed to be enjoying a mother/daughter brunch, it would be nice if you'd at least pretend to be interested in me waffling on about my love life.'

'I am interested, but speed dating hardly classifies as a love life,' Sophie protested. 'It's like calling McDonalds a proper meal. Come back to me when you're at least at the Nando's stage.'

Her mother quirked a delicate grey eyebrow. 'You're a fine one to talk. At least I don't put my love life down on a spreadsheet for everyone to look at.'

'I didn't...' she trailed off. What was the point? She'd explained this so many times already. 'Are you seeing any of those guys again?'

'Well, I thought Ronald was rather nice. Good teeth.'

Sophie burst out laughing. 'Isn't that how you judge a horse? At least my spreadsheet uses a range of criteria.'

'Your darling spreadsheet led you to have sex with a man who was very mediocre from the sound of things.'

'That's not true,' she protested. 'Johnathan wasn't mediocre. The sex was.' Truth was, she'd had a lot of mediocre sex – Johnathan's score could have been that for every man she'd dated. And really the score should be hers, because chances were, *she* was the average one.

Her mother blew out a noisy breath. 'That's because you didn't feel enough of a spark with him. I don't mind you having great sex with someone you know isn't right for you. Flings are highly underrated. But it's a tragedy to have mediocre sex with someone on the basis you think they *might* be right for you.'

'Easy for you to say. You had a good marriage with Dad, while it lasted. Children.' Eight years on, and the word still left its mark on them both. Swallowing, Sophie pushed past the pain. 'I believe it would be an even greater tragedy to keep investing time with someone who isn't right for me, just because I enjoyed the sex.'

'Investing time.' Her mother shook her head. 'Sophie dear, this obsession of yours with making every second count, it's too much. Relationships don't have to lead anywhere to be enjoyed. Recently I've had the best time with the most unsuitable men.'

Sophie thought of last night. Of dancing with Michael and that zap, that unexpected buzz. But then she thought of Will, of not just the time wasted but the hurt, the devastation of the split. Maybe her spreadsheet wouldn't have prevented that – she could hardly add a *wants a future with me* column – but wasn't it the definition of insanity to keep doing what she'd always done and expect a different result?

And with her thirtieth birthday looming, with Ava content with Ethan and Grace looking loved up with Daniel despite her insistence it was casual, she *needed* a different result to Will, and Chris before him.

'You've disappeared on me again.' Sophie gave another guilty start and focussed back on her mum. 'I asked where you are with that spreadsheet of yours.'

'Which part? I've already apologised to Patricia about the gift mix-up thing.'

'What gift mix-up?'

Damn it, why had she opened her big mouth? 'Never mind.'

Her mum gave her the steely look. 'Don't make me have to ask that ghastly woman, because I will. And I'll hate every minute of it.'

Patricia wasn't ghastly. In fact Sophie quite liked her stepmother, in short bursts. But then she wasn't jealous of the relationship she had with her dad. 'Fine. That cashmere jumper you gave me for Christmas? I gave it to Patricia because I thought it suited her more.' As her mother opened her mouth to speak again, Sophie ploughed on, figuring talking about her dates with Michael was better than getting an ear bashing. 'If you mean where am I with the love life spreadsheet, then I've put it on hold for a bit while I conduct a little trial.'

'Trial? Like you're checking out if it works?'

'More like confirming it works,' she corrected. 'I'm seeing the last guy I went out with, Michael, for a few more dates.'

'Two and half out of ten, Michael?'

The more she heard him being called that, the more she cringed. 'He's gone up to four out of ten.' Weird that now she knew him a bit better, it didn't seem enough. 'I've agreed to re-look at his score after ten dates to see if he's still less than seven out of ten.'

'And if he is?'

'I'll have proved the spreadsheet was right to red-line him after the first date.' She rearranged the salt and pepper pots on the table so they sat neatly side by side. 'I know you don't like my obsession with not wasting time, but just think, I could have spent that two months, or however long these dates take, going out with someone better.' An image floated into her brain of Michael's wry smile when he'd admitted he'd not told her why he'd been late for that first meeting because he'd been worried he'd sound arrogant. 'Someone more suitable for me,' she corrected.

'And what if this spreadsheet of yours puts him at eight out of ten?'

'Then I'll abandon the idea of using it to determine my love life.' Would she want to keep seeing Michael? Would he want to continue to see her? The thought was...surprisingly interesting.

'And what does this Michael get out of carrying on seeing a woman he knows has such a poor opinion of him?'

Ouch, that sounded callous. 'I … I suppose he gets to tell me I was wrong.'

Her mother gave her a pointed look. 'That seems like a poor reason to put himself through being judged.'

She had a flashback to last night. Of the way his face had closed up when she'd asked if he wanted to see the updated score. Shit, had that sounded really insensitive? She'd not meant him to take it so personally, or so seriously. It wasn't about the scores, but about the spreadsheet and whether it worked. Yet what *was* he getting out of this, if it wasn't the satisfaction of scorching her theory?

'I suspect most men would have told you to take a running jump,' her mother added.

'He did.' But she'd persuaded him to give it a go. *Bulldozed him*. Had he felt like he couldn't say no to her?

When she said goodbye to her mum she decided it was too nice a day for the tube so she set off walking back to the flat. The sort of walk that didn't involve raging rivers and rock climbing. The thought reminded her again of Michael and she pulled out her phone, her finger hovering over their string of messages. She didn't want him to keep seeing her because she'd forced him. She didn't even want him to keep seeing her just to prove he was right. She wanted him to see her because he'd enjoyed himself. Like, against the odds, she was starting to enjoy him.

―――――――

Michael had just dragged his cricket bag out of the boot of his car – the club was within walking distance but it was hard work with a kit bag – when his phone beeped with a message from Sophie.

> Sophie: Mum's just asked me what you're getting out of this ten-date thing. Beyond being able to say my spreadsheet is stupid, I didn't know what to tell her.

Perching on the Discovery tail-gate, he considered how to reply.

Saying your spreadsheet is stupid isn't enough?

He got an almost instant beep. Followed by several more.

Sophie: Mum said that's not reason enough to put yourself through being judged.

Sophie: Which I'm not by the way.

Sophie: Judging you, I mean.

Sophie: Like you don't already know that, but just in case it's not firmly entrenched in your brain.

Sophie: It's the spreadsheet that's being judged.

Sophie: So…

Sophie: What ARE you getting out of all this?

Damn it. Even he couldn't ignore six messages. Taking a deep breath, he went with the truth.

I get to see you.

There was no answering beep. Seconds rolled by and his palms began to sweat, his stomach to feel heavy. He'd scared her off. Made her worry that he thought they were dating for real when he knew damn well she didn't want that.

Angry at himself, he jumped off the tail gate and slammed

it shut. He was about to haul his kit bag over his shoulder when his phone began to ring.

His pulse picked up speed when he saw who was calling.

'Hey, Doc.'

He wished he didn't like the familiarity of that. 'Hello Ms Spreadsheet.'

'Ha, very good. Anyway, I was getting finger ache from all that messaging so I thought I'd do this the old-fashioned way.' Her voice sounded warm, soft and slightly breathless. 'The thing is, Mum's got me really worried that you're going through with this ten-date thing because I forced you into it. Bulldozed, even, which wouldn't be the first time I've done that. Not with a date,' she added quickly. 'But I have been called pushy.'

Did she think quiet meant *weak*? 'I'm a thirty-five-year old man. Nobody bulldozes me into anything.'

There was a beat of silence. 'Okay, that's good because I can be a bit overpowering sometimes, apparently.'

'Sometimes?' He countered dryly.

'Fine.' He heard the smile in her voice. 'Make that more than sometimes, slipping into often.' She paused, but he knew he wouldn't have to wait long for her next point. 'This probably sounds really needy, and I promise I'm not looking for you to blow sunshine up my arse or anything, but why would you want to keep seeing me after I was so mean to you?'

He leant against the car, taking a moment to order his thoughts because unlike her, he was cautious about revealing too much of what he was thinking. 'I spend my days seeing patients. My evenings with an 85-year-old. My weekends walking a dog called Princess and planting begonias. Why *wouldn't* I want to see you?'

'Ah, okay. It's not because of my sparkling personality then? Just because I get you out of the house and the begonia planting?'

Was she disappointed with his reply? Or relieved? 'Thought you didn't want me to blow sunshine?'

'I did say that.' She made a noise that sounded like a mix between a laugh and a groan. 'Maybe I was a bit hasty. A little sunshine is good for the ego. Not full sun, that can go to the head, but a bit of dappled sunlight. You'd know what I mean, being a gardener and all.'

He couldn't stop the laugh from escaping. 'How about this. When you're not making me dance, scoring me, or letting your friends interrogate me. I enjoy your company.'

The sound of her giggle sent a warm pulse through him. 'I bet you feel soooo much better for getting that off your chest. So, when are you free for date three?'

Tomorrow. Every evening next week. 'Probably when you are.'

He heard a shuffling sound. 'Hang on, let me check my calendar.'

'Not your spreadsheet?'

'The spreadsheet is the repository for everything that goes on in my life. The calendar is the schedule.' As he could hold both in his head, he kept quiet. 'This next week is pretty packed. I've got a possible on Thursday, but I should really see if Callum's free because I still owe him that apology drink.'

No, he wasn't going to ask. 'How did it go with Joshua?' Okay, looks like he was.

'Well, I think. He didn't seem too cut up about the whole spreadsheet scoring thing.'

Easy not to be annoyed with a seven out a ten. 'Is he still not getting a dinner?'

'No, he seemed fine with a drink.'

But if he hadn't been? If she'd decided actually she should have ignored her spreadsheet and kept seeing him? 'Sophie.' He halted, trying to find the words to say this without overstepping. Or sounding as jealous as he felt. 'Are you going to go out with other men while we're doing this?'

'Oh. I hadn't thought. I mean, Joshua wasn't a date.'

'I don't mean Joshua and Callum.' Though as she'd liked both more than him, it was hard not to resent them.

'Well I'm not looking to see anyone else, if that's what you mean, but obviously if either of us meet someone before the end of the ten dates, we'll just stop the trial.' She let out a soft groan. 'What am I saying? Stop the trial makes it sound so serious. And I guess, if we're calling it a trial, I should add that you can stop taking part for any reason, whenever you want. You don't even need to sign one of those waiver things.'

'I won't be dropping out.' The chance of him finding someone he enjoyed seeing as much as her ... it wasn't going to happen any time soon.

'Nor me.' Her two words should not mean as much as they did. 'Sooo, back to date three,' she continued, unaware he was silently fist pumping. 'Saturday's out because we've got a girls' shopping day. Can you do Sunday? Only you have to promise we won't be walking again because my finance spreadsheet isn't showing enough budget for a pair of proper walking boots.'

'But it is for whatever you're buying on Saturday?'

'Of course. I *need* a pair of sparkly sandals. I don't need walking boots because you're going to plan something far less demanding for my poor little feet.'

Amused, he agreed on Sunday before tucking away his phone and hauling his cricket bag onto his shoulders.

'What's put that smile on your face, lad?'

He turned in surprise to find the club president giving him a curious look. In his late seventies, Dennis was dressed, as usual, in a smart jacket and tailored trousers, despite the fact he was only going to watch a village match from the balcony of a rickety old pavilion. 'The sun is out. Great day for cricket.'

'He's been talking with his pretty new girlfriend, more like.' Betty appeared on his other side, a smug smile on her face

He should have guessed she'd be here, too. Ask her and she'd tell you she and Dennis were only friends. But they were seen together an awful lot.

Dennis chuckled. 'A pretty girl will put a smile on anyone's face. Hope you have a good game, I'll be cheering you on.'

'Thanks.' When Dennis was out of earshot, he glanced sideways at Betty. 'Out with your toy boy again, I see.'

'He's not … we're not.' She gave him a reprimanding glare. 'Don't talk nonsense.'

'I could say the same.' To take the sting out of his words, he bent to kiss her cheek. 'Sophie's not my girlfriend and you know it.'

'I like her.' This time her expression held a hint of stubbornness. 'And if you've any sense, you'll make her your girlfriend.' Before he could say anything back, she patted him on the arm. 'Have a good game, dear. With a bit of effort, you could bowl a maiden over.'

He was left shaking his head in amusement for the second time in as many minutes.

Chapter Twelve

I t had been another hectic week. On the Sunday, Sophie raised five hundred pounds for Cancer Research UK by running a half marathon – yep, an All contacts message that hadn't angered, annoyed or hurt anyone. She'd even received a donation from Michael, along with a message.

Michael: You run but you don't like walking? That sheep phobia is worse than I thought.

It had made her smile. She was starting to get him, she realised.

After work on Monday she'd begun a new piece for her Grade 2 saxophone exam and gone to Zumba. On Tuesday she'd had her roots done in her lunch hour and gone to the tennis club session in the evening. Wednesday had been drinks with an ex work colleague who she still kept in touch with because she was fun – and because she knew networking was important. On Thursday Callum had cancelled on her, so she'd had a night in with Grace, Ava and Lucifer. Friday they'd gone to The Drunk Flamingo as usual but she'd not been able to find her rhythm. A few times she'd even caught herself glancing at the door, hoping to see Michael.

That had been really weird.

Saturday she'd bought her sparkly sandals and she and the girls had celebrated with cocktails. Later they'd been joined by Ava's boyfriend Ethan and Grace's *casual hook-up but not really*, Daniel. Again, she'd found herself thinking of Michael. If she'd asked him, would he have come? Then again, had she only wanted him to come because she'd felt like a third wheel?

And now it was Sunday.

'I'm seeing Michael again today,' she told Tinkerbell, who was curled up beside her on the bed. 'You remember him? The one with the dog?' The tabby yawned dismissively, making Sophie laugh. 'I know, dogs aren't cool. But Fudge, well, she's not like most dogs. She's really well behaved and actually pretty smart. For a dog.' She gave Tinkerbell a long, smooth stroke. 'I wonder if I can wear my new shoes?' She thought of Little Brook, of what there was to do, and sighed. 'Best not. He'll probably make me walk again.'

As if there was some sort of telepathy going on, her phone began to ring and Michael's name appeared on her caller ID.

'Hey, I was just wondering if what we're doing today is sparkly sandal suitable?'

A long pause. She'd come to expect them, but even by his standards this was a loooong one. Like *I've got something difficult to say* long. It was the length of pause Will had left after she'd suggested they find a flat together. And before he'd told her that wasn't how he saw their relationship going. Unease coiled in her belly. 'I'm not seeing you, am I?'

125

'I want to see you.' He exhaled sharply, muttering something pithy under his breath. 'This spreadsheet of yours. Does it have a column for organisation ability?'

'Err, no. Though maybe it should, because it's pretty important—'

'I've cocked up,' he interrupted. 'I totally forgot I said I'd play cricket today. I was reminded this morning.'

'Oh.' Disappointment washed through her. 'Maybe you should have a spreadsheet for your cricket fixtures.'

She heard a deep sigh. 'Maybe I should.'

'Does this mean I shouldn't come over?'

'Oh no, you're very welcome to.' He let out one of his low, gruff noises. Not a laugh, not a groan, but maybe something in between. 'The question is would you *want* to?'

'Why not? I've put aside today to see you. This would be seeing you, wouldn't it?' It was worrying to realise quite how much she'd been looking forward to it.

'When I'm not batting or fielding, yes.'

'Well then, I've not watched a cricket match before. This will be fun.'

Another longish pause. 'Many people would disagree with that statement.'

'Then why do you play it?'

A huff of soft laughter. 'Touché. But playing is different to watching.'

Was there something she was missing here? 'Why does it sound like you're trying to put me off?'

'Sophie.' What was it about the way he said her name, all butter soft and deeply sexy? 'I'd really like to see you.'

There was no denying the rush of pleasure those words brought. 'And my sparkly sandals?'

The man she'd dismissed a few weeks ago as being humourless, now caused her heart to flutter when he laughed. 'Essential attire for cricket watchers.'

This time, she knew he was joking. Yet as she ended the call and began to work out what to wear, the sparkly sandals were the first things she pulled out.

Twenty minutes later, she tapped on Grace's door. Ava had stayed over at Ethan's.

'What?' Came the grumpy reply.

'Good morning to you, too. Can I come in?'

'If you mean are me and Daniel having rampant morning sex, the answer is no. He left last night. After the aforementioned rampant sex.'

Ignoring the jolt of jealousy – it had been so, so long since she'd had sex, and it had categorically never been rampant – Sophie pushed her way in. 'I know Daniel left last night. I heard your noisy goodbyes.' For a pair who weren't officially seeing each other, they did a lot of kissing. 'Can you tell me if this is suitable for watching cricket?'

Grace propped herself up on her elbow and stared over at her, bleary eyed. 'Is that the terminally boring game that goes on for days?'

'I think so? But I assume this is the shorter, less terminally dull version.'

'You hope so, more like.' Grace's gaze skimmed over the flowery summer dress she'd chosen. Short, because her legs were tanned and so currently her best feature, it had a halter neck and a nipped in waist. 'Nice sandals.'

As Grace had chosen them for her, Sophie rolled her eyes. 'What about the dress? Too much?'

Grace's gaze shifted from her clothes, to Sophie's face. 'You know you've never asked my opinion on what to wear, right?'

'Ava isn't here, so…'

Grace smirked. 'So, usually you just wear what you want, because you know you have way more of an eye for this stuff than either of us. The fact you've stooped so low to asking for my opinion leads me to conclude you must now rate the good doctor a lot more than a two and a half out of ten.'

'Four.' For some reason the word got stuck in her throat. She coughed and tried again. 'He's gone up to four.'

Grace sat up. 'You're getting all wound up about what to wear for a date with a guy you're only rating four out of ten?'

'The spreadsheet isn't there to determine whether I like a guy or not,' she protested. 'It's to determine his long-term suitability. Michael's … well, he's different to guys I normally date, and I'm kind of enjoying that for a while. But we'd never make a couple.'

'Okay, I get that.' She laughed. 'I definitely can't see you as a doctor's wife, living in some quaint village and making cricket teas.'

'Exactly.' She stared down at her dress, the sparkly sandals. Ignored the weird wriggle in her gut. 'Anyway, do I look okay?'

Grace waved a hand at her. 'You look uber chic as always. You'll have those pompous old white guys eating out of your hand.'

Sophie wrinkled her nose. 'That's who I'll be spending my afternoon with?'

'Yep, trust me. I saw this program on TV about village

cricket. When the guys get too old to play they sit on benches and watch, tossing out phrases like "where's your long john", or it could have been "long on", and "show them your googly".

Sophie's jaw dropped, her fun afternoon now looking decidedly shaky. 'Do I want to know what a googly is?'

'Not if some old guy is asking to see it.'

Michael couldn't believe he'd ballsed today up so catastrophically.

First, he'd managed to add disorganised to his humourless, unstylish, uncharismatic, unsociable – and whatever other attributes Sophie had rated him low on. But it got worse. In fact, he was breaking out in a cold sweat at the thought of the second disaster. Her turning up and watching.

She was going to hate it. Likely even more than she'd hated the walk.

Betty walked into the kitchen where he was sorting out his kit, making sure he had his boots, pads, helmet, the all-important box. See, he *was* organised. It's just that sometimes things slipped through. Like friendly matches he'd promised to play in a rash moment when he'd scored fifty and felt like a king.

Friendly matches where most of the village turned out to either play or watch.

And now Sophie was going to be one of them.

'Getting ready to play I see,' Betty remarked, surveying the kit spread across the floor.

'Yes. Just a friendly.' Maybe Betty had forgotten, like he had...

'We both know the annual Little Brook CC versus All Comers village cup isn't a *friendly*.' She tutted at him. 'Dennis would be horrified. He says Roger has pulled together a really strong team to beat you this year.'

It was a tradition that once a year the Little Brook cricket club played a team lead by ex-president Roger, which usually consisted of ex-players plus anyone else with half decent talent he could persuade to take part.

'You're coming to watch then?' He deliberately focussed on re-packing his bag so he wouldn't have to look at her.

'Of course.' Ignore the pregnant pause. Helmet, gloves... 'Why?' Thigh guard. Did he need to pack that today? 'Michael, why are you avoiding looking at me?'

God, Betty could read him better than he could read himself. Quickly he shoved everything back in the bag and zipped it up. 'Sophie's going to be there.'

'She's coming to watch you?' He nodded, still too unhinged to point out she wasn't coming to watch *him*, but because she'd already allocated today as "spreadsheet trial" time. Betty clapped her hands together. 'That's marvellous. I can introduce her to the rest of the village. Dennis said he's hoping for a bigger turn out than ever this year, what with Gill putting the advert on that clever Facetiming thing.'

'Facebook,' he muttered, feeling more and more like a man about to walk the plank.

'That's what I said. Oh, this is going to be such a good day.'

He thought it probably would be, for the village. But not for someone coming up from London. Who had no clue what she was letting herself in for.

The sound of scampering feet alerted him to the arrival of Fudge and Princess. Fudge had a sort of weariness about her when she was with Princess. Like the older tom boy forced to play dolls with her annoying younger sister.

Big brown eyes looked pleadingly into his and he smiled. 'It's alright, girl. I'll take you with me. Princess and Betty can come along later.'

Fudge had grown up with him playing cricket, so she knew to sit patiently by the steps to the pavilion. Usually there was someone, the players' kids, ex-players like Dennis, to make a fuss of her and walk her round the boundary.

His phone pinged with a message as he was hauling the kit into the car.

Sophie: On train. Researching cricket terms. Googly sounds way ruder than it is. S x

He couldn't stop the smile. Thank God Betty wasn't watching.

Sorry to disappoint.

Another beep.

Sophie: How many times have you bowled a maiden over? S x

With a shake of his head, he sat on the tail gate.

Sadly very few.

Sophie: Nooooo. I don't believe that. I think you're more deadly than you think. S x

Was she still talking about his cricketing prowess? And if not … how could she say that after she'd skewered him with her spreadsheet?

He considered his options for the reply.

I've been told I have a smooth action.

He received the fastest ever message back.

Sophie: Ha now we're getting to the rude stuff. S x

He chuckled, realising he was enjoying himself.

I'm also good with line and length.

Sophie: Umm, you talk a good game Doc. S x

Was she flirting with him? Or just teasing the man she thought was too uptight? And how sad that he didn't know. Before he could out think himself, he typed back.

I also walk the talk.

He held his breath as he waited for her answer. Had he gone too far? Shit, of course he had. She'd been teasing someone she'd started to think of as a sort of friend. He'd gone and creeped her out, his comment too suggestive.

Finally his phoned beeped.

Sophie: Sorry. Just had to pick myself off the floor. And fan myself down. See you soon. S x

His relief that she'd replied, was palpable. Was he disappointed she'd not taken his dip into flirting and run with it? Yes. But that hum of sexual tension, the see-sawing *Does she fancy me, does she not* wasn't going to happen for him because her spreadsheet had already shattered any hope. She didn't see him as boyfriend material.

With a sigh he motioned for Fudge to get into the car. One neat jump later, she performed a 360-degree swivel before lying down next to his kit bag. 'Good girl.' He gave her ears a good rub, briefly remembering Sophie's tentative *fondling*.

Nope, thinking like that was not helpful.

'Any woman who doesn't like dogs isn't worth getting all tangled up about, is she, huh?'

Fudge let out a short bark, and licked his hand.

Chapter Thirteen

Sophie nearly fell out of the train when she spotted Michael waiting for her on the platform. Wearing a white cricket shirt and navy athletic shorts, his legs hadn't lost any of their hotness since she'd seen them last.

With a heroic effort she dragged her gaze up to his face, which was also no hardship to look at.

'I didn't expect to see you.' She pointed to his cricket shirt. 'Thought you'd be, you know, taking guard, or standing at silly mid-on.'

He smiled, amusement brimming in his eyes. Was it her, or had they turned bluer? 'I see the research is paying off.'

'Hey, I know all the terms now. You can test me on anything,' she replied breezily, taking another sneaky glance at his legs. They were dusted in soft, fair hair, the muscles bunching and stretching as he walked...

'Are you looking at my legs?'

She snapped her head guiltily away. Then gave him a

134

cheeky smile. 'I'm wondering if that's what they mean by fine leg.'

His bark of laughter took her by surprise, as did the way it crinkled the corners of his eyes. He isn't just handsome, she realised with surprise. He was *sexy*. It wasn't an obvious, *Look at me, I'm covered in tattoos and wearing tight, muscle enhancing clothes* kind of sexiness. No, his sexiness was quieter, more subtle. And perhaps, she thought, feeling a giddy quiver in her belly, perhaps it was all the more potent for being so unexpected.

'You know where fine leg is then?' he asked as they walked towards a green Land Rover Discovery, a brown Labrador looking out of the rear window.

'Yep … just give me a minute.' Glad of the question so she didn't have to think too much about this new and disturbing reaction to him, she pulled out her phone and tapped on the photo of the field placements she'd downloaded. 'Fine leg is behind the wicket-keeper but kind of towards square leg. The other side of third man.' She blew out a breath. 'You do realise this game is nuts, yes?'

Another laugh, more of a chuckle this time, yet it produced the same unnerving response. When she glanced sideways at him though, his smile faded. 'Thank you for coming today. I am sorry about the muck up.'

'Don't be. I'm buzzed to be going to my first cricket match.'

He held the passenger door open for her. 'Please don't judge cricket on the basis of today. Played by professionals, it can be skilful. Exciting at times.'

'Don't expect too much, got it.' She leapt in, glancing over her shoulder to wave to Fudge, who gave her a sober, watchful look. So much like her owner, all reserved and … gentle she thought.

'I'm afraid we'll have to go straight there.' Michael settled into the driver's seat, tanned hands resting on the steering wheel. 'We're due to start in five minutes.'

'Oh, wow, you didn't have to pick me up. I could have walked from the station.'

His gaze dropped to her new flat sandals, which shimmered even in the footwell. 'I wasn't sure how walking-friendly sparkly sandals were.'

Her stomach did a little flip. There was something very sweet and considerate about the fact he'd thought of her, despite getting ready for his game. To distract herself from wondering about it, she wriggled her feet. 'See, they're perfectly good for walking. Not the sort of walks you take me on,' she corrected. 'But the normal kind that involve pavements.'

It was only a short drive to the cricket club, yet her eyes kept straying to his forearms, the roped veins and tanned skin. Then dropping to his thighs, and the flex of taut, defined muscle beneath the thin layer of his shorts.

This was not the reaction she expected towards a man her spreadsheet had clearly marked as unsuitable.

He parked up and she jumped out, grateful to create some distance. As he grabbed his bag out of the boot, she took stock of her surroundings. A wooden pavilion at one end, a few people already on the balcony. Milling around on the field in front of the pavilion were a crowd of men, all dressed in white shirts and long white trousers.

Michael waved over to them and then turned to her. 'I need to go and find out what's happening.' He gave her an awkward smile. 'Are you going to be okay? We might be batting first, in which case I'm not needed for a bit, but if we're fielding—'

'I'll be fine,' she cut in, giving him a reassuring smile, even though her stomach gave a nervous dip. What had she got herself into here?

Fudge looked up at her, brown eyes still wary.

'Do you need me to do anything with Fudge?'

'She's used to me playing cricket. There'll be plenty of people coming to make a fuss of her.' He drew in a breath, shook his head on the exhale. 'Look, if you hate it, don't feel you have to stay.'

'Hey, I'm about to watch a game I don't understand, with people I've never met. What's not to like?' He groaned, his expression pained, and she took pity on him. 'I'm kidding. Go and do your stuff. Me and Fudge will take care of each other.'

He didn't look so sure, and neither did Fudge who was still giving her this half curious, half worried look.

But then one of the guys shouted Michael's name, and with a final apologetic smile, he trotted off, bag over his shoulder. Legs she absolutely wasn't ogling, rippling with every stride.

'So then.' She gave Fudge a tentative pat, then remembered what Michael had told her and fondled the dog's ears. 'Where shall we sit?'

As if she understood – or more likely to wait for her beloved owner – Fudge began to trot towards the pavilion. Before they reached it though, she heard her name shouted behind her.

She turned to find Betty, arms clutching the little Chihuahua. Princess sported a yellow bow in her hair today, Sophie suspected to match Betty's sunflower yellow dress. The woman was the most glamorous eighty-five-year-old Sophie had ever met.

'There you are, dear. Michael said you were coming. I promised to take care of you, introduce you to everyone. You'll soon find this is a very friendly club.' Sophie opened her mouth to thank her, but Betty's attention was on a very dapper looking old man wearing a smart jacket and straw hat. 'Dennis, come and meet Michael's girl, Sophie.'

Michael's girl. The words rumbled round in her brain, sounding wrong, and yet not unpleasantly so. She wasn't Michael's girl, but she realised she didn't actually mind being called that. At least not enough to correct the mistake.

'Well, well, come to watch the man play. It must be love, eh?' He chuckled to himself, seemingly oblivious to the look of horror Sophie knew had spread across her face.

'Umm, we're not really dating,' she started to say, but neither Dennis or Betty were listening. Far too interested in greeting the constant stream of people turning up, Dennis with a handshake, Betty with a peck on the cheeks. God, it was like watching royalty on a walkabout, Sophie thought with a giggle.

'Sophie, meet Sanjay, the Little Brook vice-captain.' At Betty's introduction, Sophie smiled at a tall man with mahogany skin, salt and pepper hair and a wide smile. 'His wife Ayesha is up in the pavilion, sorting out the teas.'

'Word of warning, if you hang around here long enough, you'll get roped in.' Sanjay winked at her before heading off, presumably to play the game all these people seemed to have turned up to watch. Seriously, how many people lived in the village? Half of them at least must be here now.

Dennis let out a deep grumble of laughter. 'Sanjay's not

wrong. We're always looking for willing volunteers. And even not so willing ones,' he added on another laugh, looking fondly at Betty. 'Eight years ago, Betty started turning up to watch and now she's our treasurer.'

'Somebody has to keep you all in order.' Betty turned to Sophie, a glint in her eye. 'I happen to know this young lady is a real expert when it comes to spreadsheets. Maybe I should get her on the task of creating one for the finances.'

The suggestion was met with a murmur of agreement, not just from Dennis but from another couple, who Betty introduced as Roger and Gill.

'Are you the lass I owe an apology to?' Roger asked. Grey hair and a ruddy, weathered looking face.

'Apology?'

'For making Michael late a few weeks ago. Betty told me afterwards that he'd been on his way to see a young lady when our Gill here diverted him.'

She must have looked confused, because Gill smiled and gave her husband's cheek a gentle pat. 'What he's trying to say is I called Michael in a panic because Roger was having a heart attack.'

Roger let out a low rumble of a laugh. 'In typical Michael fashion, he calmly saved my life. Then went on to make his date.' He winked at her. 'Looks like I didn't cock things up too badly for him.'

How to reply? Apparently one wasn't needed though because she was being introduced to more people; a rather stern looking woman called Hattie, Julie, wife of one of the players and her two cute kids. Kath, who ran the Post Office and her shy daughter, Lucy. An old guy called Sid who Betty

139

apparently knew from Bingo. Maureen and Robert who she recognised from the Royal Oak.

All of them smiled, made a joke about how brave she was to turn up and watch. Then put bets on whether she'd ever watch another cricket match again.

Sophie didn't know whether to turn around and run. Or be quietly delighted these people weren't the boring old farts Grace had predicted.

Typical that he'd lost the toss – the one day Michael had needed to bat first, so he could make sure Sophie didn't feel like he'd just dropped her off and run.

From his position at slip he kept glancing up at the balcony where he had occasional glimpses of her brightly coloured sundress – and her glorious legs – as she chatted to Betty and Dennis.

He tried not to think what they might be saying to her. Of how much damage the pair could do to his already battered street cred in the space of an afternoon. And that was before he considered Roger chipping in with tales from his childhood. And Hattie treating him like her unruly teenage son.

She wasn't watching the cricket, he could tell that much. Even Fudge had abandoned her post on the boundary rope and followed Sophie upstairs. Maybe he should remind her that Sophie was a cat person.

'No looking up at the girlfriend.' Hamza, their wicket keeper, shot him a grin. 'Head in the game, cap.'

'She's not my girlfriend.'

Hamza whistled. 'That's not the impression Dennis has been giving.'

Michael's stomach knotted. 'What's he said?'

'Overheard him introducing her as Michael's girl.'

'Christ.' He just bet Sophie enjoyed that. Yet the alternative, that they were all up there laughing about how she'd given him this diabolically bad rating on a spreadsheet and was now giving him ten dates to improve on it... The knots in his stomach tightened.

The sooner they got the opposition out and he was able to do some damage limitation, the better.

Forty overs later, and with a satisfying three wickets to his name, he finally walked with the others off the field.

There was no Fudge to greet him. No Sophie, either.

He wasn't sure whether it was nerves or anticipation that had his stomach swarming with butterflies as he made his way towards the club house. Sophie was outgoing. She wouldn't be sat in the corner, grumpy faced and waiting for him to give him a lift to the station. Unconsciously his mind flicked back to Jackie, who'd also been outgoing. And who'd hated cricket. Later he might think it was funny how his girlfriend of three years had never bothered to watch him, yet the woman who thought he wasn't worth dating except to test out her spreadsheet, had bothered to get on a train to see him play. And research cricket terms on the journey. Right now though, he was more worried about what he'd find when he got to the stop of the stairs and...

Sophie was in the kitchen, laughing with Ayesha as they cut up slices of pizza and placed them on two giant platters.

'Dennis,' Sophie called out. 'Next one's ready.'

His eyes bugged out of his head. Had she got Dennis helping to serve out the teas?

Leaving his team mates to go and help themselves to the mountain of sandwiches, sausage rolls and samosas already waiting for them, he ducked his head inside the kitchen.

'Hey Michael.' Ayesha waved over at him. 'Before you say anything, I didn't strong arm her into helping me. She volunteered.'

Sophie, face flushed, grey eyes sparkling, beamed at him. 'I did. I offered. She didn't even need the thumb screws.' She raised a glass that looked suspiciously like a giant gin and tonic. 'But she did ply me with gin.'

Ayesha pointed over to where Betty was sat with Princess on her lap, holding court as he liked to think of it. 'If you think her helping me with the tea is bad, you should hear what she's agreed to do for Betty.'

'Hey, are you kidding? That's not going to be a hardship.' Sophie rubbed at her face, unknowingly leaving a splodge of pizza sauce on the tip of her nose. 'Putting together spreadsheets is what I do for fun.'

He found himself distracted by the sauce, and an almost overpowering desire to lick it off. Giving himself a shake, he forced his eyes back to hers. 'You've agreed to make Betty a spreadsheet?'

'Of course. I can't believe she's trying to do the finances without one. It'll be so much quicker once I get it up and running. All she'll need to do is pop in the numbers.' She clicked her fingers. 'Easy as pie.' Then she threw a hand over her mouth. 'Oh, look at me waffling on about spreadsheets again when I should be congratulating you. Roger said three wickets is a good … haul I think he said, for a spin bowler on that wicket.'

'He did, did he.' She'd been talking to Roger then, as well as Betty and Dennis. And helping out Ayesha. And drinking gin.

'Yes, something about the wicket being too green to turn it much.' A frown appeared between her eyes. 'I didn't get that. I mean how can you have grass that's too green?'

She was interested. His heart nearly stopped when he realised this gorgeous, fun loving, exciting woman was, at the very least, pretending an interest in the game he'd spent his whole life defending against his football loving brother. 'If the wicket is green, it means there's moisture and it plays slow. Spin bowlers like a dry, dusty surface as it grips the ball better, meaning we can get it to turn.'

'You mean to move off the pitch?'

He nodded, totally captivated by her. 'Will you come and eat with me outside?'

'Err, shouldn't you eat with the team?'

Fearing he might actually give in to temptation and lick the damn sauce off her nose, he picked up a paper napkin and gave it a quick wipe. 'Sauce.' He smiled down at her startled expression. 'And no. I want to eat with you.'

'Righty, okay then.'

She pulled out her phone and he shook his head. 'Tell me you're not checking your spreadsheet.'

'Of course I am. I'm not sure pizza is allowed this week. I'm on a … whoa, you can't do that.'

He took hold of her phone, turned it off. Then gave it back to her with a plate of pizza. 'One slice won't kill you. Come on.'

They were about to head outside when Hamza called over to them. 'Before you two slink off, we want Sophie to settle something for us.'

His stomach dropped. No good was going to come of this question. But Sophie, clearly unware of the devious look on Hamza's face, or perhaps unbothered by it, gave him a warm smile. 'Sure, ask away.'

'Are you Mickey's girlfriend, or not?'

The pavilion, a hub of conversation a few seconds ago, suddenly fell silent and Michael died a few thousand deaths as the eyes of both teams and all spectators, swivelled in their direction.

Sophie bit into her bottom lip and stared up at him. 'Err, that's an interesting question.'

No it wasn't. It was a way too personal question. 'And one he shouldn't have asked.'

To the guy's credit, his face fell as he saw the glaring *awkward* his question had caused. 'Shit, sorry mate. I was just having a laugh, you know? We've not seen you bring a girl to the cricket before. Figured you were just being coy.'

Coy? Like he was some teenage boy with his first crush? Yet he could feel himself flushing.

Betty cleared her throat, and when Michael saw the empty gin and tonic glass in front of her, he knew his day was about to go from frigging uncomfortable but potentially salvageable, to an unmitigated disaster. His gran had a minimal filter at the best of times. It vanished after a gin. 'Michael, dear, give them all a laugh and tell them about the spreadsheet and how low Sophie scored you.' She chuckled. 'Only our Michael could have managed to get himself into such a pickle on a first date.'

Beside him, Sophie muttered, 'Holy shit'.

Holy shit was the mild version. This was mortifying.

As if she sensed his humiliation, Fudge padded over to him and put her wet nose in his hand. That simple act was enough to crush his chest. In that moment it felt like Fudge was the only one who really understood him. His gran, who he loved to death, had no clue how pathetically small she'd just made him feel. And Sophie, admittedly unwittingly, had started this whole sham with her ruddy spreadsheet in the first place.

Slowly he put his plate back on the table and bent to scratch Fudge's ears. 'Come on girl, I'll take you for a walk.' He looked back at Sophie. 'I'll leave you to explain.'

Probably that was unfair. These were his friends, after all, but he couldn't stay a moment longer. And he certainly couldn't stay while everyone found out what the girl who'd come to watch, really thought of him.

As he turned to walk back down the stairs, he heard a yap and watched with resignation as Princess trotted over, daft bow in her hair, fluffy tail up in the air. She glanced up at him with a *don't forget me* expression. His wounded male pride did not need the daft dog around him right now. But she yapped again, her tail wagging. With a sigh he bent to pick her up and tuck her under his arm. 'Okay girl, you win.' He guessed he should be pleased he had two females who wanted to be with him with no ulterior motive. Even if they did have four legs and bad breath.

Just as he headed out of the door, he heard Sophie say. 'Betty's right. It is kind of a funny story.'

'She'll certainly make it sound funny,' he muttered to his canine companions. And now self-disgust vied with his embarrassment. He'd abandoned her. Left this vital, engaging,

145

brilliantly funny woman to pick up the pieces while he and his bruised ego had waltzed off like some prima donna.

'Fuck.' Sensing his distress, Princess licked his face. With a kiss to her nose, he let her down. 'I don't deserve any sympathy. I've been a self-absorbed git.'

As the dogs ran ahead of him, he set off for a walk round the boundary, hoping it would clear his head. And that Sophie would still be there to apologise to, when he got back.

Chapter Fourteen

Sophie stood on the balcony, her eyes on the tall blond figure as he scooped the tiny Chihuahua onto his lap. The sight made her smile, yet it also made her wonder about the dishy doctor. Clearly liked and respected, he had no hesitation being seen with a distinctly unmacho dog, yet he'd appeared utterly devastated at the idea of his team mates knowing some big city airhead had been dumb enough, shallow enough, to score him on a spreadsheet. And then send that spreadsheet out to all her contacts.

Betty appeared beside her. 'Thank you, dear.'

'What for?'

'Explaining away that spreadsheet nonsense without making Michael look foolish.'

'I'm the one who was stupid,' Sophie stressed.

'No more stupid than I was, bringing it up like I did.' Betty's gaze drifted over to the male figure sat on a bench, Fudge lying by his feet. Princess in his lap. His focus on the men walking onto the field. 'I embarrassed him, didn't I?'

Sophie felt a tug of sympathy for the lady who looked every one of her eighty-five years just now. 'You were only trying to help.'

'Yes, but sometimes I forget that the man he is now isn't the same as the one he was three years ago.'

'Oh?' Sophie looked again at Michael, who was now holding Princess up above his head and saying something to her. Whatever it was, it caused the dog to wag her tail enthusiastically.

'Don't get me wrong, he's always been shy, reserved. Private enough to have dismissed Hamza's question. But three years ago, he'd also have laughed off the whole spreadsheet thing as a bit of nonsense.'

'It sounds like there was a woman involved.' *Jackie*, she thought privately.

'There was, dear. And I rue the day she ever set eyes on my grandson.' Betty let out a deep sigh. 'Still, no point in regretting what's done.' She gave Sophie a little nudge with her elbow. 'I'd go down and apologise, but I think he'd far rather see you.'

Sophie wasn't so sure. She was the one who, it was increasingly clear, had delivered a far deeper wound than she'd realised with her damning spreadsheet score. Still, she had come here to see him.

As she made her way towards Michael, she slowed her stride, watching as Roger walked up to him. How must it feel to know you'd saved a man's life? That if it wasn't for you, he wouldn't be talking to you now? As she watched the interaction, which appeared to have a degree of seriousness to it, she felt a wave of fresh admiration for Michael. She liked him, no question. Yet she hadn't designed the spreadsheet to find someone she *liked*. She'd been there and enjoyed the hell out of that. She'd also been on the flip side of it though, when enjoyment turned to heartbreak because one of you – namely her – thought the relationship was heading in an entirely different direction to the other. *You're fun but I couldn't live with you, Soph. You're too loud, too much.* Will's words would be forever etched in her memory.

So no, enjoyable as it was being with Michael, like was no longer enough. She needed compatible. Someone who was as loud – she preferred spirited – as her. Who liked the same things she did.

Roger clapped Michael on the back and, as he began to walk away, Michael's attention drifted over in her direction. He seemed to jolt, as if he'd not expected to see her. Maybe even forgotten she was still here.

'Hi.' Her hand went up in an awkward *Only me*, wave.

Fudge got up and went over to sniff her, which Sophie took to be a good sign though it could have meant she was hoping for dog treats.

Michael's bright blue eyes sought hers. 'Sorry for abandoning you.'

'Don't be.' Guilt pricked at her. 'It was my fault about the spreadsheet anyway.'

'Not your fault that I've got a team mate with a big mouth.' He shot her a rueful smile. 'And a gran who opens her mouth before thinking.'

'She's really sorry.'

He let out a deep breath, shoulders sagging. 'I know.'

Silence followed, and it was so awkward Sophie had to turn to watch what was happening on the field. She was acutely conscious that he wanted to be alone. And very likely wished she'd gone home.

'I won't bite.' He patted the space on the bench next to him. 'Please, sit a minute.'

He had cricket whites on, a tiny puff ball of a dog on his lap, sporting a yellow bow no less, yet something about him was acutely, perhaps dangerously, appealing. 'Don't you have to … hang on a minute. Something about pads.' She delved into the cricket trivia she'd crammed into her brain on the train ride. 'I've got it. Don't you have to pad up?'

This time the smile he threw her way had a fond edge to it. Enough to cause a little catch in her throat. 'I'm batting number five. Only the next two batsmen need to put their pads on.'

'And their box.' She slid onto the bench next to him, and even though they'd danced together, this felt oddly more intimate. His big, muscular thigh only inches from hers.

A low laugh rumbled through him. 'That too.'

Why was she suddenly noticing how broad, how tall he was compared to her? And that his biceps were nicely defined? 'I read that the helmet was invented something like a hundred years after the box,' she rambled, needing to divert her thoughts onto something else. 'I'm not sure what that says about cricketers.'

'I think it says we're more likely to get hit in the groin.'

More silence followed his comment, but this felt easier. Rather than asking her to leave, he'd asked her to stay.

'I heard from Roger how you explained about the spreadsheet.' His eyes caught hers, held them for a beat. 'Thank you.'

Now it was her turn to be embarrassed. 'I only said the truth.'

'Maybe, but making it all about how you blundered sending it out, and how you then asked if I'd mind seeing you a few more times because you knew the score from our date was wrong and you needed to check it.' He swallowed. 'I appreciate that.'

'No worries.' Probably she should leave it at that. But what Betty had said, niggled at her. 'I know I've said this before, but that score, it is only the opinion of one, some would say unimportant, woman.'

His gaze flicked towards her. 'Your opinion isn't unimportant to me.'

Her heart gave a long, slow flip and she didn't know what to say.

'You're right though,' he added, finally breaking the quiet. 'I've overreacted. You said as much when you first called to apologise.'

'If I remember, I said it was only my opinion, based on a date where I drank most of the bottle of wine we were supposed to share. And I didn't think you'd have rated me any different.'

He cast another sidelong glance at her, and she was struck by how long his lashes were. Fair, yet dark enough that they gave a striking frame to his eyes. 'Actually, I would have.' While her brain struggled to grasp that interesting piece of information, he added an even more fascinating insight. 'I told you the last time I went out with a woman was three years ago.' She noticed his throat move, his hand tremble as it slid over Princess's back. 'What I didn't say was that our relationship ended when I found her pinned against our bedroom door, her legs wrapped around my best mate. Ex best mate,' he added bitterly.

Michael gave Princess another stroke, hoping the action would ground him. He shouldn't still care what Jackie and Ian had got up to when he'd come back earlier than planned from a conference. The moment was still indelibly etched in his memory, though. As was how Jackie had tried to defend her action afterwards.

Sophie blew out a breath. 'Sorry, that sucks giant, smelly donkey balls.' It said something about her way with words that he almost smiled. 'How long had you guys been going out?'

'Two years.' He was a private man but he wanted Sophie to understand why he'd been such an overly sensitive arse about the score she'd given him, so he added, 'Long enough for me to have proposed to her.'

'Oh shit. I presume she said no?'

'She said she wasn't ready.' Self-disgust caused his stomach to clench. 'I should have realised then something wasn't right, but I told myself she just needed more time to get used to the idea. What she was actually doing was trying out my best mate for size. Deciding which of us she wanted.' *I tried hard to prefer you, but I realised I don't want steady. Ian's more exciting. He gets my heart racing, my blood pumping.*

'That's … awful. Just awful.' Sophie's softly spoken words broke through the painful memory loop. 'I suppose I should be grateful Will said no to me straight away when I asked him to live with me.'

Michael slid another glance at her. Those clear grey eyes radiated such empathy, it was hard to look away from them.

'You were hurt so much you created the spreadsheet,' he remembered. 'To reduce the chance of it happening again.'

'And you were hurt so much you couldn't laugh off my stupid score, like you should have.' She turned to face him, and there was no other word for it. Her face crumpled. 'If only I could turn the clock back. Take a moment to check I really was sending the message to *Ava*. I mean, that's messaging 101, check before pressing send.' Her almond shaped eyes blinked a few times. 'Wait, I'd wind it back before that, to our date. I'd not talk so much, not drink so much. Not leap to conclusions before knowing the facts. Then my score for you wouldn't have appeared so horribly bitchy compared to the others.'

His lips twitched. 'I'd have taken a five.' She let out a strangled laugh and it amazed him that he was finally able to joke about it. She still looked stricken though, so he put his hand over hers. 'But then I wouldn't have seen you again.'

Her hands gave a quick jolt beneath his. 'I'm not sure that's a good enough reward.'

Alarmed by the pulse of heat that shot through his blood at their connection, he let go. 'I've enjoyed our dates.'

She smirked. 'Even the first one?'

'Even the first one.' He took a breath, chose his words carefully. 'I couldn't get a word in edgeways, but I didn't mind that. You were easy company.'

She burst out laughing. 'I'm not sure how to take that. Interesting, fun, exciting, fascinating, challenging even, but easy.' She pulled a face.

He wanted to tell her she was all of those things, and that when like him you weren't a talker, easy was meant as a compliment. But he'd only just got his balance back, and he wasn't sure if she wanted compliments from him, so he asked her instead who she'd been talking to, and for the next ten minutes they sat chatting like friends on the bench, the gentle breeze taking the sting out of the sun, the familiar sound of leather on willow adding to the contentment of the moment.

'Roger said he's got hundreds of tales he can tell me about fourteen-year-old Michael.' She giggled. 'He said you had braces and hair so long it kept getting in your eyes but you refused to get it cut because you wanted to look like the lead singer of Nickelback.'

He grimaced, remembering how desperate he'd been to try and look cool so he could fit in at the new school they'd had to join following their move here to live with Betty. And how futile that had been for the quiet, studious kid, grieving for his mother. 'I need to have a word with Roger.' Back on the field there was a shout and the umpire signalled that Sanjay was out. 'The excruciating trip through my childhood will have to stop though. Thankfully, I have to pad up.'

Together they walked back to the pavilion, dogs in tow. 'Will I see you later?'

'You mean am I staying to watch you bat? Of course. Besides, I've got to set up this spreadsheet for Betty. And Hattie said she wanted to talk to me about doing something similar for her.'

'Hattie?' He couldn't keep the surprise out of his voice. 'Practice manager, Hattie?'

'Oh, is that what she does?' He saw the moment when understanding dawned. 'Ah, so you must work with her.'

'I do,' he confirmed warily.

She looked like she was trying to fight a smile. 'You must be one of the people she was complaining about, then. She said her work colleagues drove her mad. She tried to organise them but it was like getting cats to sit on command, impossible. Of course we then had this big discussion about cats being way more intelligent than dogs as they refused to be trained, and she did admit that was part of the problem with her colleagues.'

'Consider me duly flattered.'

Sophie laughed. 'I think you should be, because Hattie sounds like a woman who knows her own mind.'

'And she isn't afraid to tell me what's on it. With alarming detail and regularity.'

'It did take me ten minutes to warm her up sufficiently to smile.'

'I've not received one in three years.'

Her eyes widened. 'Wow, the pair of you must really have a disconnect. Though maybe I shouldn't be surprised because actually you're alike in many ways, only she hides her reserved nature by being prickly.'

He wasn't sure he liked the comparison. He definitely didn't like the reminder that she still thought of him that way. The opposite of the exciting, charismatic guy her spreadsheet was geared towards. 'What were you talking to Hattie about?'

'She thought spreadsheets could be the answer to helping her organise you all. She asked if I'd help her set some up so I told her of course. Anything to help a spreadsheet fan.'

He stared at her, part awed that she'd made so many connections in such a small amount of time. Part terrified by what Hattie was planning. 'I'm not going to get away from the blasted things, am I?'

She gave him a sunny smile. 'Why on earth would you want to? They're awesome. By the way, have you noticed the way she and Hamza sort of, I don't know, circle around each other? Watching but pretending they're not?'

'I hadn't, no.'

'Are they both single?'

'To my knowledge.'

'Umm, interesting. He's a computer whizz, isn't he? Maybe he could help Hattie out, too.' She winked. 'I bet he could get a smile out of her.'

As he watched her walk away, a gentle sway to her hips, he was left with the feeling that while he'd never be converted to spreadsheets, he could easily be converted to her.

Of course Sophie would only ever think of their dates as an exercise, but maybe it was time he recognised that Betty was right. Seeing Sophie was a rare opportunity for him to have some fun. Put the sorry saga of Jackie behind him. And in the process, he might be able to prove to Sophie that he was worth continuing to see beyond the ten dates they'd earmarked.

He wanted that, he realised with a start. He wanted more time to get to know her.

Maybe while he was doing that, he'd also find the parts of himself the last few years had wrenched away from him.

Chapter Fifteen

Sophie knocked back the last of her gin and tonic as she sat on the pavilion balcony, enjoying the evening sun. Then frowned down at the empty glass.

'Have I just finished another one?'

Dennis chuckled. Sweet, affable, but deadly with the gin pouring. 'Plenty more where they came from.' He rose to his feet, looking way steadier than she felt, and started to stride towards the little bar inside.

'Oh no, no, no, no.' She shook her head, then winced as the room started to spin. 'No more gin. I need to catch a train soon.'

'It's only seven o'clock. Plenty of time for that.' Betty, sitting next to her, patted her hand. 'Besides, Michael will never talk to me again if we let you go before he's had the chance to say goodbye.'

She wasn't sure where the rest of the afternoon had gone. She'd started helping Ayesha clear up – a lot more fun than it sounded. They'd ended up using the floor mop as a microphone and singing old Abba tunes for reasons that escaped her, but had possibly been fuelled by alcohol. Then she'd set up Betty's spreadsheet, chatted to Hattie about her work at the surgery and run through some options that might help, and somewhere between all that, she'd watched Michael hit some pretty impressive fours – yep, she was shit hot with the cricket terminology now.

Talking of hot – she'd felt a real stomach swoop when she'd watched him walk out to the middle carrying his bat. There was an ease to his stride, a confidence she'd overlooked before now because it was so low key. Yes, he was quiet, unshowy, but he had a composure that was surprisingly sexy. And when he'd started to hit the ball with such assurance, such authority, butterflies had swarmed in her belly.

There was a chance she'd just been seeing him through gin eyes though, because Dennis had kept pouring them. One to celebrate Michael's fifty, then to commiserate with him getting out for sixty-three. And … she was sure there had been a third, no make that a fourth because she'd already had one before the break for tea. Oh and one with Ayesha.

Bollocks, how much had she drunk?

And was it bad form for the captain's friend – in typical Michael form he'd kept the fact he was the frigging captain, quiet – to be pissed before the game had even finished?

Ignoring her protests, Dennis handed her another full glass and as he sat down next to her, she noticed his eyes travel over to Betty, who'd moved inside to talk to Roger.

'How long have you had a crush on her?' she whispered, nodding in the direction of his gaze. At least she hoped it was a whisper. Very hard to judge the volume of her voice after a few drinks.

Dennis jolted. 'Ah.' Then he cleared his throat. 'Is it obvious?'

'Maybe a tiny bit?' Surely Betty had seen the way he was always by her side. Always looking at her as if she was the centre of his world. 'You should do something about it.'

He smiled ruefully and scratched his head. 'I'm still trying to pluck up the courage.'

Bless. Her heart reached out to him. 'Don't waste too much time waiting. Seize your chances for joy when you can.' Her throat tightened. 'You never know what's round the next corner.'

Dennis gave her a searching look, but before he could ask questions she wasn't ready to answer, not with all this gin slopping about in her, the balcony began to clap.

'That's the last four runs we needed.' Dennis let out a satisfied smile. 'Better luck next year, Roger.'

Figuring she needed a bit of air to clear her head, Sophie left Dennis to receive the winner's acclaim and headed downstairs – clutching at the handrail because it seemed way steeper than it had a few hours ago. Fudge was outside, lying on the grass, unfazed by all the petting she was receiving from the children swarming round her. Turning the corner, she noticed the players all shaking hands. Automatically her eyes zeroed in on Michael. Had he grown taller in the last couple of hours since she'd seen him?

He met her gaze and gave her what she now considered his trademark smile – a small lift of his mouth, a crinkle of his gorgeous blue eyes. From nowhere, her breath caught in her throat.

He might be all sorts of wrong for her, but she had an undeniable attraction to him.

And now he was walking towards her, broad shoulders stretching his cricket shirt, blond hair ruffled from being under his helmet. His doting canine companion bounded ahead and Sophie felt a squirming sensation in her stomach as she watched him bend to give Fudge's ears a thorough fondle.

'You won.' Inwardly she smacked her head with her hand. Duh.

Those lips curved again. 'I know.'

'Umm, yes, I figured you might, but I just wanted to show off my new cricket knowledge. Like I also know you scored sixty-three and that's quite good.'

That little huff of laughter was starting to become her favourite sound. 'Thank you. I think. Sorry I didn't come up and see you after, but I had to take over the scoring.'

'Ah yes, all those dots and squiggles. Important stuff.'

Vivid blue eyes skimmed her face. 'Are you okay? You look flushed.'

Oh boy, she could feel her cheeks heat even more. 'I may be a teeny bit drunk. But you have to blame Dennis because he kept pouring the gin and I don't think he knows what a single measure is.' She leant in, close enough she could smell the woody scent of his aftershave, mixed with a hint of clean sweat and what must be a massive dollop of testosterone because her heart skipped a beat. *Focus.* 'Did you know Dennis has a super massive crush on Betty?'

Michael's expression was part curious, part amused. 'I did.'

'Thought you must have because it's like super obvious, though I'm not sure if Betty's aware of it. Do you think she's interested? I know she used to be married to … Paddy I think? But I don't know when he died and if she's ready for another relationship but I think they're cute together.'

'Cute,' he repeated, lips twitching. 'Paddy was ten years older than Betty. He died quite a while ago, before I went to live with her.' He paused. 'Maybe you should create her a Love Life spreadsheet.'

'Wow, that would be a great idea … oh wait. You're kidding.'

'Yes, I'm kidding.' His eyes seem even bluer today. And when they locked on hers, she felt prickles race across her skin. 'When do you want to head back?'

'I'm okay for a bit. I want to help you celebrate your victory. But keep me away from Dennis. No more drinking for me, no siree. Water. That's what I need. Water and then push me off to catch my train.'

He nodded towards the changing room. 'Okay, give me a few minutes to shower and get changed?'

'Sure. I'll, err, wait with Fudge.'

As he strode off, she glanced down to see Fudge following him with her gaze, an expression that could only be described as adoration on her face. 'You love him, don't you girl?' Fudge wagged her tail. 'I imagine he's pretty easy to love, huh? Bet he's kind, patient, totally trustworthy. Takes really good care of you.'

For a moment she imagined how it would feel to have all those qualities focussed on her. Jackie must have been nuts to give him up.

Michael held Sophie's hand as she stepped onto the train. She wobbled, ever so slightly, and he tightened his grip.

'This is silly. You really don't have to do this. I'm quite capable of making my way home without a minder.' She hiccupped out a laugh. 'I've done it loads of times before and after way more to drink, though not usually gin. That was Dennis's fault. Inside that sweet and smiley exterior is a lethal gin pourer.'

He felt a ripple of concern. 'I hope you don't travel alone after you've been drinking.'

'Aw, worried about me?' She flopped onto the seat and gave him a soft, tipsy smile. 'You don't need to be, Doc. It might not look it, but I'm sensible. Ava and Grace always have my back, like I have theirs. Today was an anomly … annoim … anom…'

'Anomaly?' He took the seat opposite her, though everything inside him begged to sit next to her. Throw his arm around her and hold her close.

She started to nod her head, then groaned. 'Damn it, remind me not to do that. But yes, one of those. I told you, blame Dennis. Oooh, and Betty. She's a bad influence too.' With a contented sigh she flopped back against the seat. 'You know what, Doc? I had a surprisingly good time today.'

It was hard to take offence at the *surprisingly* when her face carried such a gorgeous dreamy smile. 'I think that's the gin talking.'

'Maybe.' She eyed him with stunning grey eyes that were just a tiny bit unfocussed. 'Or maybe it was because you looked hot in your whites.'

Jesus. He could feel a flush creep over his cheeks. 'That gin really was potent.'

She giggled. 'It really was. So when do we do this again? Not the me getting drunk and you feeling you have to take me home thing ... did I tell you how ridiculous this is? You're going to spend all tonight on a train.'

He thought of his usual Sunday evening. Walking the dogs. A glass of wine and a good book. 'But I get to sit and talk to you for half of it.'

Her expression softened. 'That's, wow. A really nice thing to say. *You're* a nice guy, Doc.'

You're a nice guy. I tried hard to prefer you, but I realised I don't want steady.

'Hey, Doc, where did you go?'

'Sorry.' He shook off the memory of Jackie's words, shoving them deep back inside. 'Are you free next weekend?'

A cloud crossed her face and she stared out of the window. 'Can't do Saturday. I've got some family birthday thing.'

'Whose birthday is it?'

'Err, mine, kind of.' Again her eyes studiously avoided his. 'But that's not really why we're getting together.'

Why did a woman he'd seen celebrate a Friday, just because it had been the end of her working week, look so upset at the thought of her birthday? 'You're meeting with your family on your birthday, but not to celebrate it?'

'Yep, that's about it.' Her voice caught. 'Not something to celebrate. Nope.'

He studied her profile, saw the pain etched on her face and felt a sharp tug in his chest. 'You know you can talk to me, don't you? About anything.'

She let out a bark of laughter. 'I bet that's one of your super powers, isn't it? You don't talk much so you get to spend loads of time listening.'

'Listening is something I get a lot of practise at, yes.' Concerned, he leant forward and put his hand over hers. 'Will you tell me why you don't celebrate your birthday? Has it got anything to do with Rosie?'

She jerked back, snatching her hand away. 'What … what do you know about Rosie?'

'Only that she's your sister.'

Her face looked paler now, her eyes standing out like shimmering silver almonds. She seemed to be struggling with something, but then she gave him a small smile. 'You really do listen, don't you? I only said her name once.'

'But you looked sad when you said it.'

She nodded, bit into her bottom lip, her eyes glistening. 'That's because Rosie isn't with us anymore. She died eight years ago, a shitty aggressive form of non-Hodgkin Lymphoma.'

'I'm so sorry.' He felt utterly useless, sitting across from her, wondering if he could even hold her hand again since she'd pulled it away so quickly. 'Did she die on your birthday? Is that why you don't celebrate it?'

'Oh no, she died November 6th. One day after she made us set up a firework display in the garden so she could watch it out of the window.'

Understanding dawned. 'She was your twin sister.'

'Bingo. My *identical* twin.' She gave him a sad smile. 'And that's why we don't celebrate my birthday, because how can we when she isn't here to celebrate it with us?'

He felt his chest crumple, not just at the sadness of her words, but at the utter loss in her expression. That this funny, irrepressible woman carried such grief inside her … it was hard to fathom. Yet so was the way she and her family seemed to be stuck on making Sophie's birthday one of remembrance, and not celebration. A fact he found he desperately wanted to redress. 'How about I see you afterwards? Or before?' Sod his cricket. This was far more important.

She looked at him like he'd said something ridiculous. 'Not a good idea, Doc. I'll be really crappy company.'

'And I haven't been?' he answered dryly.

'Well, you've had your moments I guess.' He was pleased to see a little of the mischief back in her eyes. 'Not telling me why you were late and distracted that first time we met, taking me on an intrepid hike, not drinking cocktails with us at The Drunken Flamingo.' She smirked. 'Making me watch cricket with two gin guzzling pensioners.'

'I can only apologise.' Something powerful shifted in his chest and he found he could no longer sit opposite her. Slowly he rose to his feet, giving her ample chance to tell him no. But she didn't, just kept watching him with those direct grey eyes, so he plonked himself down next to her. Then, heart pumping, he reached for her hand again. 'Let me see you next Saturday. I don't need fun Sophie, or even happy Sophie.' He gave her fingers a squeeze. 'Quiet Sophie might even be a blessing.'

She let out a strangled laugh, but he noticed she didn't pull her hand from his. And when, a minute later, she sighed and dropped her head onto his shoulder, his heart did a slow cartwheel. 'Did you know you're a comfy pillow?' she said sleepily. 'And I like holding your hand.'

The breath caught in his throat and he tightened his fingers around hers, feeling the softness of her palm, the warmth of her skin. 'I like holding yours, too.' His voice sounded rough, but she didn't seem to notice. And when she closed her eyes, he found himself unable to look away from her, instead studying the long lashes that feathered across her lids, the clear skin. The plump, soft lips that made his own tingle, as if anticipating how they would feel if they kissed.

Did she *want* that from him? Her whole spreadsheet was geared around not wasting time on unsuitable guys, and he was definitely unsuitable according to her criteria. Yet she'd already committed to ten dates with him. It left another six times to see her, enjoy her. And maybe to kiss her. If she still found him hot when she was sober.

Unable to resist, he planted a soft kiss on the top of her head, inhaling the coconut smell of her shampoo. And feeling everything inside him settle somehow.

They got off at Waterloo and she announced she was going to walk, in the hope the fresh air would sober her up. So he headed with her towards the exit.

'This is silly. I know my way.' She glanced up at the departures board. 'And your train back is in ten minutes.'

'What sort of minder would I be if I didn't escort you to your front door?'

She gave him a soft smile and didn't object when he put his arm around her. In fact she snuggled in to his side as they made their way across Westminster bridge and St James's Park, dusk settling over the familiar London sights. He wondered if sober Sophie would have done that, too. 'Tell me you would have taken the tube if I'd not been with you.'

'I would have taken the tube,' she deadpanned. But her lips twitched. 'I've lived in London for twenty-nine years. It's nowhere near as scary as the press would have you believe. In fact, according to the TV, more murders happen in those sleepy villages in the countryside.'

'In fiction.'

'If you say so.'

She finally came to a stop in front of an impressive looking old building, just off Berkeley Square. His expression must have said it all, because she laughed. 'I told you, Grace is the one who's loaded.' She bit into her lip again and God, he wanted to kiss those lips so badly he could taste them. Wanted to do way, way more with them. With all of her. 'Do you want to come up?'

Yes. He was shocked by how vicious his need was. But she was still partly inebriated. And he had a train to catch. 'Can I take a rain check?'

Did she look disappointed? Or was it his disappointment he could feel? 'Sure.' She tilted her head. 'Do I get a goodnight kiss at least?'

Immediately his eyes zeroed in on the mouth he'd been fantasising about. Or did she mean a friendly peck on the cheek? Before he could twist himself into knots second guessing her, she took the matter into her own hands. Clasping his face, she pulled him down and kissed him, no coyness, no shyness. A full mouth on mouth, kiss. Immediately he covered her hands with his, taking the reins, kissing her back. Feeling the warmth of her sizzle through his blood, the taste of her, sweet with a hint of gin, coiling round his groin. Giving it a sharp tug.

He wanted to push her against the wall, to wrap those long legs around his waist and feel the heat of her core against his now throbbing erection.

But. Would she be doing this if she was sober?

Reluctantly he drew back. 'Goodnight, Sophie.'

Her breath sounded choppy, her cheeks were flushed. 'Night, Doc. Thanks for getting me home in one piece.'

He smiled. 'Thanks for surviving your first cricket match.'

He waited until she stepped into the lift, and as he walked back to the station his step felt lighter. And the smile wouldn't budge from his face.

Chapter Sixteen

Monday morning, and Sophie was in the kitchen, the second cup of coffee finally making inroads through the dense fog in her brain. Snippets from yesterday danced around the edges of her consciousness. Gin, cricket, talking spreadsheets. Michael in his whites. Michael striding out to bat. Michael as he'd told her, eyes full of compassion, that he wanted to see her on Saturday, even if she wasn't fun Sophie.

Michael's shoulder as a pillow on the train.

Michael turning down her invitation to come up. An invitation for sex, because let's not beat about the bush, that's exactly what she'd wanted in that moment. Hot sex with the man whose hand she'd held on the train. Who'd kissed the top of her head – oh yes, she'd not been so drunk she'd missed that. And whose blazing blue eyes had seemed to want exactly the same from her in that moment.

Michael kissing her back. His hungry mouth on hers … waves of desire hummed through her and she slumped onto the bar stool, all weak-kneed and giddy.

'Well then, if it isn't the woman who came home drunk and smelling of gin.' Ava eyed her as she meandered into the kitchen, all bunched up in a fluffy dressing gown even though it was summer. 'What sort of cricket match was it, exactly?'

'The best sort.' Sophie rubbed at her head, trying to get the blood circulating again. 'Or maybe the worst sort.'

'Well, that makes perfect sense.' Ava grabbed at the coffee machine and popped a capsule in it. 'Explain. In short sentences preferably because I need to get to work.'

'I can't do short, you know me.' She swallowed another mouthful of caffeine. 'Okay, so it turns out cricket is okay, but the people who watch it are a lot more fun than Grace said. And they like to drink gin. And men look way hotter in cricket whites when they stride out to bat than I thought.'

'By men, do you mean a particular man?' Ava cut in. 'Dr two point five.'

'He's not two and a half.' When Ava just looked at her, Sophie mumbled. 'He's five and a bit now.'

'Wow, dizzy heights, huh?'

It felt uncomfortable, discussing him like this, so black and white when last night everything had got distinctly blurry, and that wasn't just the booze. 'It doesn't sound enough, but I have to be honest with myself when I mark and not let how much I like him get in the way.'

'But isn't liking him the most important part?'

'No, because I liked Will. And he liked me. In small doses.' She rubbed at her chest, the hurt still there. 'So liking someone doesn't mean they're right for me.'

'When you say *right for you*, that's according to your spreadsheet,' Ava countered with a heavy dose of irony.

'So?' She could feel herself getting defensive. 'Nice as he is,

Michael doesn't have the charisma, sociability, spontaneity, or excitement that I'm looking for in a guy.' Unbidden, an image of him popped into her head. Those hot blue eyes as he'd pulled away from one humdinger of a kiss. 'I did up his looks score to ten.'

Ava's mouth gaped open. 'You think he's that gorgeous – and I'm not disagreeing with you – yet you still believe your spreadsheet was right to red-line him? You're nuts.'

'There has to be more to a guy than his looks, Ava, or it doesn't work.'

'That is true, but this all sounds mega weird.' Ava gave her a searching look. 'You said it was the best sort and the worse sort of match. Why the worst sort?'

Unconsciously Sophie licked her lips. 'Because I kissed him.'

Ava almost dropped the mug she'd been holding. 'You kissed the hot looking man you like, but you don't want to date for real?'

Sophie touched a finger to her lips, sure she could still feel him there. 'Okay, okay I admit this *does* all sound weird.' *And I'd have gone further.* She wished she knew whether he'd turned her down because he hadn't wanted her. Or because she was tipsy and he was a gentleman. 'I also agreed to see him on Saturday.'

'Your birthday, Saturday?' Ava's jaw hung open. 'The day you never want to see anyone?'

'I know. And I told him about Rosie, warned him I'd be crappy company. But he said he wanted to see me anyway.'

Ava didn't look impressed. In fact she looked concerned. 'I hope you know what you're doing, Soph, because I certainly don't.'

'It's fine.' She thought about the kiss, how much she wanted a repeat. 'I can have a … fling. Just while we're finishing these ten dates. People have them with unsuitable guys all the time.'

Ava regarded her oddly. 'But *you* don't do flings. And do you really think the serious doctor is fling material?'

Sophie remembered Jackie, how Michael had proposed to her after two years, then not dated since, and felt a squirm of unease. Pushing it aside, she hurried through the shower yet, as she dried her hair, she kept glancing at her phone on the bedside table. The need to reach out to him again was almost palpable.

Finally, she gave up and sat on the bed.

Thank you for taking me home last night. Hope I didn't do anything embarrassing. S x

Aside from invite you up for sex and make you kiss me. Gin was clearly her nemesis.

She was dressed and ready to go when she finally received a reply.

Michael: Embarrassing? No.

Gah, the man was so minimal with his words. She bet he was a nightmare to have a real relationship with.

Anything I should know about tho'? S x

He messaged again as she was squeezing into her Mini.

Michael: We kissed.

Was that it? All he was going to say? With a squeal of frustration, she flung the phone onto the seat and was about to set off when another message came through.

Michael: But as you don't remember, next time I'll have
to do better.

The frustration evaporated, leaving a warm, happy feeling in its space. *Next time.* Like it was definitely going to happen again. She had to revise her opinion. He did communicate, he was just subtle about it.

Grinning like a fool, she typed back.

I do remember. S x

Michael: Did you score me?

Oh. That happy bubble deflated a little. This scoring thing still hung between them. With a sigh she messaged back.

I did. Do you want to know?

Immediately he pinged back.

Michael: No.

She could imagine his expression when he'd sent that. Tight jaw, hurt blue eyes. It upset her that she was adding to the crazy insecurities Jackie had given him. Before she could add something to reassure him though, she received another message.

Michael: Are we still on for Saturday?

The reminder of her birthday made her insides clench. Did she really want to see him? It was an awful day, one filled with grief, sadness, not to mention stress because it was the one time of year both parents came together.

Yet wouldn't it be nice to have a few hours to look forward to in the day?

Can do afternoon. Or evening. Seeing parents for meal at 6 pm. S x

She glanced at the dashboard clock. She really needed to get going, yet the phone wouldn't leave her hand.

Finally she heard the ping.

Michael: Plan something for the afternoon. And evening.

Well.

Her heart gave a little flutter, but as she slipped the phone back into her bag, she wondered if this … flirting … was really such a good idea when they both knew there was no future to it. Maybe that was okay though, because there was a clear expiry date.

What if the spreadsheet has him averaging more than seven by then?

The thought made her pause, yet she couldn't see how it

would happen. He was maxed out on the looks score, and even if the sex matched the kissing … heat flooded through her, settling between her legs. Okay, so that would be some scorching hot sex. Even if that happened though, if it really was the quiet guys a woman had to watch out for, it still left a lot of categories where he would always fall short.

Ava was right, it did sound crazy to be sat here feeling all squirmy and fluttery about the thought of sex with a guy she didn't want to date for real. But those butterflies had buzzed for Will, her heart had beat faster. And just when it had opened, excited to let him in, he'd stomped all over it.

No way did she want to go through that again. It was time to put her faith in the spreadsheet.

———

Michael had ten minutes between patients to eat his sandwich, check his e-mail, call Betty back because she was in a fluster about something, and go through the twenty lab results waiting for his review.

Sitting back on his chair, he stretched out his neck. Figuring his sandwich could wait, he reached for the phone to call his gran.

'Hi, it's me.'

'Oh Michael, I'm in a real dither. Dennis is going to take me to lunch but I can't find my piddling purse.'

Unbidden his mind flashed up an image of a smiling, inebriated Sophie as she'd giddily informed him Dennis had a … how had she phrased it? A *super massive crush* on Betty. 'I'm sure Dennis is expecting to pay,' he replied mildly.

'Tosh. I'm a modern woman. I pay my own way.' Her voice

faltered a second. 'Or I would if I could remember where I put that stupid purse.'

He smiled fondly, his heart full. 'I think I saw it on the coffee table.'

'What on earth is it doing there? It should be in my handbag. That's where I keep it.' He heard sounds of movement, presumably her wandering into the living room. 'Good heavens, you're right. I'm getting dafter than a brush. Thank you, dear. Sorry to be a nuisance and disturb you at work.'

She was getting increasingly forgetful, but he had to remind himself she was eighty-five, and forgetting things wasn't necessarily a sign of anything more sinister. 'You're never a nuisance. And most of the time you're smarter than I am.'

'Nonsense. But thank you for saying it.' A pause, and he geared himself up for whatever was about to come next. 'So, where did you and the delightful Sophie go after the match?'

He raised his eyes to the ceiling. 'I told you, I took her home. And as I'd had a beer I couldn't drive so we took the train.'

'Very gentlemanly of you.' He'd not felt very gentleman-like when he'd been kissing her. 'You were so late back I didn't hear you come in.'

He started to smile to himself. 'Come on Betty, say what's on your mind. You don't usually hold back on me.'

She spluttered. 'You make me sound like I'm nosey.' He kept quiet and dug into his briefcase for his sandwich. 'Fine, did you get invited in?'

'I did.' He carefully peeled off the cellophane wrapping.

'Oh, you're teasing me now you awful boy.'

He smiled. 'Where is Dennis taking you on this date?'

'Good heavens, it's not a date. He just thought I might like to try that new café that's opened.'

'Umm. So will you invite him in when he drops you back?'

'Invite him in ... whatever are you ... oh.' He heard her let out a deep sigh. 'Alright. I won't ask what's going on with you and Sophie. Just know she has my full approval.'

He wasn't surprised. Sophie was incredibly easy to like. He only had to ask anyone she'd met at the club to know that. 'And Dennis has mine.'

'He does?' She muttered something else under her breath.

'What was that?'

'I just thought ... well you might think it was silly, me dating at my age. Not that I am dating, and not that I would date someone like Dennis who's nearly ten years younger than me.'

'Seven years. And you're a very young eight-five.' At least she had been, before her fall. Now there were times she acted her age, though not, he recalled, when she was with Dennis.

'Hmph.' Experience told him she wasn't finished yet, so he waited, eyeing up his ploughman's sandwich. Hearing his stomach rumble. 'But if I did consider dating someone...'

'Like Dennis?' he prompted.

'Well yes, like Dennis.'

'Then I would shake his hand and tell him he's a very lucky man.'

She let out a half chuckle, half laugh. 'Get away with you.' She hesitated again. 'About you and Sophie—'

'There will never be a me and Sophie,' he cut in quietly. 'I like her, a lot, but we both know...' *I'm not what she's looking for.* 'Nothing will come of this.'

'I hope you're not taking that from her daft spreadsheet.'

'You didn't think her spreadsheet was daft when she was showing you how to do the cricket finances.'

'*That* was very helpful. But matters of the heart will never be decided by rows of numbers.' Her voice turned softer. 'You show that woman what she really needs in a man, not what her spreadsheet tells her she needs.'

As he ended the call, Michael sat back in his chair and let Betty's words settle. Later he'd consider them, wonder if maybe she was onto something. But for now … he looked at his watch. Two minutes to eat the sandwich. And a late finish ahead of him to go through the emails and lab results. Still, Betty had her purse, and her date.

And he had something to chew over beyond a hunk of cheese and two slices of bread.

It was after seven when Michael finished catching up. As he walked past the reception area he noticed Hattie was still there.

'Everything okay?'

She bristled. 'Of course.'

He drew in a breath. He was better than this with people. 'If you're finding you have to work this late, we need to get you more help.'

She waved him away. 'I've got Sophie on the case. That girl is a godsend.'

'Sophie?' Then he remembered the cricket match. 'Ah, the spreadsheet.'

'She said if I told her my main issues here, she'd see if she could devise something to help.' Hattie tapped away for a few beats then turned to him and smiled. Actually bloody *smiled*. 'I sent her a list this morning and she's already come back with some ideas.'

'That's … great. Let me know if there's anything I can do to help.' He sent up a silent prayer that any spreadsheets Sophie sent wouldn't implode like her previous ones.

'Thank you, I will.' Hattie inclined her head. 'Goodnight, Dr Adams.'

Maybe one day she'd call him Michael. 'Goodnight, Hattie.'

Sophie remained on his mind as he walked home. He tried to think about other things, but whether it was work, or what to make for dinner, he kept circling back to her. After ten minutes of it, his phone was in his hand, his fingers scrolling to her name.

'Hey Doc,' she answered, and he found a smile creeping onto his face just hearing her voice, and her daft nickname. 'Changed your mind about Saturday already?'

'No,' he said instantly. Emphatically.

'Ah, you say that now, but wait till you see what I have planned for us. We're going to be flying high.' Was that mischief adding to the amusement in her voice? 'I predict it'll be our best date yet.'

'Better than watching cricket?' he asked dryly.

'You know what? I actually enjoyed yesterday.'

'You enjoyed talking to everyone.' And didn't that just scream how different they were? It had taken him three years to get the same level of comfort, of rapport, that she'd achieved in a few hours. 'Which brings me to why I'm phoning. Hattie smiled at me today.'

There was short pause and he pictured her trying to make the connection.

'Ah, she told you about my spreadsheet ideas.' Sophie laughed softly. 'And I bet you're pulling a face now, huh, because you hate them almost as much as I love them.'

'I hate *one* of your spreadsheets,' he corrected her. Then wondered if it was true, because if it hadn't been for that, he wouldn't be talking to her now. And wouldn't be looking forward to Saturday, irrespective of what she had planned. 'But I thank you, and them, for giving me some brownie points with Hattie. I needed them.'

'Oh God, you're clueless, aren't you?' Sophie replied after a beat. 'And I don't know why I'm so surprised, because you're the most humble guy I've ever met.' Her voice lowered a notch. 'The thing is, and you have to keep this between ourselves, I've discovered that Hattie secretly worships the ground you walk on. She's embarrassed by her little crush on the handsome doctor though, which is why she acts like she does around you.'

'I...' he shook his head. Surely that couldn't be true?

'You don't believe me, and it doesn't matter because you shouldn't treat her any differently. Besides, I've kind of given Hamza a little push in her direction.'

'A push?' he asked, alarmed.

'Maybe I should have said a nudge. I've asked him to pop into the surgery to see if he can find any IT solutions to help Hattie.' Before his mind had a chance to grapple with that image, Sophie was talking again. 'So anyway, I'll see you Saturday?'

'Yes.' He sucked in a breath, debated whether he was pushing himself where he wasn't wanted. Or just nudging. 'If you want to go to your family do alone, I'll entertain myself for a few hours. But if you want me with you, I'm very happy to go.'

Silence. For a few humming moments he held his breath, only releasing it again when she started to speak.

'You, Mr Reserved, are happy to go out for a meal with a bunch of people you've never met? And who will either be grieving or having a snide dig at each other because Mum and Dad in the same room are not a good combination, and when we add in Patricia, my step mum, it's potentially explosive.'

For once he didn't need to think. 'If you feel me being there will help make it less explosive, or perhaps less painful, then I repeat. I'm happy to go.' He uttered the next words before he could talk himself out of it. 'I want to go.'

More silence, and he wished he could see her face. Was she annoyed that a guy she wasn't interested in seeing beyond ten dates, had tried to push himself into a very private part of her life? Or could she understand what he'd failed to say. That he hated the thought of her – bubbly, lively, vital – not celebrating her birthday. And if there was anything he could do to help her through it, he wanted to do it. Even if it meant catapulting himself into an emotionally charged family dinner.

'Looks like I'd better warn Mum to book a table for five instead of four,' Sophie said finally. 'See you Saturday, then. No ducking out now.'

Well then. He slid the phone back into his pocket and spent the rest of the walk home wondering if he – or worse, if she – would regret his rare impulse.

Chapter Seventeen

Sophie couldn't help it. She took out her phone and snapped a photo of Michael as he stared at the place she'd booked them into for their fourth date. It wasn't, as his expression suggested, a modern take on a medieval torture chamber. Nope, the flying trapeze school in Regents Park was way more thrilling than that.

Though perhaps not for everyone.

'You're not scared of heights, are you?' Too late, she realised she should have checked with him.

He turned, gave her one of his mild looks that actually said so much, once you got to know him. 'If I said I was?'

'Then obviously I'd have to find something else for us to do. We've probably still got time to get over to the Docklands and go flyboarding.'

He swallowed, and God she was starting to get obsessed with watching that sexy Adam's apple move in his tanned throat. 'Dare I ask?'

'You strap these two huge water-powered jets to your

ankles and they propel you about ten metres up in the air. It's an experience not to be missed,' she added with a grin.

'You've done both these?'

'Absolutely. And I'm still here, so nothing to be afraid of.'

He gave her another dry look. 'Except plummeting to my death?'

He was so damn cute. How had she not seen that when she'd first met him? And okay, cute appeal wasn't on her spreadsheet because it wasn't a quality she thought important in a man, but it did concern her that she'd got him so wrong at the start. He should never have been two and a half out of ten. Was the failure hers, or the spreadsheet's? 'The plummeting to death part is what the net is there to prevent,' she told him, pointing to said net before looping her arm through his. 'Come on Doc, this is going to be a laugh.'

He gave the trapeze another look, then turned back to her. 'This is how you want to spend your birthday?'

Funny, she'd successfully forgotten it was her birthday for most of the day. Ava and Grace, because they knew her so well, hadn't mentioned it, though they'd both come into her room this morning, Ava placing a vase of flowers on her bedside table, Grace handing her a tray with a mug of tea and a selection of pastries from her favourite bakery down the street. But Michael hadn't mentioned it when she'd met him, and she'd been too full of excitement about the trapeze, and yes, perhaps seeing him, to dwell on it. 'Yes, this is how I want to spend it.'

He nodded, straightening his spine and drawing back his shoulders before shooting her a small smile. 'Then let's do it.'

The smile slipped a little when he was asked to fill in the

consent form. And slipped further when they went through the safety briefing.

'Listen to the underlying message,' she told him encouragingly. 'Everything will be fine as long as you do as you're told.'

'Thanks.'

She took a moment to study his handsome face, set in serious lines as he listened. This was not his idea of a fun day out. Still, he was going to go through with it because he wanted to make this day better for her.

Something shifted in her chest. She shouldn't be surprised he was so kind – he was a doctor, after all – yet it was hard not to get emotional when she knew this was probably the last place he'd really want to be today.

As the briefing finished, he cleared his throat. 'I'm beginning to regret the bacon sandwich.'

Appreciating him, she nudged his ribs. 'Just think of it this way, if it comes back up, I'll buy you another one. And this part of the day is going to be way more fun than the next.'

'That's … not exactly reassuring.'

Sophie jumped in delight as she watched Michael perform a neat forward flip before sailing through the air and being caught by the instructor on the other bar. All with grace and a surprising power. Yep, she'd now seen those arm muscles in action, had a tantalising glimpse of flat stomach as he'd hung on the bar and – wow. Beneath the conservative polo shirt and cargo shorts she suspected he was rocking a lean, muscular body. It was also clear he was a natural athlete. And sure, she should have known that from the way she'd seen him bat and bowl, but the man was so unassuming, it was easy to overlook.

A few moments later she saw him striding towards her, his smile snatching the breath from her lungs. Never before had the phrase *lit up his face* been so aptly demonstrated. Or to such devastating effect. His ocean blue eyes sparkled, grooves slashed his cheeks. He looked so far removed from the stressed, distant man she'd first met it made her wonder which was the real Michael Adams.

'Well, you were kind of a superstar at this, weren't you?'

He laughed, adding to the whole sexy man vibe and sending a shiver of awareness through her. 'I wouldn't say that. You were far more elegant.'

'Oh no, don't give me any of that humble stuff,' she protested, wagging a finger at him. 'You were awesome and you know it. In fact I reckon you can get a job at the circus if you ever get bored of the GP gig.'

Colour flushed his cheeks and he looked away, shaking his head. 'What's the plan now?'

She'd done this activity with two other guys – one of them Callum. Both had been hard to shut up afterwards, so pumped up that they'd done it. Typical that Michael wanted to move the subject on. 'I figured we'd go back to mine and get changed.'

He fetched the rucksack he'd brought from the lock up and they walked across the park to the tube. It was a warm, sunny late afternoon and Sophie inhaled a deep breath, for once content to settle into Michael's pace; leisurely strides, easy silence.

'Thank you.'

She glanced up in surprise, only to find herself the focus of that intense blue gaze. 'What for?'

'Taking me out of my comfort zone.' His mouth curved into his trademark dry smile. 'I would never in a million years have chosen to do that.'

'No, really?'

He smiled at her gentle sarcasm. 'Really. But I have to admit I enjoyed it.'

'Worth missing cricket for?'

He appeared to give the question some serious thought. 'On balance, yes.' He glanced sideways at her. 'Though I think that was more to do with the company.'

Her belly somersaulted. Not knowing how to reply, she resorted to humour. 'Well stick with me Doc, and I'll make sure you never get too comfortable.'

He smiled again, but there was tightness to it this time and as she replayed her words, she felt a similar tight feeling across her chest. There would be no sticking with her, because there were only five more dates after this one. The thought made her sad, though logically she knew they both needed to move on and find their perfect ten out of ten. 'You know, when these dates are over, it doesn't have to be goodbye.' Why had her heart begun to thump? 'We could remain mates. If you wanted to, I mean,' she added hurriedly. 'I could continue to plan days to take you out of your comfort zone. You could plan days to calm me down.'

Silence fell between them, and it hummed with the tension that had been absent a few minutes ago.

'I don't think that would work for me,' he said finally.

Disappointment flooded through her, and hot on the heels of that, was hurt. 'Oh, that's fine. I can understand.' She forced some humour into her voice. 'You're probably looking forward to getting back to your quiet life, huh? No more having to entertain me, or put up with my idea of a good time.'

'No, that's not what I meant.' He slid his hands into the pockets of his shorts. 'I don't think I can do friends with you.' Her heart faltered as his eyes skimmed her face before landing on her mouth. 'I can't be friends with a woman I want to kiss again.'

Holy cow. Breath rushed from her lungs and Sophie found she was speechless. It was one thing talking about their kiss by text. A kiss that had happened when she'd been giddy with drink. It was another discussing it face to face, when she was sober. And he was looking at her with hungry eyes that had darkened almost to navy. 'I … umm.' Her phone rang, the shrieking tone shattering the moment. She didn't know whether to be grateful or gutted when she saw it was her mum. Awkwardly she showed him the screen.

Michael nodded and, clearly wanting to give her some privacy, walked away.

———

Well, he'd totally ballsed up today. Head in his hands, Michael sat on the soft velvet sofa in Sophie's living room as he waited for her to change. He tried not to listen to the sound of her shower, because if he did, he'd start picturing her under it. The supple body he'd watched fly through the air now naked, rivulets of water flowing over toned skin.

He felt a tightening against the fly of his chinos and swore. A woman who saw him only as a friend, did not want to see him aroused. Especially when they were about to be having dinner with her family. On the birthday she didn't celebrate because her twin sister was no longer around to celebrate with her.

Fuck.

What had he been thinking, telling her he wanted to kiss her? Ever since he'd done that, things had been strained between them. Of course she'd only kissed him because she'd been drunk. Of course she didn't want a reminder of it, or to know he couldn't look at her, couldn't think about her, without wanting to do it again.

He glanced up when he heard footsteps. And had to stop his jaw hanging open when she emerged in the doorway in a slim fitting halter neck dress with purple and yellow swirls. 'You look … great.' *Great?* He was bloody certain he once had more charm than this.

She smiled awkwardly at his inept compliment. 'Thanks. It's always a bit of an awkward dinner, so I found it helps to dress up a bit because they always do.'

He looked down at his chinos and blue linen shirt. 'Should I have worn a suit?'

Some of the tension left her face as she made an exaggerated grimace. 'Pretty sure you didn't get many marks for that.'

Why did he get the feeling she'd deliberately raised the spreadsheet to show him that was the only reason they were seeing each other? 'I do have better suits.'

'It's fine. Dad won't be in one. And you have a jacket, so it's all good.'

It wasn't though. From the stilted tone of her voice, to the stiff set of her shoulders, to the smile that had frozen on her face, he knew there was nothing good about how Sophie felt right now. He rose to his feet and went to stand in front of her, taking hold of her hand. It felt cold, and he'd like to bet if he put a finger on her pulse it would be racing. 'Please tell me this is you worrying about the meal and not about what I said earlier. About wanting to kiss you,' he added quietly when she frowned. His stomach fell as her eyes darted away from his. 'I won't,' he stated firmly. 'I realise now it's all one sided, so I—'

'It isn't.' She blew out an agitated breath. 'But I really can't deal with us right now. I have to get through this dinner and Mum's already had a minor meltdown on the phone about what to wear so she won't look dowdy next to Patricia. And Dad's annoyed because the restaurant can't guarantee the same table we always book because it's a new manager who hasn't a clue why it's so important to us. And—'

'Shh.' He cupped her face, his heart twisting when he saw her eyes well. 'Come here.' Unsure what to say that would help, he wrapped his arms around her and hugged her against his chest.

'I'm not going to cry,' she said shakily, pressing her cheek against his chest. 'Because that would be ridiculous. So if you see your shirt is wet when I step back, you must have spilt your drink down it.'

He smiled against her hair. 'I'm clumsy like that.'

'I know.' They remained like that for a few minutes, him feeling as if he was holding something very precious. But then she drew back and gave him a tremulous smile. 'Looks like Mum isn't the only one having a meltdown today.'

This was her birthday. He wasn't a man given to anger very often, but he felt it simmer through him as he thought of how selfish her parents were, making today all about Rosie, all about them. And not about this gorgeous woman standing in front of him.

Gently he wiped the tears from her cheeks with his thumb, feeling his heart swell alarmingly. The more time he spent with her, the more dangerous this all was, yet the alternative, not seeing her anymore, wasn't something he could contemplate. For the last three years he'd felt adrift, going through the motions of life. Since he'd met her though, he'd begun to wake up, to smell the roses – and hell, even the begonias. He didn't want to stop. Fear – of being hurt again, of not being enough for someone again – had held him back too long. At least this time he wouldn't be blind-sided because he already knew he wasn't enough for Sophie, that she wanted more, deserved more. In the meantime though, maybe he could help her, as she was helping him.

'Wait here a minute.' He squeezed her hand before walking over to the coat stand in the hall where he'd hung his jacket and took the little gift bag from his pocket. Planting a quick kiss on her cheek – not the kiss he wanted to give her, but a reminder that there was still a discussion to be had – he handed the bag over to her. 'I know you said you don't celebrate today, but that feels wrong. This is daft, but it's my way of saying that I think the day you came into this world *is* something to celebrate. Happy birthday.'

She bit into her lip, glancing down at the gift bag and then back up at him. 'I don't know what to say.'

He tried to smile, but the moment felt too emotionally charged to manage it easily. 'I'm sure that won't be the case for long.'

She dived into the bag in the way he'd expected – a great rush of enthusiasm. But when she found the jewellery box, she hesitated. 'Open it,' he prompted, his voice sounding gruff. 'It's not…' He exhaled heavily. 'Just open it.'

When she did, her eyes widened. And he almost sagged with relief as a smile split her face. 'Oh my God, it's gorgeous.' He knew her delight was genuine when she threw her arms around his neck and kissed him on the jaw. 'Thank you so much.' Her words were softly spoken, her breath tickling his neck and making him feel things he didn't want to feel, yet couldn't stop. Like wishing she'd stay in his arms. Or that she'd take his hand, pull him down onto the sofa and kiss him for real. His mouth against hers, their tongues dancing…

'Will you put it on me, please?' Her question shook him out of his daydream and he was very glad when she turned to present her back, giving him a moment to get his body and his head back under control.

Carefully he secured the silver catch to the necklace, then slid his hands down her shoulders before turning her back to face him. The silver charm – a sheep, fashioned out of thin silver wire curled round and round to make the body and finished with a black face and legs – settled enticingly above her cleavage. Her fingers curled round it and she grinned. 'Where did you find it?'

He wasn't going to tell her that he'd spent hours searching the internet, wanting to find something friend appropriate – because that was the box she'd put him in – yet also personal. Because that was the box he wanted to be in. 'In a local shop. So, are we good to go?'

With a sigh, she nodded. 'Let's get this over and done with.'

His heart broke a little bit at the way her shining eyes dimmed, like the joy had just been snuffed out of her.

Chapter Eighteen

Sophie couldn't help it. She kept touching her new pendant. And every time she did, it grounded her, made her smile a little inside. As did the memory of what Michael had said when he'd given it to her.

His thigh brushed hers, a warm and reassuring presence. 'How are you doing?' he asked under his breath.

She smiled, a lump jumping into her throat. 'Okay.'

The presence of a stranger had so far been enough to stop her parents from doing their usual *Let's see who can cause the deepest wound* routine. And the manager had given them the table they always sat at – the one they'd sat at for her and Rosie's twenty-first birthday, a few months before she'd died. So that had kept her father happy.

Plus she was pretty certain Patricia, sat on the other side of Michael, was flirting with him. At the very least, his presence had given her stepmother something else to focus on beside making catty remarks to her mum. So yes, all good. So far.

'Thirty.' Her mother swallowed. 'Rosie would have been thirty today.'

It was the first mention of her twin out loud, though Sophie knew her sister would have been on her parents' minds all day. And especially when they saw *her*. The very visible reminder of their loss.

Michael cleared his throat. 'Sophie *is* thirty today.' He glanced sideways at her and smiled.

Unconsciously her fingers touched the sheep. The first present she'd had since Rosie had died. 'It sounds old.'

'Well at least you got to grow old.' Her mother gave her a sad smile. 'Our poor Rosie.'

Because she could see tears fill her eyes, Sophie reached to squeeze her mum's hand. 'I know, Mum.' The familiar guilt slithered into her stomach. Why had she been the twin not to get cancer? The one still sitting here?

Again, Michael cleared his throat. But when she looked at him, he blinked slowly, then gave his head a little shake. Like he wanted to say something but had decided against it.

'We should raise the traditional toast.' Her dad lifted up his glass. 'To our dear Rosie. I hope she's having a huge party up there.'

'To Rosie.' They all lifted their glasses.

Silence descended over the table and as she wondered how to break it, Sophie felt a warm hand on her knee. It wasn't sexual, just a gentle squeeze of reassurance before he lifted it off.

'Was Rosie a fan of parties?' he asked into the now awkward quiet.

Sophie was so relieved at the question, she could have kissed him. 'She most definitely was.' She glanced over to her parents. 'Do you remember that party you did for us when we turned eighteen?'

'You mean the marquee in the garden with that awful band.' Her mum mock shuddered. 'There wasn't an inch of their skin that wasn't pierced or inked.'

Sophie laughed. 'We thought it was the coolest band, ever. Rosie had a real thing for the lead singer but he was about ten years older than her and totally uninterested.'

'It didn't stop her from dancing on the table to get his attention,' her father added dryly. 'I thought she was going to fall and break her neck.'

'You should have stopped her,' Patricia said, frowning over at him.

'Trust me, I tried. But then Linda here,' he pointed towards her mum, 'told me to stop being a killjoy.'

'I'm surprised at you, Linda,' Patricia rebuked in that way she had that always sent her mum bristling. 'I wouldn't have let my daughter do something so foolish.'

'Rosie was a live wire. There was no stopping her.' Her mum swallowed. 'Nor did I want to because she was like this angel, but a feisty angel. One who would light up a room but also make us all laugh with her antics. And drive us a little crazy, too.'

'It sounds like Rosie and Sophie were identical in more than just looks,' Michael said quietly.

When Sophie glanced at him in surprise, he stared steadily back at her, the fondness in his expression making her heart perform a little flip.

'Oh no, not really.' Her mum's voice broke the connection. 'Sophie was the quieter of the two.'

Michael huffed out a laugh before turning to her, eyes bright with amusement. 'Really?'

She nodded, the memories flooding back. But this time it was *good* memories. 'Rosie was born first, so she reckoned that made her the leader. At school she'd make me do all those twin tricks you play on the teacher, like switching classes to see if they'd notice, which they usually didn't. She once got me to sit an exam for her so she could bunk off with her boyfriend, then moaned when I only got her a C+.'

'Yes, she was always the smarter twin,' her dad interrupted.

The little buzz she'd got from relating the stories, died. 'Thanks, Dad.'

He looked taken aback. 'Hey, you know I didn't mean it like that. It's just she was smart, as well as being beautiful.'

And she wasn't smart. Or as beautiful. Or anyway nearly as good as Rosie had been. The hurt pushed up against the lid she'd slammed over it. Losing her sister had been hard enough, but in a way, she'd lost her parents, too, because how could she possibly compete with a perfect ghost?

'Again, you could be describing Sophie.'

Michael's comment brought a hush over the table. How sad, not to mention mortifying, that the same parents who were happy to gush over Rosie, were hesitant to talk about *her*.

'I realise that as an outsider this must seem odd to you,' her father said finally. 'But today is the day we get together to talk about Rosie, not Sophie.'

'And yet, with respect, today isn't just Rosie's birthday. It's Sophie's too.' Michael cast his eyes round the table, before landing finally on hers. She saw a hint of apology in them, but also defiance. 'If you'll forgive me, I would like to toast this warm, funny, gorgeous, vital, smart woman it is my honour to be getting to know.' He lifted his glass. 'Happy birthday, Sophie. May every birthday going forward have you flying as high as you did today.'

Too much emotion swirled inside her to be able to laugh at his joke, but she tried anyway, the sound she emitted was probably like something a cat would make if it fell into water.

'Flying high?' Her mother glanced at her questioningly.

She was grateful to Michael for so many things already tonight – insisting on coming with her, speaking up for her, his touching toast, keeping the conversation flowing. Yes, reserved, quiet Michael had been the one to smooth over the sharp silences. But more than any of those things, she appreciated the way he'd encouraged them to talk about Rosie in a *positive* way. To remember the good times, rather than dwell on the sad. 'We went to the trapeze school this afternoon,' she explained. 'It was the same one Rosie dragged me to on our twentieth birthday…'

———

After saying goodbye to Sophie's family, Michael took Sophie's hand, something that felt far more natural than it should, as they walked back through Hyde Park towards Mayfair. It took him a good ten minutes of striding out before he felt the tension begin to leave his shoulders. He wasn't sure he'd ever felt so angry on someone else's behalf.

How could her parents not see what they were doing to her? It was clear they loved Sophie, yet making her birthday all about the loss of her twin was rubbing salt into a wound still painfully raw because they wouldn't let it heal.

'Michael?' Sophie tugged on his hand. 'I know you think

I'm this super walker now, but really my legs are kind of short next to yours and these heels are even less like walking boots than my converses and you were pretty dismissive of those.'

'Sorry.' He slowed his pace to hers, tried to tell himself none of this was his business. He was in her life on a temporary basis only. Sure, she said they could do the friends thing, but he didn't think he could. Not when she'd be dating other guys, maybe telling him about them, what score she was giving them. Laughing over the fact that nobody had got a score lower than three...

He felt a jerk on his hand, and then her hand left his completely and she halted, hands on her hips. 'What's got into you?'

Christ, she was stunning, those grey eyes sparking with attitude, that body vibrating with annoyance. 'Sorry.'

'That's the second apology I've had in two minutes, but with no explanation for why you're turning this romantic evening walk across the park into a route march.' His pulse kicked up at *romantic* but he had no time to question it because she was still talking. 'Or for why you're not listening to a word I say, which I know is an awful lot to take in but you usually try, at least.'

Ashamed, he sucked in a deep breath and tried to centre himself. This was her birthday, for God's sake. Her parents had interfered in it enough. 'At the risk of repeating myself yet again, sorry.' Exhaling slowly, he attempted to distil his anger into something more digestible than *I can't believe how fucking selfish your family is*. 'I'm having a hard time dealing with how your family seem to have forgotten that while they were unlucky enough to lose one daughter, they are incredibly blessed to have you.'

'Oh. That's … a good answer. Really good.' She nibbled at that bottom lip again, and he felt a pulse of arousal flood through him. 'Thank you.'

'You don't need to thank me. What happened tonight, what I sense has been happening since Rosie died...' The anger started to bubble again and he glanced away, taking a moment to let it settle. 'It's not right,' he said finally. 'I'm sure Rosie was very special, she had to be, the way you all talk about her.' His eyes landed on hers and the need to touch her, to trace his finger across those soft lips, to *kiss* her, was just too much to ignore. 'But you're very special, too,' he added quietly, bringing his face closer. Giving in to that temptation and cupping her chin, running his thumb along the curve of her mouth. 'And it upsets me that you might ever think otherwise.'

Her eyes glistened back at him. 'I…' She huffed. 'That's the second time you've rendered me speechless.'

He smiled, searching those beautiful grey orbs. 'If I weren't a gentleman, I might think now would be a good time to kiss you. When you can't say no.'

Her laugh caught a little. 'Full disclosure. I wouldn't say no anyway.'

Thump went his heart against his ribs. They were in the middle of a public park, so he knew this had to be chaste, but still his pulse began to go like the clappers. Taking his time, both to savour the moment and to get a tight grip on his control, he ran his finger over the angles of her face; the wide cheek bones, the strong lines of her jaw. The slight indent where her dimples appeared when she grinned. It was a face that fitted her so perfectly, full of character, of strength and clear-eyed intelligence. Despite what her parents had told her.

'Michael.' Her voice was a husky plea, her eyes like saucers.

'I don't like to rush things,' he countered, smiling when she rolled her eyes.

'If you don't kiss me in two seconds, I'm going to scream—'

His mouth met hers, cutting off what he wasn't totally convinced was an empty threat. Unlike their first kiss, this felt bigger. A kiss he knew she wanted as much as he wanted to give it to her. A kiss that despite the public park, felt wholly intimate as he brushed his mouth across hers, revelling in the scent, the feel of her before tasting her with his tongue, his heart tripping when she opened to let him in. And wow, when she did, when he fell headfirst into the heady heat of her mouth, his body responded fully, becoming instantly and painfully aroused. Still he didn't want to stop. He didn't know when, *if*, he'd ever get the chance again. So he continued to take his fill, sliding one hand down her arm and onto the small of her back, pressing her against him. Feeling that slim, toned body move against his.

It was the sound of a yapping dog that broke him from his trance. Reluctantly he released her, willing his body to calm.

She smiled into his eyes. 'You sure know how to kiss, Doc.'

The memory of their last kiss circled through him, as did their message exchange afterwards. His awful, paralysing need to know how she'd scored him, vying with that insecure part of him that didn't want to know, because what if Jackie hadn't just left him because Ian was a more exciting personality, but was more exciting all round? In and out of bed.

'Hey.' A pair of laser focussed eyes zeroed in on his. 'What is it?'

He hung his head, ashamed he was still thinking of that blasted spreadsheet. 'Nothing.'

He tried to turn, to start walking again, but she put a hand on his arm. 'Please tell me you're not thinking of what score I'm going to give you.'

Heat burned across his face and he looked away.

'Monkey nuts.' She released a deep, painful sounding sigh. 'I hate the thought of you always worrying about me scoring you. It's … oh crap, it's demeaning and that's really not right because actually when you think of it, you're way out of *my* league.'

A bark of laughter escaped him. 'Absolutely not.'

'Well I think you are, so please, can we park all this scoring crap.' She twisted her hands in an agitated way. 'God, I wish I'd never—'

'I don't.' He pressed a kiss to her forehead. 'Because then I'd never have met you. Never have been on a trapeze.' He smiled down at her. 'And never have done whatever it is you have planned for the rest of this evening which you've been surprisingly secretive about.'

'Okay.' She inhaled, seemed to shake off the tension he'd created with his funk about the spreadsheet that he absolutely wasn't going to mention again. Ever. 'Tonight is really going to cap off a truly great day for you.'

'I'm more concerned whether it will be a great end to the day for you.'

'Oh, it will be, you don't have to worry about that.' A mischievous sounding laugh bubbled out of her, yet unlike previously when he'd worried, now he relaxed. If she was happy, he realised he really didn't care what they were doing.

'And?'

She glanced sideways, looked like she was trying not to burst into giggles. 'How do you feel about karaoke?'

If she's happy, you're happy, he reminded himself. 'I feel I can't wait to see you sing.'

That laughter burst out of her. 'Oh no, we're going to sing.' She gave him an exaggerated pout. 'You wouldn't deny me on my birthday, would you?'

Chapter Nineteen

For the first time in years, Sophie forgot to immediately update her finance spreadsheet with the money she'd spent on Saturday. It took her till now, Monday evening, to realise the error, by which time she realised she'd also forgotten to book herself the manicure that, according to her schedule, she should have had this week. The only reason she'd realised that, was because she'd been checking when her bikini wax was due.

And the only reason she'd been doing that, was because she'd been thinking of sex.

Sat on the sofa now, computer on her lap, Sophie felt her whole body flush as she remembered talking with Michael on the phone last night. He'd phoned as she'd got into bed after they'd sent a string of messages to each other all day. Nonsense messages that had started off with him thanking her for the karaoke serenade but then turned silly; him hoping Sally Sheep liked her new home in the city, her telling him she was checking out trapezes she could put in his back garden. By ten o'clock he'd picked up the phone, arguing his thumbs were tired of messaging. They'd carried on talking for another half an hour and while there had been nothing sexual in their chatter, it had felt more intimate than any conversation she'd ever had. And that was before he'd said goodnight with a husky, 'Sweet dreams, Sophie.'

Yep, she'd almost begged him to get in his car and come and join her.

That's when she knew she was in trouble. Sex with Michael would be absolutely the wrong thing for either of them. She was only booking the bikini wax because it was due.

'Hey Soph, you ready?'

Hastily she closed the laptop and jumped off the sofa. Monday meant Zumba. It also meant Jade and the question she dreaded being asked so much she'd taken the cowards' way out, making sure they turned up late and buggered off early the last few weeks. *How are things going with Michael?*

Would "fine" about cover it?

'You were going to give us more details about how Saturday went,' Ava reminded her as they piled into Grace's car. The pair of them had spent most of the weekend with their boyfriends so they hadn't all had a chance to really touch base until now.

Sophie allowed herself a small smile as she thought back to the day. 'What sort of details?'

'Come on. All we've heard so far was that you enjoyed yourself and the meal went surprisingly okay.' Grace slid her a look. 'If you tell me the good doctor took part in the karaoke I'm going to want video evidence before I believe you.'

'No, he didn't.' Had she been disappointed? Honestly, yes. Yet when she'd gone up by herself to sing – she wasn't going to miss the opportunity even if he was too shy/staid/stubborn to – the sight of him in the audience, those bright blue eyes totally focussed on her … it was quite possible she'd got a bigger buzz out of that than she'd have done singing with him. And when she'd come back to the table, the admiration in his gaze had been enough to cause a giant lump in her throat. Sophie Williams, the less smart twin, actually eliciting a look of awe from a man who spent his days, if not always saving lives, then definitely improving them.

'Well, what a shocker. Not.' Grace's voice cut through her happy memories. 'I can't believe you actually thought you'd be able to get him onto the stage.'

Had she thought that? Or had she just wanted to show him what she liked, to warn him off because she was frightened he was starting to like her? She absolutely didn't want to do any more damage than her harsh scoring had already.

Between her and Jackie, they'd hurt the man enough.

'What about that last guy you took to the trapeze, Callum?' Ava asked. 'Are you still planning on meeting up with him to apologise?'

She'd forgotten all about that. But she'd tried, hadn't she? It wasn't her fault he'd cancelled. The thought of seeing him again … it felt wrong now. Like she'd be betraying Michael somehow. 'I don't know. Oh shit.' As Grace parked up, Sophie looked at the clock on the dashboard and cringed. 'We're a few minutes early. Can we, you know, just stay in the car for a bit?'

Ava and Grace began to laugh. 'God, Soph, you're not scared of Jade are you?' Grace asked. 'I thought things were cool between the pair of you after that first time.'

'They are.' But there was Jade, walking across the car park. And heading towards their car.

'Think we've been spotted,' Ava whispered. 'No way can we hide here now, we'll look like right muppets.'

'Stick by me,' Sophie muttered as they all got out of the car. 'Talk about something, anything that doesn't involve Michael.' Sophie waved at the advancing Jade. 'Whatever you do, don't leave me alone with her.'

'Hey Jade. How's things?' Sophie gave Jade a wide smile. 'We've missed catching up these last few weeks.'

Jade eyed her suspiciously. 'I was starting to think your arriving late and scuttling out as soon as we finished, was deliberate.'

'Oh no, why would we do that?' Innocent. That's the expression she needed, though it had never been one she'd been able to pull off.

Grace burst out laughing. 'She's not buying that look Soph, so Ava and I will just, umm, go and plonk ourselves down and give you two a moment to catch up.'

'Traitors,' Sophie grumbled at their retreating backs.

Thankfully it made Jade laugh. 'Come on you don't need reinforcements, surely. I'm not *that* scary.'

'Errrr, yes, you are. Last time you were mad at me I couldn't walk properly for a week.'

'But I've got nothing to be mad about.' She put her hands on her hips. 'Not if you tell me how many dates you've had with Michael so far – I know the pair of you committed to ten – and whether you've changed your original inaccurate opinion of him.'

'Oh, wow, okay. Go straight for the jugular huh?' Sophie blew out a breath. 'We've had four dates.' She hesitated, counted again on her fingers. 'Yeah, that's all, though it seems way more than that.'

Jade's expression relaxed a little. 'That's because he's easy to be with, once you get to know him.'

He was, she realised with a start. She'd laughed at him when he'd described her as easy but actually he'd been onto something. The last two times they'd been together, it had been easy. She'd felt she could be herself, even if that meant wobbling over a birthday meal with her parents. Crying on him.

But. Sophie felt her pulse race as alarm shot through her. 'You can't think ... I don't want you thinking ... I mean neither of us are thinking...' She exhaled sharply, desperate to put her confusing, conflicting thoughts into something that might make sense to both of them. 'We both know this is just six more dates and we're done.'

So why are you planning on having sex with him?

'If you say so.' Jade gave her a very careful study. 'Promise me you won't hurt him, Sophie. He's far too nice a guy to be mucked around with.'

Something heavy pressed on her chest – guilt? Fear? Upset, for him, for both of them because it wasn't fair that something that felt so good, should be doomed?

Only doomed according to your spreadsheet. Was she so certain it was right that she was willing to jettison whatever it was that seemed to be developing between her and Michael?

'Sophie?'

Jade was giving her the stern eye now, and she found it hard to hold her gaze. 'I have no plans to hurt Michael or to muck him about. I like him, Jade. Really like him.' It's just she didn't think they'd work in the long run.

As that was a conversation to have with Michael, she gave Jade a quick smile and went inside to join Ava and Grace.

At the same time as Sophie was stepping into her Zumba class, Michael was arriving home from work. After greeting Fudge, he tossed his jacket on the hook, yanked off his tie and walked into the kitchen to pour himself a glass of red wine – it had been that sort of day. Fudge stared wistfully up at him so he filled her water bowl and poured some pellets into her food bowl before grabbing at the dog-eared copy of Delia Smith's cookbook from the shelf. It was the copy he'd given Betty when he'd been sixteen and clueless as to what to get a woman for her birthday, never mind one in her sixties.

With a furtive check to make sure Betty was nowhere in sight, he snuck into the garden.

At least she'd used the cookbook, he thought as he sat on the bench and thumbed through the pages. And he'd definitely got better at gift buying, as evidenced by Sophie's reaction to the sheep pendant.

Would she be equally delighted with his choice for their fifth date?

His shoulders sagged, guessing the answer. But while he could take her to a fancy restaurant in town, he had no doubt she'd done that with every date she'd ever had. And he had no desire to compete with the Joshuas, Callums or Wills.

A wet nose brushed against his hand and he smiled down at Fudge. 'Finished your tea, huh?' Giving her ears a rub, he looked at the recipe book. 'Am I mad to cook for her? To try and show her a different date than she's used to? One that's more personal?'

'Ah, you're planning on making Sophie a meal, are you?'

He gave a guilty start as Betty wedged herself onto the

bench next to him, Princess trotting daintily behind her and then leaping onto his lap. With a sigh he stroked her, careful to avoid today's purple bow. 'Maybe I'm deciding what to make for our dinner.'

She scoffed. 'Two years I've lived with you now, and you've never needed to refer to old Delia.'

That tickled him. 'She's four years younger than you,' he pointed out mildly.

'Hmph. Enough trying to distract me. I'm far more interested in what you and Sophie have been up to.' Her eyes might be cloudier with age, but the look she gave him was sharp as a tack. 'Anything to tell me?'

'I thought my lack of a grilling yesterday meant you'd finally accepted a man needs his privacy.'

She snorted. 'I was trying to be tactful and wait for you to say something.' Her side glance held a hint of mischief. 'But when you get to my age, waiting is a fool's game. Who knows when I might drop down dead? Though be warned, I don't plan on doing that before I see my favourite grandson walk down the aisle.'

A rush of affection, of love, swamped him. 'Favourite huh? Bet you say that to Dave, too.'

She chuckled. 'Maybe.' But then her wrinkled hand clasped his, and squeezed as tight as the arthritis would allow. 'But with you I mean it.'

He had to swallow down the massive ball of emotion lodged in his throat. 'You won't be seeing me walk down the aisle any time soon, so be prepared to live out many, many years yet.' He gave her a nudge. 'Who knows, maybe you'll beat me to it.'

'Good heavens, no, once was quite enough.'

We'll see, he thought privately, and hoped with all his heart there was a sunset romance on the cards for her and Dennis.

'Don't think you're going to side-track me, young man. Tell me how you and that lovely girl are getting along.'

He stroked Princess while he considered how much to say. 'I'm enjoying her,' he pronounced finally. 'I think you were right. It's doing me good.'

Betty beamed the same smile he remembered from his childhood. The one that had eased the crippling loss of his mother. 'I do love to be proved right. When I saw her chatting away to everyone at the cricket the other week, I thought to myself, Anne would have approved.'

Emotion caught him again, both at the mention of his mum, and the awareness that Betty was right about this, too. 'Don't get carried away,' he warned. 'Sunday will be date five of ten. Then it ends.'

'We'll see.' Before he had a chance to quash her optimism, she started talking again. 'Now what are you going to make her? She's a bit skinny for my liking, so choose something hearty. Maybe a stew with dumplings.'

He had to smother a laugh. 'I'll consider it.'

Seemingly satisfied, she rose stiffly to her feet, clutching at the arm of the bench to help her up. He knew she didn't like a fuss, so he resisted the impulse to check she was okay. At the sight of her mistress walking back into the house, Princess scampered off his lap to join her.

'Just the two of us again.' He rubbed Fudge's soft brown ears. 'What do you think Sophie would like to eat?' Fudge wagged her tail, and rested her head on his lap.

Remembering Sophie's spreadsheet obsession ran to meal planning, he slipped out his phone and messaged her.

Going to make us a meal this Sunday. Betty suggests dumplings.

He tried to ignore the disappointment when he didn't get an immediate reply. Instead he continued to read through the recipes. Something he could prep beforehand, he decided, as it was all too easy to picture him toiling away in the kitchen while Betty commandeered Sophie in the garden. Probably showing her the damn begonias again. His phone beeped and immediately he picked it up.

Sophie: Can we go out instead?!

Sophie: PS Just been worked to a sweaty pulp by Jade. I'm sure she has sadist tendencies. S x

It was hard to smile at the second message when the first felt like a kick in the teeth. His hope that she'd find his suggestion to cook impressive/endearing/interesting … he'd even take sweet at this point. Well that hope had just been crushed. But while he contemplated how to reply, he heard another beep.

Sophie: Am on Paleo diet this week. Pretty sure dumplings weren't around then.

Sophie: FYI here is spreadsheet for meal plan.

He shook his head. What on earth was she doing with all this food fad stuff? It wasn't like she needed to lose weight. Because he wasn't sure, he googled Paleo diet.

'A diet plan based on the hunter-gatherer era, the Paleolithic diet eliminates food groups not available before industrial farming,' he read out to Fudge, who looked at him with besotted brown eyes. As if he was reading how to make pork chops. 'No dairy, no grain, no sugar, no processed foods.' He exhaled heavily. 'And no fun, eh?'

He returned to the message app.

Going to pretend I didn't see this.

She had to be by her phone now, like he was, because she immediately came back to him.

Sophie: Noooooo. Are you threatening me with dumplings? Sx

That pulled a laugh out of him.

No. Threatening you with good tasty food you'll enjoy.

Her reply came back a second later.

Sophie: Is that you talking yourself up again Doc? S x

He smiled as his fingers typed back.

You'll see for yourself on Sunday.

Sophie: Looking forward to it S x

Michael: Me too.

Sophie: PS I'll be on 5.00 pm train. And wearing pavement appropriate walking footwear S x

He sank back against the bench, a satisfied smile on his face. Now all he had to do was find and cook something that would impress the hell out of her.

And at the very least, be more palatable than dumplings.

Chapter Twenty

Her mum had an uncanny knack of phoning at the most inconvenient times; when Sophie was on the loo, in a bar, with a customer. Or like now, when she was on the train. Thankfully it wasn't very full – she was one of only a handful of barmy people choosing to leave London on a Sunday evening.

'Hey Mum. I can't really talk now, I'm on the train.'

'Phooey. I'm sure the other people in the carriage won't mind you telling your mum what you've been up to all week.'

Sophie rolled her eyes, well aware what her mum really wanted to know. 'Well, let me think. Monday, I had Zumba which was really intense and I've got a sneaky feeling was a warning from the teacher to me about … well, you don't need to know. Tuesday, I had the sax lesson,' she hurried on. 'Polly said I was good enough to think about booking the Grade 2 exam which I—'

'Never mind all that,' her mum interrupted impatiently. 'Hurry along to the part about you and the handsome doctor.'

Sophie smiled to herself. 'I'm actually on my way to see him now.'

A contented humming noise echoed through the earpiece. 'You know I wasn't sure when I first met him,' her mum mused. 'Oh, I could see what you saw in him, though you usually go for the dark, moody type, but I didn't like the way he was so pushy at the start of the meal.'

A burst of laughter shot out of her. 'Pushy is the last word anyone would use to describe Michael. He was just ... concerned for me, I guess.' Her mood sobered and she added quietly. 'He didn't know Rosie.' Hadn't seen how amazing her twin was, how much brighter, bubblier, altogether better than she was.

'No, and maybe that was just what we all needed. An outsider's view.' There was a pause where her mum seemed to hesitate over what to say. 'I spoke to your father afterwards, and this is one of those rare times we're in agreement. We've done you a great injustice over the years by making the day all about your sister. It wasn't fair on you.'

'Oh Mum.'

'There's no making excuses for me, for any of us. You're our beautiful bright spark of a daughter and deserve to have us celebrate the day you came into our lives. Somewhere along the line we seem to have forgotten that.' Her voice held a palpable emotion. 'So make sure you thank that Michael from me. I'm glad he's looking out for you. I'm sure your father will say the same, when he finally gets around to it.' Her dad was notoriously bad at communicating. It was mainly the reason her parents had split up after Rosie had died. Her mum had wanted to talk about her grief. Her father hadn't. It was also why, much as she loved him, she had a closer relationship with her mum. 'Now I'll leave you to your train journey but be sure to update me later in the week.'

'On the Grade 2?' Sophie asked, innocently.

'On *everything*. But mainly about tonight, because I'm really not sure the saxophone is a good look on you, dear.'

Smiling, Sophie tucked away her phone, but it was hard not to think about what her mum had said. *I'm glad he's looking out for you.* She'd known the man, what, eight weeks? And in that time she'd managed to insult him, make him have cocktails with her friends when she knew he'd hate it, and then repeat the offense by dragging him to a karaoke bar.

In contrast, he'd agreed to help her with her spreadsheet experiment, bought her a gorgeous necklace. And somehow managed to give her a birthday to remember for all the right reasons.

Was it any wonder she was so confused about what to do about all this chemistry between them? Her head said no, learn from your mistakes. Don't waste time and emotional energy trying for a relationship that logic – spreadsheet logic – says won't last.

Her heart said why on earth are you hesitating? Here's a decent, extremely likeable guy who listens to you, slows you down, makes you think. And when have you ever had a man look out for you like that?

Plus – and it was a huge, belly full of excited butterflies, plus – he's sexy in the most adorable way, she thought as she stepped off the train. Her heart jumped in delight at the sight of man and dog waiting for her on the platform. Tall and handsome in grey jeans and a cream linen jacket, the sight of Michael was breathtaking enough, without the addition of

Fudge sat at his feet, a bunch of large daisies between her teeth.

'Oh.' Utterly flustered, she didn't know what to say. It felt like he was trying to romance her, and she'd never had a guy do that before. Not in such an old-fashioned way. Cook her a meal, bring her flowers. Meet her off the train. It was like something out of some black and white film. But she was no Audrey Hepburn.

If he'd laid the table with roses and candles, she was going to melt into a puddle on the spot.

Fudge padded over to her and Sophie reached down to take the flowers. 'Thank you, sweetie.' She started to pat her head, then remembered and gave her ears a good rub. Tinkerbell, she had to admit, would never have done that. When she straightened, her eyes caught Michael's and her heart shifted in her chest. 'Hi, Doc.'

His brilliant blue gaze locked on hers and she noticed him swallow. 'You look lovely.'

The simple words, the clear admiration showing on his face … her heart stuttered. Afraid to think what it might all mean, she defaulted to humour. 'That'll be the sparkly shoes again.'

He gave a slight shake of his head, eyes still riveted on hers. 'Pretty sure it's down to you rather than what you're wearing.'

She let out a shaky laugh, her belly all jumpy, like the butterflies in it were flapping crazily, trying to get out. 'Flowers and flattery. You'll turn my head.'

He didn't reply, just kept on looking at her, gaze dipping to her mouth for a moment before resting again on hers.

He was going to kiss her. Her hormones began to dance, her pulse to hammer. She wanted to feel his mouth on hers again so badly, it panicked her into turning away and beginning to walk.

Beside her she heard his soft exhale – disappointment? Or had she misread him?

Needing to get them back on track, she indicated the flowers. 'Is this all part of your softening up tactics so I won't be horrified by the dumplings?'

His low laugh smoothed away the remaining tension. And wasn't it just the best feeling in the world, making this serious man laugh? 'I promised, no dumplings.'

Fudge darted ahead of them, stopping every now and then to sniff at something. As they turned to go down the lane, Sophie felt Michael's hand wrap round hers, sending a flood of warmth through her. Maybe she hadn't misread him, after all.

It was so quiet. She slowed her pace from brisk London walking pace to the easy, meandering one Michael seemed content with. One that allowed Fudge to do whatever dogs needed to do. A bee buzzed past them on its way to the clump of wild flowers at the side of the road. Birds chirped. And that was it. No cars, no horns, no people pushing past.

An involuntary sigh escaped her.

He turned, eyes questioning her. 'Bored already?'

'Hardly.' She tried to analyse where it had come from and came up with a surprising answer. 'I think my body just decided to relax.'

The smile he flashed her made her blood hum; a sizzle of something, overlaying the contentment. 'Good.'

———————

Michael studied Sophie across the table he'd set up outside. Had he gone overboard on the tea lights, the flowers? Betty's napkins and best rose patterned crockery? Did she hate the scallop and shrimp linguine he'd finally settled on?

Her gorgeous silver-grey eyes caught his and he reluctantly forced his gaze away, aware he was staring. But God, she was so easy to look at. Not just because she was incredibly attractive, but because she was always so animated. He loved watching her different facial expressions, trying to work out what she was thinking.

Like at the station, when at one point he'd felt certain she'd been thinking of kissing him as much as he'd thought of kissing her.

'This is really good.' She gave him an impish smile. 'The candles, the vases of flowers, a home cooked meal out on the patio. You really know how to romance a girl.' She shook her head and let out an embarrassed laugh. 'Not that you're trying to romance me, obviously.'

They'd skirted around this, but perhaps it was time to show his hand. He made a deliberate effort to catch her eye. 'Who said I'm not?'

Alarm flickered across her face. 'Michael.'

'I know,' he cut in, disappointment settling heavily in his gut. 'That isn't what we're about. But I do still have five dates left, and I hope to use them to get to know you more.' He paused, decided tonight seemed to be a night of confessions. 'And maybe to get to know myself.'

Her eyes popped wide open. 'Yourself?'

He reached for his wine, buying himself thinking time. 'I've started to see you weren't that far wrong with your initial score of me,' he admitted after settling the glass back on the table. 'And I want to rectify that.'

She looked appalled. 'Oh no, I can't have you thinking like that. It's me who was wrong, or the spreadsheet is wrong because...' She looked away, her teeth sinking into that bottom lip again – something he noticed she did when she was unsure what to say.

'Because my score is still shite?' he finished for her, trying to keep his voice light, one of dry amusement, when inside his earlier bravado began to crumble.

'I haven't updated it for a while,' she admitted quietly. 'In fact I've slipped a bit on all of my spreadsheets. Including my Paleo diet,' she added, staring down at her plate. 'I'm pretty sure you can't hunt down linguine.'

'Should I apologise?'

She gave him a soft smile. 'Absolutely not. This is worth breaking my meal plans for.'

He frowned. 'But why bother with them in the first place? It clearly isn't to lose weight.'

'No.' Her eyes darted away from his. 'I just think it's important to look after your body. Take care what you put into it.'

There was something about her careful words that niggled at him. 'Is that how the spreadsheet thing all started, with the diet?'

'Oh no, that came later. It started with me trying to keep track of my finances.'

'Okay, that I can understand. But why expand it to so many other areas of your life?'

Again, she avoided his eyes. 'It was getting harder and harder to keep on top of everything I was doing, so I figured if it worked for money, it should work for other stuff, like what I was doing each week.'

'Ah, yes, the classes, the music and tennis lessons, the charity runs, the list of places and venues you plan to visit every month.' He recalled glancing through the spreadsheets, not sure whether to be impressed or horrified. 'You pack a lot into your life.'

'Yep, that's me. Determined to live life to the full.' Her smile had a brittle edge to it.

'And are you, living it to the full?' he asked softly. 'Or are you living it for someone else?'

'Sorry?' Her face paled, her eyes turning a wintry grey, guarded.

He had to tread carefully, he realised. This woman who seemed to laugh at everything, was hiding far more pain than he'd ever have guessed. 'Did you ever talk to anyone about how you felt after Rosie died?' Her fork clattered onto her plate and he cursed silently when he saw tears in her eyes. 'Shit, this was bad timing. I'm sorry.' Ignoring his half-eaten meal, he jumped to his feet and went to crouch in front of her, taking hold of her hand. 'You don't have to answer my question. Just, please, finish your meal.'

She gave him a watery smile. 'I think I've lost my appetite.'

'That's okay. It only took me five hours to prepare.'

She groaned. 'Tell me that's not true.'

'It's not true.' He smiled. 'It took two hours to decide on the recipe, an hour to prep and cook the first attempt which I ate on Tuesday. Another hour to prep and cook the second attempt which I ate yesterday. This only took fifty minutes because I was so practiced.'

'Oh.' The laughter that was so much a part of her, slid out

in a hiccupy waves. 'Then you should sit back down. We can't let all that effort go to waste.'

She turned back to the dish and forked up some more pasta. 'What did you mean earlier, about getting to know yourself?'

It was an obvious attempt to turn the focus back on him, and as he was the one who'd upset her, the least he could do was answer her. 'The split with Jackie, finding her with Ian, knowing they'd both been screwing me, literally and figuratively, behind my back. And I'd been blithely unaware.' His stomach cramped and now he was the one to lose his appetite. 'It gutted me. I felt betrayed, humiliated.'

She nodded, face full of sympathy. 'Anyone would.'

'Yes. But my reaction to it was to retreat even further into my shell.' Those bleak days and weeks came flooding back. 'I turned down invites to meet up with friends because I didn't want them giving me pitying looks. And then of course Betty had her fall, and suddenly the solution, me leaving Manchester and moving back down, was obvious.'

'Not obvious,' she argued. 'You weren't the only grandson.'

'No, but I was the only single grandson whose life could easily be transplanted.'

'Did you consider asking Betty to move in with you instead. Or with Dave and Jade?'

He let out a bark of laughter. 'You've met her. How well do you think that would have gone down?'

A fond expression fluttered across her face. 'I think you didn't even consider asking, because you knew she loved her cottage, her life here. And you would rather disrupt your own than make her do anything she didn't want to do.'

How odd that despite their differences, she seemed to

understand him. 'I wasn't that selfless. I didn't have much of a life to disrupt.'

'You're a humble man, Doc.' She finished her last mouthful, took another sip of wine. 'This shell of yours that you like to retreat into. Is there anything I can do to help lure you out of it?'

'You already are.' He pushed his own plate away. 'I've done more, laughed more.' He paused, searched for that bravery again. '*Felt* more, in the last two months since I've known you than I have in years.'

Her body stilled and his heart jumped into his mouth. There was a fine line between bravery and foolishness. Had he just crossed it?

Chapter Twenty-One

S ophie stared back at Michael. A man of so little words, yet the words he did use were always considered, well thought through.

So had he meant to imply he had feelings for her?

'Felt more?' She heard the catch in her voice.

He swallowed and for a few moments he looked anywhere but at her. When he finally spoke though, those blue eyes stared directly into hers. 'I like you. I like spending time with you.'

Okay, that she could cope with. 'Ditto. I like spending time with you, too, Doc.'

He cleared his throat, his voice dropping an octave. 'I also like kissing you.'

Oh shit. This was … she wasn't sure what it was. Something she'd hoped for, but… Becoming intimate with him would complicate the hell out of their next few dates because how could she stop seeing a guy who made her knees tremble from just a kiss? Who caused her insides to melt when he stared at her like he was now. So bloody handsome, his smouldering blue eyes filled with hope, with longing. And with a raw vulnerability that caused her heart to twist. Yet if she was going to stick to her plan of only dating men she believed she had a chance of building something permanent with, didn't she have to stop this?

The *want* though, oh God, that was an almost unbearable ache, a heavy feeling between her thighs, and pressing down on her chest.

'I like kissing you, too,' she admitted softly. 'But,' she waved a hand in the air, trying to find the words, the breath to say them.

'But you don't want to lead me on.' His eyes found hers, darker now, matching his sober expression. 'You don't want me thinking this could turn into a relationship.'

Feeling numb, she nodded. 'I know this sounds stupid, if it helps it sounds stupid to me too, now I'm saying it out loud. But I started this date spreadsheet for a reason, and if I don't stick to it I think I'll regret it. I think we *both* will, further down the line.'

'Because you don't think we would ever work.'

'Yes.' God, this was hard. Painful even, not just because it was awkward, but because she felt she was hurting them both. 'Relationships are such a huge investment of time, and to put that investment into something you know from the outset is going to fail...' She swallowed. 'You wouldn't do it with a business, so why do it with a relationship?'

He nodded, a muscle jumping in his jaw. 'That is one perspective. The other would be that spending time with someone you enjoy being with, getting to know them more, is time well spent regardless of how it might work out.'

She felt a vicious squeeze on her heart. 'But what if your time was limited?'

Alarm crossed his face and he stood abruptly. 'You're not … please tell me there's no reason for you to think your time is limited.'

'No, no. I'm fine.' A wave of emotion blindsided her, clawing at her throat, her chest. 'I'm the lucky twin,' she whispered, feeling her voice break. 'I'm the one who got to live her life.'

She wasn't aware she was crying until she felt his arms wrap round her. 'Oh Sophie.'

'I…' *I'm fine.* She couldn't get the words out, and even if she had they were clearly a lie because the tears wouldn't stop coming.

'It's okay, it's okay,' he murmured. 'Cry it out.'

In a blur she felt herself being lifted into his arms and carried across the garden, into his annex. Before she knew it, she was sat on his lap, her cheek pressed against his shirt as grief swamped her and she gave into wave after wave of wrenching sobs.

'Oh my God, this is so embarrassing,' she mumbled when the tears started to dry, not yet willing to raise her head from the warm, solid haven of his arms. 'I don't know where that came from.'

Are you living your life to the full or are you living it for someone else?

His words flowed back to her, answering her question.

'I suspect you've been carrying this burden around for a long time,' he answered quietly, his hands stroking gently down her arm. 'Ever since Rosie was diagnosed with cancer.'

She felt him shift beneath her. The next second, he pressed a tissue into her hand.

'Thank you,' she said, giving him a tremulous smile before wiping at her eyes. 'I don't know why the cancer chose her, not me,' she said quietly, voicing dark thoughts that had been trapped for so long. Thoughts she'd told nobody, not her parents, not Ava and Grace. 'It's not fair. She had all these plans for what she wanted to do with her life. She didn't deserve to die.'

'I know.' His lips pressed against the top of her head, the tenderness of the gesture threatening to set her tears flowing again. 'But tragic as it was, it wasn't your fault.'

'In my head I know that, but...'

'Survivors' guilt.' His arms tightened round her. 'You can't help feeling guilty you're here and she's not.'

She nodded, overcome with gratitude. He got it. Even more than that, he wasn't making her feel stupid for it.

'I suspect she'd be livid to think you've spent the last nine years trying to somehow make up for it,' he murmured against her hair. 'To live the life you think she wanted to live.'

Slowly she looked up at him. 'Is that what I've been doing?'

His smile was so kind, it nearly shredded her. 'You're the only one who can answer that.'

'I … I don't know. Rosie and I were always so alike, it's hard to tell what is me, and what is me acting on behalf of her.'

'You mean you were always this … full of energy?'

A laugh spluttered inelegantly out of her. 'Very tactful. But yes, I think I was. The pair of us were always making plans. Rosie liked to challenge herself and I guess I liked to keep up with her.' She smiled at the memories. 'Between us we must have tried every instrument, played every sport, started God knows how many classes. I was always on the arty side, she was better at languages. When she fell really ill though, I stopped everything.' Sadness clawed at her again and she felt her eyes well. 'For months after she died, I lurched between thinking I should carry on because she'd want me to, and giving up because it wasn't right that I could do these things and she couldn't.' She inhaled a shaky breath. 'Perhaps in the end I unconsciously fell in between the two, carrying on, but for her, not for me.'

He didn't reply for a while, just kept stroking her arm in a soothing gesture. 'Earlier you asked what if time was limited,' he said eventually. 'Do you worry about getting cancer, too?'

It was a question nobody had ever asked her. 'On one level yes, maybe I do. Certainly it made me realise how unpredictable life is. None of us know how much time we have left.'

'Which all comes back to you not wanting to waste it.'

'Yes.' But was she seriously saying spending time with this kind, patient, quietly sexy man would be a waste of time? She had to be nuts. Totally certifiable. Maybe everyone else was right and her whole spreadsheet thing really was stupid...

'We've already agreed to another five dates.' His voice broke through her panicked internal ramblings. And when he shifted them, cupping his hand to her jaw and gently directing her eyes to meet his, her breath became trapped in her chest. 'What if I said I was more than happy with a fling? Would you consider it a waste of time to have a fling with me?'

'Are you kidding me?' His humbleness threatened to start the waterworks off again. 'You're worth way more than a fling—'

Her words were cut off as his mouth captured hers.

Enough. He'd had enough of this tip toeing around their attraction. He got it. She'd regret seeing him for longer than their agreed number of dates – fuck, that had been hard to hear. But if he had to agree to stick to five, so be it.

He'd be her fling, her temporary experiment to help her refine her spreadsheet so she could go on to meet the perfectly compatible guy she thought she wanted. Whatever it took, he'd do it because he could no longer contain this desperate need to bury himself inside her.

'I want you, Sophie,' he whispered as he dragged his mouth away from hers and moved to planting a series of kisses along her jaw, behind her ear, down the exquisite column of her neck. 'However you'll have me.'

She groaned, arching into his touch. 'I want you over me, inside me.'

Lust shot through him, not felt for so long he'd forgotten how overpowering it was, how it could drown out every other thought. 'I can do that. Definitely.' He kissed her collar bone, revealed by her strappy top, and tasted her skin there, inhaling her striking scent – bold, spicy, it captured him by the balls, leaving him hard and aching.

'This is very sexy,' he told her, running his fingers along the silk edges, skimming past her cleavage, noticing her taut nipples. 'But can I take it off?'

Her cheeks were flushed, her eyes a shimmering silver, and when she nodded, another spike of arousal arrowed through him. 'I wish you would.'

Instantly his hands bunched up the soft material and he

was about to lift it over her head, when his mobile rang. 'No,' he groaned, seconds away from heaven.

Ignore it. Nothing is more important than this.

He blinked his eyes shut, waging an internal battle, his hands tightening on the silk even as his phone continued to ring in his trouser pocket.

'You need to answer it, don't you?'

'No.' His conscience glowered back at him and with a sigh, he released her top. 'Dammit, okay, yes. I don't want to, but...'

She smiled, touching his face with gentle fingers. 'Don't worry. I'll still be here when you've finished.'

'Cross your heart?'

Another smile, this one full of flirty promise. 'Cross my heart.'

He lurched to his feet and dragged the phone out of his pocket.

'Michael Adams.'

'Oh, thank God. I'm so sorry to trouble you but Lucy's been sick and now she's complaining of stomach ache. I tried to phone 111 and they said someone would phone me back, but that was over an hour ago and I'm really worried.'

He exhaled, concern for Lucy rubbing shamefully against heavy disappointment. 'No problem, Kath. I'll come round.'

When he turned he found Sophie had straightened her top. 'You have to go.'

'Yes.' The disappointment curdled in his stomach. 'That was Kath. She runs the post office. Her daughter's not well.'

'Then you'd better go and see her.' Sophie jumped to her feet. 'Don't worry about me, I'll walk to the station.'

'No.' Gutted, he dragged in a breath. 'I won't be long. You

can wait here … or why don't you come with me? I'm sure Kath would appreciate a friendly face while I check Lucy over.'

'If you're sure I won't be in the way?'

'I'm certain.' He placed a gentle kiss on her mouth. 'I'll just get my bag.'

It was only a five-minute walk to Kath's. The single mum to eleven-year-old Lucy greeted him with a strained smile.

'Hope you don't mind but I've brought Sophie with me.'

Kath attempted another smile, this time in Sophie's direction. 'I remember you from the cricket match. You helped Lucy put her hair up in a fancy plait.'

Sophie smiled at her. 'I did that for my sister all the time.'

It was only because he was watching her so carefully, that he saw the fleeting shadow cross Sophie's face. Once again he felt a sharp tug of sympathy for the woman who on the surface seemed so full of life, of joy, yet who was hiding a terrible heart break. He could only guess how awful it must feel to be the twin who was left behind.

'This is so good of you, Michael.' Kath turned back to him, the tremor in her voice betraying her anxiety. 'I know you're not on call, and that I only have your number because you're on the village fete committee.' She wrung her hands. 'But I'm so worried about her.'

He gave her shoulders a reassuring squeeze. 'I'd have been cross if you *hadn't* phoned me. Where is she?'

Kath directed him upstairs to where Lucy was lying on her bed. While he talked to the shy girl, feeling her stomach, checking her temperature, he was aware of Sophie and Kath talking behind him, Sophie clearly trying to distract the anxious mum by gushing over Lucy's pale pink canopy bed, and the fairy lights twisted round it.

'You were right to be concerned,' he told Kath once they'd stepped out of the room. 'I think Lucy's got appendicitis. She'll need to be admitted I'm afraid, but the hospital will take good care of her. Usually they operate but it's a standard procedure and that way it won't trouble her again. I'll call an ambulance and warn them she's coming in.'

Sophie put an arm around Kath. 'I had my appendix out when I was about Lucy's age. She'll be fine, and if she's anything like me she'll enjoy the bragging rights of having a cool scar.'

It wasn't long before Kath and Lucy were safely in an ambulance.

'I hope she's going to be okay,' Sophie whispered as they watched it drive off.

'She'll be fine.' Because he had a feeling she was remembering another girl, another ambulance, he wrapped his arm around her. She fitted, he realised with a pang. Just the right height for him to kiss the top of her head. 'Thank you for coming. You were lovely with Kath. I know she appreciated what you said.'

She waved a hand in the air. 'I had the easy job. You had to reassure a poorly girl and tell a scared mum that her daughter had to go to hospital.'

He wanted to tell her that what she'd done, the compassion, the understanding she'd shown, wasn't something to be waved away, but before he could articulate the thoughts, she spoke again.

'We lost our moment, didn't we?'

She smiled ruefully up at him, her eyes looking huge in the moonlight. Pools of silver that he dreamt of staring into as he buried himself inside her for the first time. But he didn't want a poorly child hovering in either of their minds when that finally happened. 'There will be other moments, I hope.'

'Definitely.'

Yet the opportunity for them was fading fast, he realised with alarm as they walked slowly, hand in hand, to the train station.

Only five more dates, five more potential moments.

Panic slithered into his gut. Would that be enough to show her she was wrong about him? To prove that relying on a spreadsheet was no way to decide a partner? And for her to see that the guy she thought she wanted, this extrovert adrenaline junkie, wouldn't appreciate her anywhere near as much as he did?

Chapter Twenty-Two

Sophie didn't know what she was doing in this bar, with this man. It was Thursday night and here she was, listening to Callum go on and on about his latest parachute jump. She'd been surprised to get his text earlier in the day, asking when she was going to buy him this drink she'd promised. As he'd cancelled on her last time, she'd kind of hoped he'd decided he didn't want to see her again.

She'd debated ignoring the message, but then remembered how he must have felt seeing his score, especially the three out of ten for kissing. In a rush of guilt, she'd agreed to see him tonight.

Now she was regretting her decision. She was also utterly confused as to how she'd ever managed to score Callum more highly than Michael. He might not say much, but everything Michael did say was worth listening to. And boy, was he a good listener. How else to explain how she'd told him things she'd never told anyone?

Callum on the other hand, talked like he was the only one who had anything interesting to say.

'Do you want another drink?'

She forced herself to look at him. 'I'm supposed to be buying them.'

'Okay then, I'll have another pint of whatever I had last time.'

Michael didn't let you pay for his meal. Yes, she'd hurt Callum, yes, he deserved a few beers. Still, it was hard not to make the comparisons as she walked off to the bar. Michael was old school, a gentleman. Something she'd never thought she'd value, yet she missed the discrete way he pulled the chair out for her, opened the door for her. Made sure he always walked nearest to the traffic on the pavement. Things she only noticed when she was with someone who didn't do any of that.

'Here you go.' She slid his beer in front of him.

'Cheers.' He raised his glass. 'So, are you still filling in that spreadsheet thing?'

'I am, yes.'

He nodded. 'Bit brutal, isn't it, giving us blokes a score?'

'I told you, it was only ever meant for my eyes.'

'Yeah, I get it. Can't say I wasn't really fucking angry to see you scored me a three for our kiss. You know it takes two to tango, right? Not my fault you kiss like … I dunno, what's a fish with a big sucky mouth? A carp?'

Anger fizzed through her, along with a dose of embarrassment. Did she kiss that badly? *I like kissing you.* The memory of Michael's words helped to calm her. 'You're right. It wasn't all on you. But together we didn't work.'

As if she'd summoned him, her phone started to buzz on the table, the caller ID flashing up with Michael's name.

Callum stared down at it. 'That the same Michael who was on your spreadsheet? The one who scored like a two, wasn't it?'

She scooped up the phone. 'It's none of your business.'

Callum started to laugh. 'You're going red. It must be him. What, are you so hard up for men you're seeing the duff ones again?'

A few months ago, she'd have taken her glass, poured the rest of her wine over his head and stormed out. But this Sophie simply rose to her feet and smiled. 'The only thing I'm doing with the duff ones, as you so eloquently put it, is buying them a drink to apologise. And now I'm done. Goodbye, Callum.'

As soon as she was out of earshot, she answered the phone. 'Hey, Doc. Just give me a second to find somewhere quiet.' She weaved through the drinkers standing by the bar and out onto the street. 'That's better.'

'If this is a bad time, I can call back.'

'It's not a bad time.' In fact it was perfect timing. How better to rid herself of the bad taste of Callum, than by talking to the man who always managed to put a smile on her face.

'Sounded like you were having a more exciting evening than me.'

A worm of guilt wriggled through her. Technically she and Michael weren't in a relationship but … and it was a frigging huge, but. They'd almost had sex last Saturday. 'I wasn't. Having an exciting time, I mean.' She paused, then the words came out in a rush. 'I was in a bar with Callum. You know, one of the other guys on the spreadsheet? I offered to buy him a drink to apologise ages ago, like I did you, but he kept cancelling so I thought he didn't want to do it. But then he contacted me earlier today and asked if I was free tonight. And I was, so, well, here I am. Or I was.' She'd got used to patiently waiting for Michael to speak, but this time the pause that met her garbled explanation felt uncomfortable. 'I can't tell if this silence is just you being you, or if you're cross with me. Please say something.'

'I've no right to be cross with you.'

His quiet words packed more of a punch than any harshly spoken ones. 'We nearly had sex last Sunday. You have every right.' She sighed. 'Bollocks, I'm sorry. I should have told you before I met him for the drink. Then you'd have seen it for what it was. Something I felt obliged to do, not something I *wanted* to do.'

'It's fine, Sophie.'

The heavy sound of his voice made her question if it really was. 'Well, I wouldn't have felt fine if you'd told me you'd just been out for a drink with a woman you used to date. In fact I'd be pretty angry. And hurt,' she added, her chest feeling crushed just thinking about it.

'You would?'

The fact he had to ask the question, caused a dart of shame. 'Yes, I would. God, Michael, I don't sleep with men lightly, and if we hadn't been interrupted last Saturday, that's exactly what we'd have done.'

'I didn't mean to suggest...' He swore under his breath. 'This isn't a conversation to be had in a phone call.'

'No.' She didn't like leaving it hanging though. Liked even less that she might have upset him. 'But if you leave this call with any other impression than one where I had to endure a painful hour of listening to Callum talk, and being told I kissed like a carp by the way, I'll be really bloody cross with you.'

'He said what?'

There was a bite to his voice she'd not heard before. 'Apparently the fact our kiss was only three out of ten was down to me and my big sucky mouth.'

'I hope you told him to fuck off.'

Laughter burst out of her. 'Sorry, it's just, hearing you say that word. I didn't think you swore.'

'I swear plenty when people who matter to me are slandered.'

Her heart flip flopped. 'Thank you.' She wanted to let him know he mattered to her too, but she didn't get the chance.

'As for your beautiful mouth,' he continued, voice lower, softer. 'It's the best mouth I've ever had the good fortune to kiss.'

Tears sprang to her eyes and she hadn't realised how much she'd needed to hear that, until now. 'If we were talking about the spreadsheet, which I know we're not, but if we were, I would be able to tell you I rated your kissing expertise a ten out of ten.'

She heard a huff of laughter down the phone. But then he let out a sigh. 'I wish I could see you right now.'

'Ditto. But Saturday is still on, yes? I can't wait to show you your first music festival.'

Sat on his sofa, Fudge's head resting on his lap, Michael dropped his head back at Sophie's words, blinking his eyes shut.

'About that.' There was no way to sugar coat it. This was who he was. Even if it did mean letting down this woman he desperately wanted to see again. 'Dave has asked if I can look after Olivia on Saturday.'

'Oh, yes. Jade mentioned she was off to a wedding.'

'They were going to take Olivia with them, but Dave's having second thoughts.' Absently he stroked Fudge's soft ears. 'Jade's finding this pregnancy tiring and he's worried he won't be able to help her much with Olivia because he's best man.'

'So it's Uncle Michael to the rescue, huh?'

He couldn't tell whether she was annoyed. 'I can say no, but…' He trailed off. Fact was, he *couldn't* say no.

'But it's your niece, and your family,' she supplied. 'Of course you have to look after Olivia.'

Once again he'd let her down. Once again she'd accepted it without blinking. 'I would ask you to come and help me, but I guess a music festival trumps babysitting a four-year-old.'

'Is she cute?'

He glanced at the photo of his niece he kept on the sideboard. The one of her on the slide in the park that he'd taken last time she'd stayed here. Arms aloft, mouth grinning, brown eyes wide with excitement. 'Impossibly so.'

'And you're not biased at all,' she said dryly.

'Maybe one day you'll meet her and see for yourself.'

'Maybe I will.'

But it wouldn't be this weekend. Much as he loved his niece, he couldn't help but feel gutted it would be another week before he saw Sophie again. Unless. 'If they pick her up early enough on Sunday, can I come over and take you out to dinner? Not as a date,' he added quickly.

'Not as a date?'

He heard her confusion. 'I only have five more left.' And he wanted to make each one count. 'A few hours over dinner isn't enough.'

He heard the smile in her voice. 'I agree. And yes, I'd love to see you for a non-date on Sunday if time allows.'

They said goodbye and he ended the call feeling no less settled than he had before. On the one hand he'd bagged himself a potential extra evening with her. On the other hand … Callum.

'I don't like the thought of her seeing other guys.' Fudge opened her eyes and glanced up at him, her head not leaving the comfort of his lap. 'Too possessive, huh?' Fudge closed her eyes again and Michael shook his head. 'What am I doing, talking to you? I should have talked to her about it.' The trouble was, they hadn't agreed any ground rules to what they were doing. At the beginning she'd talked about stopping the trial if she met someone, but that was before they'd kissed. Before he'd almost made love to her. Where did he stand now? Would she turn the guy down until their ten dates were over? Was that even fair to ask, when this was just a bit of fun for her?

Fuck.

Yes, he did say that word, though usually only to himself when he was feeling turned inside out, like he was now. He was falling for a woman – there was no kidding himself anything less than that was actually happening here. He was falling for someone who saw him, at best, as an interesting detour on the way to what she really wanted. Which was a guy about as different from him as it was possible to get.

His phone buzzed again, and his heart leapt in anticipation, only to settle again when he saw who was calling.

'Your legs not working anymore?'

Betty made a huffing noise on the other end. 'I was checking you were off the phone. Didn't want to barge in and interrupt.'

'Well I've finished now,' he said mildly, smiling a little as he pictured her face at his non-informative reply.

He heard a clatter, then the line went dead.

'I'm betting she'll open that door in five seconds,' he murmured to the still dozing dog.

One, two, three…

The door burst open and Betty appeared, Princess behind her. 'I thought I'd let you know I'm off to bed.'

He had to work hard not to smile. 'Okay, thanks.' He jumped to his feet. 'I'll take the dogs out before heading off myself.'

Betty narrowed her eyes. 'Everything alright?'

'Fine thanks.'

'Good.' Still, she hovered in the doorway. 'Thought I'd check, what with the phone call. And the way you hid yourself away to make it.'

He couldn't help it, he started to laugh. His gran was priceless. Feeling a rush of love, he walked over and kissed her cheek. 'I was talking to Sophie, as you probably know.'

She let out a satisfied hum. 'You've not said much about how the meal went, other than to say it got interrupted by young Lucy's appendix, and you know how I don't like to pry.' Again, he had to smother a smile. 'I was worried you might have stopped seeing her.'

'We have five more dates left.'

The wrinkles on her forehead deepened with a frown. 'But then it's over?'

'Unless I can persuade her to drop her spreadsheet idea,

yes.' That made it sound like her fixation on the spreadsheet was his only problem. Fact was, he wasn't what she wanted. The spreadsheet was just a tool to prove it.

Whatever Betty saw in his face, caused her to grasp his hand. 'If that woman's got any sense, she'll forget all this scoring nonsense and see what a great catch you are.'

'Says my grandma.'

'True, but I'm also a very wise woman. Just ask anyone in this village.' Her smile twinkled back at him. 'Where are you off to on this next date of yours?'

'We were supposed to be going to a music festival.' If he was honest, he wasn't bothered about missing it – there was a reason he'd not been to one before now. But he was acutely bothered about missing her. He'd found it hard to settle into any sort of rhythm this week, his thoughts filled with Sophie. How desperately he wanted to spend the weekend with her. In and out of her bed…

'Is that one of those romping about in mud and tents, festivals?'

Betty's voice cut through his X-rated thoughts. 'I don't think so. It's in Victoria Park. But it's not relevant now as I'll be taking care of Olivia instead while Jade and Dave go to a wedding.'

Betty's face lit up. 'We get to see little Olivia?'

'You get to play with your great granddaughter, yes.' And really, the happiness he saw on her face, the fact he got to spend time with his precious niece, the knowledge he was helping out Jade and his brother. It was enough.

It had to be enough, because in another five weeks, it would be all he had again.

Chapter Twenty-Three

S aturday morning, and instead of being excited about going to the festival with the gang later in the day, Sophie felt weirdly … flat was the only way to describe it.

She loved this festival. The music was always rocking and year after year they'd had a ball, dancing until they were so knackered they could barely stand. Yet today she couldn't summon up the enthusiasm to go.

'What's happening to me?' she asked Tinkerbell, who was curled up on the end of her bed. But her cat failed to open her eyes. 'I bet if Fudge was here, she'd listen.'

That's when it hit her. Spending time with Michael was changing her. Not only had she begun to appreciate the peace of the countryside, and to enjoy the company of dogs. Well, a particular dog. Now party-loving Sophie Williams didn't want to go to a music festival. She wanted to take a train to a quiet village and help babysit a little girl.

Pushing off the duvet, she leapt out of bed and banged on Grace's door – Ava had stayed the night with Ethan again.

'Are you awake?'

Grace groaned. 'I bloody am now.'

She pushed the door open. 'I'm not going with you guys today. I'm heading off to see Michael.'

Grace gave her a bleary-eyed look as she struggled to sit up. 'I thought he was busy this weekend.'

'He's looking after his niece, which is why he couldn't come over. So I'm going to him instead.'

'Wait, wait.' Grace held up a hand. 'You're telling me you'd rather babysit in the sticks than go to the most awesome music festival on this planet? With the most awesome group of mates a girl could possibly wish for?'

Sophie took a breath, then nodded. 'I am saying that, yes.'

Grace stared back at her. 'Bloody hell, Soph. Aren't you getting a little bit too serious with a guy you insist you don't want to date for real because he's not crossed whatever threshold you have on that frigging spreadsheet?'

'It's seven out of ten.' Her heart started racing. 'And I'm aware how it sounds.'

'Has he even reached seven yet?'

Sophie couldn't look her friend in the eye. 'Not really.'

'Not really? What the hell does that mean?'

'It means I've been cheating,' she mumbled.

Grace looked at her in disbelief. 'What, like you're giving him a ten when he should be, I don't know, a three?'

Sophie groaned. 'Exactly that.' With a sigh, she on the bed. 'This is going to sound so dumb…'

'You think?' Grace butted in dryly, then waved at her. 'But hey, keep going. Whatever you're reasoning, it can't be any dumber than using a spreadsheet to choose a guy in the first place.'

Sophie rolled her eyes at her. 'Okay, I know you're not a fan, but…' She allowed herself to think back to those dark days following the break up with Will. How she'd lost who she was for a while, not wanting to go out, not caring how she looked. Her self-confidence taking a nose-dive. 'I can't go through another bout of heartbreak. It's too painful, too destructive. I need to know if the spreadsheet works.'

Grace's features softened. 'Okay, maybe I understand that, even if you believing it's the solution to preventing heartbreak is a bit, make that a lot, suspect. But you said you're cheating?'

Sophie sucked in a breath, worried not about what she was going to say – Grace already thought she was crazy – but what it *meant*. 'I keep wanting to up Michael's scores, even though I know he's not really … what was the last one I did? I think I gave him an eight for sociability.'

Grace burst out laughing. 'That man is about as sociable as … what's a really unsociable animal? A bear maybe? I know, a wolf. He's like the lone wolf.'

Sophie let out a cry and flopped back on the bed. 'I know.'

When Grace spoke again, it was with a more serious tone. 'I'm no genius at all this spreadsheet stuff, or even the relationship stuff, but have you considered that maybe, possibly, you're measuring the wrong things?'

Sophie stared up at the ceiling. 'I don't know anymore. At the start of this I was so certain I knew what I was doing. I sat down, listed the key characteristics I wanted in a man, characteristics I knew would make us compatible, and put them into a spreadsheet. Hey bingo, I had the ideal tool to find my perfect partner. Now I'm more confused than ever.'

Grace leaned over and gave her a hug. 'But you do know

you'd rather spend the weekend with him and his niece than hang out with us cool kids at an awesome music festival?'

She swallowed. 'Yes. I know that.'

Grace gave her a push. 'Then you'd better get in that shower, woman.'

––––––––––

Butterflies swooped in her stomach as Sophie climbed off the train at Little Brook a couple of hours later. Along with the anticipation of seeing Michael again, was a very real worry. What if he didn't really want to see her today?

She'd been so swept away by the prospect of surprising him, it was only now she remembered he was careful, cautious. He probably didn't do spontaneous. Worse, she realised he'd not actually *asked* her to come and help him. Maybe taking care of his niece was an excuse to avoid going to the festival. He usually played cricket on a Saturday, and he'd already missed a match for her, so he probably didn't want to miss another one. Or maybe he didn't want to see her because he was still angry about Callum. Or maybe he just didn't want to see her...

She shook herself. It was too late to change her mind now. Whatever she found when she got to his place, she'd deal with it.

As she halted outside the cottage he shared with Betty, a childish shriek of laughter came from behind it. Automatically her shoulders relaxed a fraction. He'd not been blowing her off.

Deciding to keep with the surprise, she opened the side gate and walked towards the back garden.

The sight that greeted her caused a hard tug on her heart.

Michael was on his hands and knees, a small, curly-haired girl on his back, a furry orange toy with lots of legs tucked under her arm. She peeled with laughter as he proceeded to give her a ride up and down the garden. Beside them, Princess was yapping, as if she was trying to join in. Fudge lay in the shade, watching quietly.

It was only then that she noticed Betty sat on the bench, issuing instructions. 'Now turn around and take Olivia to the bird table.' Chuckling to herself, she turned her head in Sophie's direction. And let out a gasp of surprise. 'Oh heavens, we have visitor.'

Suddenly aware she wasn't just intruding on Michael's day with his niece, she was intruding on Betty's, too, Sophie gave an awkward wave. 'Err, hi Betty.'

Michael came to a sudden halt. 'Sophie?'

'Who's that?'

Blinking a few times, he twisted to lift his niece off his back and climbed to his feet. 'That is my friend, Sophie.'

'What's she doing here?'

Wearing a dazed expression, Michael took hold of his niece's hand and started to walk towards Sophie. 'I don't know. Let's go and find out.'

Was he happy to see her? Annoyed she'd burst unannounced into his garden? Her heart began to gallop as he neared her. When those stunning ocean blue eyes found hers, her confidence faltered and she dropped her gaze, smiling down at the little girl. 'You must be Olivia.' The girl gave a solemn nod. 'Do you know how I can tell that?' Olivia shook her head. 'Because your uncle told me you were impossibly pretty.'

'Cute,' he corrected, smiling down at his niece. 'I said you were impossibly cute.'

Olivia gave her a wide grin. 'I like pretty best.' She held out the orange toy. 'This is Squirt. He's an octopus.'

'Ah, and what a handsome octopus he is, too.' Sophie reached to shake one of the tentacles. 'Pleased to meet you, Squirt.' Then she reached for the next one. 'And pleased to meet you again.'

———————

Michael watched as Sophie solemnly shook each of Squirt's eight tentacles, making Olivia giggle.

Was he hallucinating? Had he dreamt of her so much last night he was now imaging Sophie in his garden, looking unbelievably sexy in a pink vest top and denim shorts, revealing legs he wanted to slide his hands up.

'Have you come to play with us?'

Olivia's excited little voice knocked the fantasy on its head.

'Umm, I don't know.' Sophie glanced over at him. 'It depends on your uncle.'

Olivia jumped up and down. 'Please Unkey Mikey.' She turned back to Sophie. 'Do you want to feed ducks? They like bread. Betty said we can feed them bread when she's finished her coffee.'

Eyes still on Sophie – he couldn't drag them away, not even to look at his niece – he was only dimly aware of Betty calling Olivia over. As his niece skipped away to hunt for bread he knew Betty had already organised, he smiled at their visitor. '*Have* you come to play with us?'

She grinned back at him. 'If that's okay with you.'

He twisted round, checked no old or young eyes were watching, then rested his hands on her hips, tugging her gently towards him. 'It's very okay with me.' The air between them crackled with awareness as he did a silent inventory of her face, drinking in the clear grey eyes, the soft pink lips. The tiny freckles across the bridge of her nose he'd not noticed before. 'Is *this* okay with you?' He bent to feather kisses along her jaw line.

'Umm, very okay.' Her arms slid round his neck. 'It would be even more okay if you put your mouth on mine.'

'I'll get there.' His hands slid to her bum, his mouth to kiss the soft skin behind her ear, inhaling her scent, feeling his whole body come alive.

She groaned, pushing her hips against his. 'I'm still waiting.'

'You're going to be the death of me,' he muttered, finally giving in and kissing her on the mouth, his tongue automatically seeking the wet heat of her, turning the kiss from sweet to wonderfully inappropriate in a flash. *Your grandmother and niece could be watching*.

Reluctantly he drew back, heart racing, his shorts uncomfortably tight. 'I can't believe you're here.'

She ran her tongue across her swollen lips, causing the shorts to tighten further. 'I thought I'd see if your niece was as cute as you claimed.'

It wasn't *I missed you* but he'd take it. Fact was, she was standing in front of him now. That was all that mattered. 'How long have I got you?'

'That depends. The last train is eleven. Or...' she nodded to the small red and black striped holdall on the floor. 'I've brought an overnight bag.' As his heart jumped into his throat, she bit into her lower lip. 'Not that I'm saying we should share a bed, I mean not if you don't want to, and obviously with your niece staying with you that wouldn't be right. So I'll sleep on the couch, if that works, or like I said, I can always get the last train. Or maybe the one before that, because sometimes they cancel the last one—'

He kissed her again, long enough to feel her body relax against his. 'There will be no train, and no couch.' He cupped her gorgeous face. 'I want you in my bed.'

'But Olivia…'

'Is a sound sleeper.' He kissed her again, because it was addictive. 'Now let's go and wear her out.'

Michael felt a squeeze in his chest as he watched his niece, and the woman he was falling for, laugh together as they threw bread at the ducks. Alongside them, a fond expression on his face, was Dennis. A surprise addition to their generation-spanning party.

'She's a natural with her,' Betty observed, following his gaze.

He couldn't disagree.

'So she's missing this festival of hers, then.' Betty slid him a loaded look.

'Apparently, yes.' He smoothed his hand down Princess, who'd perched herself on his lap.

'But there's nothing serious going on between the pair of you.'

'No.' He was careful to avoid her eyes.

She let out a dismissive snort. 'Your face lit up like a

Christmas tree when you saw her earlier. You can fool yourself, but you can't fool an old woman.'

Not wanting Fudge to feel left out, he fondled her ears. 'I thought we'd agreed you aren't old.'

'Maybe it's time to accept I am.' Her pale blue gaze snared his. 'And maybe it's time to admit that you're falling in love with Sophie.'

He smiled, though his stomach knotted at having to say out loud what he'd already admitted in his head. As if it made it more real. 'I know I am.' He watched as Sophie lifted Olivia onto her back, piggy-back style. 'But she's not falling for me.'

'She chose to come here rather than go to a festival with her friends? I'd say she was smitten.'

This time his smile was more genuine. 'Is that the same smitten that made your eyes light up when you caught sight of Dennis sitting on the bench?'

'Phooey.' But then she chuckled. 'What a pair we are.'

But the difference is, Dennis is besotted with you. He decided not to ruin the moment, for either of them. Instead he rose to his feet and went to relieve Sophie.

'Come on Squirt, time to ride on my back. Give Sophie a rest.'

Olivia happily swapped over. 'Can we go watch cricket wiv Dennis?'

Michael winced. So far Sophie had been submitted to a skipping competition, providing piggy back rides, having a coffee with two nosey pensioners – Dennis and Betty together were a formidable double act – and feeding ducks. He could just imagine how excited she would be over the prospect of watching cricket.

'Pleeeeaaase.'

But how could he turn down that sweet smile? He really was a total sucker when it came to the women in his life, he thought, flicking Sophie an apologetic glance. 'If you go now you can still make the festival.'

She laughed and slipped her arm through his. 'Not a chance. Who needs live music, dancing and alcohol when you can have ducks. And cricket.'

'We can supply the alcohol,' Dennis chimed in, making Sophie laugh even harder.

'Oh no, you need to steer me well away from your lethal gin and tonics. My hangover lasted for days.'

'Just the one then, eh?' Dennis offered his arm to Betty and they walked across the park towards the cricket field, Olivia settled happily on Michael's back, both dogs bounding ahead. Now and again he glanced over at Sophie, trying to work out what she was thinking. Was she staying only because she felt it was rude to go? Or was she genuinely enjoying the change of pace from her life in London? She caught him looking, and raised an eyebrow.

'Are you okay?'

Her gaze softened and she squeezed his arm. 'I'm good, Doc. In fact, I've never felt better.'

Bending slightly, he whispered into her ear. 'You've never looked better.'

She stared down at her shorts and then back up at him. 'In my tatty shorts?'

He shook his head. 'Don't get me wrong, I'm a big fan of any clothing that shows me your legs. But I meant your face. You seem happier. More relaxed than when I first met you.'

Her expression turned thoughtful, but whatever she might have said was interrupted by Dennis.

'Well blow me, they're four down already.'

'I blame the captain.' Michael shifted Olivia off his back and gave her a soft ball to throw to Fudge. 'Too busy with his niece.'

'Rubbish. The rest of them should be able to cope without falling like a stack of cards.' As Dennis started to give the amused Sophie and tolerant Betty the benefit of his cricketing wisdom, Michael had a moment to hope the lessening of tension on Sophie's face was at least in part due to their heart-to-heart the other day. Maybe now she'd start to question whether cramming so much into her life was really what *she* wanted. And even if lessening her obsession with wasting time didn't lead her to get shot of her ruddy spreadsheet, he liked to think she'd leave their relationship in a better place than when she went into it.

He knew he would.

Chapter Twenty-Four

It had been a different sort of Saturday than the one she'd planned. And yes, maybe when Sophie looked at the photo Grace had just sent of her and Ava pulling silly faces, crowds of festival goers in the background, she'd had a pang of disappointment that she wasn't there.

But not regret.

With a contended sigh she picked up her wine glass and nestled back against Michael's extra comfy corner sofa. He was upstairs, putting a very sleepy four-year-old to bed.

No doubt reading Inky Octopus to her again.

A squishy sensation rippled in her chest at the memory of how sweet they'd looked together, uncle and niece, heads bent as he'd read her the story. She wished she'd taken a photo to send the girls in reply. Instead she picked a selfie she'd taken with Olivia and Betty as they'd fed the ducks.

Anything you can do – me with the girls, Little Brook style S x

A few seconds later she got a reply from Grace.

Grace: Aww, is that Jade's daughter? So cute. Got to go, next band on. We miss you, Gx

She smiled at the next photo of all of them – Grace, Ava, their boyfriends, a few of the regulars from The Drunk Flamingo – crammed into a chaotic selfie with the huge stage in the background. Yes, she would have liked to have been with them. But she wouldn't have swapped today for it.

Looking up, she found Michael standing in the doorway between his kitchen and the sitting room, an unreadable expression on his face.

'Everything okay?'

He nodded. 'She fell asleep on page three.'

'Ah, bless her, Inky-ed out I suspect.'

He smiled, but there was something not quite right. A tension she didn't like, and if she was honest she'd noticed it start to build before he'd gone upstairs. 'Dinner won't be long. It's the same lasagne Olivia had I'm afraid, but at least it only needs warming up.'

'Hey, don't be afraid. She gave me some, it was really tasty.'

Silence descended as he walked through to the kitchen, interrupted only by the noise of the oven door opening, the clink of plates and the rattle of cutlery.

He popped his head in the doorway again. 'Can I get you another drink?'

She waved her nearly empty glass. 'Sure, thanks.'

He came back out with the bottle and poured them both a glass before sitting next to her on the sofa. Concerned now, she studied his profile. It was a good profile, hinting at the strength, and the decency that lay beneath his handsome looks. 'What's wrong?'

He shook his head, but then let out a sigh. 'One of the many things Jackie accused me of was not communicating.' His eyes caught hers. 'I don't want to make the same mistake with you.'

'Good, because I'm awesome at communicating. It's one of my superpowers, along with parking my Mini into tight slots.'

This time his smile was more genuine, though the strain of whatever worried him was still evident. 'When I came downstairs, you were looking at your phone.' He glanced away, picked up his glass in one long, careful motion. 'Your expression, it was melancholy, like whatever you were looking at was something you missed.' Finally a pair of turbulent blue eyes met hers. 'Were you messaging Grace and Ava?' Before she had a chance to open her mouth, he placed a hand on her arm, squeezed gently. 'It's okay, I understand if you regret missing the festival.' His lips tilted in a wry smile. 'To be honest, I can't believe you even considered coming today, let alone actually got on the train.'

'I can't believe it either.' She'd boasted about her communication skills, so it was time to be honest. 'But when I woke up this morning, I didn't feel that buzz, you know, that jittery excitement in the belly at the thought of what you're going to do today.'

His eyes held hers, the blue so intense it made taking a breath difficult. 'I know that feeling.'

She swallowed. 'When I got off the train, I got the buzz.'

His eyes studied hers, his expression still careful. 'You did?'

'Yep. That's when I knew I'd rather spend the day here, with you, than at the festival without you. Sure, I was disappointed we couldn't go, but that's all you saw on my expression. I don't regret choosing to come here, not for one minute.'

He smiled, giving a shake of his head. 'I've been so worried you were bored.'

'Not for a single moment.'

'Thank God.' Exhaling, he sunk back against the sofa, drawing her tightly against him.

Quiet descended again, but this felt different. Devoid of the tension, it was calm, relaxing. A gentle silence, if there was such a thing.

'It's been lovely to see you with Olivia,' she said after a while, absorbing the feel of his arms wrapped round hers, the solid warmth of his chest. 'The pair of you have such a great bond.'

'One of the advantages of my move down here. I'm lucky to be number one on their babysitter list.'

'Err, to be able to leave their daughter for the night with a doting uncle who happens to be a doctor? They're the lucky ones.' Because she felt so peaceful, she felt able to say exactly what she was thinking. 'I sometimes wonder, if Rosie hadn't died, what would she be doing now? Would she be married? Would I be an aunt?' Her voice caught on the last words and his arms tightened around her.

'You'd have made a great aunt,' he said quietly. 'And one day, when you find that perfect man of yours, you'll make a great mother.'

That perfect man. Her heart stuttered, because lying here, his strong arms around her, knowing she could say whatever was on her mind and he would listen carefully, without judgement, it felt awfully like she'd already found the perfect man.

As Michael thought of Sophie with another man, his chest felt like it was being crushed in a vice. It was all too easy to picture her a few months from now, the spreadsheet lit up with a row of tens as she began to fall happily in love with her view of the right man.

And maybe the guy who ticked all those damn boxes of hers would make her happy, but would he care for her, understand her … and yes, *love* her, as much as he'd begun to?

She moved against him, her head snuggling further into the space between his chest and his arm. A space she fit perfectly into.

'We should eat,' he murmured into the quiet, glancing at his watch. But eating wasn't what he was thinking about when her leg slid over his.

'In a minute.'

Another minute of lying here with her, and what he really wanted to do was going to be all too obvious. 'Let me turn the oven off.' He slipped away from her, adjusting himself as he flicked off the oven.

After taking a few deep breaths he joined her again, arousal humming through him as she crawled right into that same space again.

'Sophie.'

'Umm.'

He glanced down, saw her eyes were shut, and forced his body to cool. If he wasn't making love to her, sitting here holding her was the next best thing.

The time ticked away and he felt her body sink into him. As if all the tension that had been holding it together, had quietly disappeared. She was in such a deep sleep that when he lifted her into his arms and carried her up the stairs to his room, she didn't stir.

Still dressed in her top and shorts, he eased her under the duvet. He wanted to curl up beside her so much it hurt, but cuddling downstairs on the couch was one thing. How would she feel if she woke up to find herself next to him in bed?

With a final longing glance at her, he stepped out of the room and quietly shut the door behind him. With Olivia in the only other bedroom in his annex, it looked like he was spending the night on the couch.

Michael was up, dressed and eating breakfast with Olivia when Sophie walked down the stairs looking rumpled in the clothes she'd gone to bed in. Rumpled and sleepy and so damn sexy he had to turn away before his body began having ideas totally unsuitable for his current uncle duties.

'Morning.' She gave him an embarrassed look before heading over to Olivia and sitting next to her at the island. 'Umm, that looks tasty. What is it?'

Oliva grinned at her. 'Unkey Mikey's eggy toast.' She lowered her voice into a loud whisper. 'He makes it 'specially for me.'

Sophie cast him a mischievous look. 'Ah, then maybe I'll have to have cereal.'

Michael bit back a smile as Olivia frowned over at him. 'Can Sophie have eggy bread, too?'

'I think that can be arranged.' He reached into the fridge for another couple of eggs. 'As long as she understands I don't make it for just anyone.'

Olivia giggled. 'Just special people. That's what you said.'

'Exactly right.' He made sure to catch Sophie's eye. 'Just special people.'

Her cheeks flushed and his heart squeezed. She was so confident, so bold, yet she blushed at being called special, like she'd never been told that before.

The three of them enjoyed their breakfast and, after Sophie took a quick shower, they headed out to give the dogs a walk. Olivia doted on Fudge, and Sophie clearly enjoyed being around his niece because all three of them walked on ahead, leaving him with the tippy toes Princess. 'You need to learn to walk faster,' he grumbled at her.

She stuck her nose in the air, wagged her tail. And carried on her slow, dainty pace.

By the time they arrived back, Jade and Dave had arrived to pick up Olivia.

Desperate for some lone time with Sophie, he decided not to offer them a drink. His brother gave him a knowing look but he ignored him.

He might have got away with it, had Betty not decided to make an appearance.

'What are you all doing standing in the hallway? Come into the garden. I want to hear all about this wedding. Michael will make us a drink.' She flapped her hand in his direction.

'Thank you, Betty. About time someone offered to make us one.' Dave smirked in his direction.

Gritting his teeth, Michael marched into the kitchen ready to make the fastest coffee on record.

He was just filling the coffee machine with water when he felt a pair of arms slide around his waist from behind.

Body on full alert, he turned and did the one thing he'd been wanting to do all morning, hell all night, ever since she'd fallen asleep in his arms. He bent and kissed Sophie, intending it to be gentle, but the moment his mouth touched hers, it was like a tonne of fireworks exploded in his body and he couldn't slow, couldn't pull back. All he could do was deepen the connection, pushing her back against the island, his mouth greedy, his hands sliding up her naked legs until their progress was hindered by her shorts.

'Fuck.' He sucked in a deep breath and took a tiny step back, resting his forehead against hers as he tried to find his equilibrium. 'Sorry.'

'Whoa, no, don't apologise. That was…' she blew out a breath. 'Spectacular, and that's not doing it justice. Besides, it's me who needs to say sorry.' She rested her hands on his chest, and he wondered if she could feel his heart pounding. 'I can't believe I crashed on you last night.'

He smiled. 'I wasn't sure whether it meant you were bored or relaxed.'

'Not bored, definitely not.' She groaned. 'I feel terrible. I don't even know how I got into bed.' Her eyes blinked up at him. 'I presume it was your bed I slept in?'

'It was.' Remembering what he was supposed to be doing, he began to pour the beans into the coffee machine. 'Before you ask, the couch is very comfortable.'

'Oh.' She worried at her bottom lip. 'So I fell asleep before eating the lasagne you'd made for me, and then effectively kicked you out of your own bed. Turns out I'm a pretty crap guest.'

The catch in her voice made him pause. Putting down the mugs he'd been gathering, he slid his hands on her shoulders. 'For the avoidance of doubt, the hour I spent holding you in my arms while you fell asleep was the best hour I've spent in a long, long time.' He placed a soft kiss on her lips. 'And the lasagne you get to take home in a doggy bag.'

She smiled, but still looked pensive. 'What about the other part I missed out on?'

His pulse jumped, but he wasn't sure she was on the same wavelength so he turned and began to studiously arrange the mugs onto a tray. 'Which part?'

'The you and me, together, part.' She glanced up at him from under her lashes. 'In your bed.'

He was instantly hard and his voice, when he managed to find it, scraped over his throat like sandpaper. 'Let's get rid of our guests as fast as humanly possible.'

Of course it wasn't that easy. With her family around her, Betty was in her element, seemingly unwilling or unable to stop asking questions. Jade was either too polite, or in on some secret plan with Dave to cockblock him because she kept answering, the amused glint in her eyes totally matching that of her husband's.

Eventually Michael's patience ran out and he stood up. 'Sophie and I have plans for this afternoon, so you'll need to excuse us.'

'Oh, how lovely.' Betty beamed at him. 'Where are you taking her?'

My bed. Then against the wall, though maybe we'll do the wall first, or even the stairs...

He caught Sophie watching him, laughter making her eyes shimmer. 'He didn't say,' she filled in for him, clearly realising he was incapable of any further polite conversation. 'But knowing Michael, it will be spectacular.'

He let out a bark of laughter, then attempted to turn it into a cough.

His brother glanced between him and Sophie, and correctly read his *I love my family, but now piss off* expression. 'Come on gang,' he announced, jumping up from the wicker armchair he'd been sprawled in. 'We've taken up enough of my brother's weekend.' He reached to pick up his daughter, who'd been giving Squirt rides on the very tolerant Fudge. 'Come on poppet, say goodbye to Uncle Michael and Auntie Sophie and thank them for looking after you.'

Hugs were exchanged and with inexorable slowness the party moved towards the front door. Dave slapped him on the back then gave Sophie a kiss on the cheek, whispering far too loudly in her ear. 'Hope the afternoon turns out to be as spectacular as he promised.'

Sophie burst into laughter but Michael didn't have time to answer the question he could see on Betty's face. Giving her a quick hug, he took Sophie's hand and all but dragged her back to his annex.

Chapter Twenty-Five

S ophie couldn't stop laughing as Michael hurried her into his part of the house. The man was on a mission, and thank you God, the mission was her.

She couldn't believe she'd fallen asleep on him last night. One minute she'd put her leg over his, fully intending to jump him.

The next, enveloped in his arms, his chest raising rhythmically beneath her cheek, she'd fallen asleep.

Other men might have been annoyed, insulted. Michael had carried her to bed. And then been such a gentleman he'd slept on the frigging sofa.

But he didn't feel like a gentleman now, she thought giddily as he spun her round and attacked her mouth like a man starved. And considering how long he'd been without sex, probably he *was*.

He sunk deeper into the kiss, his tongue dancing in and out of her mouth, his hips rocking against hers with the same fluid motion. Arousal crashed through her, heating her blood, pooling between her thighs, making her body tight and achy.

Desperate to feel his skin, to run her hands over his chest, she began to lift up his shirt, but his hand settled on her wrist, stopping her. 'Not yet.' Midnight blue eyes pressed hers. 'Now I've finally got you to myself, I find I want to take my time with you.' His gaze, hot and needy, travelled down her body before arrowing back up to hers. 'I need to put my hands on you, strip you and kiss every inch of your skin before I finally sink into you.'

She gulped, feeling her knees weaken at the gruff, sexy words. 'I … wow. I didn't think…' She trailed off, embarrassed.

He tilted her chin, making her look at him. 'What?'

She huffed out a breath. 'I thought you'd be shy. You know, not say much, which is absolutely fine, by the way.'

His lips settled over hers again, gentler this time, but she felt the restraint. 'Don't mistake quietness for being shy. I don't like being the centre of attention, prefer to listen than talk. But I'm not hesitant when it comes to things I'm sure about.'

She couldn't help but tease him. 'That sounds like a boast.'

His eyes burned into hers. 'I meant I'm sure about wanting you.'

'Oh.' Her heart began to hammer against her ribs. 'I'm sure about wanting you, too.'

His face relaxed, a smile sweeping across it. 'Then I need to get you in my bed before you fall asleep on me again.'

Laughing, she raced towards the stairs. 'No chance. Thanks to a great night's sleep, I find myself with boundless energy today. You probably won't be able to keep up with me.'

She'd reached the top of the stairs when she felt him press against her from behind, his hands settling on her hips, the clear evidence of his desire a hot steel bar against her bum. 'Not a chance,' he whispered in her ear, then proceeded to kiss down her neck, making her dizzy with lust.

Not breaking his hold on her hips, or stopping the hot little kisses flirting with parts of her neck she hadn't realised were erogenous zones, he slowly guided them towards his room.

Once there, he lifted her onto the bed and began to undress her, unzipping her shorts and tugging them off with deft, sure movements. 'You're exquisite,' he murmured as he peeled off her bra, his hands immediately reaching to cup her breasts. 'Utterly perfect.'

She melted in a puddle of want as he began to kiss her there, toying with her nipples, sucking, nibbling in such an erotic dance her hands clutched at the duvet. 'God, please, enough foreplay. I need you inside me.'

She tried to grab at his shirt, but he pulled away. 'Don't be in such a rush,' he murmured, his breath hot against her stomach as his kisses headed south. 'We've got all afternoon.'

He'd been right, she thought as she began to drown in pleasure. She had mistaken quiet for shy, yet there was nothing shy about what he was doing with his hands, his mouth. There was only an understated, immensely sexy, self-assurance. Feeling her insides tighten deliciously, she groaned out his name. 'Michael.'

'I know.'

He continued his onslaught until she was a writhing, gasping mess of sensation, coming with a shout of pleasure as the damn burst open, leaving her blissfully spent.

'Fuck, you're sexy,' he whispered, kissing his way back up.

'And you're … unbelievably talented,' she decided, causing him to laugh softly. 'You're also wearing too many clothes.'

He levered himself up and onto his feet, stripping off his shorts and shirt in typically un-showy fashion before reaching into his bedside table and pulling out a foil packet.

'Wait.' This time she was the one to put her hand on his. 'Lie on the bed. I want to touch you.'

He blinked his eyes shut, muscles tensing, but did as she asked.

And now it was her turn to drink him in. Delighted, she ran her hands over his defined pecs, the hard ridges of his stomach. 'Wow, look at you, Doc. You're ripped.'

He let out a strangled sound. 'Hardly.'

Her fingers brushed over his dusting of chest hair. 'And no need for those Drunken Flamingo cocktails. Your body is already shrieking testosterone.' Enjoying her exploration, she kissed her way across his chest. When she licked at his nipples, he groaned.

'You need to stop. I'm holding on by a tether.'

'Aw, don't be a spoilsport. I'm enjoying myself.' Reaching inside his boxers, she clasped him, her mouth watering as she felt along his impressive length, squeezing gently to test them both. She'd never felt so powerful, so turned on by the sight and feel of a man's body.

With a growl he reached for her hand, stopping her. 'Enough.'

He must have come to the end of his seemingly infinite patience because he shoved off his boxers, ripped open the condom and sheathed himself in one deft, fast movement. Then before she knew it, she was on her back and he was sinking into her, making her toes curl, her breath hitch.

'Fuck,' he rasped, his expression one of intense pleasure. 'You feel incredible.'

She swallowed, the emotion of the moment hitting her like a runaway train. This was supposed to be fun, just a few more dates with a guy she enjoyed being with but who would never be anything serious.

Yet as she felt him pulse inside her, as he began to move, to bring them closer and closer together, as his eyes stared unblinkingly into hers with an intensity she was unable to look away from, her heart seemed to open.

'Sophie.'

The way he said her name, his voice husky, thick with emotion, caused tears to prick at the back of her eyes. She could only hang on to his gaze as the world shifted around her, pleasure coiling until she fell over the cliff, her whole body shuddering with the force of her climax.

With a grunt of satisfaction, he stiffened, then whispered her name over and over again as he collapsed on top of her.

She held him close, feeling the heat of his skin, the faint sheen of sweat. Not wanting him to move, not wanting to let go.

Not wanting to face up to the fact she might be falling in love with the man her spreadsheet insisted wasn't right for her.

Have you considered you're measuring the wrong things? Grace's words floated back to her and Sophie shut her eyes, her arms tightening around Michael.

———————

He wanted to stay buried inside her forever.

Christ, he was in trouble. He'd already stuffed himself by continuing to see her even though he knew he was falling for her. Now he'd royally skewered himself by having sex with her. There was no way he could stop having sex with her now, for as long as she'd let him. And equally no way he could do anything else over the next few dates but fall completely in love with her.

Aware her thoughts were unlikely to be anything like his, he reluctantly pulled out, quickly ridding himself of the condom before bundling her into his arms.

When he glanced down, he saw her eyes tightly shut. 'What are you thinking?' Slowly she opened them, a flush crossing her face, and his heart stuttered. 'Tell me you're not thinking what I think you are,' he said flatly, disappointment rocking through him.

'Well, yes, sort of, but…'

'At least tell me my score was higher than Johnathan's,' he interrupted, the joy of the moment gone. He'd been thinking of falling in love. She'd been mentally scoring him.

She sat bolt upright, breasts swaying as she turned to face him. As he dragged his gaze away and up to her face, her eyes flashed angrily at him. 'I wasn't *scoring* you. God, seriously, you think after what just happened I had the mental capacity to even do that?' When he just stared back at her, because he really didn't know, the anger extinguished and her expression turned sad. 'Maybe we should stop doing this.'

'Stop?' Dread settled over him.

'It all went wrong the moment I sent the stupid spreadsheet out. It's supposed to be something I do in private, just a dump of my thoughts. Not this awful thing that hovers over us, you thinking all the time about what I'm scoring you when really I haven't thought about that aspect of it once since I came here.'

His mind was stuck on the word stop. 'What are you saying? You want to stop us, or the spreadsheet?'

'I don't know.' She lifted her eyes to his, and he saw she was as confused as he felt. 'I don't want to stop us, but I'm not ready to abandon the idea of the spreadsheet either.'

'Okay.' His heart was hammering, his mind trying to grapple what was going on.

Then she placed a hand on his face, drawing his eyes to hers. 'I *was* thinking about the spreadsheet, but only about whether I'm measuring the right things.' She bit into her lip. 'You, this,' she indicated between them. 'Us. It wasn't supposed to happen.'

'Do you regret it?' He pushed the question past a throat tight with fear.

'No, God no, of course not.'

Some of the air that had become trapped in his lungs, left in a long exhale. 'Me neither.' He searched her face, wanting to tell her he was falling for her, but worried it would make her bolt. 'I can live with the idea of you scoring me, Sophie. What I can't live with is the thought of stopping now.' *Not when I want to spend every second I can with you before you call time on us.* Brushing his thumb across her cheek, he swallowed down the words. 'I'm done with being cautious, careful. We've four more dates left and I want to enjoy them.'

Finally a smile broke free. 'Me, too.'

Relief washed through him and he sat back against the headboard, drawing her into his arms, feeling his heart begin to calm. And her body to settle against his.

'It's your turn to come to me next,' she said into the quiet.

'It is,' he confirmed.

269

She glanced up at him, eyes glinting. 'I've already worked out a really cool place to take you.'

'Promise me I won't be required to sing.'

She laughed, giving him a shove. 'I promise. I've already tried to do that, and failed.'

And she wanted a man who would sing with her, he thought sadly. As his eyes roamed her face, he recalled the evening of her birthday when she'd taken him to the karaoke bar. She'd looked so sexy, so vibrant standing on the tacky stage, belting out the lyrics to Feeling Good, winking at him when she'd sung *birds flying high, you know how I feel*. 'But if I had, I'd have missed watching *you*.'

Her expression softened. 'You might be a man of few words, but somehow you always know the right ones.' Expelling a breath, she leant against him. 'And don't worry, there's no singing involved.' Her fingers traced over his pecs, and his cock twitched. 'Would you mind if we invited Ava and Grace and their boyfriends?'

I'd rather have you to myself. But that was selfish. 'Of course not.' He twisted, his fingers running over the smooth skin of her stomach, beginning his own exploration. 'You've had to endure the company of a four-year-old and a couple of pensioners. I think it's only fair.'

'Betty and Dennis are a treat. And spending time with Olivia was almost the best part of the weekend.'

Her hands began to wander downwards, finding his happy trail. 'Almost?' he asked roughly.

'Umm.'

Shit, he was rock hard and raring to go again. 'What was the best part?'

She grinned, the wicked edge to it telling him she knew

exactly what she was doing to him. 'Maybe the lasagne? Oops, no I didn't get to eat that, did I?' Her fingers slid further, curling round the throbbing length of him, and his breath hitched. 'Maybe it was feeding the ducks, or —'

She squealed as he rolled them over, and silenced her with kiss that was as hot and hungry as he felt. 'You want to know the best part for me?' he asked hoarsely when he eventually drew back. She nodded, breathing heavily. 'You.' He smoothed back the hair from her head and kissed her again. '*You* were the best part of my weekend.'

He watched her swallow, felt her heart jump beneath his hand. Was it tension, worry that he was saying more than she wanted to hear? Or did she *like* what he was trying to say?

Whatever it was, she'd promised him four more dates. He was going to focus on making the absolute most of them and in doing so, maybe he'd convince her they *could* work as a couple.

Chapter Twenty-Six

Sophie was sat at the kitchen island staring at her computer, or more accurately at her spreadsheet, when Grace and Ava burst in carrying a week's worth of groceries between them.

'Hey, what are you doing home?' Grace frowned. 'It is a Tuesday, right? Shouldn't you be trying to make a decent noise out of the saxophone?'

'I've cancelled it.'

Ava frowned. 'Are you not feeling well?'

'I'm feeling fine.' Sophie shrugged. 'I just decided I don't want to play it anymore.'

'Oh okay.' Ava dumped the bags on the island. 'What you going to do instead? Please don't take up the violin. My brother played that when we were kids and it sounded like a cat having its tail stood on.'

'I'm not going to do anything.' Ava and Grace gaped at her. 'What?'

'But you always do something every day of the week,'

Grace replied, starting to empty out the shopping. 'It's your thing. You're manic and funny, I'm loud and wild.' She waved a French stick towards Ava. 'Ava's sweet and responsible.'

'Thanks,' Ava muttered. 'Make me sound like the dull one.'

'Being decent and caring doesn't make you dull,' Sophie retorted sharply.

In an almost uncanny symmetry, both of them stopped unpacking.

'Sophie?' Ava looked concerned. 'What's happening here? First the saxophone, now you're snapping at us. It's not like you.'

'I don't know what you mean.' But she couldn't look them in the eye.

'Sophie.' Ava walked up to her and slid an arm around her. 'We're your friends, remember? Talk to us.'

She let out a long, shuddering breath. 'Sorry, you're right. I didn't mean to snap. It's just dull is exactly what I thought Michael was when I first met him. And now I'm ashamed of how shallow I must have been, thinking that. But according to this spreadsheet, if you didn't know him and just looked at the scores, you'd *still* say he was dull. I mean, he's not sociable. He is funny in a sharp, dry way but I could hardly call him fun-loving. He plays cricket and keeps himself fit.' She took a moment to recall her delight at the ripped body she'd discovered. 'But he doesn't do enough to be called interesting. And while he's caring and oh God, the way he was with his niece, the way he puts up with Princess, Betty's little dog, I could definitely say he's sweet, I can't say he's charismatic. He doesn't want to be the centre of attention, to hold an audience. He'd far rather listen, and he's so good at that, but it's not one of the things

273

I listed on my spreadsheet.' Feeling Ava's hold tighten around her, Sophie looked up at Grace. 'You asked me once if I was measuring the right things, and I don't think I am. I think I need to re-do this whole spreadsheet. Cross off charisma, and replace it with ability to listen. Remove sociability and add compassion, change sense of fun to steadiness/reliability.'

Grace gave her a searching look. 'That sounds as if you're manipulating it to suit Michael. And that's fine if you are, I mean it's your spreadsheet, you can do what you like with it. But if you're deliberately changing it so you can push the odds in one guy's favour, is there any point having it at all?'

Ava let out a small laugh. 'Wow, Grace, that's almost profound. Plus she's right.' Ava turned to look at her. 'Are you sure the things you mentioned, like ability to listen, compassion, reliability, are what you're really looking for in a guy above anything else?' She gave Sophie a nudge. 'The Sophie from a few months ago would never have said that. I mean, yes, you want a guy to be all those things, but don't you also want him to be dynamic, to live life at a hundred miles an hour like you do? To join you on the stage? Not lurk in the shadows.'

But if I had, I'd have missed watching you. 'What if I was wrong? What if that person I'm compatible with, isn't who I need to make me happy?' She drew in a breath, looking at them both. 'Or what if the Sophie you're talking about, the one who wants to live life to the full, isn't who I really am?' Emotion balled in her throat. 'I only played the saxophone because of this pact I had with Rosie about trying something new every year, but that was what *she* wanted to do, and I just followed her lead, like I always did.' Her voice wavered as she remembered the emotional conversation with Michael. 'I think I've been living my life for her, and not for myself.'

'Oh, Soph.' Both women encircled her as she started to cry.

'It's okay.' She sniffed, wiping at her eyes. 'I've already cried this out with Michael and you know what, it's loosened something inside me that has been wound tight for so long. I've not looked at my diet spreadsheet in weeks.' She showed them her hands. 'I've not had a manicure. I'm not going to get my hair cut. Tinkerbell hasn't been to the groomers in so long they've started to send me reminders. If you ask me now what I gave Patricia for her birthday I wouldn't be able to tell you because I didn't put it on the spreadsheet.' She let out a choked laugh. 'But guess what? The wheels haven't come off my life. In fact I'm sleeping better, I feel more relaxed.' She gave them both a wobbly smile. 'I'm happier than I've ever been.'

Ava pulled back, and Sophie watched as she and Grace shared some silent communication. 'Hey, no secrets between us,' she protested.

'Sorry.' Ava pulled a face. 'I was just wondering if Grace was thinking what I was.'

'Which is?'

Ava looked over at Grace, who shrugged and turned to Sophie. 'We think you've fallen in love with your two and a half out of ten man.'

'Oh no. No way. I really like him, and hate you calling him that because it isn't true anymore, but no. I'm not falling for him.' Yet even as she said it, her subconscious gave her a *Duh, who do you think you're kidding*, stare.

Grace scrutinised her face. 'I hope you're right. I mean I like the guy, don't get me wrong, and he's clearly helped you loads with sorting out your feelings over Rosie. But—'

'But you don't think we're a good long-term match,' Sophie filled in, though inside she was working out if that mattered. It might have done a few months ago, just like it mattered what the spreadsheet had said, but now she was questioning everything, shouldn't that include questioning what Ava and Grace thought, too?

'*Nobody* knows, when they start dating,' Ava corrected. 'That's the risk we all take. You were trying to minimise that risk with your spreadsheet but I guess you need to ask yourself if you like him enough to take that risk. To abandon your spreadsheet and keep dating him even after these dates are over.'

'I want to keep seeing him.' The thought of not seeing him caused her heart to falter. 'But maybe I don't need to abandon my spreadsheet.' Sophie looked back at her computer, giving it a nudge to wake it up. 'All I need to do is think hard about what this new version of me really wants from a man, and … readjust.'

Ava and Grace shared another look, but Sophie ignored them. So what if she was changing the goalposts? If she was going to go falling in love, she felt safer doing it while clinging to *something*.

Michael was at the surgery, going through the last of his paperwork when Hattie knocked on the door of his office.

'I'm just completing Mr Jenson's referral,' he told her.

She cleared her throat. 'That's not why I'm here.'

'Ah, sorry.' Wondering what else he'd done wrong, he cautiously met her eyes. 'How can I help?'

'You can't.' But then she smiled, taking the edge off her words. 'I wasn't sure if Sophie told you, so I thought I should. She made two spreadsheets for me and they're proving very useful.'

He hadn't asked, he realised, but she'd kept her promise to Hattie. 'Good.'

Her eyes darted away from his. 'She also asked Hamza to look at our computer systems to see if there's anything else that can be done to help the practice run more smoothly.'

Was she *blushing*? He tried to keep his face straight. 'Was he helpful?'

'Actually, yes.' She hitched her handbag further onto her shoulder. 'I offered to take him out for a drink. You know, to thank him.'

His lips twitched and he had to look away. 'I'm sure he'll appreciate it.'

'Yes, well, I'll leave you to it. See you tomorrow, Michael.'

He nearly fell off his chair. Three years after he'd asked, and she'd finally called him by his first name.

Without thinking, he dragged out his phone and called Sophie.

'Hey, what's up Doc?' Then she burst out laughing.

'How long have you been itching to use that line?' he asked dryly.

'So long,' she admitted, laughter still in her voice.

'Wait, I've just realised, it's Tuesday. You should be at your saxophone lesson.'

'I'm impressed you remembered.' Her voice turned quieter. 'But actually, I've given it up.'

He paused, listening to what she wasn't saying. 'Because you realised you weren't enjoying it?'

She huffed out a breath. 'Gold star. It seems you know me too well.'

He sat back on his chair. 'I'd like to know you even more.'

A beat of silence and he wished he could see her face. 'What if you don't like what you find?'

His heart crumpled at the vulnerability in her voice. 'If you think there's even the remotest chance that would happen, let me shoot it down right away. The *opposite* is happening.' He shook his head. 'The reason I'm phoning is to say thank you for waving your magic wand in Hattie's direction. She didn't just smile at me today. She called me by my first name. And I'm pretty sure she's going on a date with Hamza, though she tried to pretend it was just a thank you drink.'

Sophie squealed. 'Oooh, that's fantastic. It was obvious those two had a thing for each other. They just needed a little nudge.'

'It was obvious to *you*,' he told her, emphasising the last word. 'Because you take notice. You're a people person. I knew that on one level, but watching you interact with the cricket crowd, with Betty and Dennis, the way you put everyone at ease no matter who they are. The way you try and help in whatever way you can.' He paused, trying to think of the right words. 'You make a difference, Sophie. Not many people can say that.'

A wall of silence met his words and he worried he'd given away too much of how he felt. 'I don't know what to say,' she said at last. 'Nobody has ever said that to me.'

Nobody has ever seen you like I do. It was too deep a comment from a guy who only had four dates left with her. 'It doesn't make it any less true.'

'Then thank you. Really. I was just having a bit of a wobble, thinking about what you said the other day, about whether I'm living my life for me, or for Rosie. And if it's for Rosie, it got me wondering...' her voice began to shake and he heard her draw in a breath. 'Do I even know who *I* am anymore? I mean, do I really like karaoke, or dancing? Am I playing tennis because she was good at it or because I enjoy it? Do I have this list of places to go and do because *I* want to experience them?'

'Hey.' He so desperately wanted to hold her. 'These aren't questions you need to be in a rush to answer. We're all continuously discovering things about ourselves. I thought I'd hate flying through the air on a neck-breaking trapeze.' He heard a little snort of laughter. 'I didn't think I could enjoy dating a woman who lived her life by spreadsheets and could talk for five minutes without taking breath.'

He could hear the smile in her voice when she answered. 'And now?'

And now I can't imagine being with anyone else. But she didn't want to hear that from him. 'Now I'm really looking forward to seeing you on Saturday. Whatever you have planned.'

'Good answer. And I'm looking forward to seeing you, too.' She hesitated, then added softly. 'Thank you for what you said. You really are the easiest person to talk to. And the best listener I've ever come across. I guess you get a lot of practise, listening to all those patients.'

'Maybe. Or maybe I enjoy listening to you.' Before he could get himself in a tangle, saying too much, he added. 'I'll message you which train I'm on.'

It was becoming harder and harder to keep his feelings to himself, he thought as he walked back to the cottage. But if he said too much now, he'd scare her away. He needed to bide his time, wait for the last date. Then, when he had nothing to lose, he could tell her how he felt. He was under no illusion it would make any difference, he was never going to be her spreadsheet ten out of ten, but he didn't want their time coming to an end without her knowing how utterly special she was.

Chapter Twenty-Seven

S ophie almost squealed when she heard the flat intercom. As it was, she must have let out some sort of noise because Grace raised her eyebrows. 'A bit excited to see him, aren't we?'

'It's okay for you and Ava, you see your men during the week. I've not seen Michael since last Saturday.'

'Number one, I don't have a man. Daniel and I are just casual. Number two,' Grace rolled on, not giving Sophie a chance to point out this non-casual thing she had with Daniel had taken up two days this week already. 'Is Michael officially now *your* man?'

It was so easy to think of him as that. In her head, her heart, he was. But on her spreadsheet, the old one, he still hadn't made seven out of ten. The new one was still work in progress. 'He is for the next four dates.'

Her heart slammed into her ribs when she opened the door. Understated, sure, but the man on her doorstep giving her an openly admiring smile, his eyes vivid against his sky-blue shirt, made her breath hitch and her body tingle. 'Hi.' Funny how sometimes she lost her words when she looked at him.

His eyes skimmed over her, before resting on her mouth. Then, without saying a word, he bent and kissed her. Not a hello kiss, but a *God I've missed the hell out of you* kiss. One that had her reaching to wrap her arms around his neck, and wishing Grace wasn't inside, waiting for them.

'I've been waiting all week to do that.' He smiled, running his finger across her cheek. 'You look gorgeous, by the way.'

'What, this?' She looked down at the purple top she'd splurged on that afternoon because she wanted to look knock out for him. 'It's just some old thing.'

'About four hours old, to be exact.' Grace gave her an evil grin before greeting Michael. 'Hi again.'

'Grace.' He nodded, giving her friend the small, reserved smile she'd once thought was his only smile.

'We were expecting you to be later. Sophie said something about you having to play cricket first.'

'I swung the bat.' When they both gave him a confused look, he shrugged. 'I hit out at every ball. Figured if it came off I could win us the game, if it didn't, I could lose it.' He glanced down at her. 'Either way, I'd get to see Sophie earlier.'

'Aw.' Charmed, Sophie slid her arms around his waist, loving how he felt, slim, solid. 'So which are you, hero or villain?'

He laughed. 'Hero, actually. It nearly backfired because everyone wanted to buy me a drink. Betty had to pretend she'd left the back door of the cottage open to give me an excuse to get out.'

'Well now we've got you, let's go.' Grace chivvied them

along. 'Ava and Ethan are already there and Daniel's on his way.'

'Where is *there?*' Michael looked between the pair of them. 'Or am I better not knowing?'

Sophie gave him a quick kiss. 'Don't worry, I think you're actually going to enjoy this one.'

'Of course he will,' Grace agreed, picking up her jacket and striding towards the door. 'He's used to being scored, aren't you Michael?'

'Grace.' Sophie gave her friend an admonishing stare.

'What? He knows it's just a joke.' She looked over at Michael, who gave her a small smile.

'Ignore her,' Sophie grasped Michael's hand and squeezed. 'We're heading to a cocktail bar. The scoring she mentioned is because it's got a crazy golf course.'

'Ah.' He squeezed her hand back. 'Then my ability to get a low score will be an advantage.'

Grace burst out laughing and pointed back at Sophie. 'See, the doctor can take a joke. Now get a move on. I need a drink.'

As they hurried along to the tube station, Sophie whispered, 'I'm sorry about that.'

Michael shook his head. 'I'm not entirely humourless.'

'I know you're not.' She exhaled in exasperation. 'I just … God, I hate being reminded about it.'

He smiled, pressed a kiss on her nose. 'Forget it. I have. And you should know I'm pretty lethal at crazy golf so be prepared to be beaten.'

'Oh yeah?' She grinned back at him. 'Bring it on.'

The place was busy when they arrived, but Ava had messaged to say they were on the terrace so they headed up, past the fake green turf of the golf courses, complete with trailing vines and plastic flowers. Michael whistled and when she looked at him she saw his eyes were shining. 'I bet they don't have anything like this in Little Brook.'

'True. But we have sheep.' His eyes drifted down to the silver pendant nestled between her breasts. When his gaze found hers, it had darkened with heat. 'And that is one lucky ewe.'

Laughing, she smiled coyly. 'Maybe you'll get lucky tonight, too.'

His eyes smouldered back at her, but when he spoke, it was with quiet sincerity. 'I hope so.'

They caught up with the gang, and all decided to have a drink first before tackling the golf. As she was enjoying the first sip of her cocktail, she heard an unwelcome voice behind her. 'Well, well. If it isn't Spreadsheet Girl.'

Stiffening, she turned to find Callum smirking at her. She wanted to say *Hello three out of ten kisser*, but refused to stoop that low. 'Hello. And goodbye.'

She turned back to the group, where Ava was discussing golf with Michael. Funny how she'd not realised he played. He knew everything about what she did outside work, because he asked questions. He listened. Silently she made a promise to talk less, listen to him more.

She felt Michael's hand slide round her waist and rest on her lower back.

'That's him, isn't it.' Callum's voice again. 'The bloke who got a two.'

The gang fell silent, all attention now turned on them. Beside her, Michael's body tensed as he shifted to face the man behind him.

'I take it you're Callum?'

'That's right, mate. Think we both got skewered by this woman. Difference is, you're apparently desperate enough to keep seeing her.'

She watched Michael stretch to his full height, which happened to be several inches taller than Callum. His shoulders also several inches wider. 'No, the difference is I'm lucky enough to be given another shot with her. And smart enough to grab that chance with both hands.'

Callum stared back at him, shifting his hands to his hips, his expression one of confusion. 'Seriously? You're prepared to humiliate yourself by seeing a woman who clearly thought you sucked?'

'For the chance to prove her wrong?' Michael stated calmly. 'Absolutely.'

Callum let out a derisive laugh. 'You're nuts, mate. But because I feel sorry for you, I'm going to warn you, she kisses like a fucking carp.'

Michael stepped forward, bringing himself right into Callum's personal space, staring down at the shorter man. 'You can keep your sympathy. She kisses like an angel. Makes love like a goddess. I'm one lucky bastard.' His face hardened into an expression she'd never seen on him before. 'And if I find you talking to her again, you'll discover I can also be a mean bastard. Now get out of my sight.'

Whatever Callum saw in Michael's expression was enough for him to drop his stare. With a brief shake of his head, he sloped off, leaving Sophie dazed, and more than a little turned on.

'Well.' Even Grace, it seemed, was lost for words for a moment. 'Remind me not to piss you off.'

Michael smiled, but tension was still clear in the tight set of his jaw, the flat eyes. 'It takes a lot to do that.' His eyes narrowed as he gazed in the direction Callum had left. 'But he managed it.'

As the gang started talking again, Sophie leaned into Michael. 'Thank you,' she whispered, emotion catching her by the throat at the thought of this man, who'd been humiliated by her, defending her so resolutely. And against a man who'd somehow once scored more highly. It was blindingly obvious her original spreadsheet was flawed.

His brow furrowed. 'For what?'

'Standing up for me.'

His arm tightened around her, and when their eyes met, she was rocked by the intensity she saw in his. 'Always.'

The encounter with Callum still hung over Michael as they tackled the first hole of the Windmill Course. He wanted to lose himself in the game – crazy golf it might be, but the indoor courses were pretty impressive. It was also something he wasn't shite at, or at least no worse than any of Sophie's friends.

But he couldn't shake off the sight of that git smirking at him. Or the thought that Sophie had really thought Callum was so much better than him.

Grace screamed with delight as her ball sunk into the hole, shaking him out of his introspection.

'Hey.' Sophie wrapped her hand around his. 'Are you okay?'

He nodded, giving her a smile. 'Fine. Just working out my tactics.'

She rolled her gorgeous grey eyes, but her gaze remained on his for a few telling seconds. 'I wonder where Callum slunk off to,' she said finally as he lined up his shot.

He raised his head to look at her. 'Are you trying to put me off?'

Her mouth curved. 'Maybe.'

He bent his head again, settled his shoulders.

'Watching you face up to him.' She blew out a breath. 'Let's just say, now I know what they mean about being afraid of the quiet ones.'

It was his turn to study her. 'And now you're mistaking quiet for timid.'

Her eyes widened. 'I'm not. I wouldn't.' She stepped across the plastic grass and clasped his face in her hands. 'I totally underestimated you when we first met, I know that. But that was then. This is now.' Her voice turned soft. 'And now I think you're incredible, Dr Adams.'

Her eyes turned liquid silver, utterly beguiling, and the more he stared, the more lost he became in them. Incredible didn't mean she felt what he did, but to have this woman he was in awe of, who had suffered so much grief yet not become hardened by it … to have her admire him, was a heady experience.

He angled his head towards her, about to press those inviting lips against his, when he heard a non-too subtle bout of coughing from the two other couples.

Reluctantly he straightened. 'Sorry.' He cast a glance towards Sophie. 'My partner is distracting me.'

She pouted. 'Hey, you can't blame a girl for finding you sexy. The way you went Rambo on Callum.' She shivered. 'All quiet authority, wrapped up in a smoking hot body.'

287

He knew she was kidding, but it was a massive stroke to his ego to have her say it, especially in front of her friends. 'If you think that was sexy, wait till I get you home.'

Her cheeks flushed in a way that gave his ego another firm stroke. 'Promises, promises.'

'Come on you two love birds,' Ava called over to them. 'This is supposed to be golf, not foreplay.'

He put his hand up in apology, crouched again over the ball. And watched with smug satisfaction as it popped into the hole.

'Well, well.' Sophie slipped an arm around his waist as they walked to the next hole. 'Seems there's no end to your talents, Doc.'

He gave her a mild look. 'You do realise if you carry on flattering me like this my head will be twice as big as when I arrived.'

She halted, ran a hand gently down his cheek, causing a tremor of awareness to run through him. 'I doubt that. In fact I think I could stand here and tell you all night how amazing you are, and you'd not believe a word of it.'

His gaze jumped to hers, searching. 'You could try me.'

She smiled. 'Okay then. Here are some qualities that weren't on my spreadsheet, but arguably they *should* have been. You're steady, and I mean *rock* steady. Earlier Callum tried to goad you but you didn't let him, just stayed calm, like you were with Lucy's mum. And how Roger said you were when he had his heart attack. Then there's this whole grounded thing you've got going on. You don't care if you're seen taking Princess for a walk, or playing horse with Olivia on your back. And you're oblivious to how many women turn their heads to look at you, or how the guys at cricket have hero worship in their eyes when you walk out to bat. You *listen*, that's a given, but it makes such a huge difference to the people you listen to. Like me.' As her words tumbled around in his head, she carried on. 'And all that's before we factor in your compassion, your kindness. Or that bone dry but lethal sense of humour.' She wound her arms around his neck. 'That do you for now, Doc?'

Dumbfounded, he stared into her eyes, blinking a few times to regain his balance. But if he was all those things – if – why had Jackie chosen Ian? Why was it still not enough for Sophie?

Because neither of them had wanted steady. They wanted exciting.

The truth hurt so much he had to step away. 'Michael?'

He swallowed, trying desperately to keep in the moment. 'Sorry. I ... thank you for saying all that, really.' He swiped a hand down his face, digging deep for that very steadiness she'd talked about, when all he felt was a crushing sense of loss. It didn't matter what he did over the next three dates, she was never going to fall for him. He was only ever a change of pace, a diversion. An experiment. 'I'm going to get myself another drink. Want one?'

She shook her head, clearly worried, and because he hated that he'd confused her, he gave her a kiss. 'Later, I'll tell you how amazing *you* are.'

And when they were finally alone in her room, he did exactly that. Pushing away the grim thoughts from earlier he gazed into her eyes as she lay on her bed, naked except for the sheep necklace he'd insisted she keep on.

'You're fearless,' he told her. 'Take the way you had the guts to apologise to me in person after you knew I'd seen the spreadsheet. And you're game to try anything. Even watching cricket. We've talked about your ability to talk to people, how you try and help, but what about your strength in how you coped after Rosie died? And your enthusiasm for life?'

She smiled up at him. 'And my awesomeness at singing. And how I can beat you at crazy golf.'

'Hey, you distracted me.'

She narrowed her eyes. 'Something distracted you.'

He couldn't tell her the truth, so he told a partial one. 'When you said all those nice things about me, it triggered a memory. Something Jackie said to me.' The hurt was still there, but this time it wasn't Jackie he was thinking of when he looked into Sophie's eyes. 'She told me she *wanted* to prefer me, but in the end, she didn't want steady. She wanted exciting.'

'Then she's a bloody fool.'

Couldn't she see that her whole spreadsheet was geared towards exactly the same quality? But his time with Sophie was precious, and he wasn't going to waste it arguing. 'I don't want to talk about Jackie. Anything I once felt, is over.' His eyes dipped to Sophie's. 'You're the person who takes up all my head space.'

Pressing his hips against hers, he thrust slowly, capturing her mouth with his. As he took his fill, tasting, savouring, he clasped her hands, lifting them over her head so she was pinned beneath him. 'You're who I think about when I go to bed,' he told her hoarsely, rocking back and forwards before slipping inside her. 'Who I fantasise about until I'm hot and hard and wanting.' She inhaled a sharp breath. 'Do you want to hear what I do to you in my dreams?'

Her slender neck moved as she swallowed. 'Yes, God yes.'

'Sometimes it's just like now, me inside you, taking you

slow, feeling the heat of you envelop me, the softness of your curves slide against mine in the most intimate ways.' He bent, sucked on one of her nipples until it was tight, and she was gasping. 'But sometimes it's hard and fast, me driving into you, the bedhead banging against the wall, you screaming for me to go harder, faster.'

She groaned. 'Oh God, keep talking. I'm going to come.'

He kept talking long into the night, until they were both exhausted. And while she slept in his arms, he wondered if he could keep doing this for another three dates. Or if he should walk away now, before he fell so irrevocably in love with her, that he'd never be able to recover from it.

Chapter Twenty-Eight

The week had started well. On Monday Sophie had met her mum for lunch.

'You seem happier, Sophie,' she'd announced. 'Less brittle. Calmer.'

Sophie had objected to the word brittle, yet when her mum had gone on to talk about how worried she'd been, seeing her always so busy, like she was on a treadmill and didn't want to slow down in case she fell off, Sophie wondered if her mum had seen more than she'd realised.

'It has felt like that ever since Rosie died,' she'd admitted. 'Michael said he thought I was living my life for her, and in some ways I think I was. I felt so guilty for being the one still alive.'

Her mum's face had crumpled, and she'd apologised over and over for not realising. 'I think I was partially to blame,' she'd said sadly. 'We were so caught up in our own grief. And some of that guilt, too, for not realising sooner how sick she was.'

The pair of them had been a waste of space after that, crying and yet also laughing at the way they were crying. Finally, she'd told her mum it was time she forgave herself, too. And about time she stopped pushing men away and started to date again. 'Patricia isn't the bad guy here,' she'd told her. 'She makes dad happy, and you deserve to be happy, too.'

But though the meal had been cathartic for both of them, they'd been spotted by Trevor, who'd been on her case ever since the spreadsheet debacle, going through her week in minute detail so he knew where she was at all times. It had meant she'd had to cancel taking Tinkerbell to the groomers and do it herself. Sitting on the sofa, brushing a purring feline with long, smooth strokes had been surprisingly therapeutic and she'd decided to do it herself from now on. Which was possible now she'd dropped the saxophone lessons, and the Pilates. And didn't spend half an hour every evening revising her spreadsheets.

'So, this weekend you're back in Little Brook, huh?' Ava asked as they sat at their usual table in The Drunk Flamingo on Friday night.

'That's the plan.' The lovely habit she and Michael had got into over the last few weeks of phoning or messaging each other every day had been worryingly low key this week. He'd been distinctly subdued, his usual dry wit absent, yet when she'd asked him what was wrong, he'd insisted he was just tired. Twice he'd also blamed Betty for having to cut their chats short, the first time needing to pick her up from bingo, the second from dinner with Dennis. If true, it was great news for his gran's love life, which seemed to be going full steam ahead. She wasn't sure what it said about her own.

'Hey.' Grace tapped her on the head. 'Are you still in there?'

'Sorry, yes.' She grabbed at her drink and took a long swallow.

'I asked what Michael's got lined up for you, or is it a secret?'

Sophie recalled their quick call yesterday. 'He just said to bring warm comfortable clothes I didn't mind getting dirty.'

'Oh boy.' Grace grimaced. 'That sounds like he's taking you walking again. Or … what do they call it in the country? Yomping?'

Ava burst out laughing. 'Don't be daft, that's what soldiers do when they have to hike with equipment on their backs.'

'Well she might have to carry a rucksack,' Grace protested.

'I think you're talking about rambling.' Ava smirked. 'Which is kind of what you do a lot, only with words instead of your feet.'

Grace shuddered. 'I can't imagine dating a guy who wanted me to wear warm comfy clothes.' She looked quizzically at Sophie. 'Don't you want to go out with a guy who's more interested in ripping your clothes *off*?'

Sophie looked at her friend. 'For the record, I've never met a man *more* interested in ripping my clothes off. Or more insanely hot while he's talking about doing it. Best sex of my life, no question,' added, in case there was any more doubt. 'But returning to the question, I'm going to throw it back to you. Don't you want to spend time with a guy who's interested in you both in and out of bed?'

Grace blinked and looked away. 'I don't know.'

Sophie glanced at Ava, who shrugged.

'I think you do know,' Sophie countered softly. 'And I think it scares you so much you've decided to treat Daniel as just a hook up. But he's not, is he? You care for him.'

Grace sighed, staring down at her drink. 'Maybe I do.' She stared up at Sophie. 'But I'm not the only one kidding myself over what's happening with a guy, am I? Miss I'm Not Falling in Love. Nope. No Way. Even though you were all over Michael last weekend and you haven't stopped talking about him all week.'

Sophie put her hands up. 'Okay, point taken.' She drew in a breath, took another sip of whatever cocktail Grace had ordered them. 'I may be falling in love with him.'

'Shit, Soph.' Grace's eyebrows flew up, just as Ava inhaled sharply. 'I thought you'd deny it again.'

'There's no point. I'd be lying to myself.' She groaned, putting her head in her hands. 'Bloody hell what have I done? Rosie would have absolutely crapped herself to hear me say I'm falling for a reserved doctor who lives in a quiet village with his gran and his dog. And who spends his down time playing cricket and going for long walks.'

Ava smiled sadly. 'I don't know whether to be pleased for you or not.'

Sophie let out a strangled laugh. 'I don't, either. This wasn't supposed to happen. The whole point of the spreadsheet was to stop me from getting to the point where my heart was tangled up with a guy who isn't a good fit for me.'

'Not a good fit according to who?' Ava interjected. 'What?' she asked when Sophie gave her a look. 'It's not like you even know the spreadsheet *works*. That's why you agreed to see Michael for ten dates in the first place.'

'I know.' She sighed. 'And I've got into a right muddle with that. The original one still has Michael less than seven out of ten. The new one feels like I'm cheating.'

They both gave her a sympathetic look.

'Do you think he feels the same about you?' Grace asked.

'I don't know. Like I *really* don't know.' Tipping her head up again, she thought of their last proper conversation, the one where he'd told her she was the person who filled his head. Who he thought about all the time. 'Maybe?' But then she thought of how distant he'd been this week and some of her confidence leaked out. 'Or maybe not.'

Ava and Grace, sitting either side of her, gave her arms a comforting squeeze.

'How could he fail to fall for you?' Ava smiled. 'You're awesome.'

'Amen to that.' Grace eyed up their largely untouched cocktails. 'Why don't we park this conversation and get some drinking done? We all know everything is clearer after alcohol.'

Sophie let out a small laugh. 'If only.'

'Well, for what it's worth.' Glass in hand, Grace turned to her. 'I do like Daniel, you're right. But there's no way he looks at me like Michael does you.'

Sophie's heart bumped against her ribs. 'How's that?'

'Like he can't believe he's lucky enough to be dating you.'

Friday night, and Michael was in the garage, sorting through the camping equipment he'd brought down with him from Manchester. Fudge was watching him patiently, frowning every now and again.

'You think this is a daft idea, don't you?' Christ, what was he doing, asking advice from his dog? He gave Fudge an ear rub. 'Sorry girl, but I have to talk to someone and Betty's out with Dennis again tonight.' Fudge cocked her head. 'Yeah, I know. She's got a better social life than I have.' A better love life, too, because at least the person Betty was dating was head over heels in love with her.

He stared down at the sleeping bags, the camping stove. He'd told himself Sophie was game for anything, and he wanted her to experience something she might not have done before. Part of him wondered if this was some sort of self-sabotage on his part, though. Get her to call quits on their arrangement so he didn't have to.

'Fuck.'

He rubbed at his eyes. How had he fallen in love with a woman he'd only be seeing three more times?

With a sigh he gathered up the equipment and packed it into the back of his Discovery.

'All ready for your trip?'

He turned to find Betty walking towards him, her arm linked with Dennis. For a second he forgot his own misery to rejoice at how bloody happy she looked.

'I'm not sure ready is the right word, but I think I've got everything we need.'

'Dinner round a campfire, an evening looking up at the stars, a night under canvas.' Dennis chortled and turned to Betty. 'Shall we go with them?'

Betty probably looked as horrified as he did. 'You wouldn't get me under canvas, you daft sod. I need a nice comfy bed, central heating and an en-suite bathroom.'

Michael had an awful feeling Sophie might need the same.

Dennis gave her a sweet kiss. 'How about instead we sit in your garden under a blanket with a mug of cocoa?'

A soft expression crossed her face. 'Now that's what I call a good end to the evening.' She looked over at Michael. 'Are you joining us?'

'What? Play gooseberry to my grandmother?' He blanched. 'Thanks, but I'm good. Probably got some filing I can do.' Even poking his eyes with a rusty nail sounded less painful.

Thankfully his phone rang, saving him the humiliation of her trying to persuade him. When he saw who it was, his pulse quickened.

'Hey Doc, can you hear me?' In the background he could hear chatter, interspersed with loud laughter. 'Wait, hang on, I'm going outside because even if you can hear me, I can't hear you.' There was rustling, the lilting sound of her voice as she greeted someone she knew. 'Is that better?'

A siren wailed in the background, and traffic hummed. 'Still louder than the sound of crickets and Betty and Dennis drinking cocoa, but yes. I can hear you fine.'

She let out a bark of laughter, and it still did his ego good to know he could that. 'It's all happening in Little Brook huh?'

'About as much as usual.' But he enjoyed the quiet pace now, had settled into it. He wouldn't swap his walk across the fields with Fudge every evening for a drink in a busy bar. Unless he could go to that bar with Sophie.

'So, I wasn't going to make this phone call, but then I had a few drinks and it suddenly became a great idea, though now I'm actually talking to you I'm wondering if maybe it isn't, because I want you to be honest with me but I don't want to make things weird between us. And now you're wondering what on earth I'm going to say, so I'll just get right out and say it.' She finally took a breath. 'Did I say something to upset you last weekend?'

'No. Absolutely not.' His emphatic statement was met with an ominous silence. In deciding to pull back a little to avoid falling even deeper in love with her, had he unintentionally hurt her? 'Sophie—'

'You say I haven't, but this week I got the impression you've been trying to avoid me.'

He hung his head, ashamed of himself. Of course she'd notice. Wasn't her ability to read people, to understand them, one of the things he admired about her most?

'Do you still want to see me tomorrow?' she added, and his chest squeezed as he heard her voice break a little.

'More than you can possibly know,' he answered truthfully, staring at his car, packed to the brim with camping stuff. 'So much so, I've spent the last hour getting ready for it.'

'You have?' The returning bounce in her voice was unmistakable, and he felt like an utter git for being the cause of her losing it. 'Now I'm super intrigued as to what you've got lined up for me.'

He pictured her face, the enthusiasm he'd bet was written all over it. And then imagined seeing it vanish when he showed her the tent. 'Do you want me to tell you? Forewarned is forearmed is a popular saying for a reason.'

'And there he goes, bringing me back down to earth again. Okay, sock it to me, Doc. Where are you taking me?'

'The South Downs.' He crossed his fingers. 'Camping.'

'Oh.' The beat of silence that followed caused his stomach to pitch. *You're putting a city girl in a tent. She's not going to shriek with glee.* 'Well, that's definitely going to be one I can cross off my spreadsheet,' she said finally, the amusement in her voice making everything inside him loosen and realign. 'Rosie and I wanted to go camping when we were kids, but Mum was never keen so it didn't happen. I asked Ava and Grace a few years ago but they turned their noses up at the idea.' He heard the smile in her voice. 'Can you imagine Grace, camping? Glamping, maybe. Or, wait, is this glamping or real camping?'

'As real as it gets. A tent we put up ourselves, a stove we cook over.' Please God he wasn't putting her off with every word he spoke. 'Sleeping bags we go to bed in.'

'Bags?'

He stared back at the Discovery. 'I guess we could take a duvet.' At a push. If she sat on it. But it wasn't camping.

'No, I meant bags plural? As in one for you and one for me?'

That was what she was baulking at? 'Bags plural, yes. But with zips we can unzip. And re-zip together.' He felt a flush of arousal just thinking about it.

He heard her let out a long breath. 'That sounds … oddly idyllic.'

'Thank God.' He kicked himself for being so distant this last week. Why was he trying to protect himself when he was already head over heels in love with her? His only option now was to make the most of her, while he still could. 'Look, about this last week. I'm sorry if I seemed elusive. I was working through something.'

'That's okay.' He heard a slight hesitation in her voice. 'Did you come to a resolution?'

'Yes.' He looked back at the car. 'I've decided not to worry about it.'

Chapter Twenty-Nine

Sophie giggled as she watched Michael try to retrieve the tent pole from Princess. It hadn't been his idea to bring the little dog with them.

'But she'll miss Fudge,' Betty had argued. 'And think how much she'll enjoy all that outdoor living.'

Of course the reasoning hadn't mattered. Michael, Sophie had learnt, was putty in his grandma's hands. Sophie didn't think he was capable of saying no to her. So despite muttering something about short legs and long walks, he'd squeezed Princess's bed and her favourite toys into the back of the car.

Sophie couldn't say she'd been disappointed at the thought of having any walk curtailed. And she'd bent double with laughter when Princess had leapt into the passenger seat and sat up with a smug expression on her little face. Though her stint riding shotgun had been short-lived, her smugness had remained for the rest of the journey.

And now the pint size dog was causing more trouble for

Michael. And more hilarity for Sophie, who was watching with Fudge.

'Are you two going to help?' Michael inquired mildly.

Sophie looked down at Fudge, who stared up at her with big brown eyes that she was beginning to think were kind of adorable. 'We both think it's more fun watching.'

Michael slid his hands onto his hips. 'Since when were you and Fudge a team? You're a cat person, so you told me. I got a zero for daring to own a dog.'

'Umm, I may have got that one wrong.' She'd got pretty much all of them wrong, she now realised. Everything she thought she'd wanted in a guy had been totally upended, thanks to the man in front of her. The one with dynamite legs, showcased in his cargo shorts, his handsome face currently wearing an expression torn between frustration and amusement.

'Princess, come here.' Michael's tone was firm but soft. It wasn't a huge stretch to imagine that same tone talking to a naughty toddler. Patient, calm, dependable yet, as she'd witnessed with his niece, willing to make a fool of himself. He'd make one hell of a dad. A stab of longing tore through her as, for the first time in her life, she saw herself with a kid. A fair haired, blue eyed, mischievous son.

'Good girl.' Princess dropped the tent pole and trotted willingly into Michael's outstretched arms. He lifted her up and the dog licked his face, tail wagging, the tent pole immediately forgotten the moment she was offered a cuddle.

'You know I would help with the tent if you offered me a cuddle.'

Michael's bright blue eyes found hers. 'I'll offer you more than a cuddle.'

She felt her skin tighten, her blood thicken. God, he was so good at turning her on with just a look. 'Well, why didn't you say?' She went to pick up the errant tent pole. 'Where do you want me to put it?'

Laughter burst out of him. 'Isn't that my line?'

She gave him a push, enjoying this version of Michael. Clearly in his element outdoors, the dogs playing around him, humour alive on his face, he was so different to the serious man she'd once thought he was.

And this version of *her* was different, too, she thought a few minutes later as she sat with a satisfied thump on the picnic blanket, their tent officially up. Michael, who was filling a small kettle from the canister of water, glanced over at her, seeming to take a full inventory before ending at her feet.

'I see you've upgraded the Converses.'

She wiggled her new sturdy boots. 'I learn fast.' Yet it wasn't only experience that had led to her buying the boots and the easy-care shorts. She felt different to the woman he'd first taken for a walk at the beginning of the summer. This Sophie, with hair that hadn't seen a hairdresser in months, was happier, free from a burden she'd not realised she'd been carrying.

She watched as Michael crouched on his haunches to light a small camping stove before placing the well-used kettle on top of it.

'Do you camp a lot?'

He settled back on the blanket next to her, hugging his knees. 'I used to. Then Jackie came along and she didn't like it so I stopped. When I moved back down, I got the tent out again. I didn't go for long, just a couple of nights here and there, but enough to recharge.'

303

She inhaled a lungful of fresh air. 'I can see how that could happen. It's so peaceful.'

He gave her a quiet study. 'I wasn't sure you'd enjoy it.'

'I wasn't sure, either.' She grinned at him. 'And I don't think the Sophie you first met would have done.'

He laughed, a deep rumble that caused her toes to curl inside her boots. 'Probably not. Back then I likened you to a double expresso topped up with Red Bull.'

'Oh my God, that's so bad.' She gave him a wry smile. 'Yet also worryingly true. What would you say I am now?'

His brow furrowed. 'Maybe more of an Irish coffee.' He winked. 'You've still got that kick, but you seem mellower.'

'I am.' She settled back on the blanket, looking up at the sky. 'The Sophie of two months ago wouldn't have been able to lie here. She'd have been getting out her phone, checking Google maps and making a list of all the things to do in the area. Then adding them to her spreadsheet, ready to cross off.' She smiled over at him. 'This new, chilled version is thanks to you.'

He shook his head. 'The change is down to you learning to let go of things you'd bottled up for too long.' His expression turned serious, the blue of his eyes more intense. 'But I like to think I'm not the only one to have gained something from the last few months.'

Her heart gave a solid thump. 'What have you gained?'

His hand reached to caress her face. 'You mean aside from spending time with a warm, vital, fun, incredibly sexy woman?'

Why did she get the feeling that behind the lovely words was a sense of finality? 'Do I know her?'

He smiled, eyes crinkling at the corners. 'I've not felt so

alive in years, Sophie. It's like my life was in drab monochrome, but recently I've started to see it in rich colour with high definition.'

Before she could say anything, he kissed her. And kept on kissing her, pressing her back on the blanket, his thigh sliding between hers as the kiss became hotter, heavier.

They jumped apart when the kettle started to whistle, both of them laughing. 'Remember where we left off,' he told her, before going to make the tea.

After their picnic lunch, they trampled over the hills with the dogs. When it became too much for little legs, Michael lifted Princess into his rucksack, much to Sophie's clear astonishment.

When they returned to the campsite, he got out a pan and cooked up a simple macaroni cheese, adding a tin of tuna to give it a twist.

Now they were sitting by the small fire – thanks to a portable fire pit – and finishing off the bottle of wine he'd brought. Fudge and Princess were asleep on the rug next to them. If he'd had to pick one word to describe the day, it would be *idyllic*.

'In case you're still worried, I really enjoyed today.' Sophie gave him a side-glance. 'And that's despite the long walk. I hadn't reckoned on you being able to put Princess in a rucksack.'

He smiled. 'I didn't think she'd be so compliant.'

Sophie scoffed. 'That dog dotes on you. As long as she's near you, she's happy.'

If only he was as good with non-canine females. 'Let's hope you still enjoy camping after you've spent a night on an airbed.'

She slid him a coy look. 'Are you with me on this airbed?'

'Try stopping me.'

With a long exhale she leant into him. Automatically he slid his arm around her, feeling her warm and soft against his side. Intimate, yet it was as if they'd always done this, always been this close, this comfortable with each other. 'As long as you're with me, I'll still be enjoying myself tomorrow morning.'

His heart bumped against his ribs. How could she say such nice words to him, and still be planning on saying goodbye in two dates' time?

Silence descended and for a while neither of them spoke, Sophie seemingly content to listen to the crack of the fire, the gentle sound of Fudge snoring. As for him, his mind continued to circle back to the one thing he didn't want to think about. 'Do you still believe in your spreadsheet idea?' He asked finally into the quiet, unable to shake the thought off.

She shifted. 'I still believe in the concept, yes.' His heart sank and she must have read something on his face because worry clouded her eyes. 'You said you were okay with carrying on, but if you're having second thoughts—'

'I'm not,' he interrupted quickly, panic shooting through him as he remembered the last time they'd discussed it. And the fact she'd almost stopped seeing him. 'I just wondered if you'd changed your mind at all.'

'I think,' she said slowly, 'that the idea of using a spreadsheet to help gain clarity on whether to carry on seeing someone still has merit, as long as you're very clear on the attributes you're scoring the person on. Basically, you have to know what you want in a partner.'

And he already knew he didn't fit that bill. Disappointment curdled in his stomach and he kicked himself for souring the mood by bringing the subject up. Why hadn't he stuck to his usual default mode and kept quiet? 'I'm just going to give the dogs a final walk before we get ready for bed.'

He jumped to his feet, feeling her eyes on him. Hopefully she'd put his eagerness down to a desire to snuggle down with her, which he absolutely did want to do. Once he'd cleared his head of the negative thoughts currently spiralling.

Aware of his movement, Fudge and Princess both opened their eyes, and immediately bounded over when he signalled.

'Do you want me to do anything?' Sophie wrapped her arms around her knees, the gesture looking defensive.

Realising his abrupt departure could be misconstrued, he crouched down and kissed her. 'Get ready for bed so we can pick up where we left off,' he told her hoarsely.

She smiled. 'Okay. I'll be waiting for you.'

He kept that image, and the promise in her eyes, in his mind as he walked round the campsite, dogs scampering in and out of the bushes. It helped settle him, bring him back to the present, so that by the time he returned to the tent his gut-wrenching disappointment was, at least temporarily, pushed to the back of his mind.

She was already snuggled in the sleeping bag when he settled the dogs into their beds in the outer part of their tent. After quickly brushing his teeth outside, he stripped to his boxers, unzipped the inner tent and went to join her, making sure to firmly zip it up again behind him. The thought of having two pairs of canine eyes watching him and Sophie ... yeah, not going to happen.

'Hey.' He slipped into the bag next to her, his body jumping for joy when he found her warm and naked. 'Christ, Sophie.' He ran his hands down her body, loving the softness of her skin, the toned muscles, the way her breath hitched as his fingers settled between her legs, finding her wet and ready for him. 'You're perfect,' he whispered, meaning it in every sense, how she looked, how she felt, who she was. If he had a spreadsheet, she'd be ten out of ten on everything that was important to him.

She smiled, grey eyes smoky with arousal. 'I'm definitely not.'

'You are to me.' Her head drew back, her eyes narrowing, studying him. Because he didn't want her reading him too accurately, he averted his gaze and began to trail kisses over her collar bone and down to the gentle curve of her breasts. 'God, Sophie.' *I love you*. He almost said it out loud. But it was impossible for him not to show her how he felt, so he began to make love to her, every kiss, every press of his body against hers sucking him further under her spell as he reacquainted himself with every dimple, every freckle.

Finally, she pleaded with him to stop. 'Not that I'm ungrateful, but enough. I need you inside me.'

Gladly, joyously, he complied, thrusting deep, his body shuddering with longing as she contracted around him. 'Fuck Sophie, I can't get enough of you.'

Her reply was a long groan as he began to move, shifting his hips but keeping a slow, languorous pace. She complained, squeezing him, pressing her hands into his buttocks. 'More. Faster. Harder.'

'Patience.' He shifted so he could look deep into her eyes. 'I want this to last. I want to stay buried inside you forever.'

And damn, the words had spilled out without him realising. Ignoring the way her eyes widened, he dragged his gaze away and bent to kiss her, tangling their tongues, diving into the sweetness of her, forgetting everything but the absolute perfection of being so intimately connected to her.

Chapter Thirty

F riday night had come round again and Sophie was putting the finishing touches to her make-up. The woman who stared back at her was both familiar and different. Same angular face, same shaped eyes. Her dark hair was longer though, and her eyes brighter, somehow. She sucked in a breath as a realisation came to her. She looked more like Rosie now. Not the Rosie in her final year, but the Rosie before that. The one full of life, who'd treated every day as an adventure.

'I wish you were still here,' she whispered, touching a hand to her heart. 'I wonder what you'd have made of Michael.' Then she smiled. 'Scratch that, I know you'd have loved him. How could anyone not?'

Adding a dash of colour to her lips – red to match the short dress – she walked out of her en-suite and into the living room. Out of habit she opened up the laptop she'd left on the kitchen island and toggled to Tab 8, her social life. She'd lapsed on a lot of the spreadsheet – why on earth had she spent so much time and effort on weird diet plans? But a few of the sheets she kept up. Places she wanted to visit for one, as she still had a desire to go travelling. The social life sheet was another one she liked to update as it acted like a diary, not just in what she had coming up, but what she'd done. She smiled as she saw the entry from the camping trip last week. And then added tonight's entertainment with a flourish. It wasn't something she'd ever thought she'd be looking forward to seeing. But then she'd never thought of going camping, or watching cricket, either.

Her phone buzzed with a message.

Michael: Just got off the train. See you in ten x

Smiling, she replied with a grinning emoji, followed by a kissing face emoji.

Idly she clicked on tab 9, the original Love Life spreadsheet. Because this had all started out as an experiment, she'd kept it up after each date, even adding the camping trip entries. Even now, Michael was only on 6.5.

Proof not that the idea of the spreadsheet was wrong, but how important it was to load it up with the right characteristics. Charisma, sociability. Sense of fun, spontaneity. All interesting qualities, but why had she ever thought they were so important? *You're too loud, too much.* Yes, Will had probably had something to do with it. She didn't want someone similar to her, though, she realised now. She wanted someone who understood her, helped her grow, listened to her. Someone she could rely on to be there for her, have her back.

She wanted Michael.

KATHRYN FREEMAN

She was so immersed in her thoughts, she didn't notice Grace letting Michael in.

Nor did she realise he was standing behind her before it was too late.

'I see I still have a way to go.'

She gave a guilty start and pushed the laptop shut. 'You scared the crap out of me.' Leaping off the stool, she turned to kiss him, but he remained rigid. Alarm surged through her. 'Michael, what you saw, it wasn't the real spreadsheet. Well, it was, but it isn't now, at least not in the sense that it means anything...' she trailed off, aware she was stumbling over the words and not making any sense.

He exhaled a long, deep breath. 'Forget it.'

But the way he wouldn't meet her eyes, the tense line of his jaw, the *Keep away from me* body language. It was clear forgetting it was the last thing he could do.

She caught sight of Grace, who screwed up her face in a gesture of both sympathy and *Good luck wriggling out of that one* before she disappeared off to her room.

Reaching for his hand, she found it balled into a fist. 'Please, don't let this spoil tonight. What you saw, it's nonsense. It doesn't reflect what I feel at all. In fact I've made a new spreadsheet.'

'Jesus.' He stepped back, shaking his head, expression tighter than she'd ever seen it. 'I don't want to talk about spreadsheets.'

'No. But I need to, because I don't want you thinking—'

'I'm not what you want?' He let out a humourless laugh. 'Isn't that exactly how this started?' His eyes flickered to the now closed laptop. 'At least I've improved.'

Her heart faltered. This was terrible. He looked so

shuttered, so closed off to her now. She didn't know if she could get through to him. 'This spreadsheet is nothing to do with you, and the incredible person you are. It was me being blind, being stupid as to what I wanted. Please, Michael,' she pleaded, wriggling her fingers round his, getting him to open his hand. 'Believe me when I say you're definitely who I want.'

He inhaled, glancing away from her, and though she could see the cogs of his brain turning, she couldn't work out what conclusions they were coming to. Should she tell him she was falling for him? Yet she wasn't sure how that would be received. He'd been distant before the camping trip, and though the trip itself had been amazing, there had been moments when he'd pulled back, especially after she'd mentioned the spreadsheet. It hung over them still, as it always had from the beginning.

'Michael?' The silence had gone on for so long she was starting to panic. 'I wish I'd never started this bloody spreadsheet, but if I hadn't, I would have missed out on getting to know you better.' She swallowed. 'I can't imagine not having you in my life.'

His eyes fluttered closed and his shoulders dropped as he exhaled. Then he cupped her face and bent to kiss her. Soft lips, just a gentle press, but enough to loosen everything that had felt so very tight for the last few minutes.

'The next time I see a spreadsheet with my name on it,' he said quietly. 'I'm not going to look.'

'But you can,' she protested. 'I want to show you the other one. It's a huge improvement.'

'I think,' he stated slowly, 'it's best if I stay far, far away from them.' Taking a step back, he slid his hands into his trouser pockets and studied her with an intense blue gaze. 'You look stunning.'

She could still feel a tension, but as it appeared he wanted to push past it, she smiled. 'Thank you. I could say the same to you.' Reaching up, she smoothed the lapels of his navy jacket. 'I'm not sure what I prefer you in most, the shorts, the cricket whites, or the suit.'

'You didn't like me in one suit.'

'It wasn't so much the suit,' she protested. 'It was that it looked like you couldn't be bothered. The jacket was crumpled, the tie pulled down.' She waved a hand. 'But I didn't know you'd come straight from work, and straight from saving someone's *life*.' How shallow she'd been, to judge him on what he'd been wearing. 'And FYI, style isn't on my revised spreadsheet. I'd tell you what is, but I know you don't want to talk about it and besides, we need to get moving or we'll be late.'

His left brow quirked upwards. 'Can I ask where we're going?'

She felt good about this date. It had taken a bit of thinking, but she was pretty confident that what she'd settled on would, for once, make his eyes light up. Because that was what she wanted to do now. Life was no longer about racing to cross things off a list to fulfil Rosie's dreams. It was about taking time to enjoy herself, to do things that made her happy. And she'd discovered making Michael happy did exactly that. 'We're going out for a posh meal where they have wine waiters as well as food waiters. And candles on the table. Then on to the theatre to see Les Mis.' She waited for the smile, the tension she could still read in him to disappear, but to her horror he stiffened. Maybe he'd misheard her. 'Les Misérables,' she qualified, then groaned. 'Oh, I bet you've seen it already, haven't you? Bummer. I never thought to check. I wanted it to be a nice surprise. You know, for once you get to do something in London *you* enjoy.'

Michael stood in front of the woman he loved, who was smiling so brightly at him, so pleased that she'd arranged a date to make him happy. And he couldn't smile back. God knows he wanted to, he was trying to force his mouth to curve, but his face felt too tight.

'What is it?' The joy in her beautiful eyes began to recede. 'What's wrong?' He watched her face fall. 'Oh no, did Jackie take you to see Les Mis? Is this a horrible reminder of a magical time you had with her—'

'No.' He clasped her by the shoulders, hating that he was ruining what she'd clearly planned to be a treat. For him.

But fuck, this wasn't what he wanted at all. He didn't want her changing her spreadsheet to suit him, just as he didn't want her planning a date to suit him. He wanted to be what she needed without changes, without compromise. Not only the man she wanted for now, but the one she wanted to spend forever with. Nine dates in though, and it was blindingly obvious he would never be that person. He didn't even need the very average 6.5 out of 10 score she'd given him to know that.

Her hand settled over his cheek. 'Talk to me, Michael.'

He stared down at her, his stomach clenching in frustration when he saw how agitated she looked. Frustration at himself, for upsetting her, and at the universe for toying with him like this, showing him for nine glorious dates what he could have had. If he'd been a different man.

'Today was your choice,' he told her hoarsely. 'It's supposed to be what *you* want to do.'

'But this *is* what I want to do.'

He let out an incredulous laugh. 'You took me trapezing, to a bar where they dance on tables. To a karaoke club and a place where you drink cocktails and play crazy golf. Now you tell me your idea of a Friday night is to go out for a sedate meal and on to the theatre?'

A frown blemished her forehead and her eyes brimmed with hurt. 'I wanted to make you happy.'

Emotion balled in his throat and he had to step away, to take a breath and try and steady himself. 'But you shouldn't have to change to suit me.'

She shook her head, her frustration now mirroring his. 'I don't understand. Why are you being like this?' Her voice trembled. 'I was so excited about tonight, seeing you again, showing you a different side to London.' She raised tear-filled eyes to his. 'I just wanted to do something nice to show you how much I missed you.'

His heart splintered as tears rolled down her cheeks. 'Oh God, Sophie, please. Don't cry.' He was ruining everything. Not just tonight, but the chance of any sort of relationship with her in the future, even if it was only friends. 'I'm sorry. I'm being an ungrateful prick.' He bent to kiss her, the taste of salt from her tears deepening his shame. 'I missed you, too,' he told her, moving to trail kisses down her cheek, across her chin before shifting to her neck, burrowing his nose in her soft hair. 'So much it terrifies me.'

Her hands wound round his neck and he felt her body relax

against his. 'How about you go back outside and ring the bell so we start tonight again?' she whispered. 'I can't believe Grace answered the bloody door. She usually can't be arsed.'

He smiled, telling himself he could do this. Pretend he didn't know he was still only a six and a bit out of ten. Pretend he was in a relationship, and not on date nine of a dating experiment. Pretend he was everything this woman wanted. 'Didn't you say we were running late?'

She looked at her watch. 'Bollocks. Yes. We'll have to skip the redo and go straight to the restaurant.'

Because she still looked agitated, the vitality that was so much a part of her, now dimmed, he put a hand on her arm, halting her progress towards the door. Then he kissed her. A full on, pushing her against the island, settling his hips against hers, diving his tongue into the sweetness of her mouth, kiss. When he broke away his heart was galloping. 'How about we skip the restaurant?'

Cheeks flushed, she nodded. 'We can share a box of Maltesers in the theatre instead.'

He smiled, tucking a wayward strand of hair behind her ear. 'This from the woman who sent me a list of dietary requirements when I made her a meal.'

Clasping his hand, she led him down the hallway towards her bedroom. 'You taught me there are more important things in life.'

It wasn't until the following morning, when he sat at the island and watched Sophie fry bacon while she rattled off a whole list of other plays and musicals she now wanted to see because Les

Mis had been so awesome, that the impossibility of it all came back to hit Michael with the force of an out of control truck.

Sophie turned, picking up a plate loaded with buttered bread. 'Maybe I should ask Mum which show we should see next. She's always going…' She faltered as her eyes met his. 'Michael?'

'I'm sorry.' Carefully he took the pan out of her hands and rested it back on the stove. 'I can't do this anymore.'

'You can't eat bacon?'

He was doing the sensible thing. But why did it feel so wrong? Why did he feel sick to his stomach? 'I can't be part of this … experiment anymore. I know we've got one date left still, but I doubt you need that to prove your theory.'

'Prove my … God, is that really what you think this is about now?' Her face paled, her expression one of disbelief. 'I've stopped counting dates. I thought you had, too. I thought we were dating. For real.'

'The dates were real. What I feel for you is real.' Shit, his heart felt like it was breaking in two. 'But I can't be someone's less than perfect again.'

'What … what do you mean?' She stared back at him, looking like she'd been sucker punched. 'Please don't tell me you're talking about that sodding spreadsheet again because I told you, the old one doesn't matter anymore.'

'But don't you see, it does.' How could he make her understand he was doing this not just to protect himself, but to help *her*? 'I'm like the sofa that came with the house you just bought. It wasn't the sofa you had your eye on before moving, but it's easy to keep it because it's already there, and it's comfortable.' *I tried hard to prefer you.* Jackie's fucking words haunted him even now. 'In time though, you'll realise it's not what you wanted after all. And you'll trade it in for the one you originally planned.'

She let out a growl of annoyance. 'Why are you talking about bloody sofas? I want to carry on seeing you. If you want to carry on seeing me, what's the problem?'

Tears pricked at his eyelids. Shit, he had to get away before he caved. Before he got down on his knees and begged her to keep him. 'The problem is you want, you *deserve*, a man who scores ten out of ten,' he told her roughly, emotion clawing at him. 'Not six and a bit out of ten.'

Her eyes flashed – anger or pain? 'You're breaking up with me over some dumb spreadsheet I told you was no longer valid and you've never believed in anyway? Seriously?'

'No.' It frustrated him that she didn't understand. 'I'm breaking up with you now, to save you breaking up with me further down the line.'

'Oh right, so I'm supposed to feel grateful, am I? You're doing me a favour?' Her voice trembled, eyes glistening with tears. 'Well guess what, it doesn't feel like that.' His heart crumpled as he watched tears flow down her cheeks for the second time in twenty-four hours. 'It feels like you've had enough and you want out, but you're doing it in a really shitty underhand way.'

Christ, he really was awful at communicating. 'No, you've got this all wrong. I don't *want* out. I just … shit.' Exasperated, emotionally wrung out, he hung his head, searching desperately for the words he should be saying. But the only ones that came back to him were *I love you* and he'd already told one woman he loved her and had his words, and his heart, rejected. He couldn't eviscerate himself like that again. Couldn't give her his heart, knowing he'd wake up every day wondering if this was the day she'd give it back to him.

'You need to go.' Sophie clattered the frying pan into the sink. 'You miss out on bacon sandwiches and seeing more of me but hey, your loss.'

'It *is* my loss.' The realisation this was it. That he might never see her again, even in a friends only capacity, rocked him back and he clutched at the island for support, his knees buckling under the weight of his loss. 'This time with you has absolutely been the best time of my life.' Tears blurred his vision and he choked on the last few words. 'Thank you for giving me the chance to get to know you.'

She swallowed, her watery gaze raking his. 'That sounds like goodbye and I don't want to say goodbye. Please, let's talk about this.'

Her eyes pleaded with him, and his heart took another wrench.

But if he opened his mouth, words would come out that wouldn't do either of them any good. She didn't need to know how heartbroken he was, because she'd want him to stay, want them to carry on. And that was wrong for both of them. 'I'm sorry, I can't.'

His chest felt like a hollow shell as he lurched towards the door, and when he shut it behind him, the finality of the sound sent a wave of desolation through him.

As he made his way back to the station, all he could think was he might never see her again.

Chapter Thirty-One

Six weeks later

Sophie threw her bag on the floor, dragged off her shoes and went to collapse on the sofa.

Another date. Another frigging disaster.

'I don't want to talk about it.'

Ignoring the startled looks coming from Ava and Grace in the kitchen, she reached for the laptop on the coffee table and opened up the spreadsheet. The new spreadsheet. The one that listed all the qualities she now knew for certain she wanted in a man.

'Oh boy, I think we have another failure on our hands.' Ava's voice wafted over to her from the kitchen.

'How many do you think this one scored?' Grace's voice was deliberately loud enough for Sophie to hear. 'I'm betting on three.'

'That high?' Ava, too, was talking at full volume. 'The last one only got two point two.'

'I don't know why she bothers with the spreadsheet.' Grace again, and Sophie knew what she was going to say next because they'd said it after each of the three dates she'd had in the last two weeks. 'Kind of pointless when you've already found your ten out of ten.'

'Will you two shut up, I'm trying to concentrate,' Sophie complained as she typed a one in the Ability to Listen column. And that was being generous. Beyond telling Max her name and age, she didn't think she'd actually spoken for the first half an hour.

'Seriously, Soph.' Ava came to sit next to her. She knew she was in trouble when Grace sat on the other side. Being surrounded was never a good sign. 'This has got to stop.'

'I don't know what you're talking about,' she protested.

Gently Ava prized the laptop from her hands and put it back on the coffee table. 'Since you and Michael stopped seeing each other—'

'Since he dumped me.'

Grace sighed. 'You told us he said he didn't want out. That he was breaking up with you to save you from breaking up with him later. Correct?'

He had said both those things. She remembered it clearly. Just as she remembered him saying he couldn't be anyone's less than perfect again. Her heart faltered as she recalled his words, the look of utter devastation on his face when he'd said them. But he'd not given her a chance to tell him he was *her* idea of perfect. 'He also said he couldn't do us anymore,' she reminded them, reminded herself. 'And he walked out despite me pleading with him to talk.' That had hurt most of all. If he'd really wanted to be with her, wouldn't he have at least listened to her side of things?

'In his defence, he knew he was still a red line on your spreadsheet, Soph,' Grace argued. 'The guy must have been gutted. No wonder he figured it was time to jump before he was pushed.'

'That was the *old* frigging spreadsheet,' Sophie reminded her. 'And I told him that but he wouldn't listen. He kept banging on about sofas.' She'd not had a clue what he'd meant at the time. Afterwards, when her brain had begun to unfreeze, she thought she knew, but felt insulted by it. As if her heart was capable of falling for just anyone who happened to hang around her long enough.

'Look.' Grace took hold of her hands. 'All we're saying is since you stopped seeing Michael, you've become really weird.'

Before Sophie could complain, Ava put her hands over Grace's. 'What our eloquent friend means, is you're back to this spreadsheet obsession again, only worse. I mean, look at you, you've not even taken your coat off.'

She glanced down at the red wool coat she was still wearing and had to admit they had a point. But she didn't know how else to cope with this hollow feeling in her chest. This sense that everything in her life was now pointless. 'Spreadsheets helped me after I lost Rosie.' Emotion clogged her throat. 'I thought they could help me again.' Yet even as she said it, she could see Michael's face, eyes filled with concern. He'd be horrified to know she was going backwards, retreating into the world of crossing things off, getting them done.

'Oh, Soph,' Ava said quietly.

She felt arms encircle her from either side and for a few moments they sat there, huddled together in silence.

'You know what would help you more,' Grace said after a while.

She wiped at her cheeks, surprised to find they were wet. 'What?'

'Phone the bloody man.' Grace held her chin and forced her to look at her. 'Seriously, what are you doing, wasting your time on these dating apps when you've already found your guy?'

It sounded so simple, yet she'd been here before. She'd opened her heart to Will, asked him to live with her. And bluntly been told he liked her, but not *that* much. What if Michael felt the same? For all his words, what if they had just been his way of letting her down gently? 'I'll think about it.'

Michael was in a crowd of people, yet he'd never felt so alone. It was the cricket awards evening and as he sat on a table with Betty and Dennis, everywhere he looked, everyone he met, only served to remind him of Sophie, and what he'd lost.

What you've given up. He shoved the unhelpful thought away. He couldn't give up something he'd never had in the first place. Sophie had only ever been on loan.

'No Sophie today?' Hamza scanned the pavilion, as if expecting to see her. Beside Hamza stood Hattie, and Michael couldn't fail to spot the fact they were holding hands. He should be delighted, but the sight only reinforced his loss. Especially as it had been Sophie's magic that had helped Hamza and Hattie get together.

'No.'

He knew his answer to Hamza had been too curt when the man took a step back. 'Ooookay.'

'Michael decided he didn't want to see her again,' Betty interrupted. 'Only he can tell you why. I'm sure I don't know, since she was the best thing to ever happen to him. Can't see him finding anyone else even half as lovely as Sophie,' she added pointedly.

'Gran.' He received a glare in response to his use of the name, but uncaring, he glared back. 'While you're interfering in my business, I'll call you what I like.' She blinked, and as hurt shot across her face, shame ploughed through him.

'If you disrespect Betty like that again, I'm going to ask you to leave.'

Michael looked over in shock at Dennis. Always smiling, softly spoken, Dennis. He'd never heard the man sound so angry. Realising he'd been way out of order, Michael rose stiffly to his feet and nodded to both Dennis and Hamza. 'I apologise. Please excuse me, I'm going to get some air.' Before he left, he bent and kissed Betty's cheek. 'Forgive me, I'm being an arse.'

He rushed down the stairs and flung the door open, stepping gratefully into the cool October evening.

Fuck.

Ever since he'd ended things with Sophie, his life had been a mess. He'd been a mess. Nothing felt the same anymore. He had sod all to look forward to. Walks no longer gave him peace because they reminded him of her. He daren't get out the tent because, ditto. His weekends dragged, his evenings were spent obsessively checking his phone in case he'd missed a message. Even Fudge kept looking at him in sympathy, as if she knew he'd made a catastrophic error in judgement.

But had he? Wouldn't this awful longing, this deep ache in his chest have happened at some point anyway?

You'll never know.

And that was the crux of it, why he tossed and turned at night, unable to sleep. He'd thrown in the towel, given up on someone who had the ability to take him out of himself, make him feel lighter, happier, a man with zest. And for what? Because he'd got scared of losing her? Which is exactly where he was anyway?

A hand touched his arm, and he swirled round to find Betty looking up at him in concern. Betty, the woman who'd put her life on pause to help him through the loss of his mum. Who'd shown him nothing but love and support. And who he'd just snapped at like some ungrateful git. Emotion choking him, he wrapped his arms around her. 'I'm so sorry. Talking to you like that. It was unforgivable. Dennis should have thrown me straight out.'

She huffed. 'Nonsense. I've given him a flea in his ear for interfering.' She drew back, looked at him with such love he felt his eyes well. 'I won't have him, or anyone, coming between you and me. Besides, I was wrong to say what I did in front of everyone. I never did learn the art of thinking before speaking.'

He laughed softly, keeping his arms around her. 'Which is part of what I love about you. I always knew where I stood, if you were happy with me or cross.' He peered down at her. 'And I know you're cross with me now.'

Her shoulders rose and fell as she sighed. 'I'm not cross. I just don't understand.'

He paused, looking out across the cricket field. 'I didn't tell you, because I was too gutted, but when I went to see Sophie she didn't realise I was there at first, and she had the spreadsheet open with my score on it.' Everything inside him clenched and tightened. 'It was six and a half.' He tried to keep the bitterness out of his voice but the hurt was still there, a raw, angry wound that refused to heal. 'Not even above the seven she had as her cut off to keep seeing someone or not.'

'Oh Michael.' Her arms tightened around him, and though her body felt frail, the strength in that hug was the same as it had always been. 'No wonder you bailed.'

That's exactly what he'd done. Abandoned her. Abandoned any hope of seeing her again. Any hope that there could ever be a *them*.

'I feel like a coward,' he admitted. 'Thrown away something remarkable, because I was too scared to risk another detonating blow to my ego.'

'Your ego is too fragile for the man you are.' Betty placed a hand on each of his arms and stared up at him. '*You* are remarkable. And you deserve someone equally special. I don't know what was going on with Sophie and that silly scoring, but the woman I met didn't look at you as a man she was only with until she found someone better. She looked at you with the expression of a woman who'd found exactly what she'd been waiting for.'

He couldn't see how that was true, but he appreciated Betty's attempt to bolster his confidence.

'I'd better go back before Dennis gets it into his head to come down and tell you off again, the daft sod. Are you coming?'

He smiled at her. 'I'll be there in a minute.'

After she'd disappeared inside he went to sit on a bench. Drawing out his phone, his fingers hovered over the message app. He felt too vulnerable, too raw to show his hand, but he could at least reach out to her. Let her know he was thinking of her. See if she was still talking to him. After a long deliberation, he went with:

At the cricket awards. Everyone is asking after you. M x

Then he held his breath, watching as the message showed it had been sent. Then that it had been read.

Seconds ticked by. Followed by minutes. The bench felt cold beneath him, the back rigid and unforgiving. She wasn't going to reply.

Cold seeped into his body as disappointment took hold. But just as he thrust the damn phone back into his pocket, it beeped. And beeped again. He dragged it out so fast, it flew out of his hands and onto the grass.

Diving down to pick it up, he stared at the messages.

Sophie: Say hello to them all. And give dear Betty a hug from me.

Sophie: Oh and I'm sending a woof to Princess and an ear fondle to Fudge. S x

He let out a long, slow breath. Okay, there was no hug for him, no fondle - it was as safe as his message had been. But she had replied. Was it a start? Could he gradually build up the messages until he at least felt she was still in his life?

Only time would tell, but as he made his way back inside, a tiny part of the black cloud surrounding him, lifted.

Chapter Thirty-Two

Zumba classes weren't what they used to be. Jade still smiled at her, but it was no longer the wide, friendly smile she used to give her BM, before Michael. It was more the polite smile of a Zumba teacher to her student.

'Are you okay?' Grace nudged her as they walked together towards the sports hall. Ava had cried off today, saying she felt too tired. Sophie suspected she'd gone to see Ethan as the pair of them were so loved up now it was sickening. Okay, it was beautiful and the only sickening feeling she had was of jealousy. 'You're all twitchy.'

Sophie tried to relax her muscles. 'I'm just wondering what sort of welcome Jade will give me today.'

'Yeah, she's a bit more reserved with us all now, isn't she? It's like she's chosen a side and it isn't ours.'

'But he was the one who dumped *me*.' Sophie felt her anger rising. 'I don't see how she can be off with me for her brother-in-law deciding to end things. If it was my choice we'd still be together.' She heaved out a sigh. 'He texted me on Saturday.'

Grace snapped her head round. 'And?'

'And … nothing.' She'd been so excited to receive the message. And so let down to read it. 'He was letting me know the cricket crowd were asking after me.'

Grace snorted. 'Bollocks. He was reaching out to you.'

Sophie shrugged, her heart twisting. 'I don't want to be the person he feels he has to message now and again to make himself feel less guilty.'

When they arrived inside the hall, Jade wasn't there to greet them.

'Where's Jade?' Sophie asked as the replacement teacher – who introduced herself as Suzie – welcomed them inside.

'She had a last-minute family emergency.'

'Oh no.' Sophie looked at Suzie in concern. 'Nothing wrong with Dave or Olivia I hope?'

'Oh no. I think she said it was her gran? Or maybe Dave's gran?'

Sophie's stomach fell. 'Betty? Did she say what was wrong?'

'She just said this lady had been admitted to hospital.' Suzie gave her an apologetic shrug. 'Sorry, I can't remember if she said why. Just that she needed to go and see her.'

Worry knotted Sophie's stomach and she thanked Suzie before turning to Grace. 'I—'

'Need to phone Michael,' Grace interrupted. 'Sure, no problem. I'll grab us a place at the back.'

Sophie's hands shook as she dug her phone out of her bag. Heart in her mouth, she phoned Michael but it went into voicemail. Damn it. Ending the call, she tried Jade instead.

'Hi Sophie.' Jade answered. 'I guess you're phoning about Betty.'

'Yes, I just heard she's in hospital.'

'That's right. Michael phoned to tell us he thinks she has pneumonia. We're off to see her now.'

Sophie put a hand over her heart, feeling it gallop. 'Is she going to be okay? Did he say if it was serious?'

'He said she told him to stop being a fusspot.' Sophie could hear the smile in Jade's voice, because that was so typical Betty, but then Jade sighed. 'I could tell he was worried though.'

'I tried to phone him but it went to voicemail.'

'He's at the hospital, so maybe he's had to turn his phone off? But I'll tell him you called.'

'Thanks. Please give Betty a big hug from me.'

'I will.' She paused. 'And Michael?'

'I'm not sure he'd want one.'

Jade let out a dismissive sound. 'That's rubbish and you know it.'

'Do I?'

'Come on Sophie, that man adores you. It's just a shame you've never appreciated what a bloody great catch he is.'

The edge to her voice told Sophie she hadn't been imagining Jade's cooling off towards her. 'I *do* appreciate it,' she told her with quiet emphasis. 'Just as I appreciate he's way out of my league. Whatever you think happened between us, you're wrong.'

Jade exhaled sharply. 'Look, I'm not getting into an argument about this, it's your business. All I know is that's twice he's seen a spreadsheet he wasn't supposed to have done. And twice he must have felt he's been kicked in the teeth by you, though of course he'd never say. Before you go thinking he's been badmouthing you, I only know about the last spreadsheet because I was so livid that he'd ended things with you, I had a right go at him. It took a whole evening of me berating him before he cracked and admitted why he'd done it. At least it explained why he'd looked so frigging awful.' Her voice softened. 'But I know you care about Betty, so I promise to let you know how she is after I've seen her.'

'Thank you.' As she walked back into the Zumba class, Sophie's mind stumbled over the implications of what Jade had said. Why did Michael look so awful if ending things was his choice?

But Betty was ill, and she had to be the focus right now.

She was just about to take her position next to Grace, when her phone lit up with a call. After looking at the caller ID, she rushed back out again.

'Hey.'

'Sorry I missed your call.'

The sound of Michael's voice, low, with a slight husk to it, sent her heart cartwheeling. 'I heard about Betty. I wanted to find out how she was.'

'She's got pneumonia. Hopefully we've got her into hospital early enough.' His voice shook a little. Enough for her to know he was scared. 'Time will tell. For now she's comfortable. Of course she kicked up a stink about being admitted.'

'I can imagine.' It wasn't hard to picture Betty pointing out all the reasons she shouldn't be taking up a precious hospital bed. 'And you, Michael. How are *you*?'

'I'll be better when I know she's on the mend.'

Her heart ached for him. Betty wasn't just his grandma. She was his mum. The woman he'd centred his life around. 'She's going to be okay. There's no way Betty will let something as mundane as pneumonia knock her back for long.'

His exhale sounded weary. 'I want to think that.'

'What can I do? How can I help?' *Please ask me to come and sit with you.*

The following silence felt heavy with emotion. When he finally spoke, the break in his voice was unmistakable. 'Send her some of your sparkle, your boundless energy. Your positivity.'

Tears welled in her eyes and Sophie had to blink several times before she could talk. 'Consider it done. And Michael. If you need someone to talk to, any time of the day or night, phone me. I'm here for you.'

'Thank you.' She heard him drag in a breath. Imagined him thrusting a hand through his hair. 'That means more than you can possibly know.'

When he ended the call, she slumped against the wall of the hall and gave in to the tears that had been building since she'd first heard his voice. She didn't want to be here, on the end of the phone. She wanted to be there, with him. Holding him, giving him the strength he'd given her when she'd cried over Rosie.

But he'd ended them, and whatever his real reason for doing that, didn't she have to respect his wishes?

———

Michael was sat by Betty's bed in a small room at the back of the ward. Whether it was a perk of being the relative of a doctor, or just hospital policy considering her age and condition, he didn't know but he was grateful for the privacy.

And for the ward staff agreeing to let him stay with her tonight.

He nearly jumped out of his skin when Dave put a hand on his shoulder.

'Here you go, the shot of caffeine you requested.'

Gratefully he took the proffered coffee. Experience told him it would taste like engine oil, but he needed the pick me up. And he needed the heat because though the hospital was warm, inside he felt cold as ice.

'I'm afraid we need to go back now, bro. The babysitter can't stay beyond ten.'

Out of habit, Michael glanced at his watch and saw it was already nine o'clock. Where had the day gone? 'Of course.' He stood to hug his brother, and Jade who was hovering in the doorway. 'Thanks for coming. I really appreciate it.'

'No problem. You know you can go home, too.' Dave nodded over at Betty, who seemed so frail against the white sheets of the bed. She had an oxygen tube up her nose, machines monitoring her vitals, a drip running into her hand. It crumpled his heart every time he looked at her. 'She's stable. The staff will let you know if anything changes.'

'But what if she takes a turn for the worse and I'm not here?' Fuck, his eyes were burning again. He wasn't afraid to cry, but he absolutely refused to do it in front of anyone. Even his brother.

Dave exhaled heavily. 'Fine. I can hardly tell you not to worry, when you're the bloody doctor.'

That was the trouble. Michael knew exactly how serious pneumonia could be in someone Betty's age. The risk of complications: pleurisy, respiratory failure, sepsis. He could drive himself crazy thinking about it.

She's on antibiotics. She's being monitored 24/7. He chanted the words silently to himself.

'But she will be okay,' Dave asserted firmly. 'No way would she let something as common as pneumonia defeat her.'

Michael felt a pang in his chest. 'Sophie said the same thing.'

'Ah.'

'What's *ah* supposed to mean?'

His brother shrugged. 'Nothing. Just interested that the pair of you are still talking.'

'We're not.' He rubbed at the bloody great knot he could feel at the back of his neck. 'She phoned to ask about Betty, that's all.'

'Okay, okay.'

Jade cleared her throat. 'So that's not Sophie I saw sitting in the waiting area outside?'

'What?' Michael swung his head round to look at her.

'Sophie's waiting round the corner, Michael.'

His heart lurched. She'd come? When he'd asked her to send some of her sparkle, he'd never for one moment imagined she'd do it in person.

Dimly he was aware of Jade and Dave saying goodbye. For a few minutes after they left he remained sitting by Betty's bed, head in his hands, trying to get his emotions on an even keel. 'I'm not sure I can do this,' he told the sleeping Betty. 'I'm terrified when I see her I'll embarrass us both and burst into tears.'

Of course she couldn't hear him, but he imagined if she could, she'd tell him to stop thinking, stop hesitating and just go to see the person he needed more than anyone else.

His heart tumbled into his throat when he caught sight of the lone figure sitting on a plastic chair. Hair longer than he remembered, which suited her, softened some of the angularity of her face. That same gorgeous face looked up when she heard him, and he was so undone by the fact she was here, his knees almost buckled.

'Michael.' She stood up abruptly and rushed over, but when she reached him she stopped, as if unsure what to do next. 'How is she?'

His hands itched to hold her, his body craved to be held, but he forced the emotion back, unwilling to push himself where he wasn't wanted. 'Asleep. Comfortable,' he added, to reassure her.

Sophie twisted her hands. 'I'm sorry, but I couldn't keep away.' She glanced down at her vivid purple leggings. 'I was about to go to Zumba but when I knew what had happened I couldn't do it, so I jumped on a train. I wasn't sure about visiting hours but saying your name was apparently enough to let me in.' Her gaze drifted up to his. 'I wanted to find out how she was for myself.' She swallowed. 'And I wanted to see you.'

Whatever she saw in his expression was clearly enough reassurance of her welcome because she reached up and did the one thing he needed. She wrapped her arms around him and hugged him tight.

Gratefully, he melted into her embrace, inhaling the sweet scent of her, absorbing her warmth, her strength. That feeling of coming home, where everything was safe. Everything would be alright.

He couldn't say how long they remained like that, holding each other. Only that when he finally drew back, he felt less alone, less fragile. 'Do you want to see her?'

'If that's okay?'

He nodded. 'Of course.'

He heard Sophie's intake of breath when she first saw Betty, and he gave her arm a squeeze.

'Sorry,' she whispered. 'It's hard to see her without that twinkle in her eyes, a smile on her face.' She shook herself and gave his arm an encouraging squeeze. 'But give her a couple of days and both will be back.'

'Yes.' His throat felt like it had a boulder wedged inside.

As he watched silently, Sophie went up to the bed and planted a soft kiss on Betty's hand – the one without the cannula. He was on emotion overload seeing one of the women he loved showing such clear affection for the other.

Because his legs felt shaky, he drew up another chair and motioned for Sophie to sit next to him.

'How long have you been here?'

The concern in her expression suggested his brother had been right when he'd eloquently told him he looked like shit. 'Since early this morning.' He didn't think he'd ever forget the panic at seeing Betty so breathless when he'd knocked on her bedroom door with her usual morning cuppa. 'She didn't want to come here. I had to practically push her into the car.' His heart lurched at the memory. Maybe it was because he was shattered, maybe it was Sophie's presence, but before he knew it, words tumbled, uncensored, out of him. 'What if I didn't get her here early enough? I knew she'd been unwell the last few days but she kept telling me she was okay.' His insides clenched and he hung his head. 'I call myself a doctor yet I took her word for it. I didn't like the sound of her cough yesterday but I didn't listen to her chest.' His voice cracked as shame washed through him. 'I didn't even take her fucking temperature until this morning.'

'Stop it.' Sophie clung to his arm. 'She wasn't ready to go to hospital yesterday – she'd have fought you tooth and nail. The fact she's here now, receiving the care she needs, is down to you. If she'd been living on her own she'd not even have phoned for the doctor.'

The truth of her words soothed him. 'Thank you,' he said after a few minutes.

She smiled. 'I like being thanked, but what for, exactly?'

'For being here.' He risked taking her hand. 'It means a great deal.'

She leant against him, her fingers tightening around his. 'For me, too.'

Was that because she wanted to be here for Betty? Or was there a chance she wanted to be here for him, too?

Chapter Thirty-Three

On Saturday Sophie once again took the train to Little Brook – this time to visit Betty. Nostalgia swamped her as she saw Michael waiting for her on the platform. But there was no Fudge with daisies between her teeth and no hand holding. Only a strained smile and an unsatisfyingly polite peck on her cheek.

Some of her anguish was soothed when she saw the transformation in Betty. Back at home now, she was sat on the sofa with her feet up, a smile on her face and that adorable twinkle back in her eyes. According to Michael, who'd given her regular updates since putting her on the train Monday evening, Betty still coughed and tired very easily. According to Betty, who she'd phoned yesterday, her grandson was being melodramatic and she was right as rain.

Either way, Betty was most definitely on the mend. And back to ordering her grandson around.

'We need some nice cakes,' she told Michael now. Sophie was pleased to see he also looked a lot better than he had on

Monday, his face back to handsome instead of haggard. There was still a tension she didn't like though. Especially as she thought she might be the cause.

But sod it, so what if he didn't want her here? *Betty* had invited her.

Michael gave his grandma a long-suffering look. 'We have biscuits.'

Betty waved a hand at him. 'I don't want biscuits. I want a nice cake, and so does our guest, don't you dear.'

Sophie, biting back a smile, nodded. 'Absolutely. One with fresh cream, preferably.'

'Nice. With fresh cream.' He sighed, giving them both a mild look. 'Fine.'

'And take the dogs with you. They could both do with the exercise.'

'I took them out this morning,' he protested. Then raised his eyes to the ceiling. 'Why am I even trying to argue?'

She watched him whistle to the dogs, Princess immediately scampering over to him, tail all a flutter as she realised she was going out. Fudge walked sedately over, receiving an ear fondle. Sophie's heart tugged. God, she wanted those hands fondling her so much she ached.

Once the trio had stepped out, she turned to ask Betty if she'd seen Dennis recently, only to find the old lady with a smug expression on her face. 'What?'

Betty gave her an approving smile. 'You're in love with him.'

'I...' Sophie frowned, not sure she wanted to give herself away. 'Why do you think that?'

'I only had to look at your face as you watched him. The question is, what are we going to do about it?'

'We?' Sophie burst out laughing. 'Aren't you meant to be recuperating? Taking things easy?' Suddenly she realised what had just happened. 'You didn't want the cakes, did you? You were getting him out of the house so you could grill me.'

Betty nodded in satisfaction. 'I knew you were smart. Now prove to me just how smart by telling me why you're still scoring him down on that daft spreadsheet of yours when we both know you think he's the best man you're ever going to come across.'

'Wow, I can see you're not going to hold any punches.'

'I want him happy.' Her face softened, her eyes glistening. 'He's very precious to me.'

'Oh Betty.' Sophie jumped out of her seat and went sit next to her. Wrapping her arms around the old lady, she whispered. 'He's very precious to me, too.'

Betty sniffed and fumbled around on the coffee table for a tissue. 'I know, dear. That's why I wanted to get you alone so I could give you a push. I tried pushing Michael but he got very defensive and told me to leave it alone. Of course then I phoned Jade to find out what was going on, and she said she'd prized it out of him that he'd seen your spreadsheet again.'

'He saw my old spreadsheet.' Sophie exhaled in frustration. 'I wanted to show him the new one, the one where he's a ten out of flipping ten, but he wouldn't listen to me. In fact he said he *couldn't* listen to me. Then he walked out.'

Betty patted her hand. 'And I'm sure that must have hurt.'

'It devastated me.' Sophie felt her own eyes filling now and grabbed at one of the tissues. 'But he's the one who wanted out, not me, so it's him you need to talk to.'

Betty nodded, but her expression was achingly sad. 'I'm very afraid he won't listen.' Heaving out a sigh, she settled back on the sofa. 'When he was a boy, he was such a happy thing, so carefree even after his father walked out. But then my dear daughter died, leaving him and his brother orphans. I did my best to given them a home life, but I confess I did rather depend on Michael, who was the oldest. My Paddy had died the year before and I suppose I started to treat Michael as the man of the house. Of course being Michael he didn't complain, just took on the responsibilities of helping me and his brother, but I realise now it must have taken a toll on him. Deprived him of the rest of his childhood and made him grow up too fast.' She smiled sadly. 'That carefree young boy was no longer. The Michael who lived with me was a far more serious soul.'

'Hey, don't you start being hard on yourself. You gave two grieving boys a home.' Sophie nudged Betty. 'Michael has nothing but utter adoration and love for you, so you must have done something right.'

She smiled. 'Ah, he's not hard to please. Just needs someone to love him.' Betty paused, looking at Sophie. 'But I'm afraid he's not had much success on that front. Jackie broke his heart, not only going off with his best friend like she did, but by making him feel he was inadequate.'

Sophie bristled. 'I don't know who this Ian bloke was, but no way was he a better man than Michael.'

'Of course he wasn't. But as Jackie pointed out, Ian was more outgoing, more fun to be with.'

Sophie felt her insides shrivel. 'And then I came along and reaffirmed exactly what Jackie had said. Made him feel he was boring.'

'I'm afraid so.'

Sophie put her head in her hands. She'd known Jackie's betrayal had hurt Michael, but it was only now she realised the full extent of how much her own scoring of him must have damaged his already fragile confidence. *Jackie didn't want steady, she wanted exciting.* He'd told her that, yet she'd not fully appreciated what he was saying. He thought she was like Jackie, and why wouldn't he, because that's exactly what her first spreadsheet had been geared towards. 'But he's far, far from boring.' She sat up and looked Betty in the eye. 'He's the most incredible man I've ever met, and even if he doesn't want to get back with me, I'm going to make him see that.'

Betty clasped her hands. 'Thank you, dear. And trust me, whatever he says, that man adores you. When he was going out with you, I was even starting to see the boy I knew again. He was so *happy*.' She blew her nose. 'That's all I want, to see him happy again.'

'Me, too.' Sophie hugged Betty close. 'Me, too.' She let out a watery laugh. 'But I'd kind of like to see both of us happy, too. Speaking of happy, how is Dennis?'

Betty's whole face lit up. 'He's popping round later, so you can see for yourself. The hospital only allowed me out because I lived with my doctor grandson, and there was this daft old man who promised to look after me when Michael was at work.'

'Dennis won't thank you for calling him an old man.'

Betty chortled. 'Probably not, but if he's willing to play nursemaid to a woman in her eighties, he can't object to daft, can he?'

Sophie eyed Betty fondly. 'He's far from daft, Betty. In fact I'd say knowing you've found your person and fighting for them is the sign of high intelligence.'

And she was going to prove that Dennis wasn't the only one with a brain.

Michael settled the bakery box onto the kitchen worktop. Inside were six cream cakes – one of each variety because he didn't know what defined a "nice" cake.

Princess looked up at him, nose in the air, but he shook his head. 'Not for you.' Then, because she frowned – yep, he hadn't realised until he'd been introduced to the chihuahua that dogs could do that – he bent to pick her up. 'Come on you, let's go and find Betty.'

He halted outside the living room door, watching as Sophie and Betty talked animatedly. It was so good to see his gran coming back to him. At the beginning of the week he'd been terrified of losing her, but she was clearly made of sterner stuff than he'd given her credit for. Thank God. Because he had a feeling there was a few more chapters left in her life yet. Chapters including a twilight romance.

'Ah, there you are, dear.' Betty waved him in. 'I was just telling Sophie how I'm going to take a nap before Dennis comes round.'

'You are?' She'd not done that yesterday, despite him insisting. 'What about the cakes?' That he'd just walked nearly two miles to fetch.

'Oh, I'll eat them later. Rest is what the doctor ordered, isn't it?' She gave him a serene smile and began to push up onto her feet.

Immediately he lunged forward, but he was beaten by Sophie, who held onto Betty's arm. 'Here, let me help you.'

His action had propelled him into close proximity, and as Sophie's familiar scent invaded his nostrils, he took a deep breath. He'd missed her. Not in a *What a shame he couldn't phone her* sort of way but in a *total mind and body deep, painful longing* way. His life had gone back to monochrome.

Once Betty was on her feet, she shooed them both away. 'I'm perfectly capable of making my own way to my room.' She glared at him. 'Especially now my grandson has transferred my bed downstairs.'

Because you found it hard enough climbing the stairs before the pneumonia. He held back the comment, not wanting to draw attention to her frailty. 'It's better down here. You have a lovely view of the garden.' And double doors he could open and let the garden in, even if she wasn't up to going out.

'I suppose.' She raised her chin in the air. 'But I'm not ready to be labelled "frail old woman" just yet.' Her gaze transferred to Sophie. 'You'll stay for dinner, won't you dear? Michael's trying to tempt me to eat and he's promised to make me a fish pie tonight.'

He had to hand it to Sophie, if she didn't want to stay, she made an excellent effort of hiding it. 'I'd love to, thank you. Enjoy your rest.'

'Rest my arse,' Michael muttered as he watched Betty shuffle off to what used to be the old TV room.

Sophie caught his eye and started to laugh. 'She's deliberately manipulated things, hasn't she? First to get you out of the house so she could talk to me. And now to make us talk to each other.'

'Yep, that's a fair summary.' Feeling awkward, he shoved his hands into his pockets. 'Did you want—'

'I think we should—' Sophie waved a hand in his direction. 'Oh, sorry, you first.'

'I was going to ask if you wanted one of the *nice* cakes I was made to buy.'

Christ, that smile. It hit him like a punch to the gut. How bleak his life was without it. 'I think it would be rude of me not to try one.'

'Is a sugary, calorie laden cream cake in your spreadsheet?' It was an attempt to be funny, yet the moment his words were out, her face fell and a horrid tension filled the room.

'I've stopped doing the faddy diets,' she replied quietly.

'Good,' he said gruffly, trying to work out how to get them out of this conversational quagmire and onto firmer ground.

'But I'm back to filling in all the other spreadsheets.'

He swallowed, his stomach plummeting so fast he felt it might land by his feet with a loud thump. '*All* of them?'

She nodded, her eyes darting away from his briefly before she seemed to come to a conclusion and looked him in the eye. 'I'd like a chance to talk to you. There were things I wanted to say the morning after the theatre but you walked out before I got the opportunity.'

Not his finest hour, but if he'd stayed, he'd have crumpled, given in to whatever she'd suggested. And ultimately be in even more of a mess than he was already. 'Okay.' He glanced towards Betty's room. 'Maybe we should go to my place.'

Sophie gave him a small smile. 'You think she's got a glass to the wall?'

'I wouldn't put it past her.' He nodded over to the kitchen. 'I'll grab the cake box.' Though the thought of eating one now, made his stomach turn over.

Back at his, he busied himself making them both a coffee, more to help calm himself than because he wanted the drink. When he brought it out to his sitting room, Sophie was sat on the sofa with … was that her laptop in front of her?

'Are you going to take me through my final score?' And

yes, from the way she recoiled, he'd definitely overshot light and breezy and ended firmly in heavily sarcastic.

'I brought it so I could catch up with some work on the train, but as I have it with me, I thought I could show you the spreadsheet I tried to discuss with you before.'

'The new spreadsheet.' As if it made any real difference. He slumped onto the other end of the sofa from her.

'Yes. Or at least the same spreadsheet, but a change in some of the qualities I'm looking for.' Her eyes met his. 'You're not going to be able to see it from over there.'

He wasn't sure he wanted to, but he looked like a coward if he stayed where he was, so he shuffled closer. And froze when he saw the score, and the inevitable red line.

'That's not you,' Sophie interrupted quickly, correctly interpreting his dismay.

'Okay.' He let out a slow breath, but his mind kept racing. 'You've dated since we split?' His gut gave a vicious twist. Of course she had. Just because he was utterly devastated, unable to contemplate ever dating again, it didn't mean she felt the same way. How many days had it taken her to go from upset to relieved that he'd ended things? One, two?

'I tried to, yes.' She aimed a hard look in his direction. 'You dumped me, remember? What did you want me to do? Wallow in misery for a year, wondering what was wrong with me?'

'God, no.' He'd done exactly that after Jackie. And for longer. Yet that had been different. 'You have to know I think you're perfect. That there's nothing I would change about you.' He flicked a hand towards the computer. 'Except for your fascination with these.'

Her slim shoulders rose and fell. 'I didn't know. How could

I? You told me you didn't want to be with me anymore, then refused to listen to anything I had to say.'

'I'm sorry.' He leant forward, resting his arms on his knees, staring at the floor while he assembled his thoughts. 'I knew if I stayed, if I listened, I would carry on seeing you. And that would have been bad for both of us.'

She gave a vehement shake of her head. 'Why?'

'You don't need me to tell you.' He pointed at the spreadsheet. 'You have that to do it for you.'

'But *this* tells me the opposite.' She clicked and opened up a new page. 'You told me you couldn't be someone's less than perfect again, but *this* tells me you're absolutely perfect for me, too.'

Curiosity got the better of him and he peered over at the screen, seeing his name at the top. His heart bounced at what he saw beneath it, but he clamped down on the bubble of joy. 'That's not your spreadsheet. I know, because I saw it.' Why was he focussing on that devastating memory, and not on the row of tens he could see now? *Because you know what's happening.* 'That's your head getting muddled by sex, thinking I'm the person you want and adapting the spreadsheet to suit.' He drew a hand down his face, determined not to give in to the hope currently butting up against his protective guard of realism. 'In a word, it's cheating.'

Chapter Thirty-Four

Sophie gaped at Michael. She'd just shown him how much he meant to her – and she could not have done it any more eloquently than in the sight of that row of tens on her spreadsheet – and all he could do was accuse her of cheating?

She was starting to think Betty was wrong. Michael didn't want her, he wanted out. And he was going to use her spreadsheet as a way of doing it.

But then she searched his face, saw the tiny but unmistakable dart of hope in his eyes, and realised what was happening. 'My head isn't muddled by sex,' she told him quietly. 'If it's muddled by anything, it's by love.'

His whole body jerked upright, as if he'd been electrocuted. 'You can't mean that.'

'Why can't I?' Remembering her promise to fight for the man she loved, she inhaled a deep breath. 'You say it's cheating, changing the attributes on the spreadsheet, but the reason I changed them is because *I've* changed.' She reached for his hands, clasping them in hers, feeling how tightly he was clenching his fists. 'Can't you see I'm not the same person I was when we first met? That you helped me start living the life I wanted, not the one I thought Rosie would have wanted?'

He glanced away. When he finally looked back at her, the intense blue of his gaze hit her forcibly in the chest. 'If I made a positive difference to your life, then I'm glad. But it's nothing to how deeply you affected mine.'

The humbleness of the man. Tears welled in her eyes. 'For once, you're not listening to me.' She took hold of his right hand and placed it over her heart. 'The man I thought I wanted when I first met you? That charismatic, sociable guy who was always so full of energy?' She shook her head in disgust. 'What was I thinking? He would never have listened to me, like you did. Never have got my parents to see how using my birthday to remember Rosie was piling the survivor guilt onto me. Never have helped me make peace with Rosie's death.' Raising her other hand, she traced the familiar lines of his face. The creases at the side of his eyes, the strong jaw. 'You did all of that, at the same time as teaching me how to relax, to unwind and enjoy simple pleasures. Crikey Michael, you make me happy. With you I'm not looking for the next thing to fill my time. I'm blissfully content doing everything or nothing with you.'

'Except walking.'

Feeling him start to lose some of that awful tension, she smiled. 'I hate long walks. Short walks, to a pub, are absolutely on my to-do list.'

A small curve of his lips. 'I see you're still making lists.'

'Of course, I've not had a total personality transplant.' But then she put a hand on either side of his face, forcing him to look at her. 'I love you, Michael Adams. I love *everything* about you. Your looks – that was never a problem. Your style – yep, the polo shirt and chinos have grown on me. Your dog – I promise I didn't see that one coming.' She pressed a soft kiss to his lips. 'Then there's your strength, your kindness, your humility, your frigging awesome sense of humour. I could go on, but what's the point because if you don't believe the spreadsheet, you're not going to believe what I'm saying.'

His beautiful eyes pressed hers. 'I want to believe you.' She watched as he glanced away, his Adam's apple bobbing in his throat.

'But you still think you're a sofa?'

He let out a strangled laugh. 'Okay, it was a bad analogy.'

'What if it isn't?' If sofas were the way to convince him, she could do that. 'What if my taste in sofas has changed? Sure, first I thought I wanted a garish modern sofa that would be a talking point with my friends, but then I started to realise there were more important attributes to a sofa than being the centre of attention. Things like how strong it was, how comfortable. Whether it was a sofa I could just shrug off my work clothes and relax on. Be myself with.'

The blue in his eyes started to warm. 'Am I still the sofa?'

'Absolutely.'

'And you're throwing off your clothes and sitting on me?'

His eyes were getting brighter by the second. 'I said my work clothes, but sure. I can throw off all my clothes if it helps.'

'You being naked definitely helps.' But his expression turned serious. 'You shouldn't have to change to suit me, Sophie. I love you exactly as you are.'

She bit into her lip. 'You love me, huh?'

He groaned, bending to kiss her, his lips soft. 'Yes, if it's not been clear until now I apologise. I love and adore you, Sophie Williams.'

Her heart lifted, filling out her chest. She hadn't realised how much she'd needed to hear him say it. 'To be clear, I'm not changing to suit you. I'm still going to drag you to bars, make you do crazy stunts, push you out of your comfort zone.'

'Can we have a strong no on karaoke?'

'Absolutely not.' She prodded him. 'One day I'm going to get you up on that stage, singing with me.'

He groaned. 'What have I let myself in for?' Yet when she examined his face, she saw only humour. And love.

'You've shown me I can enjoy quieter pursuits as well, though,' she added softly. 'Lying under the stars with you, watching you play cricket. Taking the dogs for a walk with you. A *short* walk,' she tagged on quickly. 'The common theme, if you've not sussed it already, is doing things with you.'

His lips curved at the corners and in a flash he was lifting her up, shifting them round so she was lying on top of him. 'Okay then. If you're serious about this, we need to practice the sofa thing. See if you'll want to sit on me not just now, but in the future.' His eyes held hers, blue and silver swirls of pure emotion. 'You need to be absolutely certain, because I'm not talking months. I'm talking the rest of your life.'

Oh God. Just when she thought she'd get through this without crying. Tears spilled freely down her cheeks. 'I'm happy to practise. And keep practising. But know this.' She pressed a kiss to his beautiful mouth. 'I'm not as stupid as Jackie. I am never going to want to trade you in. So if you're planning on making that statement a little more … formal one day, you need to be certain, too.'

Joy flooded his face. 'Noted. But for now.' His gaze zeroed in on her mouth. 'For now we'll practise.'

Michael wanted to stay in this exact spot for the rest of his life. Lying on his sofa, a naked Sophie tucked against him, a blanket thrown over them which added to the cosy, loved-up feeling.

'Did I tell you that I love your hair?' He ran his hands through the soft lengths, enjoying the feel of it tickling his skin. 'Longer suits you.'

He felt her smile against his chest. 'I always did wear it long, but after Rosie died I chopped it all. Every time I looked in the mirror I couldn't see my face any more. Only hers.'

His heart shifted. 'I wish I could have met her.'

'Me, too.' She raised onto her elbows to look at him. 'She'd have loved you. In fact I can see her now, giving me that cheeky smile and telling me I've really punched above my weight.'

Laughter burst out of him. 'It's me who's punching.'

She touched his face, angling it so he looked straight into her eyes. 'You're not. One day you'll realise how bloody incredible you are. But by then it will be too late, because I'll have welded myself to you so you won't be able to leave me.'

He shook his head. 'As if me leaving you would ever be an option.' How had he got this lucky? How had he managed to get this spectacular woman to love him? And yes, a part of him still worried she'd come to her senses, but he wasn't giving in to those fears again. He was going all in.

'About this practising.' He started to kiss the soft skin above her breasts. 'I think we have time…' The hairs on the back of his neck pricked. As if someone was watching. When he looked up, he saw two pairs of brown eyes staring at him from the doorway. 'Seriously? Can't the pair of you entertain yourselves for a bit longer?'

'A bit.' Sophie giggled. 'Yet again you underestimate yourself.'

She yelped as Princess let out a couple of yappy barks and leapt up, wedging herself firmly between them. Thank God for the blanket. Fudge, far more respectful of boundaries, padded over and gave his hand a nudge with her wet nose before lying on the floor.

'I guess practice time is over.'

Sophie kissed him. 'There will be plenty more.'

Yes … but. A little of the joy trickled away as he thought of the practicalities. 'I can't leave Betty.' Unconsciously his arms tightened around Sophie. 'I would move to be near you in a heartbeat, but Betty's life is here.' He bent to kiss the top of her head, inhaling another delicious waft of her shampoo. 'I'm afraid that leaves us hopping on trains and spending less time together than I'd like.'

Sophie shuffled up, and when his attention was immediately drawn to her naked breasts, she shook her head and covered herself with the blanket. 'No getting distracted. What I'm about to say is important.' She waited until he met her eyes. 'Number one, I adore Betty, so absolutely she is the priority. Number two, and this is going to sound really pushy, but I'm going to say it anyway. I'm sure I could find a job out here. If you wanted me to live closer.'

'*If?*' He stared at her. 'You'd move out of London?'

'Duh, of course.' She tapped her fingers on his chest. 'What part of *I love you* do you not understand? I wasn't kidding about wanting to be with you, Doc.'

He wasn't sure his heart could expand any further, feel any fuller. 'But you're a city girl,' he reminded her, repeating the words she'd said to him when they'd first met.

Under the watchful eyes of Princess, she gave him a long, deep kiss. 'I'm *your* girl. Sure, I'll drag you into London on dates, and to catch up with Grace and Ava but I want to be where you are.'

'Where I am.' Heart in his mouth, he swept back a lock of her hair. 'Would that include not just in Little Brook, but here in this house? With me. And Betty.' He looked down at Fudge who'd pricked up an ear. And then at Princess who was watching him with a tongue lolling out of her mouth. 'And two dogs, one mildly annoying.'

A wide, radiant smile crossed Sophie's face. 'Why, Michael Adams, are you asking me to move in with you?'

'I'm going to ask a lot more than that from you,' he warned. 'But yes, for now, when you're ready.' He sank into another kiss, unable to stop touching her, imagining a time when he'd be able to do that every day. He'd been ready to commit to Jackie, but now he realised what a huge favour she'd done him, choosing Ian. He thought he could have been happy, but what he'd felt for Jackie, and what he felt for Sophie, were like two ends of the love spectrum. Plus, where Jackie had tolerated the quiet, reserved parts of him she didn't like,

Sophie embraced them, yet also challenged them. Life with her would never be dull. She wouldn't let it be.

'Whoa.' She pulled back, breathless, giving Princess a wary glance. 'Impressionable canine watching.' Her hand came to rest on her heart, and she smiled. 'I'll move in as soon as I can find myself a job.'

He nodded, studying her. 'If you could do anything you wanted, what would it be?'

'Easy. I'd do exactly what I do now, advising people on colour schemes, only I'd expand it to the full interior design service. It's so frustrating only looking at paints and wallpapers, and only one brand at that.' Her face became animated as the words rolled over each other. 'And I'd do it freelance so I was my own boss. No more having to put up with the likes of Terrible Trevor, watching the sales figures like a hawk, being all snotty about taking a lunch break to get my bikini wax.'

'Ah yes.' He cleared his throat. 'That was definitely one of the items on your spreadsheet that stood out.'

She glanced at him quizzically. 'Well, well, you must have read it pretty thoroughly, huh?'

He laughed. 'Little did I realise that I'd be lucky enough to see the result.' He caught her chin in his hand. 'You should do it.'

'It's not been *that* long since I last had it done. Of course I used to have a spreadsheet that told me exactly when the last appointment was, and when the next one was due...' she trailed off as he simply stared at her. 'Ah, you're not talking about the bikini wax, are you?'

He laughed gently. 'I'm talking about moving here and setting up your own business.'

'But I don't have the contacts here, at least not as many as I have in London. It could take months to get it going, years to build it into anything likely to make a decent living.'

'We've got time.' He framed her face with his hands. 'Please, you're the one making the huge compromise to move here. I want you to get something out of it, too.'

'I get you.' She said it like there was no contest. Like he was worth the sacrifice. It almost cut him in two. Then she smiled. 'But okay, we'll talk about it. And I'll definitely do it one day. I already have a company name. *Excelling at interiors*. Do you get it? Excel spreadsheets will be the cornerstone of the business. They'll be how I maintain my customer base, how I manage stock, how I…'

He quietened her, very effectively, with a kiss.

Chapter Thirty-Five

One year later

Sophie had to smother a laugh as she watched the expression on Michael's face as Grace showed him the outfit she'd selected for him. A sequined shirt and black leather trousers.

'This is a joke, yes?'

Solemnly Grace shook her head. 'Did you or did you not, put me and Ava in charge of Sophie's birthday celebrations this year?'

He visibly swallowed. 'I did.'

Ava nodded down to the outfit in Grace's hand. 'So, you need to wear this when you sing.'

His head snapped back. 'Sing? God no. There are people who sing, and people who watch. In case there's any confusion, I'm in the latter category.'

Grace huffed out a breath and turned towards Sophie. 'Tell him, Soph.'

It was no wonder she enjoyed winding him up. He was so adorably sexy when he was on the back foot. 'What Grace and Ava are trying to say, is karaoke isn't a spectator sport.' Fighting not to laugh, she beamed at him. 'It's only fun if everyone takes part.'

He looked between them all, clearly suspecting another set up. He took the pranks in good part, and it was a source of constant delight to her how well he got on with her friends. Not all their jokes had ended up only as pranks, mind you. He'd actually been disappointed to find the parachute jump had been one, so he'd organised for them to do a tandem jump on their next date – yes, even though they lived together now, they continued taking it in turns choosing somewhere to go every week. Alas karaoke was, in his words, "still a hard no".

'I *will* be taking part.' He slid his hands into his pockets and took a look around him. 'I'll be getting my eardrums tortured listening to this lot.' His glance fell on Hamza, who'd come with Hattie. Another pair who shouldn't work on paper – or perhaps on one of her spreadsheets – yet who had defied logic and remained very much together. 'Promise me you'll put the microphone on silent when he gets up to sing.'

'I'll do no such thing.' Grace smirked. 'But I will promise to let Betty go before him.'

Grace received exactly the reaction she'd been looking for, and Michael's eyes widened in horror. 'No, please, don't let her grab the microphone. You'll never prize it off her. She'll have us all singing *Roll out the Barrell*. Followed by *We'll Meet Again*.'

As he excused himself, muttering something about finding Betty, the three of them fell about laughing.

'That man is so cute.' Ava smiled. 'Maybe your stupid spreadsheets weren't so stupid after all.' When Sophie opened her mouth to protest, she would defend her spreadsheets with her last breath, Ava waved her away. 'You'll never convince me that the Love Life one works, but I can't argue with the end result. You got your man, Soph.'

She did, Sophie thought smugly. And that was all that mattered.

'Now, in the words of Pink's song, let's Get The Party Started.'

Sophie jumped up and down like an excited toddler. When Michael had first suggested organising something for her birthday, she'd figured on a meal, maybe in London, maybe with Betty and Dennis. But then he'd told her he'd put Grace and Ava in charge. 'I want it to be a celebration to make up for all the birthdays you missed,' he'd explained in that low, deep voice of his that still sent shivers through her. 'And organising that requires someone more outgoing than me.'

Between them all, they'd hired out the cricket club (Michael's idea), invited her parents and Patricia, plus Betty and Dennis (Michael again). Also invited Jade and Dave (who'd brought their *two* daughters), the London gang and the entire cricket team (Grace and Ava had decided if they were having a party, they were going big). Ava had hired the outside caterers after Michael had informed her Betty was threatening to make stew and dumplings. It was Grace who'd decided on the karaoke machine, though she'd been actively encouraged by Betty.

Finally, *finally*, the day had arrived, and the cricket club was filling up with the most diverse party crowd it had probably ever witnessed. Hip young Londoners mixed with village pensioners, party animals with those who preferred a quiet pint, her parents and Patricia were laughing with Dennis and

Betty, Olivia and some of the cricketers' kids were chasing Princess, or was it the other way round? Fudge was helping herself to a sausage roll that had fallen on the floor. Dave was rocking his second daughter to sleep in her pram. Jade was looking on with a blissful expression on her face.

It was a perfect mix of both their lives.

A warm body sidled up behind her, fingers twining with hers as the subtle scent of aftershave and sexy male drifted up her nose. 'Is this okay? What you wanted?'

'Exactly what I wanted.' With a contented sigh she rested against him. 'The only thing that will make it more perfect is watching your face as you listen to Betty sing.'

He groaned, kissing the nape of her neck. 'More perfect will come later, when I get you to myself.'

A shiver ran through her. 'Yep, you win. Your perfect beats mine.'

He let out a soft laugh, his breath fluttering her neck. 'Of course I win.' He twisted them so she faced him, his eyes shining right into hers. 'I get to go home with you.'

'Oh God. You make my knees weak, Doc.' She leant forward, melting against him, undone yet again by the look in his eyes. Never had she felt so utterly adored.

The tap of the microphone broke the spell and they both looked round to find Grace grinning at them. 'If the birthday girl would stop canoodling for a moment…' Laughter echoed round the pavilion, along with a few whistles.

'This is not me canoodling,' Michael muttered to anyone who would listen. 'If I was canoodling, the birthday girl would know about it.'

More laughter, and she didn't miss the way his arms tightened around her, protective, possessive. Loving.

'I'd like to declare this party officially open,' Grace announced. 'Help yourselves to drink and to food … and then we sing!'

Cheers erupted and from the raucous nature of them, it sounded like many had helped themselves to the bar already.

'What about a chorus of happy birthday now?' At the quietly spoken words, Sophie looked over with a start towards her dad, who smiled at her. 'It seems far too long since we sang it to my daughter.'

Before she could take a breath, her parents started singing the first line, and then everyone else joined in. Dazed, she looked around the room, seeing the affection on people's faces as they sang wholeheartedly. But it was the love on the face of her parents that brought tears to the surface. This was their way of apologising.

'You okay?' Michael whispered, hugging her to his side.

'Yes.' She swallowed. 'I know it's my party, but I'm absolutely not going to cry.'

She felt his body shake with laughter. 'Good to know.'

———

Michael stared down at the sequined shirt Grace had left for him in the men's changing room. This had to be the most stupid idea he'd ever had.

There was a light tap on the door, and Ava and Grace barrelled in.

Ava frowned. 'Why aren't you changed?'

'I think that's obvious.' Grace narrowed her eyes at him. 'The good doctor is having second thoughts.'

'Absolutely not.' He let out a deep exhale. 'But can't I do it without the leather and sequins?'

'I suppose.' Grace pouted. 'But this is payback for taking our favourite girl away from us.' She smirked. 'And you know how much Sophie would appreciate you wearing them.'

And there it was, the push he needed. He'd seen Sophie try not to laugh when Grace had shown him the outfit. Of course Sophie thought the joke had been on him, though his horror at exactly what Grace had chosen, had been a hundred percent genuine. 'Fine.' If he was going to make an arse of himself – and he was, no question – he might as well go all in. Sophie deserved him to go all in.

He started to unbutton his trousers, then realised Ava and Grace were watching him. 'Err, a bit of privacy?'

They smirked, but obediently turned around.

The leather trousers fitted way too snuggly for his liking, but it was when he put on the shirt he couldn't help but let out a muttered oath. 'Jesus.'

Grace giggled. 'You said you wanted something flamboyant.'

'I didn't say see through.'

Immediately both of them turned and he had to resist the urge to shove his other shirt in front of him like a prude, though he did cross his arms over his chest.

They both high fived each other. 'You might not like it, but Sophie will love it,' Ava announced.

Grace nodded. 'She'll agree to anything once she's seen you.'

'You really think so?' He heard the vulnerability in his voice and apparently Grace did too, because she gave him a soft smile.

'Of course. She loves you. Why else would she have left our awesome company to live with you?'

His gaze jumped between the two friends. 'You're never going to forgive me, are you?'

'We might.' Grace gave him an impish grin. 'Once you've done your penance by wearing the sequins.'

Ava touched his arm. 'What Grace really means is of course we are. We already have. You make her happy. Besides, with me moving out to set up home with Ethan, and Daniel moving in to live with Grace, it's all change anyway. Our three Musketeers have grown into six.' She let out a satisfied sigh. 'Okay, our work here is done. Walk behind us and we'll smuggle you into the kitchen. Betty's up next and she's promised everyone will be looking at her.'

All too easy to believe. He nearly swallowed his tongue as he slipped into the pavilion behind his female shields and caught sight of Betty on the stage. She'd gone all out. Feather boa in place, a silver top that easily out glittered his, she was belting out *Do You Think I'm Sexy*. He should have guessed she wouldn't be predictable.

Everyone in the place was in hysterics, and Michael knew with absolute certainty nobody was going to notice him. It gave him a few minutes to settle his nerves, and to appreciate his gran and her enthusiasm for life. No wonder he'd fallen for Sophie. She was a younger version.

Betty milked the applause, giving a curtsey unsteady enough to cause Dennis to leap off his chair with the alacrity of a thirty-year-old and rush over to help her off the stage. That's when Betty turned and gave Michael a huge wink.

His heart jumped into his mouth. Show time.

Grace popped up to the microphone. 'Next, we have a

surprise addition to the line-up. Please welcome *Dr* Michael Adams.'

Christ, he didn't need them all being reminded he was supposed to be a pillar of the community.

As he walked onto the small stage he heard gasps, followed by laughter and applause, but it was all just a dim background noise to him. His focus was on Sophie, who gaped at him, then bit into her bottom lip, mouth curved in a wide grin, eyes showing both shock and delight.

He cleared his throat and spoke into the microphone. 'I once told Sophie karaoke was a hard no.' He glanced down at his ridiculous outfit. 'Never thought I'd wear sequins either.'

A few bursts of laughter.

'They look good on you, Doc.' He caught Sophie's eye, saw the encouragement on her face, and relaxed a little.

'Thanks, but I know you're lying.' Then he swallowed, felt his pulse kick up a gear. 'I'm going to attempt to sing to you now.' He nodded to Grace, who started the music.

He didn't need to read the lines. He'd learnt them off by heart. And though the words of Bruno Mars weren't perfect, he hoped Sophie would get the gist.

'*It's a beautiful night,*' he croaked out, his eyes on her, and only her. '*We're looking for something dumb to do.*' Her eyes widened and he shook his head. 'Stick with me.'

'*Hey baby,*' he sang again, watching as she put a hand over her mouth in shock, clearly working out the next words of the song. '*I think I wanna marry you.*'

The music carried on, but he ignored it, jumping off the stage with the microphone and walking towards her.

'*Don't say no, no, no, no, no.*' Stood right in front of her, he picked up the lines. '*Just say yeah, yeah, yeah, yeah, yeah. And we'll go, go, go, go, go.*' Heart pounding now, he stared into her eyes. '*If you're ready, like I'm ready.*'

Bruno had more words to say, but Michael was done. As he felt the eyes of everyone on him, the collective holding of breath, he'd never felt so exposed, so vulnerable. So utterly out of his comfort zone. Why had he thought it a good idea to do this in public? *Because this is you, showing her how much she means to you. Giving her your heart.*

Tears rolled down her face as she clasped his face. 'Yeah, yeah, yeah, yeah, yeah.'

The place erupted in cheers, but Michael barely heard any of it, he was so caught up with Sophie, the love shining out of her eyes. 'You mean it?'

She started to laugh. 'You think I could possibly say no after *that*?'

'That was the plan.' He bent to kiss her, far too brief, far too tame but it would have to do until he got her alone.

'So all that stuff with Grace and Ava earlier, saying you weren't going to sing…' She gave him a playful push. 'And I thought we were playing a trick on you!'

'Trust me, the horror at the outfit was genuine.'

Sophie started to laugh. 'Oh my God, I can't believe you just sang Bruno Mars to me on a karaoke machine, wearing tight leather and sequins, in front of the whole village. You crazy man.' Her expression changed from highly amused to something that looked a lot like besotted. 'You do know I'm head over heels in love with you, yes? A simple, *hey Soph, will you marry me?* while we were eating breakfast would have done.'

'No. It wouldn't.' He tucked his finger under her chin, fastened those glorious silver grey eyes on his. 'I wanted a proposal you could laugh about with your grandkids. A proposal out of the ordinary, for someone utterly extraordinary.'

She shook her head, tears beginning to roll again. 'It was certainly that.'

Betty marched up and wrapped her arms around them both. 'Congratulations to two of my favourite people. Who knew my grandson would be such a karaoke star, eh?' She kissed Michael's cheek. 'You must get your singing genes from me, dear.'

Michael stared back at her. 'God help me.'

They all fell about laughing.

Acknowledgments

Where do I start? Writing a book is, for a large part of the time, such a solo venture. Just me at my desk, typing away. Oh and frowning/sighing/pulling my hair out, deleting… then typing some more. Yet there are many other people involved in the process, right from the initial idea, all the way through to the final book that gets into your hands. Without them all, this book would not have made it.

So let me start at the beginning; the idea for the book. It's impossible to write a book without one. Equally though, it's impossible to enjoy writing a book without a really great idea, one that, as the writer, grips you enough that you want to sit down at your desk every day and craft a story around it. So thank you Hannah Todd, not just for being an amazing agent, but for the idea to base the book around a woman whose obsession with spreadsheets leads her to use them to improve her Love Life. As a fan of spreadsheets myself – though only for finances I hasten to add – I totally bought into the concept and had a ball writing the story.

Next on my thank you list is the team at One More Chapter. I could not ask for a more creative, professional, supportive group of people to write for. This includes my editor Charlotte Ledger, who has been an incredible source of advice and encouragement ever since she was brave enough to invite me to write for One More Chapter. I owe her so much – none of this romcom series would have happened without her.

A big thank you also to the rest of the One More Chapter team who work seamlessly behind the scenes to shape this book into something ready to be read, and who gave it the fabulous title and cover (you are awesome, Lucy Bennett).

This is also my chance to thank the friends and family who have put up with me talking about my writing, and about my books, for over ten years now - and still haven't told me to shut up. The roll call includes my dear mother-in-law Anne (Mum 2), cousins Shelley, Karley, Kath, Kirsty and Hayley, my sis-in-law Jayne, nieces Maddi, Tiggi and Gracie, friends Charlotte, Laura, Sonia, Jane, Carol, Tara and Priti. And of course my dear mum, who at eighty-eight, finds it harder and harder to keep up with all my books, but who still asks me every day how my writing is going.

Thanks too, to my cricket experts; hubby Andrew and sons, Harry and Ben. I put all the cricket in for you guys – now you have to read the book!

I'm not sure where any of us writers would be without the amazing book bloggers who are kind enough to read and review our books, so a massive thank you to everyone who's given me a shout out on social media, taken part in a blog tour or just taken the time to read my books. Your support is priceless.

Finally, the most important thanks of all go to YOU. I am forever grateful that you chose one of my books to read. I really hope you enjoy Sophie and Michael's story, and that it rates closer to Michael's final score than his initial one...

ONE MORE CHAPTER

YOUR NUMBER ONE STOP
FOR PAGETURNING BOOKS

The author and One More Chapter would like to thank everyone
who contributed to the publication of this story...

Analytics
Emma Harvey
Maria Osa

Audio
Fionnuala Barrett
Ciara Briggs

Contracts
Georgina Hoffman
Florence Shepherd

Design
Lucy Bennett
Fiona Greenway
Holly Macdonald
Liane Payne
Dean Russell

Digital Sales
Laura Daley
Michael Davies
Georgina Ugen

Editorial
Arsalan Isa
Charlotte Ledger
Jennie Rothwell
Tony Russell
Caroline Scott-
Bowden
Kimberley Young

Marketing & Publicity
Chloe Cummings
Emma Petfield

Operations
Melissa Okusanya
Hannah Stamp

Production
Emily Chan
Denis Manson
Francesca Tuzzeo

Rights
Lana Beckwith
Rachel McCarron
Agnes Rigou
Hany Sheikh
Mohamed
Zoe Shine
Aisling Smyth

**The HarperCollins
Distribution Team**

**The HarperCollins
Finance & Royalties
Team**

**The HarperCollins
Legal Team**

**The HarperCollins
Technology Team**

Trade Marketing
Ben Hurd

UK Sales
Yazmeen Akhtar
Laura Carpenter
Isabel Coburn
Jay Cochrane
Alice Gomer
Gemma Rayner
Erin White
Harriet Williams
Leah Woods

**And every other
essential link in the
chain from delivery
drivers to booksellers
to librarians and
beyond!**

Not an expert, not even close, not in any of this. But nobody will try harder than me to make you happy.

Sally is a classic romantic and Harry is a classic cynic, but when a drunken bet leads the new flatmates to (badly) recreate 'the lift' from Dirty Dancing, and the video goes viral (#EpicRomcomReenactmentFailure), they both realise there's potential financial benefit in blundering their way through the romcom lexicon for their suddenly vast social media following.

Now, as Harry and Sally bring major romcom moments to new life – including recreating that classic diner scene – their faking it turns to making…out and suddenly they're living a real life romcom of their own! But like all the greatest love stories, the road to happily ever after is paved with unexpected challenges for this hero and heroine…

Available in paperback, eBook, and audio!

A year in a gorgeous Italian castle…

When Anna Roberts' life implodes, an online search leads her to an ad for the ultimate dream job – management of a gorgeous castle on the shores of Lake Como, accommodation included. The only catch? Anna can't do it alone…

…With the last man on earth she'd choose!

The castle owners will only accept a couple as caretakers, which means Anna needs a man on her arm at the interview. Enter her neighbour, Jake Tucker. Though Anna and Jake have never seen eye-to-eye, Jake's had a rough few years and an escape to Italy sounds ideal. Yet, when they get the job and jet off, Anna and Jake face an unexpected challenge. Pretending to be a couple is difficult … but pretending the tension simmering between them doesn't exist is quickly proving impossible!

Available in paperback and eBook!

When Lottie Watt is unceremoniously booted out of her uptight book club for not following the rules, she decides to throw the rulebook out the window and start her own club – one where conversation, gin and cake take precedent over actually having read the book!

The Beach Reads Book Club soon finds a home for its meetings at Books by the Bay, a charming bookshop and café owned by gorgeous, brooding Matthew Steele, and as the book club picks heat up, so too does the attraction between Matt and Lottie.

If there's anything Lottie has learned from the romances she's been reading, it's that the greatest loves are the ones hardest earned.

Available in paperback, eBook, and audio!

YOUR NUMBER ONE STOP

ONE MORE CHAPTER

FOR PAGETURNING BOOKS

One More Chapter is an
award-winning global
division of HarperCollins.

Sign up to our newsletter to get our
latest eBook deals and stay up to date
with our weekly Book Club!
<u>Subscribe here.</u>

Meet the team at
<u>www.onemorechapter.com</u>

Follow us!

 <u>@OneMoreChapter_</u>

 <u>@OneMoreChapter</u>

 <u>@onemorechapterhc</u>

Do you write unputdownable fiction?
We love to hear from new voices.
Find out how to submit your novel at
<u>www.onemorechapter.com/submissions</u>